"[W]orks beautifully as a tale of suspense as well as a conflicted romance that blooms slowly under most difficult circumstances. I'm giving it one of RRT's rare *Perfect 10s*."　　—*Romance Reviews Today*

## SECRETS OF A RUNAWAY BRIDE

"A fantastic follow-up to Bowman's dynamic debut . . . an enchanting, smart romance that shines with laugh-out-loud humor, delectable dialogue, smart prose, wit, and wisdom. This entertaining and highly satisfying romp is a pure joy and delight to read."
　　—*RT Book Reviews* (4½ stars! Top Pick!)

"A fun . . . yet emotionally poignant late-Regency romance which succeeds on every level."
　　—*Kirkus Reviews*

"This was an absolutely delightful book and an author that I look forward to reading more from."
　　—*Night Owl Reviews*

"The tale overall is incredibly charming, the writing dramatic, and the characters bold."
　　—*Romance Reader*

"Absolutely delightful."　　　　—*Fresh Fiction*

"A sexy, quirky, altogether fun read, Valerie Bowman's *Secrets of a Runaway Bride* is everything a romance should be. Block out a few hours for this one . . . once you start reading, you won't be able to stop!"
　　—*New York Times*
bestselling author Sarah MacLean

"Valerie Bowman pens fabulous, sexy tales—it's no secret she's a Regency author to watch!"

—*USA Today* bestselling author Kieran Kramer

## SECRETS OF A WEDDING NIGHT

"The most charming and clever debut I've read in years! With her sparkling dialogue, vivid characters, and self-assured writing style, Valerie Bowman has instantly established herself as a romance author with widespread appeal. This engaging and sweetly romantic story is just too delightful to miss."

—*New York Times* bestselling author Lisa Kleypas

"Clever, fun, and fantastic!"

—*New York Times* bestselling author Suzanne Enoch

"Ms. Bowman is quite the tease. How I love a good society scandal. The hero is absolutely yummy!"

—Award-winning author Donna MacMeans

"Bowman's engaging sense of characterization, gift for creating sexual chemistry, and graceful writing style give her debut romance a splendidly satisfying emotional depth."

—*Booklist* (starred review)

"This fast-paced, charming debut, sparkling with witty dialogue and engaging characters, marks Bowman for stardom."

—*Romantic Times Book Reviews*

ALSO BY VALERIE BOWMAN

*The Accidental Countess*

*The Unexpected Duchess*

*Secrets of a Scandalous Marriage*

*Secrets of a Runaway Bride*

*Secrets of a Wedding Night*


NOVELLAS

*A Secret Proposal*

*A Secret Affair*

*It Happened Under the Mistletoe*


ANTHOLOGY

*Christmas Brides*

# The Unlikely Lady

VALERIE BOWMAN

St. Martin's Paperbacks

This is a work of fiction. All of the characters, organizations, and events portrayed in this novel are either products of the author's imagination or are used fictitiously.

THE UNLIKELY LADY

Copyright © 2015 by June Third Enterprises LLC.

All rights reserved.

For information address St. Martin's Press, 175 Fifth Avenue, New York, NY 10010.

ISBN: 978-1-250-04209-5

Printed in the United States of America

St. Martin's Paperbacks edition / May 2015

St. Martin's Paperbacks are published by St. Martin's Press, 175 Fifth Avenue, New York, NY 10010.

10  9  8  7  6  5  4  3  2  1

*For my mother, Judith Hammond Bowman Rhodes, who instilled in me not only a love of historical romance novels but also a gift for storytelling. Anyone who has ever heard her tall tales about mountain lions and pack rats knows this is true.*

*My mother once told me that having a romance novelist in the family was her greatest dream come true.*

*I love you, Mom.*

# ACKNOWLEDGMENTS

This particular book would not be what it is without a handful of wonderful people who generously gave their time to read it and give me their opinions. I would like to thank . . .

Mary Behre for her always insightful and honest feedback on my characters and their motivations and for saying, "Nope. That's not gonna work," when she needs to.

Ashlyn Macnamara for her knowledge of the time period and humoring me and my rompish, outlandish plots. I don't call you the "Regency Google" for nothin'.

KC Klein for reminding me to give my characters a little hell now and again.

Virginia Boylan for her absolutely spot-on read and editing critique that have made my writing stronger.

Holly Ingraham, whose unwavering support and excellent editorial direction continue to make every book I write even better.

# CHAPTER ONE

*London, April 1816*

"Oh, for heaven's sake, Mrs. Cat, show yourself and let's get this over with, shall we?" Jane Lowndes wiped the dark, wet hair from her eyes. It was raining. Hard. The downpour had begun nearly five minutes ago and she'd been standing outside the mews behind her father's town house for nearly ten.

Jane could live with the rain herself. Who cared about hair or clothing being ruined? She could even stand the fact that her spectacles were foggy. But her book was getting wet and *that* was not acceptable. She'd tucked the leather-bound volume under her arm as best she could while she balanced a wooden bowl in her hands, but she truly needed to get the book inside and dry it by the fire.

Jane squinted into the gray mist. A soft meow signaled the arrival of the cat. The brown, mangy-looking animal must have heard her. The cat came running along the stone wall at the far side of the stables, heading straight toward Jane. Apparently, even rain wasn't enough to keep the feline from her free meal.

"There you are." A soft smile touched Jane's lips, despite her best efforts to stifle it. She didn't *want* to smile at this cat. She didn't want to be responsible for it at all, really, rain or shine. She'd noticed the thing a fortnight ago when she'd come to the mews after a mount to ride in the park, and then she'd had the misfortune to go and discover that the cat had *kittens* of all things. She'd seen one of the furry little things peeking from behind a bush in the alley, obviously awaiting her mother's return. A lone cat was one thing, but kittens were another matter entirely. Add to that the mama cat's scrawniness and obvious hunger, and Jane couldn't stop herself from making a trip to the kitchens to request a bowl of scraps.

Two weeks later and she and Mrs. Cat had a standing appointment here every morning. Today was the first time it had begun raining while Jane waited. She'd have to remember to leave her book inside next time.

Jane stooped and set the bowl near the wall, remaining in a crouched position. The cat licked her lips and charged toward it, hungrily plunging her face into the meal and gobbling.

"My, you're a greedy one." Jane shook her head slightly. "Reminds me of the manner in which I used to eat when I was a child." She laughed. "I suppose I must continue to feed you so you can keep those babies healthy, but you certainly don't make it easy for me by arriving late in the rain."

She patted the cat's head, ignoring her thoughts of fleas or worse. She'd promptly wipe her hands as soon as she returned to the comfort of the house.

"How are the kittens?" Jane asked, raindrops sliding down her nose.

The cat's only answer was more hungry smacking.

"I imagine you're quite busy," Jane continued,

readjusting her book under her arm. "I don't envy you. Having to keep food on the, er, table for your children with nary a paw lifted from Mr. Cat, I presume."

The cat continued to eat, steadfastly ignoring her provider.

Jane clucked her tongue. "I completely understand. Exactly why I intend to remain unattached and further the cause of women in Society, Mrs. Cat. Just like Mary Wollstonecraft."

The cat paused and eyed her askance, her green eyes narrowed, as if she understood what Jane had said.

Jane hiked her eyebrows. "I know what you're thinking. Mary Wollstonecraft was married. I know. Of course I know. But that doesn't mean *I* have to be. I rather think I'll accomplish much more for the cause if I'm not distracted by a man and his children."

The cat looked up from her meal and blinked at her. Was that judgment in the cat's eyes? Had this cat become acquainted with Jane's mother? Jane swiped the rain from her spectacles.

"Speaking of marriage," Jane continued, as the cat returned to concentrating on her breakfast. "My friend Cass is getting married and I am leaving today for the country to attend the wedding. I won't be around for a bit."

The cat swished her tail.

"Don't blame me," Jane went on. "I couldn't talk her out of it. It seems Cass is madly in love with Julian and *some* people apparently are meant to be together forever. Lucy seems to think so, too, and Lucy, of course, is a duchess now as a result of falling in love." The last three words were uttered with a fair bit of mockery.

"But don't worry," Jane said. "I've asked Anna, the cook's assistant, to check on you while I'm gone. She's promised to bring you all the best scraps and—"

"Miss Jane?" Anna's voice came floating through the rain and fog.

Jane quickly stood and turned toward the sound. "Anna, is that you?"

Anna soon materialized around the side of the mews. She held a newspaper over her head to shield herself from the rain as she squinted through the fog. "Miss Jane?" She stopped when she saw Jane. "There you are. I thought I might find you out here. Your mother is looking for you. She and Eloise are turning up the house searching."

Eloise was Jane's lady's maid. The poor woman was often taken to task if Jane's mother couldn't find her only child. "I'd better get back quickly then. Poor Eloise. Good-bye, Mrs. Cat. I'll see you when I return. And I hope to see your kittens fat and healthy. Anna will take good care of you. Won't you, Anna?"

Anna's smile spread across her plump cheeks. "Of course, miss."

The cat lifted its head and blinked.

Anna readjusted the paper atop her head. "Miss, I heard your mother tell Eloise it's quite important that she and your father speak with you before you leave for the house party."

Jane scrunched up her nose. Drat. An audience with her mother was never a good thing and if she was dragging Papa into it, it was serious. "I wonder what she wishes to discuss."

Anna stooped down and patted the cat on the head. "I heard her say something about Mrs. Bunbury."

Jane gulped. "Mrs. Bunbury?"

"Yes. She is your new chaperone, isn't she, miss?"

Jane blinked rapidly. "Yes. Yes, she is." Jane, the book still cradled under her arm, broke into a decidedly un-ladylike sprint back toward the house, heedless of the water splashing onto her skirts from the many puddles in the courtyard.

Mrs. Bunbury was indeed her new chaperone. The chaperone who would be accompanying her to Cass's wedding house party in Surrey. If her mother wanted to discuss Mrs. Bunbury, there might well be trouble.

For Mrs. Bunbury didn't exist.

# CHAPTER TWO

Garrett Upton turned over the letter and stared at it. Hard. He let out a long breath. It contained what it always did, a bank draft, an inadequate message, a hefty dose of guilt.

"Sir, the coach awaits you."

Garrett glanced at the butler who stood at attention in the doorway to his study. The two roan spaniels lying on either side of his chair lifted their heads and wagged their tails.

"I'll be there in a moment, Cartwright."

Cartwright nodded once.

Garrett's gaze returned to the desktop and the letter that had occupied his attention this morning. He finished sanding it, sealed it, and stamped it with the heated wax in front of him.

Garrett didn't have much time. The coach was waiting. He hadn't got much slept last night either, but that was nothing new. The dreams were always there, the nightmares, haunting him.

Garrett stared at the address.

*Mrs. Harold Langford*
*12 Charles Street*
*London*

Every two weeks Garrett sent a similar letter. He'd sent it like clockwork, ever since he'd been a young man of one and twenty, nearly ten years now. While it always included the same contents, conspicuously, there was no mention of Harold, his friend who had died in the war.

Garrett shook his head and pushed out his chair. The dogs scrambled up from their resting spots. He stood and made his way toward the door, the letter in his hand. He'd worked the last fortnight to catch up with his business matters to ensure he could enjoy the time in the countryside. Today, he was off to his friends' wedding house party in Surrey. The new Earl of Swifdon, Julian Swift, was finally marrying his bride, Lady Cassandra Monroe. The six months of grieving for the earl's older brother, Donald, had passed.

The wedding would be grand. The house party before the wedding, more intimate. Garrett's cousin Lucy would be there with her new husband, the Duke of Claringdon. Cassandra and Swifdon would be there, of course. Miss Jane Lowndes. Garrett rolled his eyes. Miss Lowndes usually exasperated him, argued with him, maddened him, or a combination of all three, but he could stand her company for a sennight, he supposed. Why Lucy insisted on remaining such close friends with that know-it-all bluestocking, he'd never understand.

Cartwright remained standing at attention near the door.

"Ensure this goes out today," Garrett said pointedly to the servant, handing him the letter.

"As you wish," the butler replied, taking it.

Garrett crossed back over to the large mahogany desk,

pulled his coat from the back of his chair, and shrugged into it. The dogs watched him intently. Then he turned and strode out the door. The dogs followed close on his heels. He made his way past the butler, who fell into step behind him. He marched down the corridor and into the foyer. Cartwright scurried to open the front door for him as Garrett turned to pat each of the dogs on the head. Their tails wiggled vigorously.

"Take good care of them, Cartwright."

Placing his hat on his head, Garrett strode out into the street, where he climbed into the waiting carriage. He settled into the velvet seat and gazed out the window, taking one last look at his London residence.

It was a fine house. Garrett might be the heir presumptive to the Earl of Upbridge, but the town house in Mayfair and its servants and contents were currently paid for by money his mother had brought to her marriage to the second son of an earl, and an inheritance from his maternal grandfather. Garrett was a wealthy man in his own right.

The coach started with a jerk. Mr. Garrett Upton was off to spend a week at a country house party in Surrey.

# CHAPTER THREE

"Young lady, I refuse to allow you to leave this house until you answer these questions to my satisfaction." Mrs. Hortense Lowndes's dark hair shivered with the force of her foot stamping against the carpeted floor in Jane's father's study.

Jane adjusted her spectacles upon her nose and stared at her mother calmly. Mama was in a high dudgeon today. She hadn't even mentioned the fact that Jane had arrived dripping wet upon her father's carpet and then hurried over to place her soggy book by the fire.

"Are you listening to me?" her mother prodded.

Jane glanced at her bespectacled father, who gave her a half-shrug and a sympathetic smile before folding his hands atop his desk and returning his attention to his book. Papa obviously wished this entire debacle was playing out elsewhere instead of interrupting his reading. Jane didn't blame him. She looked longingly toward her own book. *I do hope it dries and the pages aren't adversely affected.* Oh, wait. She should be paying attention to her mother.

"Of course I'm listening, Mama."

Her mother crossed her arms over her chest and glared at her suspiciously. "Why are you wet?"

Jane pursed her lips. "I thought this was about Mrs. Bunbury." Distraction. It always worked on Mama. Without taking his eyes off his book, Jane's father smirked.

"Yes. Mrs. Bunbury," her mother continued. "That's exactly right. I have several questions about her."

Jane took a deep breath. She carefully removed her spectacles and wiped them on her sleeve. Stalling. A second tactic that usually worked on her mother.

"Mama, we've discussed this. I'm no longer a child. I'm twenty-six years old. I'm a bluestocking, a spinster." She refrained from pointing out that her mother's refusal to accept that fact was exactly why she'd had to invent this preposterous Mrs. Bunbury scheme. That would not be received well. Not at all.

"You most certainly are not!" Her mother stamped her foot again. "Why, I cannot believe my ears." She whirled toward Jane's father. "Charles, are you listening to this?"

Jane's father's head snapped up. He cleared his throat. "Why, yes. Yes, of course. Bluestocking spinster, dear."

"No!" her mother cried. "Jane is *not* a bluestocking spinster."

"No, of course not," her father agreed before burying his head in his book again.

Hortense turned back to face Jane. She pressed her handkerchief to her lips. "We've spent a fortune on your clothing and schooling. We've ensured you've received invitations to all of the best parties, balls, and routs. I do not understand why you cannot find a husband."

"I don't want a husband, Mama. I've told you time and again."

"If you'd merely try," Hortense pleaded.

As usual, her mother refused to listen. Hence, the need for Mrs. Bunbury.

Jane carefully replaced her spectacles. "I'm going to the house party, aren't I?" Logic. It usually served to placate her mother, if temporarily.

Her mother made a funny little hiccupping sound. "You won't enjoy yourself. I know you won't. I think I should come with you and—"

"No." Jane could only hope she successfully kept the panic from her face. If Mama came to the house party, it would be a disaster. It was bad enough that she would be arriving at the end of the week for the wedding itself. "Of course I won't enjoy myself, Mama. Not the party part, at least. I'm bringing a great many books and I intend to—"

Her mother tossed her hands into the air. "Books, books, books. That's all the two of you ever talk about, ever think about." She turned sideways and glared accusingly back and forth between her husband and her daughter.

Jane stepped forward and put a comforting arm around her mother's shoulder. She felt a bit sorry for her. The poor woman hadn't given birth to a daughter who loved people and parties and clothing and fripperies like she did. Instead she'd given birth to a girl who took after her intellectual father. A man who'd been knighted by the Crown for his genius at economics, having successfully invested a great deal of money for the royal family. Jane even *looked* like her father. Dark hair, dark eyes, round cheeks, round face. The slightly round backside may have been more due to her love of teacake than her father's doing, but that hardly mattered. In all things important, Jane took after Sir Charles Lowndes.

"I'm sorry, Mama," Jane murmured. She hugged her pretty mother. Hortense was sweet and kind and meant well. It was hardly her fault that she'd had the terrible misfortune to have a bluestocking for a daughter.

Hortense blinked at her. "Sorry for what?"

Jane let her arm fall away. "Sorry I spend my days reading Socrates instead of *La Belle Assemblée*, reading the political columns instead of shopping for fabric and fripperies with you, attending the theater instead of visiting with friends."

Her mother's shoulders drew up and then just as quickly relaxed. She worried the handkerchief in her hands. "Oh, Jane, if you'd only *try*."

Jane sighed. She'd tried. Oh, how she'd tried. How many times had she wished she was petite and beautiful with good eyesight, someone who loved nothing better than to attend parties? It just wasn't her, and it never would be. The sooner Mama accepted that fact and let go of her dream of Jane making a splendid match, the better the two would get on.

Her mother had left her no choice. Today's little episode notwithstanding, Hortense had shown few signs of giving in. Hence, Jane was about to employ her secret weapon: one Lady Lucy Hunt, Jane's closest friend. Lucy had promised Jane she would use her considerable talent with words to convince Lady Lowndes that Jane should be left in peace. Jane wanted nothing more than to live out her days reading, studying, lobbying for the rights of women, and hosting the occasional intellectual salon. She wanted to be free, to no longer be forced to attend an endless round of social events that made her feel anything but social.

To that end, Jane had employed the second-best weapon in her arsenal, her new chaperone, Mrs. Bunbury. The idea had been inspired by Jane's other friend Cassandra Monroe's unfortunate incident last autumn when Cass had been obliged to pretend she was a nonexistent young lady named Patience Bunbury. It had been unfortunate only because in so doing, Cass had been forced to deceive the man she had desperately loved for the last seven years and . . . well, the entire charade had been a bit questionable after Captain Swift had discovered Cass's duplicity. It had all ended well enough, however, hence Jane's journey to their wedding festivities today and her subsequent need for a fictitious chaperone.

"I'm going to the house party, Mama. As for Mrs. Bunbury . . . didn't Lucy write and tell you all about her?" Jane stepped closer to the door.

Jane's father squinted up at her and arched a brow. He knew she was making her escape.

Her mother nodded vigorously. "Yes, but I find it highly suspect that I've yet to meet this woman and I—"

"Didn't Lucy vouch for Mrs. Bunbury's high moral character and excellent references?" Jane continued, with another step toward the door.

The frown lines on her mother's forehead deepened. "Yes, but I cannot allow my only child to—"

"Didn't I tell you I'm going directly to Lucy's town house where I shall meet Mrs. Bunbury and travel with her and Lucy to the house party and I shall be properly chaperoned by them the entire time?"

Her mother opened her mouth and shut it again, reminding Jane of a confused frog. "You did, but I refuse to—"

"Won't Eloise be with me the entire ride to Lucy's house?"

Her mother closed and opened her mouth a few more times. She'd apparently come to the end of her list of rebuttals. If one lobbed enough reasons at Hortense Lowndes without stopping to take a breath, one might overwhelm her with the sheer volume of logic and then . . . success was merely a matter of time. Jane could almost count the moments to her victory. One . . . two . . . three.

"I simply— I don't think—" Her mother wrung her hands and scanned about as if she'd find the answers she needed lying on the floor of the study. "Charles, what do you have to say about all of this?"

Jane's father looked up and adjusted his own spectacles. "I think Mrs. Bunbury sounds quite capable, dear."

Jane nodded, a bright smile on her face. She could always depend upon Papa.

Hortense, however, continued to wring her hands. Hmm. Apparently, this particular situation called for one more volley.

Jane folded her hands in front of her serenely. "Won't you and Papa be coming for the wedding next week, where you'll be able to see for yourself how well I've behaved and meet all the new acquaintances I've made?"

This last bit was the most important. Jane's mother liked nothing more than for Jane to meet new acquaintances, preferably of the single, titled, male variety. Of course Jane had no intention of doing anything of the sort, but her mother needn't know that.

"I shall have the opportunity to meet Mrs. Bunbury next week?" A bit mollified, her mother lowered her shoulders and her face took on a bright, hopeful hue.

"Of course. Of course." Jane nodded. Crossing her fingers behind her back, she made her way toward the door. "Now, I'm off to change my gown before Eloise and I go to meet that darling Mrs. Bunbury."

Half an hour later, Jane and Eloise marched down the steps to the waiting coach. A footman trailed behind them carrying Jane's trunk. Jane breathed a sigh of relief. Apparently, Mama was mollified for the time being. Jane lived by a steadfast rule: solve one problem at a time, preferably the one right in front of you. Worry about the others later.

The footman helped both her and Eloise into the coach, where Jane settled in the forward-facing seat and looked out the window toward the house. Her mother peered out the front door. "Good-bye, Mama. See you next week." She waved a gloved hand and smiled brightly.

Jane leaned back in her seat and let out a long sigh. She grinned at Eloise. "We're free."

Eloise sighed, too. "It'll be nice to see the country, miss."

"I'm greatly looking forward to it." Jane wiggled her shoulders and cracked open her book. It would only be a matter of hours before she'd be in the company of her closest friends, Lucy and Cass. She did so look forward to seeing them. No doubt Lucy's cousin, Upton, would be there, too. So be it. She could handle him. She always enjoyed setting him back on his heels a bit.

The coach pulled away with a jolt. Miss Jane Lowndes was off to spend a blissfully unchaperoned week in the Surrey countryside.

# CHAPTER FOUR

*Surrey*
*The country estate of the Earl and*
*Countess of Moreland*

*Thwunk.* The arrow hit the bull's-eye with a solid noise, and Jane opened her one closed eye and smiled widely.

"Another perfect hit," Lucy called from across the wide lawn. Lucy, with her slim figure, black, curly hair, and different-colored eyes—one was hazel, the other blue—was perhaps the most beautiful lady in the land. To Jane she'd always just been her friend, her fellow wallflower, and the young woman with whom she was quite often up to no good.

"Well done!" called Julian Swift's younger sister, Daphne, who was also whiling away the afternoon with Jane and Lucy.

"I quite like shooting," Jane replied, pulling another arrow from the quiver that rested next to her. "I can pretend that Lord Bartholomew is standing dead center."

Lucy's crack of laughter bounced through the field.

"Who is Lord Bartholomew?" Daphne's brow was wrinkled.

"He's one of the most vocal members of Parliament in staunch opposition to the rights of ladies," Lucy replied. "Let's just say that Jane is *not* an admirer of his."

Jane shrugged. "I'm telling you, shooting is good for one's soul. I feel quite refreshed."

Lucy laughed once more. "Hmm. Perhaps I should try it again. I've been a dismal failure at it to date. I confess I've yet to pretend an enemy is standing there. The thought definitely holds more appeal."

Daphne laughed, too. "If that's the case you must allow me to try after you're done, Miss Lowndes."

"First of all, you must call me Jane," she said to the younger woman. "Secondly, you cannot possibly have any enemies at your age, dear."

"You'd be quite surprised," Daphne said. "I may be nineteen, but there is someone I'm quite peeved at presently."

"Do tell." Lucy stepped closer, a conspiratorial grin on her face. "And you must call me Lucy, too, dear. None of this 'Your Grace' nonsense."

Daphne sighed. "I'm afraid I can't tell. But suffice it to say, I have good reasons for wanting to shoot him."

"A lady of mystery? I like that." Lucy nodded slowly.

"Him?" Jane arched a brow. "That's the part I like."

Daphne gave her a small smile and a shrug.

Jane watched the girl. Daphne was a tiny little blond thing with a plethora of energy. She'd made her comeout last year and suffered a horrible bout of sadness after her elder brother died the following autumn. It was impossible not to like Daphne. "Pretending to shoot at men or not, I'm pleased you're out today, Daphne. The fresh air is good for you," Jane said.

"I must thank you both for making me smile, and laugh. It's been so long," Daphne replied, a faraway look in her sparkling gray eyes.

Lucy crossed over the lawn and gave her a quick hug.

"My dear Daphne. We're happy to make you laugh. In fact, it's our specialty. Besides, we're practically sisters. You're one of us. Jane and I love Cass as dearly as if she *were* our sister."

"Thank you, Jane and Lucy." Daphne's mouth quirked up in a shy smile. "I couldn't be happier to have Cass joining our family. Mother and I adore her."

"Julian too," Lucy replied with a wink.

"Of course," Daphne agreed. "Julian too."

Jane faced the bull's-eye again, pulled back the bow, closed one eye, and let it fly. Another direct hit. It nearly split the previous arrow in two. "Take that, Lord Bartholomew."

"Well done," Lucy said.

Daphne clapped her hands. "Why, the only other person I've seen shoot an arrow so precisely is Captain Cavendish."

Jane and Lucy exchanged a glance over Daphne's head. Daphne had mentioned Captain Rafferty Cavendish, her brothers' friend who had been with Donald when he died, on several occasions of late.

"How is Captain Cavendish doing, dear?" Lucy strolled to where Daphne stood near Jane.

"All better, or so he says. He's recovered from his wounds in such short order, the doctors are amazed."

"Will he be able to attend the wedding?" Lucy prodded while Jane readied another arrow.

"I do hope—I mean, I think so." Daphne tugged at her gown.

"You're not *peeved* at him, are you, dear?" Lucy ventured.

Jane took a quick look at Daphne. The poor girl was blushing.

"No, wait. Don't answer," Lucy continued. "I'd hate to deprive you of your mystery."

Daphne's shoulders relaxed. "Thank you."

"One more and then you can try, Daphne," Jane said. She lined up the arrow and let go. Again, the missile whipped through the air and hit the bull's-eye in the center.

"Imagining anyone's head? Not mine, I hope," came a sarcastic male voice.

Jane lowered the bow and swung around to watch the man heading across the lawn toward them. She narrowed her eyes as he approached. "If you care to stand in as my target, Upton, that can easily be arranged."

Lucy pulled up her skirts, and rushed to greet her cousin. "Garrett, I'm so glad you're here. I worried you wouldn't get away in time for the house party."

Garrett greeted Daphne before he replied to his cousin. "I rearranged some things on my schedule."

"Ah, a wonder. Who knew drinking and gambling were so easily rearranged?" Jane gave him a tight smile. She caught Daphne's gaze and rolled her eyes. Daphne giggled.

"It's nice to see you, too, Miss Lowndes," Garrett replied. "I'll forgo standing in as your target, as tempting as that offer is. I see you have your ever-present book."

Jane squinted at the spot on the grass where she'd placed her book. "I'm surprised you recognized it, Upton, you not being a *reader*."

Daphne stepped closer to Jane and took the bow from her hands while Jane made her way over and scooped up her book.

"Reading is quite overrated if you ask me, Miss Lowndes. Besides, you do enough reading for both of us," Upton replied. "What is it you're reading this time?"

Jane gripped the book. "It's *Montague's Treatise on the History of Handwriting and Graphology,* if you must know."

"Good God, that sounds every bit as dull as I expected," Upton shot back.

Hands on her hips, Lucy glanced between the two of them. "You two, don't start. We're here for Cass and Julian's wedding, I'll have you remember, and we have a sennight to get along and enjoy ourselves before the festivities. Let's start off on a good foot, shall we?"

Upton turned to Jane. "That is entirely up to Miss Lowndes and whether she chooses to employ her razor-sharp tongue. Seems I've already become her target without the benefit of the bow and arrow." He gave her a long-suffering look. "Shall we, Miss Lowndes?"

Daphne paused in pulling an arrow from the quiver to wait for Jane's answer.

"Shall we what?" Jane asked.

Upton tilted his head to the side. "Shall we call a truce? For Cassandra's sake? For the sennight?"

Jane shrugged one shoulder. "I've no desire to cause strife during Cass and Julian's wedding. Though if I were you I'd stay out of my line of fire, Upton. I'm awfully good at shooting." She turned back to Daphne, a small grin that Upton couldn't see planted firmly on her lips.

Daphne smothered her smile behind her raised arm.

"That didn't sound like a yes to me," Upton replied.

Jane rolled her eyes where only Daphne could see. "That's because it wasn't a yes, Upton. Do try to keep up."

Lucy shook her head. "Ignore her, Garrett." Then she waved her hands in the air. "Please tell me Aunt Mary will be here." She turned back to Daphne. "That's Mr. Upton's mother. You did know he and I are cousins?"

Daphne nodded.

"Yes, Mother is coming next week for the wedding," Garrett replied.

Jane was truly glad to hear it. Garrett's mother was a

lovely woman whom Jane had had the pleasure of getting to know last summer when the friends spent time at Garrett's summer house in Bath. A pity its owner had to be there. Garrett Upton was the unfortunate addendum to Jane's friendship with Lucy. Jane had never taken to the man. In fact, the two had disliked each other nearly upon sight. They'd met at a performance of *Much Ado About Nothing,* after which the blowhard had eviscerated the play and the performance whilst Jane had defended it, and so it had been between them ever since. Attending the theater was one of her most treasured pastimes. She refused to allow some overly entertained reprobate to spout off on a subject he knew little about.

If the rumors about him were true, Upton was a rake, a gambler, and a general profligate, and Jane had little use for men who spent their time so frivolously. If those transgressions weren't enough to condemn him in her eyes, he also seemed to enjoy nothing better than to tease her about her bluestocking tendencies and education, another unforgivable sin. Though Jane had little use for Garrett Upton, Lucy and Cass adored him, and so, suffer his company Jane must.

"Wonderful," Lucy replied. "It will be so grand to see Aunt Mary." Lucy tapped a finger to her lips. "I do hope Mother is civil to her. She and Father will be here next week, as well."

Jane spied Upton out of one corner of her eye. A wide grin spread across his face. Also annoying, because Upton wasn't entirely . . . unhandsome, especially when he smiled like that. The man was tall with dark, slightly curly hair, high cheekbones, a perfectly straight nose, and hazel eyes that turned a mossy green when he traded barbs with her.

"Don't worry," Upton replied. "Mother can defend

herself. I've yet to see her in a situation she cannot handle."

At least the ass had respect for his mother.

Daphne let her first arrow fly. It shot off in a wide arc, landing in the grass nowhere near the target. "Oh, Jane, you must show me how you do it."

"Happy to," Jane replied. She set her book back on the grass and strode toward Daphne.

"Allow me." Upton made it to Daphne's side before Jane.

Just like Upton, trying to show her up. Jane crossed her arms over her chest and eyed him through the narrow slits her eyes had become.

Upton slid another arrow from the quiver and put his arms around the diminutive Miss Swift. He helped her align the arrow and pull back the bow. "You must keep your eye on the target."

Daphne let the arrow fly. *Thwunk.* It hit the target a bit off center.

Upton whistled. "Well done."

"Yes, well done. Both of you," Jane called, feeling uneasy. Good heavens. She'd just wondered what it would feel like to have Upton's arms around her, showing her how to do anything. *Not* that she needed him to. Never that.

"Thank you so much for your help," Daphne said, smiling sweetly at Upton.

Upton let his arms fall away from Daphne. He turned his head to look at Jane. A small, not uncharming smile rested on his firmly molded lips. "Thank you, Miss Lowndes. Coming from you, that is quite a compliment."

Lucy pressed a hand to her throat in a mock gasp. "What's this? The two of you actually being *civil* to each other?"

Half of Jane's mouth quirked up. "I can be civil . . . when I choose to be."

"I'm extremely glad to hear it," Upton replied. "I have to admit I've doubted it."

Waving away a servant, Daphne strode across the lawn to retrieve the arrows, leaving the others alone for the moment.

"This house party may be extraordinary indeed, if we're off to such a fine start," Lucy said.

Upton arched a brow. "I do hope this is a great deal different from the last house party we all attended."

Lucy pretended to study her gloves. "The one last autumn at Upbridge Hall?"

Upton gave her a skeptical look. "Yes, the one last autumn at Upbridge Hall."

"What was so awful about it?" Lucy asked.

Jane shook her head. "Really, Lucy?"

"Must I count the ways?" Upton added.

Lucy pushed up her chin. "I take great exception to that, Garrett. I think it worked out splendidly. We're here at the wedding, aren't we? A wedding that might not have happened if we hadn't had that house party last autumn."

"All's well that ends well, eh?" Upton pulled at the cuff of his sleeve.

"Exactly." Lucy nodded so forcefully that one of her black curls flew out of her coiffure and bobbed on her forehead.

"I would give a warning, Lucy. Don't try any of your antics during Cassandra's wedding," Upton said.

Jane had been expecting such a speech. Upton was known to be the voice of reason when his much more exuberant cousin got a scheme in her head. Lucy's "antics" always seemed to work out for the best, but there was usually trouble before they were over.

"Nonsense." Lucy tossed a hand in the air. "I would

never do anything to cause trouble during Cass and Julian's wedding."

"Lucy." A note of warning sounded in Upton's voice.

Lucy pursed her lips and regarded her cousin. She blinked innocently. "Yes?"

"I do not for one moment believe you'd do anything with the *intent* to cause trouble at Cassandra's wedding, but we all know that if you're up to something—"

"Up to something?" Lucy faked outrage with the best of them.

"Yes. Up to something. *Are* you up to something?" Upton asked.

Jane had to swallow her laughter. "Now is probably not the best time to mention my new chaperone."

"New chaperone?" Garrett put a hand on his hip.

Lucy looked at her cousin out of the corners of her eyes. "Never mind that. Suffice it to say, I do intend to help Janie here with her little problem, but that has nothing to do with Cass and Julian and will not cause them a bit of trouble."

Upton's dark brows shot up. "Jane's little problem?"

Jane shaded a hand across the top of her bonnet in an effort to look as if she were watching Daphne's progress in retrieving the arrows. Jane wasn't about to explain anything to Upton, of all people.

"Yes, it's Jane's turn, after all," Lucy responded.

"Turn at what?" The expression on Upton's face could only be called skeptical.

"Why, our pact of course." Lucy shrugged as if it were common knowledge. "We made one last summer, Jane, Cass, and I."

Upton scrubbed a hand across his cheek. "I don't think I want to hear this."

"It's nothing scandalous." Lucy flicked the curl off her

forehead. "We merely agreed to help one another, using our particular skills."

"And those are?" Upton prodded.

"First, I helped Cass rid herself of the Duke of Claringdon," Lucy said.

Upton's eyes widened. "You mean your husband?"

Lucy pursed her lips. "He just so happened to be perfect for me, but I hardly knew that at the time we made our pact."

"Then we helped Cass in pursuit of Julian," Jane added, smiling sweetly at Upton.

Garrett's mouth twisted grotesquely as if he'd just swallowed an eel. He turned to Lucy. "Don't tell me you're turning your talents toward finding Miss Lowndes here a mate."

"Don't be a nitwit, Upton." Jane crossed her arms over her chest. "And please don't say 'mate' like that. It sounds so . . . barbaric."

"Of course not," Lucy interjected before Upton could reply. "We merely intend to ensure Jane's mother leaves her alone to be a spinster. Just as Jane wishes."

"Oh, really?" Upton replied, giving Jane a sardonic look. "How exactly do you intend to accomplish that?"

Lucy didn't take a breath. "Jane's been suffering at her mother's insistence that she marry and we've a plan to put an end to it. It's quite simple, really. Nothing that will cause trouble at the wedding."

"Lucy." The note of warning was back in Upton's voice. "What are you planning to do?"

Lucy waved her hand in the air. "Nothing that requires your assistance, dear cousin. You needn't warn me this time. I've everything perfectly under control."

Upton studied Jane. She merely shrugged. She'd been patiently waiting her turn for Lucy's, er, expertise, and she wasn't about to allow Upton's cautiousness to up-end her Mrs. Bunbury plot. Lucy always managed to think of some way to get what she wanted, and this time, Jane intended to be the happy recipient of that skill.

"Don't worry your pretty little head, Garrett," Lucy replied, patting her cousin's arm. "Besides, after I help Jane here, I may turn my attentions to you."

"Me?" The whites of Upton's eyes showed.

Lucy tossed the recalcitrant curl off her forehead with one finger. "Yes. You."

Upton squinted one eye, pressing his fingertip to his forehead as if he had a megrim. "How could you possibly help *me*?"

Lucy's grin was wide and unrepentant. "Why, you're obviously in need of a wife."

# CHAPTER FIVE

"In need of a wife. Absolutely ludicrous," Garrett mumbled to himself minutes later after the three ladies had excused themselves and returned to the house. The last thing he needed was his troublemaking cousin trying to matchmake for him. Why, Lucy had already spent the last few years convinced he was in love with Cassandra. Lucy had been entirely wrong about that, of course, but it had taken no small bit of discussion to convince her.

Garrett grabbed up the bow and arrow and took aim at the bull's-eye. He released the bow, letting the arrow zing its way to the target. It hit right off center. Damn. Not quite as perfect as Miss Lowndes's arrows, but he'd never give her the satisfaction of knowing it.

Miss Lowndes. What was she up to? Lucy was meddlesome. That was her nature. Apparently, Miss Lowndes was encouraging her meddling. Garrett had nearly asked them to explain whatever Miss Lowndes meant by that comment about her new chaperone. Could he survive another mad house party with Lucy up to her old tricks? He sighed. Something told him he was about to.

He plucked another arrow from the quiver and sent it zinging behind the last one. He grinned. Aha! That hit even closer than Miss Lowndes's best shot.

"Well done."

Garrett swiveled toward the sound of clapping to see Derek Hunt, the Duke of Claringdon, striding toward him.

"Claringdon, good to see you."

At well over six feet tall, Claringdon was taller than Garrett though not by much. He was big, dark, and strong, a former army lieutenant general before being granted his dukedom for his decisiveness in the Battle of Waterloo. But for all of Claringdon's recommendations, the thing that mattered most to Garrett was that the duke made his cousin Lucy happy.

"How have you been, Upton?" Claringdon asked as he moved to stand a few paces away from Garrett.

"I've been well." Garrett pulled a third arrow from the quiver.

"Why do I question that?" Claringdon's deep voice held a note of skepticism.

Garrett gave him a half-grin. Claringdon was wise. The man could obviously tell that Garrett wanted to broach a certain subject with him. An image of Harold Langford flashed across Garrett's mind. His death. His screams. Garrett's chest tightened in that familiar way it always did. Guilt, his constant companion. "I wanted to speak with you about the bill that Swifdon is proposing."

Claringdon arched a brow. "The one for the soldiers who fought in the wars?"

"Yes."

"What of it?"

Garrett took a deep breath. "I intend to help him rally for it, of course, as best I can. But I want it to do more."

Claringdon squinted against the afternoon sun. "More?"

"That's right." Swifdon's interest in passing a bill for the veterans had given Garrett a new purpose. He'd spent the last years since he'd returned from war being the perfect caricature of a Society male, a future earl. He'd gone drinking, gambled, flirted with ladies, even taken a few of the widows to bed. All in an effort to forget. Not that any of it had worked. In addition to sleepless nights plagued by awful dreams and memories, he'd been unable to fill the void in his soul. A generous bank draft made out to Harold's widow each fortnight had done little to staunch the tidal wave of guilt that followed him wherever he went. Now, with this bill, Garrett finally had a chance to do something. He was not yet a member of Parliament himself, but he had two close friends who were, Claringdon and Swifdon.

"What did you have in mind?" Claringdon asked.

"I want to expand it. Make it so that not only the soldiers are taken care of, but their families, as well."

The edges of Claringdon's mouth drew up in a frown. "You know it's going to be a fight for the soldiers alone."

"I know." Garrett nodded. "But I think it's important."

"I don't disagree with you," Claringdon said with a firm nod. "We'll speak to Swifdon."

"Thank you," Garrett replied. "Care to try your luck with the bow?"

Claringdon stepped forward. "Don't mind if I do. I actually came here to see Lucy. She told me that she and Daphne were shooting."

"They just left. They had Miss Lowndes with them."

Claringdon took the bow and pulled back. "Jane?"

"Yes."

Claringdon shook his head. "I do hope those two think

things through a bit more before they get themselves into trouble."

"Trouble?"

"Yes. Didn't Lucy tell you? She's hired a new chaperone for Jane. A Mrs. Bunbury."

"Bunbury?" Garrett cursed under his breath. It wasn't the first time he'd heard that name.

# CHAPTER SIX

"How is the beautiful bride?" Jane asked an hour later, as she and Lucy entered Cass's bedchamber in the large manor house. Cass's room was as lovely as she was, all pink and white and cheery. There was a gorgeous four-poster bed in the center of the room, a delicate white-washed bookshelf that took up an entire wall and made Jane nearly salivate, and watercolors of flowers on the wall that Cass had painted herself.

Cass stood from her writing desk to greet her friends, her honey-blond hair cascading over her shoulders. She was still wearing her dressing gown. "The bride? I'm nervous," she responded with a tremulous smile. "And I have a horrible red spot on my nose that had better be gone before the wedding or I don't know what I shall do."

"A red spot? Let me see." Lucy hurried over to Cass and examined her nose. "It's not that bad, truly."

"Not that bad? It looks as if I have a third eye." Cass touched her fingertip to the offending spot.

"No doubt it's caused by nerves," Jane said. "Try not to worry so much, Cass." Poor Cass. The girl was as anxious as a cat in a room full of rocking chairs. She always had been, and the wedding was only making it worse. Of course, Jane couldn't sympathize, having never been engaged to be married and having the entire *ton* about to descend upon her home for the wedding. Jane could only imagine the courage it took Cass to face all of this. Especially with her overbearing mother in the way, but the outcome, the wedding itself, was certain to be beautiful.

"That's right." Lucy twisted a black curl around one of her fingers. "There's nothing to be nervous about. Everything shall be splendid. I've been helping your mother with all the planning and—"

"*You've* been helping Mother?" Cass's hand fell away from her face and her cornflower-blue eyes widened.

"Yes, dear," Lucy replied. "Don't you know? She's quite forgiven me, now that you're to be a countess."

Jane laughed. "I suppose that would do it."

Cass's mother had held a grudge against Lucy for her part in dissuading the Duke of Claringdon's pursuit of Cass last summer. Lucy had done so at Cass's behest, of course, because Cass had always been in love with Julian, but that hadn't mattered to Cass's status-hungry parents. They'd disliked Lucy immensely for months, until Julian returned and unexpectedly became an earl, that is. Julian's older brother, Donald, had been killed last autumn while working for the War Office in France.

"I've been practically forced to hide from Mother," Cass said. "I've never seen her so prone to hug me. She does so at every opportunity."

Jane laughed again. "Ah, she's about to claim a countess as a daughter."

Cass sighed. "Yes, and it makes me absolutely heartsick that it's at poor Donald's expense. The only good thing about it is that since Julian is an earl, he's able to use his position in Parliament to promote the bill for the veterans."

Lucy laid a hand on Cass's. "I know it's been difficult for Julian and Daphne since Donald died."

Cass's eyes briefly filled with tears but she shook them away. "I promised Julian we'd be joyful this week and I intend to be joyful. I *am* joyful, but still, being so happy under such tragic circumstances is difficult. Mother is so utterly callous about the reason for Julian's elevation."

"She's happy that her darling daughter is getting married. Perhaps you should look at it that way." Jane adjusted her spectacles upon her nose.

Cass raised a skeptical brow. "Darling?"

Jane shrugged.

Lucy cleared her throat. "Regardless, I've been helping your mother with the planning and we've everything arranged, including all the festivities leading up to the wedding."

Cass's nose reddened and she pressed her handkerchief to it. "The wedding," she echoed. "Oh, I just cannot believe that I'm about to marry Julian next week. After so many years and then the last six months of waiting and— Will one of you pinch me, please? I'm so frightened that this is merely a dream."

Jane rubbed Cass's shoulder and gave her an encouraging smile. She was delighted for her friend. Cass was as beautiful inside as she was out and Jane was happy that Cass had found the love of her life. Apparently that did exist . . . for some people. "No need for pinching. It's all quite real, I assure you, and no one deserves happiness more than you and Julian."

Cass bowed her head slightly.

Lucy quickly hugged Cass. "Of course it's real, dear. It's real and it's wonderful."

"The size of this wedding has my nerves in knots," Cass continued. "There will be dozens of guests!"

"An earl is getting married, dear," Lucy replied with a warm smile.

"Yes, but I had no idea it would be so large. Normally these things are small, quiet affairs. You married a duke and didn't have half so many in attendance, Lucy. It's no wonder I have a red spot on my nose. The wonder is that I don't have several."

"When a war hero earl marries his true love, who just happens to be the daughter of another earl, the entire *ton* wants to celebrate it," Jane added.

Cass bit her lip. "I don't want to be a spectacle."

"Be a spectacle, darling." Lucy flourished her hand in the air. "And have the time of your life while you're at it."

"Well said," Jane agreed with a nod.

Lucy hurried over to Cass's wardrobe. "Now, I've got your costume for the masquerade and—"

Jane's head snapped up. "Masquerade?"

Lucy turned her face and blinked at her. "Yes. Masquerade. Two nights hence. I thought I told you. Oh, Janie, please say you've remembered to bring a costume for the masquerade?"

"No, I have *not* remembered to bring a costume for a masquerade. I've never even *been* to a masquerade. Why in the world would you think I owned a costume for one? And why are we having a masquerade at a house party where everyone knows everyone?"

Cass and Lucy laughed and shook their heads simultaneously.

"Everyone does not know everyone. Many guests haven't even arrived yet," Lucy said. "Don't worry about your costume. I've a gown you may wear and we'll see to making you a domino. I think Mother has one. I'll send one of the servants over to Upbridge Hall for it."

Jane sighed. Drat all the luck that Lucy's and Cass's parents were neighbors, making it easy to send to Upbridge Hall for a domino mask. Growing up as neighbors, Cass and Lucy had become friends despite their differences. Lucy was a tomboy with a sharp tongue and matching manners and Cass was the soul of demure, ladylike perfection.

Jane fell somewhere in between. She'd never been much for demure ladylikeness, but she also couldn't quite be bothered to not follow Society's rules. She was too busy reading. She loved her friends fiercely, mostly because they did the lion's share of the talking while she was left to blissfully read. Oh, she could offer a pithy comment now and again, but usually was quite happy to allow Lucy and Cass to sort out everything and tell her the relevant facts.

Too bad the latest relevant fact happened to be a masquerade ball. Jane sighed again. She would be a good sport for Cass's wedding festivities, but really, a masquerade?

"Don't worry. It's certain to be fun, Janie." Cass patted her hand.

"Of course it will." Jane replaced her thoughts with a bright smile for Cass's sake. If Cass wanted a masquerade during her wedding celebration, Jane would procure a domino and be there.

"Tell me," Cass asked. "Have any other guests arrived since I've last been downstairs?"

"Upton's here," Jane announced, trying—though not particularly hard—to keep the disdain from her voice.

Cass clasped her hands together. "I'm so glad. Having the three of you with me makes me feel ever so much better."

"Why must you include Upton in 'the three of us'?" Jane scrunched up her nose.

Lucy gave Jane a warning look. "You promised to be civil," she whispered.

"Very well," Jane whispered back.

"You know Garrett is one of my dearest friends." Cass made her way to the looking glass to examine her nose again. She poked at the red spot.

Jane crossed to the window and pulled back the curtain to view the sweeping landscape behind the manor house. Upton was still on the lawn, practicing his archery. Jane eyed his form. She'd like to challenge him to a round, show him just how superior ladies were. "A wonder he came, considering his feelings for you."

Cass turned abruptly toward Jane. "Whatever do you mean?"

Jane pushed up her spectacles. "I mean Upton wanted to marry you, himself."

"Yes, but—" Lucy began.

Jane turned to see her friends exchange a glance.

Lucy nodded toward Cass. "You should have been there, Cass. I told Garrett that after I help Janie with Mrs. Bunbury, I'll help him find a wife."

"You did?" Cass smothered a laugh with her hand.

"She did, indeed." Jane turned back to the window.

"What did Garrett say to that?" Cass wanted to know.

"He gave me some more dire warnings of what would happen if I caused any trouble at your wedding and then spouted some nonsense about how he doesn't need a wife. The man is going to be an *earl* one day. Of course he needs a wife. The sooner, the better if you ask me."

Jane snorted. "Very best of luck finding someone who could stand him long enough to marry him, but we're focused on Cass, this week, not Upton."

"That's absolutely right," Lucy agreed.

"And we must plan what we'll say to Mama when she

arrives next week looking for Mrs. Bunbury," Jane continued.

Cass tugged at her long hair. "What exactly do you intend to do?"

Lucy's eyes lit with the mischievous glee they always did whenever she was explaining one of her schemes. "The idea is that if Jane has a chaperone who doesn't exist, she might go to the circulating library or an intellectual salon instead of making calls and attending parties. There would be no one to contradict her assertions about where she has been."

"But how will you ever keep up the charade back in London?" Cass asked.

Lucy tapped a finger against her cheek. "Admittedly, we haven't thought it through much more than that. We were merely worried about this house party at present."

"Yes, one problem at a time," Jane said.

"However, Jane and I intended to devote a good portion of the next week to coming up with the solution to the problem," Lucy added with a resolute nod.

Cass ran her hands down her sleeves. "Your mother thinks you're here with Mrs. Bunbury, Jane?"

Jane nodded. "I was able to leave the house with Eloise, but Mama insisted she be introduced to my new chaperone when she arrives next week."

"Don't worry, Jane. We'll think of something," Lucy assured her.

"You two always do." Cass turned her head from side to side in the mirror. "Perhaps I can wear a veil over my face for the next few days until this spot goes away."

"The veil will just draw more attention to it." Lucy turned to Jane. "You arrived here successfully, didn't you?"

Jane nodded. "I did, indeed, arrive successfully. I agree about the veil."

Cass sighed and backed away from the looking glass. She turned to her friends.

"Cass, you are not to worry yourself on the matter at all," Lucy said. "You are the bride and it is your wedding party. Jane and I will handle the Mrs. Bunbury business."

"That's right," Jane agreed.

"Did you tell Garrett about Mrs. Bunbury?" Cass asked.

Lucy shook her head. "No. Not yet."

Cass's eyes widened. "You plan to?"

Lucy smoothed her skirts. "With Garrett, it's best to admit to things. He has an unfortunate habit of finding out eventually, and it's better for everyone if he's in on it from the first."

"Yes, he did help when Owen arrived at the house party last autumn," Cass admitted. "But still, even though it's my wedding week, I want to help with Jane's situation. It will keep my mind off my nerves, and my mother. And my spot." She pressed at the offending bump again with the tip of her finger.

Jane tugged at her lower lip. "I've been thinking . . . Perhaps we can have Mrs. Bunbury write Mama a letter and tell her she's come down with an illness and had to leave. She can add that she is quite certain I should despair of making a match. Perhaps we can convince Mama to abandon hope when it comes to my marital prospects."

Lucy wrinkled her nose. "I'm not certain your mother would take one woman's word for it, Janie, dear."

"And a woman she hasn't met at that," Cass added.

"You're right." Jane paced across the rug. "Perhaps Mrs. Bunbury could commence a campaign of letters on the subject, begging Mama to desist in her attempts to marry me off lest she become the laughingstock of the *ton*."

"Better," Lucy conceded, pacing in the opposite direction, "but it still lacks a certain . . . something."

Cass tucked a blond lock behind her ear. She stared out the window. "You could always involve yourself in a scandal. Your mother would be forced to keep you behind closed doors. If it were bad enough, that is."

Jane stopped pacing. "Scandal?"

Cass turned her chin to her shoulder and laughed. "I was only teasing."

"No. I liked it, quite a lot actually," Jane said.

"A scandal," Lucy echoed, her unusually colored eyes twinkling.

Cass twirled to face them. "Oh, Lucy, no! Don't get that look. No scandals, please."

"What sort of scandal would it have to be?" Jane asked, her attention riveted to Lucy.

"No, Janie. No scandal! Certainly not at my wedding. Please," Cass begged.

"We would never dream of doing anything to disrupt your wedding, Cass, dear," Lucy said. "But *after* the wedding . . ."

"Yes?" Jane prompted, certain she had the same twinkle in her own eye.

Cass rushed to stand between them. "Oh, Jane. Being a wallflower is one thing, but a scandal is quite another. And I—"

Jane patted Cass on the shoulder. She and Lucy needed to plan this alone. Poor, anxious Cass had enough to fret over. "Don't worry. It won't be a hideous scandal, just a small, effective one."

# CHAPTER SEVEN

"You shall be a beautiful bride," Garrett told Cassandra that evening over drinks before dinner in the drawing room. He bowed over the hand she presented to him.

When he straightened up again, he scanned the room. Miss Lowndes watched him through narrowed eyes. Miss Lowndes was always watching him through narrowed eyes. If she was paying him any mind at all, that was. He inclined his head toward her and her scowl deepened. Just as expected, he'd annoyed her simply by smiling at her. Ha.

It was too bad, really. Miss Lowndes might be attractive—pretty even—if she wasn't such a know-it-all with a razor for a tongue. She was of medium height and looked as if she might be very well formed indeed from what he could tell. Which wasn't much because she'd never deigned to wear a ladylike garment. Instead, she insisted on dressing herself in serious-looking blue wool morning and day dresses that left everything to the imagination. What was it about bluestockings and their complete lack of femininity? Would it kill her to reveal a bit of skin once in a while?

Garrett shook his head. This was not a good thing to be thinking. Miss Lowndes had a round face, bright, intelligent brown eyes that sparkled with mirth—usually brought on by a joke at his expense—and were only to be seen behind a pair of silver-rimmed spectacles she never removed. She also had rich, dark brown hair that was always pulled into a severe knot on the top of her head. It was as if she thought a bit of her intellectual superiority would seep out if a hair was out of place.

He had the sudden urge to pull the pins from her topknot and watch her hair spill over her shoulders. Wouldn't that make her run for her smelling salts? No. She was more likely to slap him across the face. He rubbed his cheek as if she'd done it.

Dragging his thoughts from the queen of the bluestockings, Garrett turned his attention to the other occupants of the room. Not all the guests who had been invited to the prewedding festivities had arrived yet, but there was a large crush. Cassandra, Lucy, Miss Lowndes, and Garrett had managed a few moments alone before going in to dinner with the other guests. Cassandra had insisted Garrett join them instead of having drinks in the study with the other gentlemen.

Cassandra blushed. "Thank you for saying I'll be a beautiful bride, Garrett."

"Only stating the truth, Cassandra," he replied with another bow. He glanced up. Had Miss Lowndes rolled her eyes at his comment?

"It's too bad Mrs. Bunbury is under the weather this evening," Miss Lowndes said with a laugh.

Lucy clapped her hands. "Yes. Let's discuss." She

entwined her arm through Miss Lowndes's and made as if to take her off into the corner to have a private discussion.

Garrett gave Cassandra a questioning stare. She winced.

Garrett narrowed his eyes on his cousin and Miss Lowndes. This was his chance to get to the bottom of this ludicrous scheme. He held up a hand. "Just a moment. Did I hear you say 'Bunbury'?"

The two stopped their journey across the room. "Yes, what of it, Upton?" Miss Lowndes gave him a look that could melt marble.

Garrett cleared his throat. "Isn't *Miss* Bunbury the name Cassandra used last autumn when she was pretending to be a nonexistent person?"

Lucy's eyes shifted back and forth. "Yes, it was." She turned again.

Garrett blinked at Cassandra. She winced for the second time.

"Would this *Mrs.* Bunbury be any relation to *Miss* Bunbury, then?" he asked.

Miss Lowndes sighed heavily and pushed up her chin. "Of course they aren't related, Upton. Neither one of them exists." She gave him a look that clearly indicated she thought him an imbecile.

Garrett turned to Cassandra, the only one of the three who could be counted on to explain this nonsense adequately. He arched a brow in her direction.

"Mrs. Bunbury is Jane's chaperone," Cassandra said simply, as if that explained it.

"That's right," Lucy offered.

"But she doesn't exist?" Garrett clarified.

"Of course not," Miss Lowndes replied. "What is the use of a nonexistent chaperone if she existed?"

Garrett put one hand on his hip. "I'm going to regret

asking this, but why do you want a nonexistent chaperone?"

Miss Lowndes pushed up her spectacles and gave him a tight smile. "The better question is, of course, why would I want an *existent* chaperone?"

Lucy seemed completely at ease with that answer and the two ladies continued to chat until Garrett cleared his throat again. "Why do I have the feeling that one of Lucy's schemes is at work here?"

Cassandra folded her hands and searched the room as if desperately looking for something to do other than meet his eyes.

"Don't worry about it, Upton," came Miss Lowndes's tight reply.

"On the contrary, I cannot help but worry about it if Lucy is doing something she ought not to."

Lucy turned to face him this time. "Garrett, you may relinquish your role as the sensible one for the remainder of the house party. As my husband, Derek is only too willing to see to it that I don't get up to too much trouble. He knows all about Mrs. Bunbury."

Garrett clasped his hands behind his back and allowed the hint of a smile to pop to his lips. "Yes. I know. He told me."

Lucy's eyes went wide. "You already knew?"

"A bit," Garrett replied. "But with all due respect to the duke, I don't think Claringdon is fully aware of the extent of trouble you can get up to, dear cousin."

"Isn't he?" Lucy batted her eyelashes.

"Be that as it may," Miss Lowndes interjected, "it's none of your concern, Upton."

Garrett turned back to Cassandra. There was little hope of getting Lucy or Miss Lowndes to crack, but Cassandra, Cassandra would only take a bit of prodding. "Cassandra?" He drew out her name.

"Don't look at me!" Cassandra replied. "I told them causing a scandal was a bad idea. A very bad one indeed."

Garrett slapped his thigh and turned back to face the other two. "A scandal?"

Lucy's brow was furrowed in a deep frown. "Cass, why did you say that?"

Cass bit her lip and wrung her hands. "I'm sorry."

"Don't try to change the subject," Garrett replied. "What type of a scandal are you trying to cause?"

"Nothing too large or awful," Lucy replied. "And nothing until the wedding is past. We promised Cass."

Cass nodded. "Yes, thank you for that, but I still think it's a bad idea."

"It's an awful idea." Garrett tried his damnedest to keep from raising his voice. "I assume this scandal would affect Miss Lowndes's reputation?"

"Yes," Miss Lowndes said. "But we plan to—"

"What?"

"Control the size of the scandal."

"Control the size?" Garrett shot back. "You've been around the *ton* long enough, both of you. Those vultures seize upon any bit of gossip. The smallest incident could quickly grow out of proportion."

Miss Lowndes's expression was bored. "Thank you for your interest and concern, Upton. But despite what you may think, a lady doesn't always need a man to tell her what to do."

Garrett's jaw tightened. "By God, it's not about my being a man. It's about common sense, and I—"

"Think you have the monopoly on common sense because of your gender," Jane finished for him.

"No I don't," he growled through clenched teeth. No one could make him more angry more quickly than Jane Lowndes and her know-it-all female-equality attitude.

Especially since he didn't have a bloody problem with female equality. He had a severe problem with know-it-alls, however.

"Don't you?" Miss Lowndes answered sweetly. "I seem to remember you telling Lucy last autumn that she desperately needed a man to come to Upbridge Estate for the house party and see to things."

His jaw remained tight. "That house party was ill-advised and—"

"Because a man wasn't running it?" came Miss Lowndes's swift reply. She blinked at him innocently.

"No. It had nothing to do with—"

"I don't believe you, Upton. I think you are overly impressed with yourself because you happen to be male, a sad trait among your sex, to be sure. But I don't share your regard for your innately superior intellect and am happy to rely upon my own in all matters. No one asked you."

Cassandra's eyebrows both shot up.

Garrett took a long, deep breath. "I never said anyone asked me, but I'm damn well going to tell you if I think you are making fools of yourselves and—"

Miss Lowndes raised her nose and addressed her remarks to Lucy. "Did you ask him, Lucy? I didn't."

Garrett narrowed his eyes on Miss Lowndes. The woman was entirely too smug. "If you would allow me to get in a word edgewise, I could tell you that—"

"Now, now," Lucy interjected. "Let's not argue in the middle of the wedding party. You are upsetting Cass. And you promised to be civil."

Garrett searched Cassandra's face. She was wringing her hands and the shimmer in her eyes told him that she was on the verge of tears. Damn it. Lucy had a point. He shut his mouth, turned away, and downed a healthy portion of his drink. Very well. He'd bide his time and take this discussion back up with Lucy and Miss Lowndes later.

"Yes, let's change the subject," Miss Lowndes agreed. "I find this one extremely distasteful." She gave Garrett a tight smile.

Cass breathed a sigh. "Oh, please, let's." Her gaze scanned the room as if looking for a suitable subject. She pointed a finger in the air. "Garrett, I nearly forgot to tell you. Mrs. Langford is coming."

Garrett nearly spat his drink. "Pardon?"

"Mrs. Langford. Mrs. Harold Langford. She mentioned you specifically in her letter."

"Her letter?" Garrett set his drink on the nearby table and braced his palm against the top. The walls were closing in around him.

"Yes. Apparently, Mrs. Langford's deceased husband knew Julian and Donald and, well, she nearly invited herself to the wedding. I was put off by her forwardness until she mentioned your name."

Garrett tugged at his cravat. The room was stifling.

"Mrs. Langford invited herself to your wedding? And she's coming?" he managed to choke out, his finger lodged between his cravat and neck.

"Please don't think it was a bother. Any friend of yours and Julian's and Donald's is more than welcome. It just seemed a bit odd at first," Cassandra replied.

"She's coming?" Garrett echoed. Having his hand braced against the table didn't stop the room from spinning.

Cassandra nodded. "Yes, I invited her to the house party as well. It was a bit awkward because she'd mentioned you were coming. I decided if she already knew about it, it would be rude not to invite her."

"It sounds as if Mrs. Langford is the rude one," Miss Lowndes pointed out with a sniff.

Garrett stared unseeing into the fireplace. How the devil did Isabella Langford know he'd been planning to come to the house party? He certainly hadn't mentioned it in any of the notes.

"Is she—" He swallowed. "Has she arrived?"

"Not yet." Cass shook her head. "I believe she intends to arrive first thing in the morning."

# CHAPTER EIGHT

Garrett shut the door to his guest bedchamber behind him. He made his way over to the wing-back chair in front of the poster bed. He sat and shucked off his boots. Then he stood and strode to the window, flexing his toes. He looked down on the courtyard below, a sweeping expanse of gravel in front of the manor house.

Two words kept repeating themselves in his brain.

*Isabella Langford.*

She was Harold Langford's widow. Harold Langford had been one of Garrett's closest friends in the army. Harold had not returned from Spain. But Garrett had, and he'd done what he could—inadequate though it may be—to see to it that Isabella and the children were taken care of ever since.

Isabella was coming? Here? It made him . . . uneasy. He'd spent years distancing himself from those years at war. Even though the nightmares woke him with a cold sweat each night, he'd done an admirable job of keeping his Society life separate from his memories.

Lately, that was becoming more difficult. He'd seen

Isabella at an increasing number of Society events in town. A fortnight ago, he'd even run into her when he was out and had been obliged to escort her home. She'd invited him in for a drink. He'd declined.

If he didn't know better, he'd think she'd been flirting with him. It made him bloody uncomfortable. Now she had managed to wheedle an invitation to Cassandra's wedding? Something about it seemed not quite right. And mentioning the house party? Had he even told her about it? He was certain he had not.

He scrubbed his hands through his hair. Deuced uncomfortable. He'd been looking forward to a bit of relaxation this week, but now that Harold's widow was arriving, it would be anything but relaxing.

Garrett's thoughts turned to Lucy and Miss Lowndes. Jane. Funny how he called Cassandra and Lucy by their Christian names but he'd never done so with Jane Lowndes. She, however, referred to him only as Upton. As if she couldn't spare the word "mister." He was quite certain if he said "Tory," Miss Lowndes would say "Whig" just to spite him. Lucy insisted her friend was truly a nice young lady, once one got to know her. Perhaps she was . . . to other young ladies, but she'd been nothing but irascible to him.

Miss Lowndes assumed that anyone who didn't have his nose permanently wedged between the pages of a book was an idiot. A rake, she called him. A profligate. What did Little Miss Bluestocking know about profligate rakes? Typical. Those who had no fun in life were constantly criticizing those who did. Perhaps Miss Loudmouth might benefit from a bit of rakishness and profligacy from time to time. He had to admit to a reluctant—very reluctant—admiration for her quick wit and biting sarcasm. He appreciated intelligence as much as the next person. Too bad the sting of her barbed words was too often aimed in his direction. Regardless of his issues with the woman, she was Lucy's friend. She had been loyal to Lucy when few others would speak to her, before she'd become all the rage as the Duchess of Claringdon. He would give Loudmouth that.

Now, when Lucy had a party, half the *ton* clamored for an invitation. What a difference a year made. But true to her character, Lucy had kept her dearest friends, Cassandra Monroe and Jane Lowndes, close to her and the three remained inseparable. Yes, Garrett could abide Miss Lowndes if he had to. She made Lucy happy, and that was what mattered.

As for the scheme the two were cooking up, Garrett would have to get to the bottom of it sooner rather than later. A scandal couldn't end well. How could they believe otherwise? Those two women, always so certain of themselves. Damn it. He'd had enough experience with Lucy's schemes to know that they often lacked preparation and ended poorly or at least caused a great deal of havoc before ending happily. The Mrs. Bunbury plot alone sounded as if it were quite enough trouble. What else could they possibly dream up in the way of a scandal? Garrett scrubbed his hand through his hair again. Best not to answer that question.

He turned from the window and walked to the bed where he slid onto the mattress and lay facing the wood-beamed ceiling. He rubbed his temples. Sleep had long been a jest to him. He couldn't remember the last time he'd actually slept through an entire night. He hadn't made it through a night in the last ten years without waking in a cold sweat, hearing Harold Langford's screams.

Garrett closed his eyes. He was tired, suddenly, exhausted. Isabella would be arriving tomorrow. She'd come and meet his friends. What would it be like to have his two worlds together? He'd spent the last ten years ensuring they remained far apart. His past in the army in Spain, his present as the heir presumptive to the Earl of Upbridge. They were entirely different circumstances populated by entirely different people. Well, except for Claringdon and Swifdon, that is. Both of them had been in the army in Spain with him. Good men.

Garrett had spent a great deal of time wishing he'd died in Spain. He probably should have. He'd had no business buying a commission and leaving for war. Not since his cousin Ralph was dead and the Upbridge title would pass to some unknown cousin or revert back to the Crown if Garrett died as well. But he'd done it, just the same. Done it and lived. Lived with his regrets.

He groaned. The prospect of the house party had been mildly amusing before. He was happy to see his good friends Swifdon and Cassandra marry. Marriage wasn't something he'd given much thought to before but he didn't begrudge others from making a happy match.

Speaking of marriage, Lucy had said she would turn her sights to finding him a suitable wife after she finished with Miss Lowndes. He rubbed his temples again. It made his head hurt to think about that. Cassandra was lovely and accomplished and would make a fine wife, but she wasn't his sort. Not that he *had* a sort, but if he did, she would be more of someone who stood up for herself, argued a bit, was spirited . . .

He groaned. Damn it. He'd just described someone a bit too much like . . . Miss Lowndes. At least if Lucy was preoccupied with her Mrs. Bunbury scandal plot, she'd leave him and his marital prospects alone for a bit. Perhaps he ought to keep his nose out of it. It rarely ended well for him when he attempted to thwart Lucy's plans. He certainly didn't want to draw attention to himself and Isabella Langford. What if Lucy got it into her head that she should make a match between him and Isabella? It would be beyond awkward. Though discomfiture was no doubt in store for him one way or another, once Isabella arrived.

Garrett flung an arm over his forehead. The next week wouldn't be easy. Not only would Isabella be there, he'd be busy watching what Lucy and Miss Lowndes were getting up to, and to add insult to injury, there was to be a bloody masquerade ball. What more could go wrong?

# CHAPTER NINE

Mrs. Isabella Langford arrived the next morning at an ungodly hour. Jane had been roused from bed far too early given the fact that she'd been up nearly all night reading a novel. She'd been forced to come downstairs and greet the woman along with Cass, Lucy, and Cass's mother.

"Aren't you the least bit curious?" Lucy asked, as Jane stifled a yawn while they stood in the foyer, waiting for Mrs. Langford and for the servants to unload her trunks from the carriage.

"Not particularly," Jane replied with as much enthusiasm as she could muster. If she was honest with herself, she would admit she did wonder why Upton's voice had seemed a bit strained last night when Cass had mentioned Mrs. Langford. Jane also wondered why the woman had used Upton as an entrée to the house party. It seemed quite forward. But there were scores of socially ambitious people in London who would use any excuse to gain an invitation to an earl's wedding.

It wasn't particularly surprising. Jane was more interested in reading the last of her good book than wondering why a widow was coming to Cass's wedding under the guise of her friendship with Upton of all people. Upton's acquaintances were none of Jane's concern. But Cass had requested her presence this morning and Jane was committed to making Cass's wedding week the best it could be. Lack of her own sleep notwithstanding.

"She's the wife of a deceased army captain," Cass whispered, staring out the door at Mrs. Langford's entourage. "Do you find it odd that she has such a fine carriage and servants?"

"Cassandra, that's hardly polite," her mother interjected.

Lucy was on tiptoes, craning her neck to see everything. Jane scanned the scene. Indeed, Mrs. Langford had a footman and a lady's maid with her and enough trunks to fill Jane's bedchamber in London.

Lucy snorted. "She does know she's only staying a week, doesn't she?"

Cass elbowed Lucy.

When the lady herself emerged from the coach, Jane sucked in her breath. Mrs. Langford was ethereal. She was nearly as good-looking as Lucy, and that was saying quite a lot. The woman had a cloud of black hair and the palest white skin, with red lips that looked like a cherry set perfectly under her pin-tip nose. While she might have been a year or two older than Jane, she was not much more.

She was escorted into the foyer by Cass's mother, Lady Moreland, and as soon as the widow saw the three of them standing there, Mrs. Langford's beautiful face broke into a wide smile revealing perfect white teeth.

She had pale green eyes, Jane noted once she'd come close enough. Yes, she looked like a princess. Well, not Princess Charlotte, but some sort of princess, a fairy-tale, breathtaking sort.

"Lady Cassandra!" Mrs. Langford said in a voice Jane found far too exuberant for such an early hour. People who favored the morning were so often too loud. "It's so lovely to see you. You didn't need to trouble yourself with coming to meet me."

"It's my pleasure, Mrs. Langford. I wanted to see you had a proper welcome. Do you know the Duchess of Claringdon and Miss Jane Lowndes?" Cass gestured to her friends.

Lucy nodded regally, something she'd been practicing ever since she became a duchess. "Mrs. Langford," she intoned.

The widow curtsied formally. Once she straightened she said, "Your Grace. It's so lovely to meet you. I am quite overwhelmed with gratitude that you would come and greet me."

"Not at all," Lucy responded, barely inclining her head. "I was anxious to meet the friend of my cousin Mr. Garrett Upton."

Jane nearly took off her spectacles and rubbed her eyes. The look on Mrs. Langford's face the moment Upton's name was mentioned was downright . . . coy? Shy? Flirtatious? Her cheeks turned a lovely shade of rose, and she averted her gaze. "It's an honor to call Mr. Upton a friend," she said, still not meeting Lucy's eyes.

Jane snapped her brows together. An honor? To call Upton a friend? Upton? Were they speaking of the same man?

"I'm certain Garrett is looking forward to seeing you," Cass replied.

There was that coy blush again. It seemed so misplaced on the cheeks of a woman who had to be at *least* thirty.

"I hope you don't mind," Mrs. Langford said, "but I brought my footman, Boris, with me. I couldn't go anywhere without him. Why, he's nearly as precious to me as my maid."

The maid and footman stood several paces behind their mistress. Boris was tall and dark with slightly curly brown hair. He had wide-set dark eyes and a look on his face that was a bit too arrogant for a footman. The maid, however, had bowed her dark head and cast her eyes downward. She reeked with obsequiousness. Jane had never taken such a dislike to servants upon sight. Good heavens, she was up far too early if she was bothered by innocent servants.

"It's perfectly fine," Cass's mother replied graciously. "We'll be happy to find a place for your footman to sleep and of course your maid is always welcome."

A bright smile flashed across Mrs. Langford's face. "You are too kind."

"I do hope you've brought something to wear for the masquerade tomorrow night," Cass added.

Mrs. Langford's ever-present smile turned nearly predatory. "Yes, indeed. I'm *great*ly looking forward to it."

Cass's mother went about ordering the butler to take Boris under his wing and show the maid and Mrs. Langford to their rooms. A team of footmen from the Moreland household materialized to unload Mrs. Langford's trunks from the overburdened carriage.

"Poor horses," Jane mumbled under her breath.

"What was that, dear?" Lucy asked.

"Nothing, nothing at all."

Mrs. Langford swept toward the staircase, escorted by the Morelands' servants. She turned to look over her shoulder at the three ladies still standing in the foyer. "I do hope we shall all become the best of friends this week. Any friend of Mr. Upton's is a dear, dear friend of mine."

Jane narrowed her eyes. Who exactly was this Isabella Langford?

# CHAPTER TEN

Garrett spent the morning riding out to look at the Moreland lands with Swifdon, Claringdon, and Cass's brother, Owen Monroe, the future Earl of Moreland.

Like the others, Swifdon was also a large man. A former army captain himself, he was blond with a quick smile and friendly gray eyes that matched his younger sister Daphne's. Monroe was also tall and blond but with the same deep blue eyes as his sister and a much more rakish air.

They'd already discussed livestock, farming, estate managers, and the like when Swifdon turned toward his future brother-in-law. "Your estate here borders Upbridge Hall?"

"Yes," Monroe replied. "That's how Cass and Lucy have been such fast friends all these years. They grew up together."

Garrett cleared his throat. "If Lucy and Cass became friends because of the proximity of their homes, how did Miss Lowndes end up in their little group? Her father only has a house in London from what I understand."

Now where had that come from? It was a question he'd never bothered to ask the ladies, but suddenly he was quite interested in knowing the answer.

"Ah, this is a story I know," Claringdon replied.

"Really?" Swifdon said. "I don't think Cassie's ever mentioned it to me. I hadn't thought much of it, honestly."

"I've never known," Monroe admitted. "I assume they met at a party somewhere."

The men navigated their mounts along the line of trees that bordered a long meadow.

"Yes," Claringdon said. "It was at a party. Lucy and Cass's come-out ball. Miss Lowndes had already been out for a Season."

Miss Lowndes was a year older than Lucy and Cass? Garrett hadn't known that.

"They met at a come-out, nothing too special about that." Monroe shrugged.

"Yes, but it was the *way* they met that is typical to Lucy. To all of them, really."

"What happened?" Garrett mentally cursed himself for the note of curiosity in his voice.

"Cass, of course, was the belle of the ball," Claringdon said.

Swifdon grinned at the mention of his bride. "Of course."

"She had a queue of suitors lined up to dance with her. Her mother was beside herself with excitement," Claringdon said.

Owen snorted. "Mother should have saved herself the trouble. If only we'd all known that Cass intended to reject every last one of them because she was pining away for you, Swifdon, waiting for you to return from the war."

Swifdon's grin widened. "I can't help it if I was un-forgettable."

Garrett and Claringdon laughed out loud at that.

"Apparently, in addition to warding off the suitors in whom she had no interest, Cass was preoccupied with Lucy's lack of success. As you said, Monroe, they were great friends and Cass has a kind heart. She couldn't abide the fact that Lucy was wilting in the corner with the other wallflowers."

"Ah, enter Miss Lowndes," Garrett said with a smirk.

"Yes," Claringdon replied. "Apparently, Lucy marched over to Jane and demanded to know why she was reading a book in the middle of a ball."

Garrett snorted this time.

" 'Look around you,' Jane replied, 'see anything better to do? I assure you my dance card is entirely blank and this book is far more fascinating than watching all the gentlemen vie for Lady Cassandra Monroe's attention,' " Claringdon continued.

"That sounds like Jane Lowndes," Owen Monroe said with a grin, one that made Garrett feel a twinge of annoyance.

Claringdon kept talking. " 'Cassandra is a dear,' Lucy said to Jane. 'I'm certain she is,' Jane said to Lucy, 'and I am not. Which is why gentlemen are not lined up to dance with me. Now, if you intend to stand there, would you mind moving a bit to the right? You'll block the view of my mother and she detests it when she finds me reading a book at a ball.' "

"Then what happened?" Swifdon asked, his gray eyes lit with amusement.

"Then Lucy burst into laughter, moved to the right to accommodate Jane, and asked her if she had another book in her reticule that Lucy could borrow. They've been inseparable ever since."

All of the men laughed and Garrett shook his head. That story did sound exactly like Jane and Lucy. A wonder he'd never heard it before. He'd come to Lucy's come-out later in the evening and danced with her. Lucy had told him he was the only gentleman to do so. Garrett had thought she'd been exaggerating. Apparently, she had not. For all her beauty, Lucy had already garnered a reputation for ripping men to shreds with her tongue. The men of the *ton* had been duly scared off, until Claringdon arrived and gave as good as he got from her.

"You know, Jane Lowndes is considered a bluestocking by some, but I think she's actually quite an attractive young lady," Monroe said.

Garrett's eyes narrowed on the future earl.

"That's rich coming from you, Monroe. I don't think there's a lady alive whom you couldn't charm or find attractive in some way," Swifdon replied.

Monroe had a rakish grin on his face, a bit too leering for Garrett's taste. "I'm merely saying she's easy on the eyes. I'd like to see her with those spectacles off and a bit of—"

"My home isn't far from here." Garrett cleared his throat loudly. "Shall we ride over and I'll show you the property?"

Monroe shrugged, but the wolfish grin remained on his face.

"In addition to your home nearby, one day you will call Upbridge Hall home, Upton," Claringdon pointed out.

"Yes." Garrett studied his leather gloves where they gripped the reins. It was inevitable. He would be the Earl of Upbridge one day, but damn how he wished his cousin Ralph had lived. It wasn't that he didn't want to be the earl. He didn't want to be the earl at his cousin's expense, not to mention the fact that his uncle had detested him his entire life as a result.

"Lucy's brother died of fever when he was nine," Monroe added for Swifdon's sake.

"Yes, Cassie told me," Swifdon replied. "Damn shame. But I know you'll do the Upbridge name proud, Upton."

Garrett's grip tightened. "My thanks, Swifdon. I hope I'll be able to help you in Parliament one day. But as my uncle is in good health as far as I know, it won't be in time to assist with the veterans' bill."

"Ah, yes. Derek mentioned that to me earlier this morning. I quite like the idea of expanding it."

Monroe led the way toward Upton's property. The other men followed in line.

"I'm glad to hear that," Garrett replied.

"Does your interest in the bill have anything to do with Isabella Langford?" Claringdon asked.

Damn that Claringdon, nothing escaped his notice.

"Her husband died. I was there . . ." Garrett murmured.

"I remember," Swifdon said quietly.

Garrett quickly shook his head. "Yes, well, that reminds me. Cassandra told me last night that Isabella Langford is coming to the house party."

"Is she?" Claringdon's voice held a note of surprise.

"Apparently she informed Cassandra that she and I are acquainted," Garrett continued.

"Getting some unwanted attention from the widow?" Monroe said with another leering grin that Garrett didn't appreciate.

"Yes, actually," Garrett replied. "Her attention is unwanted."

"If I remember her correctly, Mrs. Langford is a great beauty. Just say the word," Monroe replied, still leering. I'm only too happy to distract her for you if you like."

Garrett straightened his shoulders. Monroe's rakishness was usually either an annoyance or an amusement, but today it might actually prove useful. "Thank you, Monroe. I'd like that."

# CHAPTER ELEVEN

Garrett took a deep breath before placing his hand on the handle, opening the door, and strolling into the drawing room that evening before dinner. He'd done an admirable job of remaining with the gentlemen all day in an effort to avoid encountering Isabella Langford. When they'd returned to the manor for tea in the afternoon, Garrett had declined. But dinner was unavoidable. He must face Isabella eventually. He wasn't usually uncomfortable around women, quite the opposite, actually. But being around Isabella brought back the memories of Harold—his mistake, his death. Guilt gnawed at Garrett especially viciously when Isabella was near.

He strode into the opulent rose silk–wallpapered room to see Cassandra, Lucy, and Miss Lowndes all busily talking to Mrs. Langford. The knot in his gut tightened.

The moment she saw him, Mrs. Langford's pale green eyes lit with a smile. "Mr. Upton, how good to see you." Her joy made the guilt all the worse.

"Mrs. Langford," he replied, with a nod and a bow. He did his best to smile. She wore a dark blue silk gown that hugged her figure. Isabella was gorgeous. There was no denying it, but he noticed it the same way he'd note his own sister was a beauty, if he'd had a sister. Well, Lucy then. Lucy was a beauty by all accounts, but to him she was just his cousin, the little ragamuffin of a girl who had chased him around and got dirty with him in his youth. Isabella may not have known Garrett as a child, but she was Harold's widow and that made her as undesirable as any sister or cousin would be.

"Wherever have you been this evening, Garrett?" Lucy asked, turning to greet him. "We've been waiting for you to go into dinner."

"I'm sorry to have made you wait." Garrett gave his cousin a kiss on the cheek.

"Yes, well, now that you're here, won't you escort Mrs. Langford into the dining room?" Cassandra requested prettily. No doubt she assumed he would be eager to renew his acquaintance with the widow. "I've seated you next to each other," she added.

Garrett kept the smile pinned to his face. He glanced at Miss Lowndes who, thankfully—and unusually for her—remained silent. She merely raised her dark brows over the rims of her spectacles and gave him a look that told him she was wondering about the nature of his friendship with Isabella. Bloody perfect.

"By all means." Garrett gestured toward the door where the other couples were lining up to make their way into the dining room. He looked back to see Miss Lowndes on the arm of Owen Monroe. Damn it. Why wasn't Monroe up here trying to charm Isabella as promised?

Garrett offered his arm to Isabella, who took it eagerly. They fell into step behind the others. The procession made its way into the dining room with its long polished mahogany table and dark green damask-covered chairs. Lord and Lady Moreland took their places at the head and foot of the table. Cassandra and Swifdon sat to their hostess's immediate right and left. Lucy and Derek, the Duke and Duchess of Claringdon, were next, seated across from each other. A few other guests filled in the space between, then Isabella, then Garrett. He took his seat and looked up to stare into the smugly smiling face of Jane Lowndes.

He wasn't certain exactly what a bluestocking face was, but surely it would look like Miss Lowndes's. She was the type of young woman who would argue with a gentleman about things like horses and history and theater and essentially any topic that came up in polite conversation and a few that did not. She *would* be sitting across from him all evening while he was forced to make awkward conversation with Isabella.

Of course, perhaps it was merely a coincidence that Isabella was here. Perhaps she'd only used his name to gain entrée to a much talked about social fete. It wasn't her fault that she reminded him of his guilt. He pasted a smile on his face and turned to Isabella.

"I trust your journey here was a pleasant one," Garrett said to Isabella as the footman shook out her napkin and placed it over her lap.

"Indeed, it was," she replied demurely. "It was kind of Lady Cassandra to invite me."

"We're all greatly looking forward to the wedding next week." He felt like a complete ass. A footman poured Garrett a glass of wine. Wine. He'd never been so bloody happy to see a glass of wine.

"Such a lovely occasion and reason for the Swifts to come out of mourning," Isabella murmured.

How long had she been in mourning for Harold?

The footmen began serving the first course, a watercress soup. Garrett sat with his back ramrod straight, racking his brain for a sufficiently pleasant yet simple topic to keep the conversation going. Thankfully, Miss Lowndes had turned to Owen Monroe. They appeared deeply interested in their conversation.

Garrett glared at Monroe. Was that reprobate flirting with Miss Lowndes? Since when did Monroe have a bloody dimple? And his eyes were—dare he think it?—sparkling. Garrett did a double take. He'd never seen *anyone* flirt with Miss Lowndes before. He narrowed his eyes on the couple. It was not possible. He was imagining things. He'd seen some of the women Monroe kept company with in London. Despite what he'd said today on the ride, it was unimaginable that Miss Bluestocking was Monroe's sort. Never. Besides, Monroe, that blighter, had agreed to flirt with Isabella. He was doing a bloody poor job of it so far.

"I hope you don't mind that I've come," Isabella whispered to Garrett, dragging him from his thoughts.

Garrett forced himself to look away from Miss Lowndes. He cleared his throat. "No. Not at all." What else could he say? "I do admit I wasn't aware that you and Lady Cassandra were . . . friends."

Isabella peeped up at him from beneath her long dark lashes. She had the grace to blush. "I must admit that we are not, Mr. Upton." She took a deep breath. Her lips trembled. "I . . . I . . . wanted to see *you*."

With that astonishing bit of information, she turned her attention back to her soup.

Garrett reached for his wine glass and took a long, deliberate drink. He went to place the glass back on the table, thought better of it, and took another long drink. The footman rushed to refill his glass.

This was what he had feared. That Isabella admired him. That she was flirting with him. That perhaps she wanted something more from him. Something he couldn't give. Not with the memory of Harold's death burned into his brain. He wanted to kick Monroe under the table, get his attention, signal to him to use his infamous charm on Isabella, but that oaf would probably only ask why he'd been kicked.

Garrett was about to reply with some innocuous bit of wording when he caught Miss Lowndes laughing at something Monroe had said. Her laughter was . . . not unpleasant. He couldn't take his gaze from her. Something about the way she'd tossed back her head and laughed as if she didn't care a bit what anyone thought about her. And those blasted spectacles. For the second time he had the urge to rip them from her nose. They made her look too prim, too proper, too . . . Miss Lowndeslike.

He forced himself to return his attention to Isabella. A brief flash of supreme annoyance crossed the widow's face. If Garrett hadn't been looking, he might have missed it.

"What's so amusing?" Isabella leaned toward Miss Lowndes and cupped a hand behind her ear.

Miss Lowndes looked a bit startled to have been addressed by Isabella. "Lord Owen was just telling me the most charming story about a mutual acquaintance of ours in London."

"Monroe is the soul of charm," Garrett grumbled under his breath, glaring at Monroe.

Monroe seemed to finally remember his promise. He leaned toward Isabella and flashed her a rakish grin. "Do tell us, Mrs. Langford. Do you know Sir Roderick Montague?"

A small pout formed on Isabella's lips. "I'm afraid I do not, my lord. I know only a few people in Society. Mr. Upton here is one of my dearest friends. I am quite thankful for his friendship."

Miss Lowndes's eyebrows rose, but otherwise she looked as if she were ready to turn back and continue her discussion with Monroe. Isabella cleared her throat. "In fact, I was just telling Mr. Upton how greatly I've been looking forward to this party. It's such a pleasure to see him again."

Miss Lowndes mumbled something that sounded suspiciously like "I find that difficult to believe." Then she pasted a smile on her bluestocking face and said more loudly, "How exactly are the two of you acquainted, Mrs. Langford?"

Garrett froze. The tone in Miss Lowndes's voice, the way she'd said "acquainted," implied something he didn't want to contemplate.

Isabella brought her napkin to her red lips and blotted their fullness before directing her gaze to Miss Lowndes. "Mr. Upton knew my late husband during the war."

Miss Lowndes turned her bespectacled gaze on him. "You served together, you and Mr. Langford? In Spain?"

Garrett plucked at his cravat. It was stifling in here tonight. He nodded and reached for his wine glass again. That footman had better stay alert. "Yes. I had the pleasure of serving with Captain Langford. A better soldier I've never known."

Miss Lowndes narrowed her gaze on him. That was another thing about her. She had a way of looking at people, a way of studying them that made it seem as if she knew all their secrets, as if she could see through them and pick them apart one by one.

"Do you have children, Mrs. Langford?" Miss Lowndes continued, smiling a bit too sweetly at Isabella.

Isabella nodded. "I do, a boy and a girl. They are in London with their tutor and governess."

Miss Lowndes cocked her head to the side. "Ah, one of each. How efficient."

"I suppose so." Isabella's smile remained tight. "How exactly do *you* two know each other?" she countered, staring at Miss Lowndes and then glancing at Garrett.

A wry smile tugged at Miss Lowndes's lips and Garrett found himself looking forward to what was certain to be a highly sarcastic answer. "Unfortunately for both of us, Upton and I have a mutual friend in the Duchess of Claringdon."

Isabella's brow furrowed. "Unfortunately?"

"Yes. It is unfortunate because we often cannot stand to be in the same room with each other. I think Cass is punishing us by seating us near each other tonight."

Owen Monroe stifled a chuckle.

"However," Jane continued, "if I hadn't got this seat, I wouldn't have had the opportunity to speak with you, Mrs. Langford, and what a pity that would have been."

Isabella smiled and nodded and returned her attention to her soup. "You're too kind."

"I'm not kind at all," Miss Lowndes replied, making Garrett wince. "I'm quite fascinated to learn how you've managed a friendship with Upton."

Isabella narrowed her eyes on Miss Lowndes. "I find Mr. Upton's company quite charming."

"'Charming'? I suppose that's one word for it. Forgive me, but are you quite certain you know what 'charming' means, Mrs. Langford?"

Owen Monroe's bark of laughter caught the attention of many of the other guests.

Garrett grabbed his wine glass, nearly sloshing the red liquid over his sleeve. He took another deep drink. God help him. This night was already too long by half.

After their drinks, the gentlemen met the ladies in the drawing room. When Garrett entered, he scanned about, appraising the situation. Thankfully, Isabella was caught up in conversation with Cassandra and Lucy on one end of the long room. Garrett made his way in the opposite direction. He couldn't stop thinking about what Isabella had said to him at dinner, that she'd wanted to see him. Any man would be flattered to have a woman like her flirting with him, but she was also Harold's wife. Harold. His friend. *His dead friend.* There was no possible way Garrett could have any sort of a relationship with Harold's wife. It would be a betrayal of his friend all over again. He'd done wrong by Harold once, he wouldn't cuckold him—or whatever the equivalent of cuckolding was once a husband was dead.

By the time Garrett looked up to see who was sitting in the corner, it was too late. Miss Lowndes was perched on a bench in front of a small card table. Blast. How had this happened? He'd barely escaped her barbs at dinner unscathed and here she was again. Thankfully, she appeared invested in her game of solitaire as if trying to beat an actual opponent. It was so like Miss Lowndes to be competitive with *herself.* But even Miss Lowndes's company was preferable to another awkward encounter with Isabella.

"Miss me so soon, Upton?" Miss Lowndes raised her nose in the air in that way she did. Ah, so she had noticed his approach. She did not, however, remove her gaze from the cards in front of her.

He sighed. "Don't tell me you didn't know that Lord and Lady Moreland have a vast library. It's just down the corridor. Surely you would be more comfortable there."

She was usually to be found in the libraries of all houses. She excused herself early and often from all polite conversation and social nicety and went in search of the library. When she wasn't in a library, she had a book in front of her head and her spectacles perched on her face in the insouciant way they were perched at present. What would she do if he reached over and plucked them from her little bluestocking nose?

"No doubt I would be more comfortable, Upton, especially if you intend to remain standing next to me. However, I've promised Cass that I will force myself to remain sociable for the remainder of the house party and wedding." She smiled at him tightly. "It seems you're stuck with me."

He returned the tight smile. "Pity. Though I relish the opportunity to watch you attempt to be sociable. It'll be like a comedy of errors. And if my standing bothers you so much . . . May I?" He gestured to the empty seat on the bench next to her.

"By all means." Miss Lowndes scooted over to allow him more space.

"Why aren't you with Lucy and Cassandra?" he asked as soon as he took his seat.

She flipped over two cards. "Because Lucy and Cass are speaking with Mrs. Langford at present, and despite her close association with you—or perhaps because of it—I find her a bit . . . much."

"We don't have a close association," Garrett bit back, perhaps a little too harshly.

One of Miss Lowndes's dark eyebrows arched over the top of her spectacles. "Oh? Mrs. Langford overstated the friendship at dinner?"

"No, she didn't. I— We—" Blast it. How in the devil had Miss Lowndes put him at a loss for words? He needed to regain control of the conversation immediately. Was there more wine to be had in here? He searched about for a footman. It was time to change the subject. "How is your scandal progressing?"

Her dark intelligent eyes sparkled. "It isn't. I haven't thought of anything sufficiently scandalous yet."

"I'm certain it's only a matter of time. Perhaps your Mrs. Bunbury might allow you to overeat teacake and call into question your gluttony. Speaking of teacake, isn't there one here somewhere that you're looking for?"

Miss Lowndes seemed to perk up. In addition to baiting him, she adored teacake. She could always be seen with a plate full of them at every social event. Lucy and Cassandra often teased her about it. He wondered how she was able to maintain her figure with the amount of teacake she consumed— He rubbed the back of his neck. Damn it. *What* level of hell had caused him to think about Miss Lowndes's figure of all things? First the spectacles, now her figure. Blasted teacake.

"It's not teatime, Upton, or haven't you noticed?" she replied nonchalantly, placing a card on the table in front of her. "While we're on the subject of refreshments, isn't there a glass of wine somewhere that *you're* looking for?"

He sucked in a deep breath. That comment hit too close to home, but he refused to let her win this war of words. "I'm certain the cooks will fetch you some teacake. Why don't you wander down to the kitchens and ask them to?"

"You shan't rid yourself of me that easily, Upton. Besides, I'm intrigued." She flipped over another card.

He made a show of tugging at his cuff. "Intrigued? By me? Surely you're jesting. Either that or you've sustained a recent head injury. Did you suffer a fall while practicing your archery yesterday? Where is your Mrs. Bunbury when you need her?"

"I admit it turns my stomach as much as it does yours,

but yes, I'm intrigued, with no head injury to speak of," she replied.

He turned his face and grinned at her. "Don't keep me on tenterhooks. Do tell. How exactly have I intrigued you, Miss Lowndes?"

She remained focused on her game. "You've intrigued me, Upton, by your complete unwillingness to discuss Mrs. Langford. Then there's the little matter of her arrival at this party, despite being barely able to claim a passing acquaintance with Cass. And finally, Mrs. Langford's apparent flirtation with you over dinner, though I daresay that turns my stomach perhaps the most of all."

He managed a shrug. "Unwillingness to discuss Mrs. Langford? I don't know what you mean."

"Don't you, Upton? You've changed the subject often enough. Tell me, why do you think she's come?"

"I'm sure I don't know. I thought perhaps she was a friend of Cassandra's."

"I'm sure you do know. And you know Cass didn't know her before meeting her this morning."

He leaned back against the cushions that rested on the wall behind them and crossed his legs at the ankles, working diligently to appear nonchalant. "You've been reading too many novels, Miss Lowndes. Your imagination has quite got the best of you. Mrs. Bunbury is quite lax in her patronage."

"It's not possible to read too many novels, Upton, and I can only hope my imagination *always* has the best of me."

"Why don't you tell me, then, Miss Lowndes? Why do you think Mrs. Langford has come?"

Miss Lowndes flipped over two more cards. "I win!"

"Was there ever any doubt?" he replied with his usual sarcasm.

She arched another brow at him, but her smile was a

bit distracting. "Don't change the subject, Upton. I have no idea why Mrs. Langford came all the way from London to spend time in your company. It seems entirely illogical to me. But then again, several things about Mrs. Langford seem illogical to me."

He did his best to sound bored. "Like what?"

"You don't find it odd that a war widow has a governess and a tutor, lives on Charles Street, and has more trunks than Lucy does?"

He cleared his throat. Damn Miss Lowndes and her uncanny intelligence, not to mention her curiosity. "I'm not certain that's any of my business," he offered.

"Isn't it?" Miss Lowndes shuffled the cards in her hands. "You seem to be preoccupied with *my* Mrs. Bunbury. It seems only fair that I pay a bit of attention to *your* Mrs. Langford."

"That is patently ridiculous. Mrs. Bunbury doesn't exist."

"Which is precisely why my task shall be much easier than yours." Miss Lowndes smiled at him sweetly. "I have no idea why Mrs. Langford followed you here from London, Upton, but I intend to find out."

# CHAPTER TWELVE

The following evening, Jane stared at her reflection in the looking glass in her bedchamber. Dull brown hair and plain brown eyes stared back at her. She sighed. She'd never be as slender and lovely as Lucy, or Mrs. Langford, no matter what she did. Tonight she'd actually made an effort. She'd allowed Lucy's maid to help her dress. She'd spent more time preparing herself for the evening's festivities than she ever had for a social event before. But why?

The day had been spent playing croquet on the lawn with the ladies while the gentlemen went shooting. Mrs. Langford had been mildly pleasant though the narrowed-eyed stares she'd given Jane every time she'd noticed her looking were a bit disconcerting. Mostly the woman spent her time trying to sidle up and be friendly with Lucy and Cass. Apparently, she wanted to be liked by Upton's closest friends. Jane was only glad she wasn't considered one of them. She'd left the widow to her efforts in the afternoon. Jane had forgone tea to sneak upstairs and read another novel.

But tonight, tonight was something different entirely. Her hair had been pulled back in a loose chignon, much different from her normal tight bun. Her cheeks had been rubbed with the smallest hint of pink rouge, and she'd even allowed Lucy to spray a bit of perfume in her general direction. Jane had made a show of coughing and gagging as if she would die from it but she wasn't unpleased with the result. Lilacs had always been a favorite scent of hers.

"This perfume is said to drive gentlemen wild," Lucy said with a sly smile. "The perfumer told me so."

Jane gawked at her. "Then I'm washing it off, immediately."

"Don't be such a ninny," Lucy countered, her eyes full of mischief. "Don't you want to see what comes of it? I daresay you could do with a bit of driving gentlemen wild."

Jane crossed her arms over her chest and glared at her friend. "What gentlemen? And why in the world would I want to drive any of them wild?"

Lucy set down the vial and plunked her hands on her hips. "Seriously, Jane? Must we have *the* talk? I was under the impression you already knew a good deal about what goes on between a man and a woman behind closed doors, but if I must explain—"

"No. No. No. Thank you very much," Jane rushed to reply. "I've read all about that subject and am well educated on the—ahem—ins and outs of it. I simply mean that *I* have no cause to drive a gentleman wild. Tonight or any night."

Lucy rolled her eyes. "I'm certain the perfumer only said it so I'd purchase a larger vial. It worked, too, though I daresay I don't need perfume to drive Derek wild, I just have to—"

"That is quite enough, thank you." Jane resisted the

urge to put her hands over her ears. Thankfully, Lucy gathered up her vial of wild-making perfume and left with a wink and an "I'll see you downstairs."

Now Jane was alone with her lilac scent, borrowed gown, and reflection in the looking glass. She sighed for a third time. A masquerade. She was not looking forward to it. She blinked at her reflection. What would it be like to be as beautiful as Lucy . . . or Mrs. Langford? She pulled the fan her mother insisted she carry with her at all times out of her reticule. She snapped it open, held it in front of her face, and batted her eyelashes at herself over the top of the silk folds. "Good evening, my lord. Why, of course you may have this dance." She giggled. That was just ridiculous. Eyelash batting and fan snapping. She closed the fan and stuffed it back into her reticule. The reticule was lighter tonight. She'd left her ubiquitous book on the bedside table. She'd promised Cass she would be social and social she would be, pretend chaperone notwithstanding.

Jane leaned in closer to the looking glass and eyed her freckles. She'd tried to scrub them off like bits of dirt when she was a child. Other children had teased her about them. Now they'd faded into small flecks beneath her wide brown eyes but they still remained, mocking her. Reminding her she would never be a beauty. It was just as well. As if the fact that she'd been a large child hadn't been enough to drive the other children away or cause them to make fun of her. "Plump" was the word her mother had used. Thank God she'd shed the extra weight as she'd grown into a young woman. Her mother had been relieved, but Jane had never divested herself of her love of sweets and teacake. She might not be the plump little girl she'd once been, but she'd never be the willowy thin thing that Cass was or have Lucy's dimin-

utive shape. Mrs. Langford's goddesslike perfection?
Hardly.

Jane had spent her childhood telling herself she didn't
care that the other children didn't want to play with her.
She'd always been more interested in reading and learning and going to galleries and museums than making
herself up and going to parties. She gazed down at her
gown, a gorgeous ice-blue concoction that made her look
more—ahem—voluptuous than she'd ever looked before. Her breasts were about to make their own debut.
Lucy's maid had spent the last two days taking out the
seams to make the gown fit Jane. On Lucy, it had been
a bit flowy. On Jane, it was anything but. In fact, the
effect was quite a difference from anything she'd ever
worn before. Despite its scandalousness, Jane had little
doubt her mother would adore this gown. If Mama believed Jane had a chance at finally attracting a suitor,
she'd no doubt add more rouge to Jane's cheeks and suggest even lower décolletage.

Jane straightened her shoulders. She'd stared at herself long enough. It was time to go. She reached for the
matching ice-blue domino mask Lucy had procured for
her. It looked quite decadent with a large white feather
sweeping across one side. Domino masks and spectacles did not mix. Jane took one last look in the mirror
and pulled her spectacles slowly down her nose. She
blinked at the blur of pale skin and blue fabric and brown
hair reflected in front of her. Her eyesight was hopeless.
She could barely see her hand in front of her face without her spectacles.

She stood and carefully made her way to the door.
At least she thought it was the door. It was the big blur
of brown in the middle of the wall with the gleaming
golden blob in the middle. This would not do. She had

to use her spectacles. She hurried back and pulled them
from the tabletop. Then she held them up as best she
could in front of her mask and made her way down to
the ballroom. Just outside the entrance, she folded the
spectacles and tucked them into the white satin reticule
that swung jauntily from her wrist. Funny how being
without her book made her feel shy, vulnerable. It was
a first for her. Tonight she would stay, and dance, and
attempt to have a grand time. At a ball. She shook her
head. Who was she becoming?

No doubt Upton would have some impertinent comment to make about the fact that she wasn't holding a
book for once. She scowled. Why was she thinking about
Upton of all people? Upton would probably be so distracted by Mrs. Langford, he wouldn't spare Jane a
second thought. What did she care?

Upton.

Why had she challenged him last night with her vow
to find out why Mrs. Langford had followed him? Other
than the fact that he'd angered her the day before, telling her how to run her life. She wasn't a fool. She knew
Lucy's schemes could end up causing trouble. She'd been
around for the last two, hadn't she? As long as she kept
Lucy's imagination from running wild, they might manage a small, simple, *controlled* scandal. But Upton had
been so certain of himself. She'd wanted to take down
his smug demeanor a notch. After all, how did *he* like
it when someone meddled in *his* affairs?

Enough about Upton. Jane had more important things
to concentrate on, like not tripping and falling flat on
her face in front of a ballroom full of the *ton*'s best.
She lifted her chin. Tonight the entire ballroom would
see a new Jane Lowndes. One who wore beautiful ice-
blue gowns with daring décolletage, and feathered
domino masks, and elegant chignons, and was sans

both book and spectacles. Tomorrow she would go back to being the bluestocking spinster they all knew she truly was.

Daphne Swift was the first to see her when Jane hesitantly entered the ballroom. The younger woman squealed. Truly *squealed*. "Jane, is that you?"

Daphne was a lovely blur of yellow silk, her golden hair piled high atop her head. She gave Jane the impression of a glowing candle. "Daphne, is that you? I cannot be certain without my spectacles."

Daphne's tinkling laughter followed. "Yes, it's me, Jane."

Jane nodded. "Very well. I would be ever so grateful if you would point me in the direction of Lucy and Cass."

Daphne laughed again and entwined her arm through Jane's. "I'll take you to them."

The two made their way through the blur of the crowd. Jane was ever so glad for the assistance. This was why bluestocking spinsters who wore spectacles did not attend masquerades with domino masks. Incidents might occur. Embarrassing ones like talking to a plant all evening or tripping and falling headlong into a duke. Though, to be fair, she believed Derek Hunt was the only duke in attendance and he would no doubt be forgiving, but still, the entire prospect was fraught with peril. Though that might be just the sort of scandal she was looking for. Hmm. Perhaps talking to a plant wasn't scandalous enough. Not to worry. A scandalous opportunity would present itself when the time was right. She was certain of it.

"I must say, Jane, you look absolutely stunning this evening," Daphne said as she pulled Jane along. The other guests were merely blurs passing by. "I almost didn't recognize you. I've never seen you so . . . so . . ."

"Blame it on Lucy," Jane replied. "She allowed me to borrow the gown and the mask. There's perfume, too, but don't ask about that."

"I had a feeling Lucy was involved," Daphne replied, with a knowing tone.

"Lucy's always involved when there is trouble."

Daphne stopped her. "Is there to be trouble?"

Jane sighed. "I cannot see a pace in front of me and I'm wearing an embarrassingly low-cut gown. I'm quite convinced trouble is imminent." No need to admit to Daphne that she was looking for a scandal.

Daphne laughed and they resumed walking.

A tall blur approached them. "Lady Daphne," a male voice said. "You look ravishing this evening. Who is your friend?"

Jane had heard the voice before but couldn't quite place it. Oh, perfect. She was going to make a complete cake of herself tonight if she didn't recognize anyone. Though, she supposed, that was the entire point of a masquerade, was it not? She took a deep breath. She might as well relax as best she could. Speaking of cake, she made a mental note to have Daphne point her in the direction of the teacake, later, as well.

"You're not supposed to know it's me, Lord Owen," Daphne replied. "And I'm not about to reveal the identity of my beautiful friend."

Ah, so it was Owen Monroe. Hmm. If she'd managed to fool the biggest rake in London, she just might be as ravishing as Daphne said she was.

Owen's laughter followed. "You're not supposed to know it's me, either, Lady Daphne," he replied. "Very well, keep your secret."

He bowed, a blur in front of Jane, and pulled her hand to his mouth. Good heavens. His actual lips brushed against the tender skin on the back of her hand. Even through her glove it was hot. She jumped a little.

"Until we meet again, my mysterious lady," he said, before drifting back into the crowd.

Daphne giggled. "My goodness, Jane, you just caught the attention of Owen Monroe. He had no idea who you were. Why, the only other person I know who is a bigger rake than Owen Monroe is Captain Cavendish."

"Daphne! How do you know words like 'rake'?"

"I know much worse words than that, Jane Lowndes," Daphne replied, giggling.

Jane had to smile. Daphne Swift was a spitfire. Cass and Lucy had told her so, but she hadn't quite seen it until now. Jane liked Daphne. She liked her a great deal.

"I daresay this evening is certain to be diverting, if you're fooling the likes of Owen Monroe," Daphne added.

Jane considered Daphne's words. It was diverting, wasn't it? This must have been how Cass felt last autumn when she was pretending to be Patience Bunbury. Cass had mentioned to Jane that it had actually been freeing to pretend to be someone she was not. As Patience, Cass said, she could act however she liked and the devil may care about the consequences.

The mask on her face and the loss of her spectacles made Jane feel a little lost, but also a little reckless, a bit free. As if tonight she was not Miss Jane Lowndes, wallflower extraordinaire, but Miss Ice Blue Domino-wearing Party Goer. And Miss Ice Blue might get up to absolutely anything. Especially while in the care of a nonexistent chaperone.

What did it matter that she could barely see a thing? Tonight, she intended to enjoy herself nonetheless. Now, where was a teacake when she needed it?

Daphne helped her maneuver through the crowd until they came upon two blurs speaking to each other. She recognized the voices of her closest friends. Lucy was a blur of crimson and Cass a blur of pink.

Lucy spoke first. "There you are, Janie. I've been searching for you. You wouldn't believe how many handsome gentlemen are here this evening. I daresay Captain Swift, er, I mean Swifdon, has good-looking friends."

Jane nearly snorted. "Indeed, I would not believe it, because I cannot see anything. I wouldn't have made it at all if Daphne hadn't helped me find you. They might as well all be trolls as far as I can tell."

Cass laughed. "You poor dear." She squeezed Jane's hand and turned to Daphne.

"Tell me, and please be honest, how horrible is this red spot on my nose?" Cass asked her future sister-in-law.

"It's barely noticeable," Daphne replied.

"I doubt that. I fear we'll be obliged to set another seat at the banquet table on the day of the wedding to accommodate it," Cass said.

"It's hardly that bad," Jane replied. "I cannot even see it."

"Yes, but you're blind as a bat," Cass replied. "And as to that, thank you for helping Jane find us, Daphne."

"My pleasure," Daphne replied. "Doesn't she look like a dream? She even caught the eye of Lord Owen." Daphne's voice took on a subtle cajoling tone.

"Owen?" Cass replied. "You must be jesting."

"I take great offense to that," Jane replied. "I might not be able to see anything, but I can still *hear* you."

"I beg your pardon," Cass said, true regret in her voice. "I just cannot believe . . . Well, you do look entirely different from how you normally do, Jane. But Owen, he's a—"

"No need to explain," Jane replied. "I was hardly attempting to attract his attention. I was looking for you two and then teacake . . . in that order."

Lucy's tinkling laughter followed. "When I gave you that mask earlier, I completely forgot about your spectacles. Take it on my good authority that there are indeed a large number of good-looking gentlemen here. It's really too bad you're a confirmed spinster." Lucy sighed as if she really did think it was too bad. "I'd be ever so much more efficient at finding you a husband than at convincing your parents you're to remain unattached. Your mother is quite single-minded."

"Don't I know?" Jane replied. "Now, would one of you kindly point me in the direction of the refreshment table?"

"I shall do even better than that. I shall escort you there myself," Lucy replied.

Jane supposed the flesh-colored blur that appeared at her side was Lucy's arm, so she wound her hand over it and allowed her friend to escort her toward the teacake. Jane waved in Cass and Daphne's general direction as she left them behind.

"Don't get up to too much trouble," Daphne called.

"Yes, and you may want to avoid Owen," Cass added, with a laugh. "He can be quite charming when he sets his mind to it, or so I'm told."

Lucy dragged Jane toward the refreshment table before stopping short. "Ooh, there's Garrett. I wonder if *he'll* recognize you."

# CHAPTER THIRTEEN

Garrett should not have allowed Owen Monroe to talk him into a stiff bit of straight liquor. "To toast the happy couple," Owen had said, and of course, one small drink had turned into two and two into three, and that in addition to the brandy he'd drunk earlier. Garrett was feeling very little pain. He detested small stiff drinks. Owen Monroe, however, never met a drink he didn't like. Nor was there a bottle of liquor he wasn't intimately acquainted with.

That's what Garrett got for spending time in Owen's company. He'd wanted to clear the air with Monroe after that hand of cards last autumn and forcing him to pretend his sister was *not* masquerading as a woman named Patience Bunbury at Lucy's house party. Owen had insisted he was no longer angry with him. Garrett had won fair and square, after all, but Garrett suspected Owen was getting a bit of his own back by ensuring Garrett awoke tomorrow morning with a devil of a head.

Drinking was Owen's forte. Garrett should have refused that last drink. Or three. He had to get away from the study and the drinking to clear his head a bit. Now here he was wearing a bloody emerald-green demimask along with his black evening attire and staggering into the Morelands' ballroom.

He braced a hand against the wall and scanned the crowd. Bloody difficult to tell who was who with everyone wearing blasted masks. Thank Christ, Isabella had stopped him earlier and identified herself. She was wearing a ruby-red gown that was a bit too . . . distracting for his taste. He'd quickly excused himself without asking her to dance, which she was clearly hinting at, and made his way to the study where Monroe had got him in his drunken clutches. At least Garrett knew enough to stay away from the ruby-red gown he saw bobbing along the far side of the room, besieged by a contingent of hopeful male escorts.

"Garrett, there you are!" came Lucy's bright voice. He pulled his hand from the wall and turned to face his cousin.

"You must meet my friend Miss . . . Blue." Lucy turned in a wide circle, obviously looking for her friend. "Now where did she get off to? I swear she was just here."

Garrett grinned at his cousin. "Are you certain she exists? She's not like Miss Bunbury, is she? Or *Mrs.* Bunbury?"

Lucy plunked her hands on her hips and scowled at him. "Of course she exists. I'll just go find her and be back. I'm greatly looking forward to you meeting her."

Lucy had a smile on her face that indicated she was up to something, but at the moment, Garrett's dizzy head was more pressing than whatever scheme Lucy had concocted. No doubt this was her inelegant attempt at matchmaking. "Fine. Go and fetch her. I'll just be . . . over here."

A large potted palm rested near the wall across the

room, a tufted chair situated behind it. Garrett had spied the space earlier. He intended to seek it out and relax for a moment.

Lucy quickly blended into the crowd while Garrett headed for the palm. When he reached it, he realized, to his chagrin, it was already occupied by a woman. A woman wearing a stunning shade of light blue with a domino mask to match.

"Good evening," he said, bowing to her.

"Good evening," came the woman's steady reply.

For a moment he wondered if she was Miss Blue. In his head, she was. Garrett bowed to Miss Blue again. Frankly, she'd looked like a blue blur to him at first. But when he lifted his head and took her hand, he was immediately intrigued. Miss Blue had dark-brown eyes, soft dark hair that framed her face, a pretty face from what he could see of it behind her mask, and was—ahem— well endowed. Quite well endowed. He forced himself to look away from her décolletage. But really, what red-blooded male could keep from looking at *that*?

"Do I know you, sir?" she asked.

There was something familiar about her voice, but with the ringing in his head, he couldn't quite place her. "No, I don't know you, and you don't know me. This is a masquerade, is it not? As it should be." Where all that nonsense had come from he had no idea. He was being charming. On purpose. Quite a shock, especially to him.

"Then I suppose it's nice to meet you, whoever you are," she said with a musical laugh. It sparked a memory he couldn't quite place in his hazy brain.

"The pleasure is entirely mine, my lady," he replied with the most roguish grin he could muster, the one that made him popular with the ladies in London.

Miss Blue opened her mouth to speak. "Oh, I'm not a lady, I'm—"

"Shh," he said in a husky voice, daring to put his finger to her lips. They were warm and soft and— He shook himself. Best not to think about that. "You're a lady tonight. You're Lady Blue."

Her laughter followed again. "Very well, and you are? Lord Green?"

"I like that name. I like it very much." He executed a sweeping bow, though how he managed to right himself afterward was anyone's guess. "Would you care to dance?" Dancing probably wasn't the best idea, but how could Garrett resist a pairing with a charming, lovely, well-endowed young woman?

He offered his arm and Lady Blue merely nodded and took it without saying a word. Garrett pulled her into his arms just as a waltz began to play. Thank God for his many drunken nights of revelry in London. He had experience dancing and appearing to be sober when he was anything but, though mostly in his much younger days.

Lady Blue, it turned out, was a young lady of few words. Pity that. Weren't the loveliest ladies the ones who rarely spoke? The most annoying ladies, such as Miss Lowndes, were the ones who wouldn't *stop* speaking. He shook his head. Why was he thinking about Miss Lowndes at a time like this? Where was that woman at any rate? No doubt she'd begged off, claiming a headache, and was ensconced in the library with a book. He searched the ballroom. At least Isabella was still far across the room.

This was exactly what he needed, a harmless flirtation with a lady. His guilt over Isabella and his annoyance with Miss Lowndes had him feeling out of sorts. He was usually charming with ladies. Charming and friendly, certainly welcomed. Miss Lowndes was the only woman who seemed to dislike his company and

Isabella was the only beautiful woman he could remember whose company he rebuffed.

For all that Lady Blue didn't speak, she was a proficient dancer, but the waltzing was making his dizziness worse. He needed to stop before he spun this divine young woman straight into the refreshment table. Bad form, that. "Would you care to go for a walk?"

"A walk?" Her voice was slightly breathless. The niggling feeling in the back of his mind remained. He'd heard that voice before.

"Yes. I find that dancing is a bit too . . . much for me at present," he replied.

She hesitated. "Where shall we walk to?"

"The gallery?" he offered. A walk in the cool corridor outside the upper floor might be just what he needed. He could pretend to show her the portraits on the walls and hopefully shake off this stupor.

"Very well," she agreed magnanimously.

Garrett pressed his lips together to keep from sighing his relief. She was gorgeous and agreeable. A delightful combination.

They stopped and moved off the dance floor. Garrett put his hand against the small of her back and ushered her in front of him out of the ballroom and into the quiet corridor. "This way." He pointed toward the right where they rounded a corner and proceeded up the staircase to the gallery.

"Do you know the Monroe family quite well then?" the lady asked. She leaned on his arm a bit heavily and he could have sworn she tripped a little on the way up the stairs. Was she in her cups too?

"Yes, actually. I've known them for years. I was raised not far from here. How long have you known them?"

"I've only known Lady Cassandra since her come-out. She's marvelous."

Another familiar niggle, but he brushed it aside. He was certain he'd know *this* beauty if he'd met her before. The alcohol was doing funny things to his mind. *Blast that Monroe.*

When they came to the end of the corridor, Garrett stopped and gestured to the portraits. "Here we are."

"There are so many of them. Though I must admit, I find them difficult to see. Who's that?" She gestured to one in particular.

"It's the second earl, I believe. There's an even better rendering of him in this drawing room." He pointed toward a door down the corridor. "Care to see it?"

Jane didn't know what to think. First, the handsome stranger in the green mask had asked her to dance. Well, from what she could see of him, he was handsome. Then he had asked her to view the gallery with him. Now, if she didn't know better—and she *didn't* know better— she'd think he was asking her to go into a drawing room with him, *alone.* It was beyond scandalous and inappropriate.

And it was absolutely perfect. She'd wanted a scandal to present itself and present itself it had, in the form of Lord Green.

Jane shivered. What was it about taking off her spectacles that made her feel so . . . scandalous? Perhaps it was because a handsome gentleman had never shown the slightest interest in her before? Perhaps it was because she'd never had the slightest inclination to return that interest? But there was something about this tall, dark man that made her want to go into the drawing room with him alone . . . even if they were only going to view an old painting. Not that she didn't like paintings—she adored the British Museum and spent absolute days there getting lost among the displays, carefully studying the lines of the Rubenses and the strokes in the Gainsboroughs. She could examine a Botticelli for hours on end. But she seriously doubted a painting of Cass's ancestor would keep her attention longer than a moment or two. Not to mention she couldn't see a thing at present. No, it was Lord Green who was keeping her attention.

Who was he? Scandal or no, she should know his name before she took off into the drawing room with him. Shouldn't she? "I should like that, Mr. . . ."

Instead of replying, he took her by the elbow and ushered her toward the drawing room. "As I said. One of the advantages of a masquerade is to be incognito." He flashed a grin. She could only see a white streak in the blur that was his face but it didn't matter. The man might look like an ogre for all she knew but he *seemed* handsome, indeed, and that was enough to pretend with tonight. And wasn't he correct? One of the advantages of a masquerade *was* to be incognito. She didn't want to give her name either, now that she thought on it. He might have heard the name Jane Lowndes linked to "wallflower" the way "indulgence" was linked to the Prince Regent. Inseparable, those two. If Lord Green pressed her, she would give the name Bunbury, or Wollstonecraft, perhaps. Yes, Miss Wollstonecraft. Perfect. That had been her pretend name at the infamous house party last autumn. For now, she was content remaining entirely anonymous.

Lord Green pushed open the door to the drawing room. The space was dark save for the faint glow coming from one small candle. He left her near the entryway and went to fetch the candle, bringing it back and shutting the door. Hmm. She'd been right about him. He *was* attempting to get her alone with him. She had no experience with such things. What happened next? Would she be forced to slap him? Should she use the words "Unhand me, sir?" or threaten to have her brother call him out? *That* would be scandalous, but perhaps a bit too scandalous. Of course, she didn't have a brother, but he didn't know that. An insignificant detail, really.

"The painting is over here," Lord Green said, grasping her hand and pulling her gently behind him. Jane nearly gasped at the touch of his warm fingers. Even through her glove she could feel it. Perhaps she didn't have to slap him. Perhaps she didn't have to pretend she had a brother to call him out. Perhaps she could . . . kiss him. That would be scandalous too. Quite scandalous. The thought made a hot knot unravel in the pit of her belly and somewhere . . . lower. She took a deep breath and trailed along behind him.

They stopped in front of a large portrait of a man wearing a uniform. At least Jane thought it was a man wearing a uniform. Blobs that looked like epaulets rested on what appeared to be giant red shoulders. The painting was so large, even Jane could make out a bit of it, but she was standing far too close.

"You may have a better feel for it from this vantage point." She turned at the sound of Lord Green's voice, to see him standing next to a blob she decided must be the settee in the middle of the room. He was looking toward her and the huge portrait.

"If I didn't know better, my lord, I'd say you were trying to lure me over to the settee."

"You don't know better," he said in a voice that sounded entirely too charming.

She slowly crossed the wide carpet toward him, her mouth going dry. Would she really do this? Allow this stranger to kiss her if he tried? Was she that daring? That Lady Blue?

She sat, spreading her skirts on the settee, but he smoothed them aside and leaned close. His warm breath smelled of alcohol, but his own scent, a mixture of soap and something that smelled like autumn leaves, left her breathless.

"What if I admitted that I was?" he asked.

Jane's brain was blurry. "Was what?"

"Luring you to the settee."

"I'd say you succeeded." She hated the sound of her shaking voice. Bluestocking spinsters never had occasion for their voices to shake. Bluestocking spinsters never had occasion to trade witty jibes with handsome gentlemen—unless her wordplay with Upton counted and that was entirely— Oh, God, there she went thinking of Upton again at a time like this.

She clasped her hands in her lap and concentrated on not breathing too heavily. Was her breath pleasant? Or did the lilacs override that? Oh, the lilacs. She'd forgotten all about the lilacs. The lilacs were working. For heaven's sake. Of all amazing things, a handsome young gentleman was actually flirting with her. Flirting! With her! A thrill shot through her. She'd read about these sorts of things, of course. She took another deep breath and made her decision. This was it. If she handled this correctly, she just might experience her first kiss and get her scandal in one fell swoop. The kiss would be strictly for educational purposes, of course. Nothing more. First she must flirt with him. *Flirt*. Flirt! She couldn't believe it, even as she had the thought.

She leaned closer. "I should warn you, I don't kiss gentlemen whom I've just met and certainly not alone in drawing rooms."

"I should warn you, I'm quite persuasive . . . and a very good kisser."

"Really . . . ?" Her voice was breathy, a mere whisper. "Persuade me, then."

His lips met hers, dry but firm. What was next? Was this all there was?

Then his mouth opened and slanted across hers, and Jane forgot to breathe. For heaven's sake, what was the man doing? His tongue plummeted between her lips and a shudder racked her body. He tasted like some sort of spicy alcohol. Her fingers went up to tangle in his dark hair. His mask and hers briefly rubbed against each other.

She'd never felt anything like it before. Lust, hot and powerful, shot through her. It must be lust. She'd read about it. Even thought about it if she was being honest, but she'd never experienced it. Never imagined she'd have the opportunity to experience it. His mouth shaped hers and his tongue plunged again. Again. She was mad for him. She wrapped her arms around his strong, warm neck. He pulled her tight against him. His body was all hard muscles and planes and perfectly *male*. His strong, warm hands came up to cup her cheeks, his fingers lightly caressing the sides of her face. He kissed her again and again, not letting go, not stopping. Her lips were swollen, hot, wet. So were other parts . . . lower parts of her body. His mouth moved off hers and trailed a damp path to her ear. His tongue skimmed over the edge. Her entire body quivered.

"Easy," he whispered huskily into her ear. "I won't hurt you."

She didn't reply, only found his mouth again blindly with her own and coaxed his tongue back into contact with hers. She rubbed herself against his thigh, lightly whimpering, wanting to feel more, more, more.

The kisses slowly wound down and became more languorous. His tongue replaced by the feel of his warm, strong lips against hers. He kissed the side of her mouth, once, twice, and pulled himself away. Was he shaking a little?

So was she.

"As much as I'd love to finish what we started," he said in a voice that was *definitely* shaking, "we should probably get back, my lady."

All she could do was nod unevenly.

He took a deep breath. "My cousin might be wondering where I've got off to. Lucy's one to come looking."

Jane's stomach plummeted. She gasped and held her breath.

*Oh, my God. I just kissed Upton!*

# CHAPTER FOURTEEN

Jane gulped. Not only had she just kissed Upton, but she'd liked it! Worse, she was about to kiss him again. Because even though he'd said they should get back, Upton's hands were pulling her back to him, and his mouth found hers again.

She was mindless, thoughtless, as if she were suspended in time, completely unable to stop the whirlwind of lust she'd been swept into.

*This is madness. This is madness. This is madness.*

She repeated the words to herself over and over, even as she met each of Upton's thrusts with her tongue, and let her fingers tangle in his dark, curly hair again.

Oh, God. Upton was not only handsome and seductive, he was driving her wild with his mouth. How was this happening?

*But it's Upton. It's Upton. It's Upton.*

Rational thought told her she should push him away immediately, but rational thought was long gone from this room. All she could concentrate on was the feel of his warm hand on her breast and how it intensified the ache between her thighs.

"Tell me to stop," he demanded against her mouth.

"No," she answered mindlessly, still cupping his slightly stubbled cheeks in her hands and kissing him back with a fervor that frightened her.

Upton seemed to have no idea who she was, and thank God for that. She'd never live it down in her own mind, regardless. Imagine how much worse it would be if he knew it was she and pushed her away.

Or did he know and was only pretending not to know, as she was? No. That couldn't be true. But how could he not know? It made no sense. At least not until she reminded herself that until two moments ago, she hadn't realized who *he* was. His voice was slurred, that was it. That's why she hadn't recognized it. It had been differ-ent from his normal clipped tones. Not to mention the man had obviously been drinking. God knew how much. What in heaven's name was her excuse? At the moment she wished she'd had a swig too.

She'd wanted a scandal? She'd just scandalized her-self!

He pulled her under him and lay atop her, his knee riding between her legs, and she was mindless again. His hips pressed against her most intimate spot and his mouth owned hers. The stark evidence of his arousal nudged against her thigh. When his hand came up to touch her breast, a shiver racked her body.

"Easy," he whispered against her mouth. "I won't do anything you don't want me to."

"That's the problem." Her voice trembled.

He laughed a little against her mouth. It was arous-ing. Arousing? Upton? Oh, God, what was happening to her? She had turned into a mindless, lust-crazed beast.

His thumb lightly pressed against her nipple through

the stiff fabric of her gown, and Jane's head rolled back. His lips found the pulse in her neck, and she moaned deep in her throat. "You're gorgeous," he whispered. "Let me remove your mask."

"No!" With strength she didn't know she possessed, Jane shoved him away and pulled herself from under him. She scrambled to the far end of the settee and sat there, staring at him no doubt with wild eyes, still panting from his kisses.

"My apologies," he said, still breathing heavily himself. "I didn't mean to— You don't have to take off your mask if you don't want to."

Jane winced. Her response had been nearly involuntary, but she should have thought it through a bit more. Surely her wild reaction would make him wonder why she was so adamant about keeping her mask in place.

"No, no," she hurried to reassure him. "It's not that . . . It's just that . . ."

"I frightened you, didn't I?"

"Yes." She nodded. Truly, she'd scared herself, but he didn't need to know that. Right now, now that she was on the other side of the settee, and a modicum of common sense and decency was returning to her brain, she needed to concentrate on getting out of this room quickly and with as little interaction between the two of them as possible. The more she spoke, the more she did anything, the greater the chances of him discovering her identity. *That* she could not live with. She would have to move to India, perhaps farther, to live this down if Upton ever discovered who she was and what he'd just done.

She'd have to find another scandal. Not this one. This one wouldn't do at all.

"I'm sorry, my lady," he said, and Jane heard a tinge of true regret in his voice. "I couldn't control myself. It's entirely unforgivable and I—"

"There were two of us here tonight," she answered, lowering her voice in a desperate effort to disguise it. "Neither is more at fault. But it's true, we should get back." She took another deep, shaky breath. "Right away."

He stood, adjusted his clothing, and held out his hand toward her. "Allow me to help you up."

God help her, she took it. Perhaps it was the part of her that wanted to enjoy this last moment of scandalous behavior. Perhaps it was the part of her that knew something like this would never happen again. Perhaps it was the part of her that knew that Upton, when he knew who she was, would never be this kind, considerate, and solicitous of her. That was the part that made her feel a little sad for a reason she couldn't describe.

Instead, she took his hand and allowed him to pull her to her feet. Before she could turn to go, he pulled her into his arms one last time and placed a warm kiss on her cheek. "To an evening I'll never forget, Lady Blue."

Jane's throat inexplicably tightened. She couldn't answer.

She didn't have to. The click of the door handle across the room had them both spinning toward it.

"What was that?" Jane asked, her eyes as wide as an owl's.

"I didn't see anyone," Upton replied. "But let's hope if someone was there, that they didn't see us."

Jane pressed her fist against her mouth. "Or if they did, they didn't know who we were."

# CHAPTER FIFTEEN

Jane awoke to a pounding head. She had tossed and turned for what felt like hours before sleep finally overtook her. She'd awakened every bit as full of nerves and doubt. What in heaven's name had she been thinking last night? She'd *known* it was Upton. Known it! Perhaps not the entire time, but long enough to make it reprehensible that she hadn't stopped kissing him. Which was more than she could say for him. He'd clearly thought she'd been some mystery harlot, but she'd discovered who he was and she'd *still* allowed him to kiss her.

She had no excuse. Absolutely none. The worst part was, she could only hope Upton wouldn't put it together and realize he'd been passionate with *her*.

What was her excuse? Could she blame it on the lack of spectacles? Obviously that had played a part in her not recognizing him sooner. Was it the gown? The lilac perfume? Blast and damn that lilac perfume. It had attracted a gentleman all right, but the entirely wrong one. Not that there was a right one, but that was hardly the point.

She sat up and hugged a pillow against her chest. She'd kissed Upton last night. Kissed him and liked it.

Not to mention the fact that someone—God knew who—may well have seen them. After they'd righted their clothing and Jane had done what she could to secure the loose pins in her chignon, they'd left the drawing room. The corridor had been empty but Jane had had the feeling someone had been there. Hopefully, it had merely been a servant. A discreet servant. Likely that's exactly who it had been, but Jane couldn't shake the feeling that the scandal she'd been courting may have found her before she'd had the opportunity to properly plan it. The only thought that kept her from a fit of apoplexy was the knowledge that a servant, even a nosy, indiscreet one, wouldn't have known who she was in the demi-mask. If it had been another party guest, that same possibility existed. Perhaps she'd picked a good night to be scandalous. A good night indeed.

She took a deep breath, pressing the pillow closer to her chest. The more concerning issue of the two that confronted her at present wasn't whether a servant had recognized her. It was keeping Upton from finding out it had been her last night. To that end, she must treat Upton with the same barely concealed distaste she always did. Upton was no fool. He might be a profligate rake who seduced young unknown ladies in drawing rooms, but a fool, no. She had no idea how she would manage it but she had to. She just had to. Upton must never, ever guess that it was she. The embarrassment, the mockery. She couldn't live with that.

Garrett groaned and rolled over in his bed. The sunlight pouring through the window told him it was morning, the pounding in his skull reminded him that he'd had far too much to drink last night. Far, far too much. The only good thing about it was that he'd passed out and apparently managed to sleep through the night. No nightmares for once.

The previous night's events came rushing back at him. Drinking with Monroe, dancing with the lady in blue, taking her to the upstairs drawing room and . . . Blast it. He hadn't acted gentlemanly last night. Something about her scent and her gown and her . . . assets had combined to make him more than a bit . . . libidinous. But who was she? Who? There weren't many possibilities. He knew most of the members of the house party. At least he had until last night. Had someone else arrived for the ball? The lady last night had seemed like a dream woman. This morning he realized it was only a matter of narrowing down the list of guests.

At least he could be sure she was not Isabella. The mystery lady's hair had been dark, but definitely brown, not black. The mystery woman's eyes had been dark too, which ruled out Isabella. Not to mention Isabella had been wearing red. Thank Christ. He did not need that sort of guilt adding to the heaping pile already on his conscience.

Wincing, he rang for a servant, and when one appeared, he asked the chap to get him a concoction for his head. Swifdon swore by some awful drink the Marquis of Colton had invented. This morning Garrett would consider drinking horse piss if it would stop the pounding in his skull. While he waited, he leaned back against the pillows and closed his eyes, running down the list of female guests and quickly discarding those who did not have brown hair and brown eyes. His mind's eye traveled around the dinner table from two nights ago as one by one he mentally checked off each name.

Daphne Swift was blond. Isabella had raven-black hair. Lucy and Cass would hardly be cavorting with a man in a drawing room. There were a handful of other guests, blond, redheaded, brunette, but none with those dark, soulful brown eyes. No one except . . .

Garrett's eyes flew wide open. He braced both palms against the mattress and shot straight up in bed, his head hammering. His heart hammered louder. No. It could not be. It couldn't possibly be.

Bloody hell. Of all people. Of all the blasted women in the world. He had done all of those things, every last inappropriate, unforgettable one of them, with *Jane Lowndes*!

# CHAPTER SIXTEEN

"I agree. If I had not seen it with my own eyes, I daresay I would not believe it, myself." Lucy trotted behind Cass as she paced in front of the wide Palladian windows in the upstairs drawing room. The space smelled of the logs that burned slowly in the large fireplace and of spring flowers that had been placed on the side table by one of the maids.

"I'm at a complete loss for words." Cass pressed her hands to her cheeks and turned in a swirl of peach skirts. Lucy noted with a bit of a smile on her face that Cass had given up the nasty habit of tugging on the ends of her gloves when she was nervous.

"It was Jane, wasn't it?" Lucy asked, wishing she might have been dreaming the entire episode last night.

Cass nodded, a blond curl bobbing against her forehead. "Yes. It certainly was."

"And it was Garrett, wasn't it?" Lucy continued, smoothing her hands over her own green skirts.

"I don't know who else it could have been. I spoke to

Garrett earlier. He was wearing that emerald pin in his cravat and a matching mask."

"That's what I was afraid of." Lucy stopped pacing and plunked down on the amber velvet settee. "There's no way around it. We have been witness to Jane and Garrett sneaking off together."

Cass's brow was furrowed. "Perhaps they were only speaking about something . . . something about the wedding."

"Like what?" Lucy sat forward on the edge of the seat, genuinely interested.

"Like . . . like . . . Oh, I have no idea whatsoever."

"I cannot imagine what they'd have to speak about. They can barely tolerate each other. *He took her hand,* Cass. I was certain my eyes would pop from my skull."

"I almost wish I hadn't seen it. The world would still make sense." Cass plucked at the silver bob that dangled from her ear.

"There is only one thing to do." Lucy rested her elbow on her knee and plopped her chin on her palm.

"What's that?" Cass stopped pacing and stared at her.

"We're going to have to discern what's going on. Learn the details."

Cass nodded. "Yes, I'll go fetch Jane. We'll ask her."

"No. We cannot allow her time to come up with an excuse. We must go to her immediately and ask her what happened. Confront her directly. That's the only way we'll know the truth."

Cass nodded again. "Very well. Let's go."

The knock at Jane's bedchamber door nearly scared her half to death. Oh, God, it wasn't Upton again, was it? Come for more of the same? She might not have the willpower to tell him to go. No. That made no sense. Upton didn't know it had been her. He wouldn't come to her room, and she doubted that even Upton, rake though he may be, would be trolling the halls in the morning looking for another assignation. Very well. It was no doubt safe to open the door.

Though one couldn't be too careful. "Who is it?" she called, smoothing down her hair.

"Lucy," came her friend's voice.

"And Cass."

Jane breathed a sigh of relief. Grabbing her spectacles from the bedside table and placing them upon her nose, she hurried to the door. She paused along the way to stare at her reflection in the looking glass. Her white linen dressing gown was perfectly pressed. Her hair was in place. Her cheeks had no rosy glow. She looked normal. Not guilty at all.

It would be best if she could admit what happened to her friends, and she would have. If it had been anyone other than *Upton*. Ugh. It was a complete disaster. She didn't even like Upton. How in the world had this happened?

She briefly considered telling Lucy and Cass the story, substituting an unknown gentleman—she could pretend that she didn't know who he was either. But she quickly discarded that thought during the journey to the door. She knew Lucy and Cass. If her friends learned that she'd engaged in such an escapade with a gentleman at the house party—any gentleman—they wouldn't rest until they discovered his identity. Not to mention they'd ask her a barrage of questions about what he looked like and what he'd been wearing, and it would all be discovered soon enough. There were only about two dozen gentlemen at the house party. Two dozen, and the one she happened to share a passionate interlude with had to be Upton. She shook her head.

"Are you in there, Janie?" came Lucy's impatient voice.

"Coming," Jane replied in the most normal, guiltless tone she could muster. She had to pretend that nothing unusual had happened last night. If Lucy and Cass wanted to know where she'd gone off to, she'd simply tell them she'd been in the library reading. She would apologize to Cass for being unsociable. Better to be thought unsociable than to be discovered being *too* sociable with the wrong person.

Jane pulled open the door and smiled widely at her friends. "To what do I owe the pleasure so early in the morning?"

Lucy and Cass entered stealthily as if they were sizing up the situation, much like Mrs. Cat when she'd first come to breakfast.

"We're sorry if we woke you, Jane," Cass said. "I know how much you like to stay up late reading."

Jane shook her head. "It's quite all right. I was awake."

Lucy crossed her arms over her chest. "Where did you go off to last night, Janie?"

Jane's palms began to sweat. She pressed them against the front of her dressing gown. Did they know something? No. They couldn't know anything. She and Upton had been completely alone. She was certain of it. They hadn't been the ones who'd closed the door. She'd decided that had all been a figment of her guilty imagination. Besides, Lord knew, if Lucy had been the one to discover them, she wouldn't have silently shut the door and backed away. She would have burst in and demanded an explanation. No. Lucy didn't know, but her question had been quite direct. Guilt was making Jane read too much into it.

"I was—erm, in the library, reading," she offered.

"Reading? In the library?" Lucy continued, walking in a slow circle around her as if she were a barrister examining a witness.

Cass remained silent but her bright eyes were trained on Jane's face and she looked worried.

"Yes." Jane didn't meet Lucy's gaze. Lucy was clever. She might discern that Jane was lying with one glance. "The music from the masquerade ball was a bit too loud for me. I'm sorry, Cass. I tried to stay. I truly did."

Cass ignored that last bit. "How many teacakes did you eat last evening?"

Jane blinked. She wrapped her dressing gown more tightly around her waist. "What does that have to do with anything?"

Cass managed a half-shrug. "I usually see you occupied with a plate of teacakes and I didn't see that last night."

Jane snorted. "What are you accusing me of, Cass? Not being hungry enough?"

Lucy crossed her arms over her chest again and paced across the carpet. The look on her face was entirely suspicious. Oh, lovely. They suspected something. Upton hadn't mentioned anything, had he? No. He hadn't known who she was. How many times must she remind herself of that?

"So, you ate no teacakes and you went to the library where you spent the rest of the evening reading?" Arms still crossed, Lucy tapped her fingers along her opposite elbows.

"I didn't say I ate no teacakes," Jane replied, pushing up her chin. "I adore teacakes. I ate three before I went to the library."

"The library?" Lucy looked down her nose at Jane.

"Yes, the library." Wasn't her philosophy to solve one

problem at a time? That was all there was to do now. Lie and stand firm. Even though Lucy and Cass obviously suspected something, they had no proof. Did they? Had they gone to the library and not found her?

"The library?" Cass echoed.

Jane considered the possibilities. It was all or nothing. She had to see this through. "Yes, the library. You do know where the library is, don't you?"

"Of course I know where the library is." Cass plunked her hands on her hips.

"Did you count the teacakes?" Jane asked, her lips twitching from suppressed laughter.

"What a silly question," Cass replied. "Of course I didn't count the teacakes. You're free to eat as many teacakes as you like."

"I'm glad to hear it because it seems the two of you are accusing me of something. Perhaps something duplicitous, involving teacakes?"

"Accusing you of something? Whatever do you mean?" Cass put her hand to her throat, but she was a rubbish liar. It was obvious she was attempting to play ignorant.

"What might we be accusing you of?" Lucy interjected.

"I don't know," Jane answered. "You tell me."

They faced off, staring at each other, Jane daring Lucy to ask a bold enough question to get to the bottom of this interrogation. Surprisingly, Lucy broke first. "We merely came up to ensure you were well, Janie. We were quite worried about you when we couldn't find you last night."

Jane breathed a sigh of relief. "Thank you for checking on me. I'm quite fine."

Cass crossed over to her and gave her a quick hug. "I'm so glad."

Lucy whirled and narrowed her eyes on Jane. "Did you, ah, happen to see Garrett last night?"

Jane pressed her palms together to keep them from shaking. She counted three and took a deep breath. They knew something. But she'd come this far and she refused to back down. "Upton?" she said in the most disinterested voice she could muster. "Are you asking if I saw Upton in the library? Because the answer is most assuredly no. I doubt Upton even knows what a library is."

Lucy's smile was catlike. "You didn't see Garrett at all then?"

"If you're interested in Upton's whereabouts last evening, you might try asking Mrs. Langford. She seems to be quite taken with him, though goodness knows why."

Distraction. It usually worked on her mother. Would it work on Lucy?

Obviously dissatisfied with that answer, Lucy opened her mouth to speak, but Cass patted Jane's hand. "We'll see you later for the picnic on the lawn, won't we, Jane?"

Lucy plunked her hands on her hips and glared at Cass.

"Yes, of course." Jane smoothed her hand over her hair. "I think I'll just pop back to bed for a bit more sleep. I'll be down for the picnic around noon."

"Have a good rest," Lucy called as she made her way to the door, Cass trailing behind her.

The two disappeared nearly as quickly as they'd come, leaving Jane staring after them perplexed. Just what did they know?

# CHAPTER SEVENTEEN

Garrett had been summoned. Summoned to the gold drawing room where Lucy and Cassandra were apparently holding court. The entire house party—or at least those who were inclined—were to have a picnic lunch in a meadow on the estate at noon. While most of the guests were assembling in the foyer to make their way out together, a footman had delivered a note asking Garrett to meet Lucy and Cassandra in the salon directly before the group departed.

Thank God that hideous concoction of Colton's had done its work. Garrett's headache was gone. The sick feeling in his stomach was now caused only by the knowledge that he'd done things with the most unlikely lady in the kingdom last night. He could only hope she hadn't realized it was him. Or had she? No. That wasn't possible. First, it was surprising that Miss Lowndes would ever do any of the things they'd done last night. Garrett wouldn't have guessed she had it in her. He wouldn't believe for a moment she would have done them had she known she was doing them with *him*.

He opened the door to the gold salon and strode inside. Lucy was at the window staring across the front lawn. Cassandra was perched on the settee near the fireplace.

"Garrett," Lucy said, spinning around. "Don't you look handsome today?"

He glanced down at what he was wearing. Gray trousers, white shirt and cravat, black boots, burgundy waistcoat. Nothing particularly different from any other day. "Thank you, Lucy."

He made his way over and kissed her cheek. Then he made his way to Cassandra and leaned to do the same.

"How are you holding up?" he whispered to Cassandra. "Nerves not getting the best of you, I hope."

She smiled and shook her head softly. "No. I'm quite fine."

"Excellent." He returned her smile before turning back to Lucy. "Now, what is it the two of you wanted to see me about? I can only imagine. Please tell me it has nothing to do with your Mrs. Bunbury plot. I refuse to be a part of it."

Lucy crossed her arms over her chest and strode toward him. "It's nothing to do with that. We just wondered where you'd got off to last night."

Garrett narrowed his eyes on his cousin. Did they know? No. They couldn't possibly.

"'Off to last night'?" he repeated, shoving his hands in his pockets in his best effort to appear casual.

"Yes, we didn't see you at the ball after a bit. We were looking for you," Cassandra added.

"I had a great deal to drink last night. Thanks to your brother. I believe I retired earlier than usual."

"Ah, so you went to bed?" Lucy prodded.

"Yes, after a bit," he replied.

"What were you doing before that?" Lucy asked.

Cassandra's cheeks flamed bright pink. Oh, bloody hell. They knew something.

"I was . . ." He took a breath. "I went to the upstairs drawing room. I was looking at the portraits."

"Looking at the portraits in the upstairs drawing room?" Lucy repeated, making "looking at the portraits" sound positively lascivious.

"Yes. I was quite fascinated by them." Wasn't it time to leave for the picnic? He tugged at his cravat. It was hot in here. He needed fresh air.

"Fascinated by the portraits?" Lucy echoed.

He opened his mouth to speak but Cassandra interrupted. "Were you with Mrs. Langford last night?"

His eyebrows shot up. Holy Christ, is that what they thought? "What exactly are you asking, Cassandra?"

Cassandra's cheeks turned pinker. "I mean, were you, were you looking at the portraits with her?"

"No."

"Who were you looking at the portraits with?" Lucy countered.

Garrett narrowed his eyes on both of them. "Why are you two so interested in what I was up to last night?" If they knew what he'd actually been doing, and with whom, they wouldn't be asking these questions. He was quite safe.

"No reason," Cassandra answered quickly, but Cassandra was a rubbish liar. They were both suspicious of . . . something.

"Lucy," Garrett said in a warning tone, "I hope this has nothing to do with your promise to find a wife for me after you're done with your whatever-it-is with Miss Lowndes. I assure you I'm in no need of a wife and there is absolutely nothing going on between myself and Isabella Langford."

Lucy raised her brows, too, but the skepticism was apparent on her face.

"Promise me you'll leave any sort of matchmaking on my behalf well and truly alone."

Lucy shrugged one shoulder. "I have absolutely no intention of matching you with Mrs. Langford. Not to worry, my dear cousin."

"Thank you," Garrett said. "Now, I'm going out to the foyer to join the others for the picnic."

"We'll be along," Lucy replied simply, studying her gloves.

"Yes." Cass nodded rapidly.

"Good." Garrett made his way to the door as quickly as he could without looking as if he were trying to be quick about it. He had no desire to answer more questions from these two busybodies. Not today.

He breathed a sigh of relief as the drawing room door shut behind him. What did they know? Or did they only suspect? He sent up a prayer to the heavens, hoping it was merely conjecture.

After the door shut behind Garrett, Lucy turned to Cass and raised one eyebrow. "We have just been lied to."

Cass took a deep breath. "It does appear so, yes."

"And not just by Garrett, but by Jane as well," Lucy added.

"Do you think it's possible they each don't know it was the other? They were both wearing dominoes, and Janie wasn't wearing her spectacles."

Lucy tapped a finger against her cheek. "It's possible, I suppose, but if they didn't know, they wouldn't be working so hard to keep it from us. Garrett might, as he'd hardly be one to kiss and tell, but Janie, no. Janie is deliberately keeping this from us."

Cass's eyes were wide as saucers. "You don't suppose they kissed, do you?"

"I don't know. I can't imagine it. But I do wonder what they did together after they sneaked off. Obviously something they don't want either of us to know about."

"Perhaps they're embarrassed to tell us because we've always known they can barely tolerate each other. They can hardly admit to sneaking off together." Cass gulped. "But you don't honestly think—"

"As difficult as it is to believe, I do think so. They kissed."

Cass gasped. "No."

"I admit it's difficult to conceive of. But the signs are all there." Lucy counted off the points on her fingers. "They were incognito. They left together. They were alone for a time in the upstairs drawing room, and neither will admit they were there together."

Cass pressed her palms to her cheeks. "But if neither of them will admit it, how will we ever discover what happened?"

Lucy paced in front of the windows, tapping her cheek. "This calls for a plan, Cass."

"Oh, no. Not a plan."

"Yes. A plan! To get to the bottom of this, to flush them out. If Garrett and Jane did sneak off together and kiss, they cannot be half as indifferent to each other as they pretend."

"Yes, but— Oh, Lucy, you know what happens when you come up with one of your plans."

"Yes! Things get done." Lucy's eyes gleamed. "Are we not about to celebrate your wedding? An event that came about as a direct result of one of my plans?"

"I cannot argue with you there, Luce." Cass pinched

the bridge of her nose. "You've already come up with this particular plan, haven't you?"

Lucy's catlike grin had returned. She rubbed her hands together with obvious glee. "Of course I have, and we're going to need Daphne and Owen to help us."

# CHAPTER EIGHTEEN

A picnic was the last place Jane wanted to be. Sprawling on the grass in the sun was not her sort of a pleasant time. She preferred the quiet coolness of a house and the sturdiness of a table and chair, but Cass wanted a picnic, so a picnic she would have. So Jane put on her favorite day dress, the white one with small flowers embroidered on it, and made her way downstairs.

The truth was, Jane had hidden. She'd hidden in the front drawing room until the large group of picnickers had all assembled in the foyer and then dutifully trotted out to the gravel drive in front of the grand manor house. They were to follow the trail to the left of the house into the meadow. While Jane intended to accompany them, she also intended to ensure Upton was at the front of the line and she at the back. She couldn't be certain how she would react in his presence. She needed time to think, and staying carefully away from him at the picnic was quite a good start.

She'd watched through the window until Upton had got safely on his way—with Mrs. Langford simpering on his arm, Jane noted with a bit of pique—then Jane counted twenty and marched out of the salon, through the front door, and onto the gravel drive.

"Janie, there you are!" Cass exclaimed the moment she appeared outside.

"I told you I'd make it to the picnic," Jane replied with her own smile. "A lady has to eat sometime, doesn't she?" She opened her white parasol and waited for Cass and Julian to precede her down the path. The day was beautiful, and the smell of freshly scythed grass and bluebells wafted along the slight breeze.

"Where's Lucy?" Jane asked as she turned to hear a ruckus behind her. Lucy brought up the rear, her handsome duke of a husband accompanying her.

"What took you so long, Lucy?" Cass asked.

Lucy shrugged. "I was just . . . planning a few things."

Jane glimpsed Daphne Swift and Owen Monroe coming out of the house. They all followed Cass and Julian down the path.

Jane didn't have time to wonder what her friends had been up to. She was far too preoccupied as she kept her eyes trained ahead for any sign of Upton. If the man doubled back, she might be forced to jump into the hedgerow and explain herself later. Thankfully, Upton remained far ahead during the entire stroll to the meadow.

Once they entered the field, Jane realized the picnic would not be quite as rustic as she'd envisioned. A team of servants bustled about half a dozen large tables with benches lining each one. White awnings were spread across their tops and each table had wide white linen cloths spread with decanters of wine and baskets holding loaves of bread, cheeses, grapes, strawberries, and an assortment of meat slices. "Thank goodness," Jane breathed. "I'd thought I'd have to slap ants from my stockings."

"Don't be ridiculous," Cass replied. "Who wants to sit in the grass?"

"Not I." Jane stalled, wandering around in a useless little circle staring at the cloudless sky and trying to whistle, hoping Upton and Mrs. Langford would sit first and then she could choose a seat far away from them. She was thwarted when Lucy and Cass beckoned her to their table. "Come sit, Jane," Lucy called.

Jane wrinkled her nose. Upton stood only a few paces away engaged in conversation with Mrs. Langford and another guest. It was too soon to tell where he would sit. All Jane could do was hope it was not at the same table.

"Garrett, we've saved you a seat," Lucy called, waving to her cousin.

*Blast.* Jane cursed under her breath.

"What was that?" Cass asked, her forehead wrinkling into a frown.

"Nothing." Jane shook her napkin into her lap with much more precision than she had heretofore ever given the task.

"Is there a seat for Mrs. Langford as well?" Garrett called back.

Jane lowered her eyes and kept her gaze trained on her napkin. *Please don't let there be a seat for Mrs. Langford. Please.* She prayed to a God she wasn't certain she believed in.

"Yes, of course. We'll make room," came Lucy's cheerful reply.

Moments later, Jane found herself looking up into the grinning face of Garrett Upton, the man she'd accidentally—not so accidentally—shared a passionate interlude with the night before. To make things worse, she was intensely aware of how *handsome* he happened to look today. His eyes were particularly green against the backdrop of the grass of the meadow and his slightly curly dark hair was a bit mussed as usual. She'd never realized how handsome he was. Why? Why had she never noticed how strong his jaw appeared? Or how straight his nose? For heaven's sake, what was happening to her? She should have worn her spectacles last night. Had she not traded them for a domino mask, she might not be waxing poetic about Upton's looks at the moment.

Jane cleared her throat and kept her gaze trained on her lap. That seemed the safest way to stop thinking about the man's firmly molded lips and dark brows. When she dared a peek, Upton immediately looked away. She took a tentative sip of the wine a footman had just poured. She'd never been so pleased to see a glass of wine.

Mrs. Langford broke the awkward silence. "Where did you get off to last night, Miss Lowndes? I didn't see you after the dancing." Was there a bit of a sneer in the lady's voice or was Jane imagining it?

Jane nearly spat her wine. "I— We— I mean, I—"

"Jane was in the library reading," Cass, that dear, offered. Thank heavens for Cass. Jane loved Cass.

"Ah." Mrs. Langford's green eyes narrowed. "The library?"

Jane squinted at the woman, not liking the tone she continued to use. Not one bit. "Yes, the library."

"That's right," Mrs. Langford added. "I nearly forgot you're a bluestocking. Where else would you be but the library?"

Jane straightened her spectacles. She'd begun this encounter a bit embarrassed to be sitting across from Upton, but if this woman intended to be rude to her, she could give as well as she got.

"A fact of which I'm infinitely proud." Jane gave Mrs. Langford a tight smile.

"As you should be, of course, dear. If one cannot find a husband, one ought to make the most of one's intellectual ability." Mrs. Langford's eyes were barely slits.

Jane clenched her jaw and waved her wine glass in the air. Why was this woman being so awful to her all of a sudden? "Funny. I've always thought if one cannot use one's intellectual ability to any effect, the only option would be marriage."

"Who would like some bread?" Cass's overly enthusiastic voice rang out.

"I would!" was Julian's immediate reply. Cass set about handing her future husband a basket of bread that had already been sliced into big, fluffy pieces by the servants.

"Well," came Mrs. Langford's silky voice, still directed toward Jane. "Perhaps you learned something about attracting the interest of a man while you were in the—ahem—library last night? Any books about that in there?"

Cass gasped. Lucy's head swiveled back and forth between Jane and Mrs. Langford. Garrett studied his wine glass. Julian and Derek shifted in their seats.

"I wouldn't know," Jane replied sweetly. "If such a book did exist, I'd be singularly uninterested in it."

"You've never taken a fancy to a man?"

Jane pressed her lips together. Something in the smug look on Mrs. Langford's face made her think the woman knew something. Or seemed to suspect. Twenty-four hours ago, Jane could have said "no" without a shadow of guilt on her conscience, but considering that last night she'd just had her first kiss . . . and more, she wasn't able to stand on the moral high ground any longer.

Once again, Cass, the dear, waded into the silence for her. "Jane is a confirmed intellectual. She's not interested in marriage at all."

"A pity." Mrs. Langford pulled a piece of bread from the basket that had made its way to her. She set the slice on her plate. "Marriage can be ever so agreeable, if it's done with the right partner." She turned toward Upton and batted her eyelashes. "Wouldn't you agree, Mr. Upton?"

Upton cleared his throat. "Considering that I am a bachelor, Mrs. Langford, I wouldn't know."

Jane hid her smile at his answer behind her wine glass but inside she was simmering. The nerve of that woman. What was Upton about, bringing this odious person into their midst? He couldn't possibly relish her company, could he? Oh, no. He didn't . . . He couldn't have thought that *she* was Mrs. Langford last night, could he? A knot formed in Jane's belly and sat there like a hard, jagged rock. She glanced up to see Upton's gaze sliding away from her again.

"I'm quite certain marriage is ever so agreeable," Julian said, a sparkle in his eye as he pulled Cass's hand up and kissed the back of it. Cass beamed at him.

Derek tightened an arm around Lucy.

Jane found herself fighting back . . . tears of all things. It wasn't as if she'd never *thought* about marriage, never considered it. As a younger woman, she'd been inclined to daydream, to wonder what it would be like to be swept off her feet by a handsome stranger, told she was beautiful, fall in love. Those things were not for her. She preferred solitude to parties, books to fripperies. She was plain and dowdy, not fashionable. Nothing like her gorgeous friends Lucy and Cassandra. Jane had never had one suitor. Not one. Not even the hint of one, the whiff of one.

Upton had said she was gorgeous last night. Had he meant it? Or was that what rakes said to all of the ladies they had assignations with in drawing rooms? More than asking her to remove her mask, telling her she was gorgeous had caused her to push him away. He couldn't mean it. It wasn't true. She wasn't gorgeous. The thought that he'd lie to her like that, that any man would lie to a woman like that, had made her go cold inside.

She was plump and plain. Well, perhaps not plump, not any longer, but she'd always be plump in her head. And the plainness, that would never go away. Perhaps with the demimask on her face and the large quantity of alcohol Upton had obviously consumed last night, he'd been momentarily lulled into the belief that he was with a beautiful woman. But nothing about last night had been true. That's why she hadn't told Lucy or Cass about it. That's why she could never let Upton suspect it was her. It wasn't just the potential embarrassment. It was because it was only a figment of her imagination, or might as well have been.

Garrett glanced away every time Miss Lowndes, uh, Jane—he needed to think of her as Jane now that he'd kissed her senseless last night—looked at him. He was beginning to feel conspicuous about it and was certain she'd noticed. Jane was intelligent. She may have already realized it had been him last night. He couldn't look at her. But he did. Again. As if his eyes were drawn to her. He wanted to see her, really see her. In the past he hadn't given a passing thought to her looks. She was just Miss Lowndes, Lucy's friend who drove him a little mad with her know-it-all attitude and penchant for making fun of him.

Now, all he could think about was her luxuriant hair, the smell of her perfume. Lilacs. Why did it have to be lilacs? That little spot just under her chin that tasted so damn sweet. Christ, what had come over him? The urge to snatch off her glasses and pull the pins out of her hair and look upon her face and see the woman he'd been with last night was nearly overpowering. If they were alone, if they weren't at a table full of people in the open air, he just might do it. What would Miss Lowndes do if he dared?

He tried to concentrate on chewing and swallowing his food. Somehow that had become a difficult task. It was a mad, mad day already. Why was Isabella being so unpleasant to Jane? At first, he suspected Isabella had been as bothered by Jane as he always had been. Jane didn't back down from a fight and Isabella had got a taste of Jane's sharp tongue. But he couldn't help feeling admiration for Jane when she stood up to Isabella. It truly was none of the other woman's concern why Jane preferred to remain unmarried. He'd always had the same preference, and felt a sort of closeness with her. He needn't have worried. Jane had promptly snapped back a volley of replies that had surely left Isabella thinking she just might do better to keep from engaging Miss Lowndes in a battle of words in the future.

He'd been in his share of word fights with her, himself, and often came out on the losing end. He smiled to himself and looked at her once more. She turned to speak with Owen Monroe, who happened to be sitting next to her again. She didn't notice Garrett's slow perusal of her. Today she was wearing a white gown that did nothing for her considerable assets. It was the type of thing she normally wore. Where in God's name had she got that blue gown she'd been wearing last night? It had transformed her.

Garrett took a long sip from his wine glass and watched her over its rim. He growled under his breath. Owen Monroe was sitting a bit too close.

# CHAPTER NINETEEN

Garrett was sitting alone in the library, reading, with his booted feet propped on an ottoman and crossed at the ankles when Cassandra found him that evening just before dinner. There was to be a dinner and a dance—not a ball, Lucy had insisted, just a dance. Garrett looked forward to neither.

"Garrett, there you are. This is the last place I expected to find you," Cassandra said, a bright smile on her face. Her blond hair was swept up atop her head and she wore a fetching lavender gown with pearls at her neck.

Garrett quickly uncrossed his feet, stood, and bowed. "Don't tell Miss Lowndes. It may ruin the bad opinion she has of me and my lack of reading habits."

"I won't tell if you won't," Cassandra said in a conspiratorial voice.

"Agreed," he answered.

Cassandra made her way to him and sat on the settee across from him.

"It's interesting that you bring up Jane, however"—

Cassandra plucked at her sleeve—"because that's precisely who I wanted to speak with you about."

Garrett's gaze snapped to her face. "Jane?"

"Yes." Cassandra calmly folded her small hands and placed them in her lap.

"What about her?"

"I wanted to say . . . It's come to my attention . . ." Cassandra blushed beautifully and glanced away.

"Yes?" he prompted.

"It's come to my attention that, well, there's no easy way to say it . . ." Her words fell from her mouth in a mad rush. "It appears that Jane is madly in love with you."

Garrett's jaw dropped. All he could do was blink. "Jane is— Pardon?"

Cassandra didn't meet his gaze. Her hands remained unmoving in her lap. "Yes. She is."

Garrett stood and scrubbed his hands through his hair. He strode to the fireplace. "That is preposterous. That is ludicrous. Why, that is—"

"Impossible?" Cassandra supplied.

He turned to face her. "Yes. Impossible."

Cassandra's deep blue eyes rose to meet his. "I'm afraid it's quite possible and we, Lucy and I, thought you should know."

Garrett narrowed his gaze on her. "Lucy is often wrong about these things, Cassandra. You know she was convinced I was in love with *you* until recently."

Cassandra fluttered a hand in the air. "I know. And it's not like that. This is different. It's quite confirmed."

"Confirmed, how?" His eyes remained narrowed.

Cassandra cleared her throat. Her voice went up a notch. "By Jane."

His hand dropped like a leaden weight to his side. "Jane said that? She *said* she loves me?"

Cassandra bit her lip and nodded. "As I said, Lucy and I thought you should know."

Garrett leaned back against the window frame; the air rushed from his lungs. It was as if he'd been slammed to the earth. He struggled to breathe. It couldn't be true. Could *not* be true. It made no sense.

But if Jane had told Cassandra . . .

He stared unseeing into the fireplace and rubbed a hand roughly across his forehead, squeezing his eyes shut. "Thank you for telling me, Cassandra." Not that he knew what the hell to do with the information.

Cass hurried out of the library, wringing her hands.

"Psst." Lucy motioned to her from behind a potted palm at the far end of the corridor. "Over here."

Cass peeked over both shoulders to ensure no one would see her before picking up her skirts and hurrying to join her friend behind the tree.

"Did you do it?" Lucy asked, her multicolored eyes sparkling.

"Yes. I did it." Cass groaned. "Heaven knows I shall be struck dead by a lightning bolt for being such a fibber. I deserve this red spot on my nose. I deserve another for what I've done. I deserve an entire face full of them. I detest lying."

Lucy's dark eyebrow rose in a semblance of skepticism. "Oh, really? You detest lying? After pretending to be Patience Bunbury last autumn? If that didn't cause a face full of red spots, nothing will."

Cass scowled at her fiercely. "Point taken, but we should have asked Derek or Julian to tell Garrett that awful lie instead of me."

"We've been over this," Lucy replied. "Derek and Julian wouldn't have agreed to this in a hundred years. They would have given us a lecture about how it isn't the right thing to do. And it's not an awful lie. Not really."

"Perhaps it *isn't* the right thing to do, Lucy. Lying to our friends feels wrong."

"Look at it this way." Lucy pushed a palm frond away from her forehead. "You're not fibbing so much as you're helping them. You saw how Garrett and Jane acted at the picnic. Something is definitely happening between them. We're simply giving them a small push. Now, tell me, what did Garrett say?"

Cass tugged at one of the leaves on the palm tree. "He was shocked to be sure, quite shocked."

"Did he believe you?"

Another tug on the long green leaf. "I do think I was able to convince him, though he was skeptical for certain."

Lucy clapped her hands together. "Perfect. The first phase of the plan has gone off splendidly."

"What about you?" Cass let go of the palm leaf. It sprung back into place. "Have you told Jane yet?"

Lucy shook her head. "I'm on my way to speak to Jane now. The second half of the plan is to commence shortly. I call it *Much Ado About Something*."

# CHAPTER TWENTY

"You *must* be jesting," Jane said five minutes later as Lucy sat on the end of the bed in Jane's guest chamber. "I cannot believe for a moment that Upton is in *love* with me."

"I didn't believe it either, at first," Lucy said with a nonchalant shrug, "but Derek and Julian both told me the same thing. When Garrett was in his cups the other night, he admitted it to them."

"Then he's a loon when he's in his cups," Jane replied, shaking her head.

Jane's voice was protesting, but her mind was preoccupied with examining this news. It couldn't be true. Could it? Garrett? Garrett Upton? Rake, gambler, and general profligate, in *love*? With *her*? If Lucy had told her this news two days ago, Jane would have laughed her out of the room. But today. Today was the day after she'd nearly been ravished by Upton on the settee in the upstairs drawing room—and liked it. Today was the day she'd gone on a picnic and noticed Upton glancing at her every time she looked at him. Today everything had changed and Lucy's story didn't seem quite so far-fetched.

"Correct me if I'm wrong, Lucy, but wasn't Upton madly in love with Cass until recently?"

Lucy twisted her lips. "Oh, ah . . . about that . . ."

Jane narrowed her eyes on her friend. "What?"

"It seems I was mistaken about that." Lucy traced her fingernail along the pattern in the bedspread.

"Mistaken?"

"Yes."

"Upton wasn't in love with Cass?"

"No."

"Ever?"

"Never."

Jane crossed her arms over her chest. "How did you make such a mistake?"

Lucy raised both palms toward the ceiling and shrugged. "He was always there, you know, sitting next to her and being nice to her, and well, Cass is so pretty, and accomplished, and so . . . Cass. I just assumed . . ."

Jane pushed up her spectacles and nodded sagely. "That explains it. You're only assuming now, aren't you? Upton's no more in love with me than he was with Cass."

"No, this time I'm quite sure." Lucy nodded firmly.

Jane narrowed her eyes. "Sure, how?"

"I told you, he admitted it to Derek and Julian."

Jane searched her friend's face, arms still resolutely crossed over her chest. "But did he tell *you*?"

Lucy didn't meet her eyes. "Telling Derek is as good as telling me."

Jane had to concede that point. She was skeptical, but even Lucy, egregiously behaved Lucy, wouldn't *lie* about such a thing. She might hint at it. She might heavily imply, but coming right out and declaring that her husband had told her the exact words, that was too much even for the most outlandish of all of Lucy's plots.

"Now that you've told me, Your Grace, what do you suppose I *do* with this information?"

Lucy leaned back on her palms. "Nothing, obviously. You're a confirmed bluestocking spinster, after all. I just thought you should know. In case Garrett is perhaps"— she eyed Jane carefully—"acting differently toward you or something of that sort. Is he?"

"Is he what?" Jane's words were a bit too rushed.

"Acting differently toward you."

Jane let her hand slide over the copy of *Montague's Treatise on the History of Handwriting and Graphology* that sat on her writing table. "No, not that I recall." Oh, yes he was. But she'd die of embarrassment before she'd tell Lucy about it.

"Not a bit?" Lucy prodded.

"Not that I've noticed." *Liar.*

"Very well, then. I suppose you should just go about your business as usual and pretend as if you don't know. In the meantime, we should discuss our plan for Mrs. Bunbury's introduction to your mother in a few days."

Jane shook her head to clear it of the prior subject. In the wake of this news about Upton, her plan to fool her mother didn't seem quite as pressing, but Lucy was correct. Jane's mother would be appearing in a few days and they needed to have a solid plan in place. Jane's first attempt at scandal had ended hideously. She was wary of a second attempt.

"I, er, I cannot think of a sufficient scandal," Jane mumbled.

"We'll need a secondary plan in the meantime. Here is what I propose." Lucy stood and shook out her skirts. "Between the three of us, you, Cass, and myself, we shall endeavor to keep your mother guessing. 'Why, Mrs. Bunbury was just here not five moments ago, didn't you see her? No, she's not here now, but I just saw her near the refreshment table a bit earlier.' That sort of thing."

It sounded insane. But then again, most of Lucy's plots sounded insane. That was the beauty of them, but even Jane had to admit they usually worked.

"Very well, we'll take turns," Jane agreed.

She had come to Surrey a few days ago, convinced that her Mrs. Bunbury plot was the most complicated thing in her life. Now she wasn't certain about that. Not certain at all.

# CHAPTER TWENTY-ONE

Garrett scrubbed a hand through his hair. There was only one way to get to the bottom of this. He was going to bloody well ask Jane Lowndes himself. Was she or was she not in love with him? First, he would ask her to dance. The Morelands were having a dance tonight. A plain little dance. No dominoes, no hidden identities. It was quite simple.

He hadn't been able to get what Cassandra had told him earlier out of his head. Jane Lowndes was in love with him? Could it be? It was true that she had been quite . . . *congenial* with him the other night, but that had been when they didn't know who the other was, hadn't it? Or had she known all along? No. It couldn't be.

He was tired of guessing. He would ask her to dance, they would talk, and he would be able to tell by her reaction whether she was in love with him. It would be simple enough. Didn't women who were in love simper and bat their eyelashes and that sort of thing? He could hardly imagine Miss Lowndes doing something like that. Normally, if she did anything of the sort, he'd probably ask her if she had something in her eye, but that wasn't the point. The point was that there must be some sign, some tell, of a woman in love, some indication of whether Miss Lowndes, Jane—why was it so difficult to remember to think of her as Jane?—was such a woman. He would know soon enough.

Garrett squared his shoulders and took a deep breath, then made his way to the refreshment table where Jane hovered near the teacakes. She wore a light pink gown that wasn't at all hideous. In fact it enhanced her figure. Had he ever seen her in pink before? Bloody hell, this was going to be awkward enough without him thinking about her figure again.

"Miss Lowndes?"

She swiveled on her heel and turned to face him, a large, telltale lump of teacake pushing out her cheek. She had the look of a hare trapped in a game warden's snare. Pure fright.

She had the grace to chew and swallow before she responded. "Upton," she said, gulping down the last bit. "What can I do for you?"

He bowed slightly. "I've come to ask you to dance. Would you do me the honor?"

She glanced back as if she expected another lady to be standing there. "Me?" She pointed to herself, eyes wide.

He had to smile. "Yes, you."

Without looking, she set her empty plate on the table, pushing it behind her with a flick of the wrist. "I suppose I can dance with you."

He bowed to her. "Thank you." He held out his arm. She took a step forward and put her hand on his arm. He led her to the dance floor.

Was her hand trembling?

He pulled her into his arms as a waltz began to play.

He'd tipped the musicians a goodly sum to play this waltz. It afforded the perfect opportunity to speak with Jane.

He spun her around. "Are you having a good time?"

Again, she had the look of a hare caught in a trap. Her eyes were wide and she *was* trembling. "Here? With you?"

"I meant at the party in general," he said.

"Yes, of course." She didn't meet his eyes. A sign of a woman in love, was it not?

He laughed. "You're lying. You've never enjoyed a party before in your life." Her throat worked. Another sign of a lady in love?

"Then why did you ask me? I'm doing my best, Upton. Don't I deserve credit for that?" She met his gaze this time and her dark brown eyes were bright and full of mischief. Quite charming, actually. Damn it. Now *he* had to look away.

He smiled at her. "You do indeed. Tell me, how is your plan coming? Done anything scandalous lately?"

Jane blinked at Upton. She'd spent the last several minutes desperately attempting to interpret everything he'd said and done. He'd made his way directly to her and asked her to dance, hadn't he? Very not Upton-like. That had to be a sign he was in love with her, didn't it? He hadn't mentioned her teacake consumption. Also quite un-Upton. Now he was being nice to her and laughing when she said something funny, a third entirely probable sign that the man was madly in love with her.

This was difficult. Why couldn't it be something tangible to interpret like, say, handwriting? She'd learned a great deal about handwriting of late. For instance, if a letter written to someone contained wide, scrolling letters, it meant the author was infatuated by the recipient.

Would it be odd to ask Upton for a sample of his hand-writing? It would, wouldn't it? She shook her head and refocused on his question. "Something scandalous?" she managed to ask in a tone she hoped sounded noncha-lant.

"Yes, the scandal you and Lucy are hell-bent on creating."

"Oh, we've been . . ." Good heavens, was she perspir-ing? She removed her hand from his shoulder and waved it in the air briefly. "Considering our options."

"I see," Upton continued. "And what of Mrs. Bun-bury?"

Jane had to concentrate on his words, because other-wise she was thinking about his shoulder. Specifically how good it felt under the tips of her fingers, even through her glove. The man was surprisingly muscled for being Upton. He wore impeccably tailored black evening at-tire with a sapphire waistcoat and a starchy white cra-vat that looked enticing against the bit of stubble from his chin that had scraped the soft skin of her cheeks last night. That, coupled with the heady scent of him, and she was finding it altogether too difficult to follow the thread of the conversation.

She sucked in her breath. "Mrs. Bunbury? Yes. We have made progress there."

"What do you intend to do?" he asked.

Jane squeezed his shoulder just barely. She couldn't resist. "Lucy says we should keep Mama guessing by constantly acting as if Mrs. Bunbury has been in our presence and left just before Mama arrives."

He arched a dark brow. "Truly? That's your plan?"

"Yes. For now." Why did Upton have to smell so good?

"Seriously?"

Jane trained her gaze over his shoulder. Why did

Upton have to have such heavenly hazel eyes? Or more specifically, why had she had to *notice* that Upton had such heavenly hazel eyes? She'd been quite satisfied with barely noticing them before, thank you very kindly. Though now he was questioning her plan, much more Upton-like of him. Good heavens. Perhaps Lucy had been mistaken about his being in love with her and now Jane was stuck thinking about the blasted color of his eyes.

"Yes," she answered with a nod. "Between Lucy, Cass, and myself, we believe we can make it work. At least for the day or two of the wedding until we leave for London again."

Upton's mouth curved into a smile that made her want to kiss him. Blast it.

"How will you explain that Mrs. Bunbury isn't traveling back to London with you?" he asked.

Why did Upton insist upon asking a lot of questions about Mrs. Bunbury? Jane could barely concentrate on his words. Instead, she'd been staring at the sensual curve of his lips. Confound Lucy for telling her anything. "Because Mrs. Bunbury is going to become horribly ill the night of the wedding and leave before Mama has a chance to check on her."

"Poor Mrs. Bunbury." Upton shook his head.

Jane wanted to thread her fingers through his thick, dark, curly hair. "Don't worry. Mrs. Bunbury shall recover." Though Jane might not.

Upton smiled again, flashing his perfect white teeth at her. Since when did she notice that Upton's teeth were either perfect or white?

"It's ludicrous, of course," he said. "But you and Lucy are so confident about it. That is her secret, isn't it? Lucy makes things work because of her supreme confidence in their working."

Jane returned his smile. Was he thinking her teeth were perfect and white? She didn't know about the perfect part, one of the teeth on the bottom was a bit crooked, but they were white. Weren't they? "I'm not certain what Lucy's secret is, but she does have confidence. To spare."

Upton sighed. "I suppose it will give even more credence to the story if I mention to your mother that I've met Mrs. Bunbury and she's a lovely woman and an apt chaperone."

Jane blinked at him. "You'd do that for me?"

A resigned smile tugged at his lips. "I've learned that going against Lucy when her mind is made up is a losing battle. Being a former soldier, I like to have the field in my favor."

Jane spun around and around in the dance, barely hearing his words. Garrett Upton was going to do *her* a favor? Without being asked? Without being begged? Oh, heavens. The man was indeed madly, madly in love with her.

# CHAPTER TWENTY-TWO

There was nothing, absolutely nothing, redeemable about Isabella Langford. Perhaps her beauty, but beauty was fleeting. Awfulness lasted forever.

Jane eyed the woman the next day as the houseguests took a walk to the lake. Lady Moreland had promised there would be rowboats available. Finally, the one enjoyable outing since the house party began. Enough of picnics and balls. Jane could truly enjoy herself relaxing in a rowboat under the shady willow trees, reading her book. She'd tucked a novel in her reticule and marched down here with the rest of them. She wore a serviceable yellow morning dress. No more low-cut ball gowns for her. A white bonnet completed her ensemble and she felt quite returned to her natural element, that of a bluestocking spinster.

Mrs. Langford, however, was dressed like a doxy. Jane watched the woman laugh and smile at every word Upton said. Quite nauseating. Mrs. Langford's hair was swept up in a set of black curls, held in place by the tiniest hat Jane had ever seen, and a small gown to match her tiny hat. The gown was small in that it had very little fabric covering her chest. It would be more in place at a demimonde banquet than a friendly little rowboating venture at a country house. *I hope she gets a sunburn.* Not to mention it was a garish shade of red. Though Jane had to admit it brought out the rosy color of Mrs. Langford's full lips.

By the time their party made its way to the lake, Upton had managed to extricate himself from Mrs. Langford's clutches. When Jane peeked up from the book she'd been attempting to read while simultaneously attempting not to trip, Upton was strolling alongside her, his hands in his pockets.

They all stopped at the line of newly painted white rowboats that sat in front of the calm, green lake like fat little ducks. "Would you do me the honor of accompanying me?" Upton asked.

Jane snapped her astonished mouth shut, then opened it to ask, "Me?"

"Yes." He smiled and made a sweeping gesture toward the rowboats.

Jane glanced around. There was no doubt. He was talking to her. The man was *so* in love with her, poor sop. She might as well take pity on him and do him the honor of accompanying him about the lake.

Jane closed her book and made her way toward an available rowboat with Upton leading the way.

"Mr. Upton, wait for me!" That harlot Isabella Langford's voice rang out at the last possible moment. She waved her hand as she came scurrying up to them. "Do you have room for one more?" The shameless widow batted her eyelashes at Upton.

Over Mrs. Langford's head, Upton gave Jane a

long-suffering look. "Yes. Of course we can fit one more." Jane returned his chagrined expression. He'd had to say it. He would hardly be a gentleman if he refused. But Jane wasn't about to get stuck in a rowboat with Upton and Mrs. Langford, of all odious partners.

"I'm happy to allow the two of you to go. I'll just find Lucy or Cass." Jane scanned the bank. Confound it. Lucy and Cass had already pushed off in two separate rowboats being captained by their respective mates.

"Nonsense, Miss Lowndes, do come with us," Mrs. Langford purred, malicious triumph etched upon her features.

Jane stifled the urge to remind the woman that Upton had invited Jane first and Mrs. Langford was, in fact, coming along with *them*. Jane turned in a frantic circle searching the riverbank. Wasn't there someone else with whom she could row? Confound it, again. Daphne had already set sail with Owen Monroe and Lord and Lady Moreland were together. Jane watched in growing terror as one by one each boat set out until there were none left except the one she was standing in front of. Upton stared at her with a boyish charm Jane wished she hadn't noticed.

"It's quite all right." Jane backed away from the grassy bank. "I'll just sit under a tree and read. I'll be perfectly fine, I assure you."

Mrs. Langford looked eager to accept this excuse and opened her mouth to no doubt issue an appropriate reply when Upton interjected.

He held a hand out toward Jane. "Please, Miss Lowndes, come with me."

It was that last word that was Jane's undoing. If he had said come with "us," Jane surely would have refused, but he had said "me," clearly indicating to Jane that Mrs. Langford was the interloper.

"Very well," Jane replied softly.

If Mrs. Langford was at all affected by Upton's choice of words she didn't let it show. Instead, she smiled her obsequious smile and held out a hand to allow Upton to help her into the small boat.

Jane waited for Mrs. Langford to get settled, complete with a false attempt at tripping and falling into Upton's arms, something Jane couldn't help but roll her eyes at. Upton had seen the widow do it. That shameless woman obviously didn't care. Jane gazed back at the willow tree along the bank with real longing as she mentally counted off the ways in which this could be any worse. There could be ants. Or water snakes. Or two Mrs. Langfords instead of one.

Upton turned to Jane and held out his hand. "May I help you?" He said it in such a charming voice that Jane momentarily forgot Mrs. Langford was there.

Jane braced her hand against Upton's strong warm arm and allowed him to help her onto the wooden bench in the back of the rowboat. Upton had maneuvered them so that he sat in the middle, facing Jane. Mrs. Langford was perched in the bow of the vessel, craning her neck to get Upton's attention. Jane sighed. Very well, perhaps she could suffer a turn or two around the lake and then she would go in for her afternoon nap, and later there would be teacake. One must always look upon the bright side, mustn't one?

Jane spent the first several moments in the boat trying not to notice how good Garrett's muscles looked outlined in his shirtsleeves. He'd removed his jacket in order to row more effectively. He'd worked up a bit of a sweat on his forehead and that, combined with the scent of him, his spicy cologne she'd become intimately acquainted with recently, was making her uncomfortably warm. She turned her bonneted head away in an attempt to catch the slight breeze coming off the water.

She made a mental note to scold Lucy and Cass for leaving her alone with Upton and Mrs. Langford. What could they have been thinking? That she would enjoy herself with these two? Even if Lucy was making a poor attempt at matchmaking, it made no sense for a threesome to be on the water together. Hardly romantic. *Not* that she wanted to be romantic with Upton. Er, again. Certainly not. *Definitely* not.

"It's a lovely day for rowing," Mrs. Langford said.

Jane nearly breathed a sigh of relief. Perhaps the widow would stick to such inane comments and Jane might be left to read her book in peace. Though she couldn't help but glance up at Upton from time to time, just to try to determine if he was indeed in love with her and perhaps to catch a glimpse of those muscles.

"It is indeed," Upton replied just as innocuously.

Jane pulled her book up to her nose.

A gasp came from Mrs. Langford's general direction. "*Don't* tell me you intend to *read* during this lovely boat ride, Miss Lowndes."

Jane didn't care for the way the woman pronounced the word "read," as if it might be interchangeable with shaking babies or kicking puppies. She didn't even spare the woman a glimpse. Nor did she lower her book. "That's precisely what I intend to do."

"Egad. I cannot imagine a less interesting way to pass the time," Mrs. Langford replied. "The only things I read are fashion magazines."

"Why does that not surprise me?" Jane murmured under her breath, peeking over the top of her book momentarily to give the widow a disdainful stare.

"What was that?" Mrs. Langford pushed herself up

from her reclining position, bracing both hands on either side of the boat, presumably in an attempt to gain a better vantage point from which to hear Jane.

"I'm not certain that browsing through fashion magazines can be equated with reading, but it sounds like a valiant attempt," Jane replied. "At any rate, this particular chapter of this particular book is quite compelling. I do hope you'll excuse me while I get back to it." Jane could have sworn she saw Upton smother a smile.

"What book is it?" he asked.

Jane's head snapped up to face him. She lowered the book. "Pardon?"

"What book is it?" he repeated.

"What does it matter? Isn't one as boring as the next?" Mrs. Langford added in a supercilious tone, tittering at her own joke.

Jane rolled her eyes, but she refocused on Upton and his surprising question. If she didn't know better, she'd say he sounded as if he actually cared. "*The Mysteries of Udolpho*."

Upton nodded. "Ah, Ann Radcliffe."

Jane's mouth fell open. "You know of Ann Radcliffe?"

"Yes, I've read the novel twice."

"Ann Radcliffe, the *female* author?"

"Yes," he replied. "Since Ann is traditionally the name of a female, I had my suspicions."

Still attempting to absorb that astounding information, Jane glanced over his shoulder to see a pout on Mrs. Langford's face. "Tell me you're jesting, Mr. Upton."

"Not only have I read it twice, I've also read *The Romance of the Forest* and *The Italian*. Though I must say I prefer *The Mysteries of Udolpho*."

"You do?" Jane narrowed her eyes on him. Was he jesting? Teasing her? Had he lost his mind? Or was he lying?

"What is your favorite part of this book?" She held it up.

"Is this the first time you're reading it?" he asked.

"Yes," she replied, eyes still narrowed.

"Then I shan't give away the ending but I'll simply say that Sister Agnes may not be the sweet nun she appears to be."

Jane's eyes narrowed further. Very well. That might be true. But she had already read one of the other books. He could not trick her with that one. "What did you think of *The Romance of the Forest*?"

"I thought it was a great deal of trouble to get up to instead of paying one's debt. Not to mention the fate of poor Adeline. I do sympathize with the lady, considering how entirely she was at the mercy of a lot of awful men."

Jane braced her free hand against the side of the boat. The world was spinning. Upton, handsome, merrymaking Upton, had read the works of Ann Radcliffe? And could speak intelligently on the subject? It was beyond comprehension.

And had he just defended the rights of females?

"I do enjoy *some* books," Mrs. Langford hastened to add from her perch in the front of the boat.

"Like what?" Jane couldn't help herself.

"I read *Secrets of a Wedding Night* recently."

"That's more of a pamphlet really," Jane pointed out. She refused to tell Mrs. Langford that she'd not only read it, she'd actually enjoyed it too.

Mrs. Langford's voice dripped with ire. "We cannot all be devotees of Shakespeare and Ann Radliffe, like you are, Miss Lowndes."

"More's the pity," Jane replied. "And it's Rad*c*liffe."

Mrs. Langford nearly snarled at her. "Let's talk about

something else, shall we? Such as the parties in London. I, for one, cannot wait for the Season to get under way. Are you going to the Hathaways' ball, Mr. Upton?"

Upton glanced at Jane before he replied to Mrs. Langford. "I am."

Jane pressed her lips together. The thought of those two together, in London, being good-looking and drinking champagne and dancing and laughing and— It made her positively . . .

By God, was she actually getting . . . jealous?

No. It was not possible. Horrifying thought.

"Will you be in London for the Season, Miss Lowndes?" Mrs. Langford asked.

"Not if I can help it," Jane replied, her book back in front of her nose.

"Is that supposed to be funny?" Mrs. Langford replied, her voice taking on an irritated edge.

"It was supposed to be," Jane replied. "Though perhaps not to you."

Mrs. Langford replied with a grunt. "I've found that people who think themselves intelligent also tend to think themselves funny."

"What do unintelligent, unfunny people think of themselves?" Jane asked, lowering the book to face the widow as if extremely interested in the answer. "Do tell."

"We ought to be getting back," Upton interjected. "It looks as if a storm might be coming up and the others seem to be heading in."

Jane turned her attention to the sky. She'd been so involved in her battle of words with Mrs. Langford she'd failed to notice the dark clouds moving in. They were indeed gathering over the lake in an ominous gray mass. The other boats were quickly rowing toward the shore.

"Too bad," Mrs. Langford said with a pout on her lips.

Yes, too bad the widow wouldn't be able to spend the rest of the afternoon sniping at her in the boat.

Upton rowed quickly to shore. The small boat skimmed along the water until it hit land. Upton stood, braced one foot against the muddy shore, and then leaned down and dragged the boat a bit closer to the grass before turning to help Jane disembark first.

Jane allowed him to take her hand and help her to stand on the grass. "Be careful," she said, motioning with her chin back toward the boat and Mrs. Langford. "I'm convinced she bites."

Upton slipped her a wry grin.

Jane turned back to watch Mrs. Langford. The lady had already stood and was teetering precariously as the boat lurched from side to side. "Be careful," Upton called. "Let me help you." He lunged for her but was too late. Mrs. Langford, tiny hat and gown and all, plunged over the side of the rowboat into the shallow mud and water.

"Goodness me!" she exclaimed, and from the tone of her voice, Jane knew the widow had done it on purpose.

Lucy and Cass hurried over. Derek and Julian and the others were seeing to the boats.

"Mrs. Langford! Are you all right?" Cass asked, genuine concern marring her porcelain features.

"She's fine," Jane muttered as Upton waded in to retrieve the woman from the water. He scooped her into his arms and lifted her, then strode onto the grass where he set her down and wrapped his coat around her. "Are you all right? Nothing broken?"

"I don't th—think so," Mrs. Langford said in the most false-sounding, sad voice Jane had ever heard. "I'm so clumsy," the widow added for good measure.

Jane fought the urge to roll her eyes. She ran her fingertips along the top of her book. At least it hadn't got wet.

"Stay here," Upton said to Mrs. Langford. "I'll get a

mount from one of the footmen. I'll take you back to the house on horseback."

Lucy and Cass fawned over the poor little invalid while Jane went back to reading her book. Udolpho's mysteries were *much* more interesting than this charade.

"I do hope the damage is only to your clothing, Mrs. Langford," Lucy offered.

"And to my pride," Mrs. Langford said simply, adding a wistful sigh to her list of transgressions.

*Ha.* Jane kept her nose firmly ensconced in her book.

"We'll have one of the maids clean your things as soon as you get back to the house and change into new garments," Cass assured her.

"Thank you so much, Lady Cassandra," Mrs. Langford said fawningly. "I do so appreciate your assistance."

"Will you be all right with Garrett taking you back?" Cass asked.

This Jane *had* to see. She lowered the book and eyed the widow. Mrs. Langford's eyes grew dark and she looked down, allowing her eyelashes to splay against her cheeks in a display even Jane had to admit was fetching. "Yes. Of course. It's for the best that *Mr. Upton* be the one to take me home in my disheveled state."

What the devil did *that* mean?

Cass and Lucy exchanged shocked glances.

Mrs. Langford stepped closer to Lucy and Cass, but Jane was still able to hear what she said next. "Because Mr. Upton and I are close. Quite close indeed."

The book nearly toppled from Jane's hands. She grabbed for it and righted it just as Upton strode back to them, a horse in tow. "Let's get you back to the manor house," he said to Mrs. Langford. He led the widow by the hand and readily helped her onto the mount. From her position in front of Upton, Mrs. Langford gave Jane a smug smile. Jane nudged at her spectacles.

Upton tapped the horse with his heels and the pair took off, leaving Jane, Lucy, and Cass to stare after them, wide-eyed.

Jane let her arm holding the book fall to her side. "Ladies, you don't suppose all this time we've been in the presence of Garrett's mistress?"

# CHAPTER TWENTY-THREE

When the gentlemen joined the ladies after dinner that night, Mrs. Langford kept her sultry gaze trained on Upton. Jane couldn't take any more of the two of them. She'd been a complete fool telling Upton she'd get to the bottom of why Mrs. Langford had come. It had been obvious the entire time! If Jane hadn't allowed first her dislike of Upton, then her scandalous interaction with him, and finally her suspicion that he was in love with her, to cloud her judgment, she would have seen it from the start. Upton, the cad, had managed to invite his *mistress* to his friends' wedding. Even worse, he'd kissed *Jane,* too. Was the man so overcome with his base instincts he couldn't limit his sexual appetite to only one woman at a house party? What would Mrs. Langford say if she knew the man keeping her had been kissing another lady in the upstairs drawing room the other night? It was disgusting to contemplate.

Of course, there was no chance Jane would be the one to tell Mrs. Langford about her lover's defection. Jane would be admitting to being the other woman, and she'd rather die. No. She would keep Upton's dirty secret.

What nonsense of Lucy to tell her Upton loved her. Utterly ridiculous. How could he possibly be in love with her and invite his mistress to the house party at the same time? Lucy had informed Jane that Upton obviously had decided he'd fallen in love with her after Mrs. Langford's arrival, but the entire thing was sickening. If this was Upton's type of love, Jane had no use for it.

The worst part wasn't realizing what a degenerate the man was. The worst part was knowing she didn't have the right to be angry. Upton hadn't known it was her whom he'd kissed. He'd been kissing a stranger during a drunken masquerade ball. He probably hadn't given it a second thought. How many women did Upton consort with? Regardless, she was through with him. She'd have to suffer his company for the remainder of the house party, but then Jane would make it clear to Lucy that if she wanted to spend time in her cousin's company, she would do so without Jane.

Surprisingly, Upton made his way directly over to where Jane sat on a settee in the far corner. He'd searched the room when he'd entered as if looking . . . for her? Mrs. Langford was on the opposite side of the salon, no doubt being catty to Daphne Swift. Poor Daphne, it looked as if the young woman had purposely engaged the widow in conversation.

Jane watched Upton's approach out of the corner of her eye. He stopped a few paces from her. He cleared his throat and she tilted her head to look at him. He gestured to the seat next to her. "May I?"

She opened her mouth to reply, just before Owen Monroe materialized directly behind Upton.

"Always getting to Miss Lowndes before I do, Upton," Owen said, flashing a smile.

Upton turned his head and scowled at Owen. Jane raised her brows. Was it possible that Owen Monroe wanted to spend time in her company as well? What was in that perfume Lucy had allowed her to borrow? Jane had dabbed it beneath each ear tonight before she'd come to dinner. Apparently, it was attracting rakes hither and yon. Potent stuff, that.

Jane nodded her assent to Upton to sit and then said, "Lord Owen, please join us."

Upton's frown deepened. Jane's grin widened.

"Don't mind if I do," Owen replied, pushing up his dark coattails and sitting on the opposite side of Jane.

She glanced from side to side. She was properly squeezed between the two large, handsome men. As if her blasted stays weren't enough.

"What did you wish to speak to me about, Upton?" she asked without turning toward him.

He, too, kept his gaze focused on the wall across from them. "Why do you think I had something specific to say?"

She turned to him and was immediately aware of how close he was. Their thighs nearly touched. "You've sought out my company during two events now. I thought perhaps there was something you wanted to say to me. Otherwise, I'm certain Mrs. Langford is missing your company. Perhaps she might take a tumble from the settee and require your assistance helping her to her bedchamber."

Owen snorted.

Upton's confident smile fell just a bit. He glared at Owen. "No, I'm quite content here but perhaps *you'd* like to go spend time with Mrs. Langford, Monroe." Upton jerked his head in the widow's direction.

Owen calmly shook his head. "No, I'm content here as well."

Upton took a deep breath and turned toward Jane finally. "Very well. Miss Lowndes, allow me to apologize for Mrs. Langford's—for some of the things she said earlier."

Jane fixed him with a stare over the top of her spectacles. "Only *some* of what she said?"

Owen's gaze bounced between them, his handsome face full of amusement.

Upton cleared his throat. "Some of the things she said were . . ."

Jane arched a brow. "Rude? Ignorant? Wrong?"

"Inappropriate," Upton finished.

"That too," Jane allowed.

Upton shifted a bit closer to her. "I'm sorry she came with us in the boat. I'd hoped to—"

"Not to worry, Upton. I wouldn't expect better behavior from a *friend* of yours." She smiled at him sweetly. Neither of the gentlemen could possibly miss the emphasis she'd placed on the word "friend."

Owen whistled. "Point one, Miss Lowndes."

"She's *not* a friend of mine," Upton growled. "She's just—"

Jane kept her smile pinned to her face. "I'm sorry. I was under the impression she was invited here expressly because she mentioned her friendship with you. Was I mistaken?"

Upton scrubbed a hand across his face. "That's true, but—"

"Point two, Miss Lowndes," Owen added.

Upton leaned forward and gave Owen a condemning glare.

Upton began again. "She's more of a longtime acquaintance than a friend and—"

"So a lady you've known for over ten years, a lady with whose husband you served in the war, is only an acquaintance? My. I shudder to think how you'd describe me then. I've only known you for four years and that is because of my friendship with your cousin. What am I? A stranger?"

Owen winced. "Point three, Miss Lowndes."

Upton clenched his jaw and turned sharply toward Owen. "Must you?"

"Yes, I must," Owen replied with a laugh. "This is highly entertaining, watching Miss Lowndes hand you your arse. Please do continue."

Despite his vulgarity, Jane smiled and nodded at Owen. In this particular instance, Owen was entirely correct. Nice chap, Owen Monroe.

Upton turned back to Jane. "I merely wanted to offer my apologies if anything Mrs. Langford said offended you."

Jane folded her hands in her lap. Now he was apologizing on behalf of his mistress? Speaking of vulgar. "It *did* offend me, Upton, but then, her mere presence offends me. However, I'd prefer it if the apology came from the lady herself and something tells me that is not about to happen." Jane glimpsed Mrs. Langford sauntering toward them. "Ah, look, here she comes. Right on cue. While it's been a pleasure arguing with you as usual, Upton, I am not about to sit here and listen to any more of her ignorant vitriol. Nor am I inclined to watch her pretend to trip and fall into your arms again. Therefore, I am off to the library, where I can find much better company than Mrs. Langford in the inanimate objects."

"Game, set, match to Miss Lowndes," Owen said.

Jane nodded to him. "Good evening, Lord Owen." She stood, smoothed her skirts, and marched away.

"Jane, don't go." Upton's voice held a vulnerable quality she'd never heard before. The tone stopped her. The use of her Christian name stopped her. She turned slowly to face Upton again. Owen's brows had shot up. Apparently, Upton's use of her Christian name had surprised him too.

"Yes?" she said, doing her best to keep her face blank.

"Don't go," Upton repeated. Why did he have to look almost boyish? But even at his most charming, he couldn't keep her here to watch him interact with his mistress, of all people.

Jane stepped closer so only he could hear her reply. "In case you haven't noticed, Upton, Mrs. Langford is much more interested in your company than I am. I'm not about to compete with her for your attention. Not to mention how disgusted I am by your relationship."

His brow knotted into a frown and Jane turned again just as Mrs. Langford sidled up.

Upton placed a hand on Jane's elbow. "Stay," he pleaded.

"No, thank you."

She took a step, but he grabbed her arm and pulled her close to whisper in her ear. Gooseflesh pebbled her neck. She tried to will it away, but Upton's deep voice vibrated along her nerves. "Don't walk away from me, Lady Blue."

# CHAPTER TWENTY-FOUR

Jane had no recollection of how she managed to make it to the library. In fact, she had no memory of retrieving her jaw from the floor, let alone fleeing, but less than five minutes after Upton had fiercely whispered those shocking words, she was lying on her back on the settee in the empty library, one hand resting upon her forehead, wondering how angry Cass would be if Jane left the house party before the wedding actually took place.

She could not face Upton again. Ever. She could *not*. She made a mental list. Things she would never do, ever: travel to Egypt and view the frightening tombs of mummies, sleep outside on the ground with insects, give up teacake for Lent, and face Garrett Upton *ever* again. Yes. Quite a good list, actually. And a plausible one. She could just stay here, in the library, her happy spot. There was a window that overlooked the village church in the distance where the wedding ceremony was to be held. Perhaps Cass would allow Jane to view the nuptials from her safe little perch here. Teacakes could be served here, couldn't they?

Jane rubbed the back of her hand against her forehead and blew out a long, deep breath. When had everything become so complicated? When she'd kissed Upton, that's when. The good thing about being a spinster bluestocking was that one didn't ever do anything to embarrass oneself. The bad thing about being a spinster bluestocking was that when one *did* do something to embarrass oneself, one had no resources or experience with which to deal with said embarrassment.

Very well. She'd got herself in this predicament. She'd get herself out. One problem at a time. All she had to do was think. Think. *Think!* She removed her spectacles and rubbed her temples.

*Slam.*

Jane jumped.

The door to the library had opened and closed with a resounding bang. Sliding her spectacles over her nose again, she sat up quickly and leaned over the back of the settee. Who was it?

"Jane, are you in here?"

Upton. He had followed her. *Oh, God. Oh, God. Oh, God.* She wasn't ready to face him. Most likely she would never be ready but she certainly was not tonight. Not *now.*

"No," came her weak reply. She mentally cursed herself for such a woeful response.

He strode to where she sat huddled on the settee at the far end of the room, knees pulled up to her chest. His boots pounded on the wood floor as he approached. She pressed her forehead to the back of the settee, covering her eyes, spectacles and all. It was going to be embarrassing enough to speak to him, let alone *look* at him. Yes. Looking at him was asking far too much.

It was weak of her to hide, but at present she just didn't care.

The thud of his boots stopped behind the settee.

"I want to speak to you," he said, sounding both breathless and a bit cross. "I had more to say."

Jane's murmured reply was muffled by the velvet couch cushion. "And I fled from you. I thought you might have cottoned on."

He ignored the jibe. "We need to talk."

"Do we? Must we?" She dared a peek at him. Oh, she shouldn't have. He looked far too handsome. He was wearing well-cut dark gray evening attire with a sapphire-blue waistcoat and a snowy white cravat that matched the bright white of his teeth. He stood with one hand on his narrow hip. The other hand was rubbing through his dark hair, making the slight curls stand on end. It was charming. She hid her smile behind the back of the settee.

"Yes," he said, simply. "We must."

She grasped the back of the settee with both hands, her fingers clutching at the velvet. "You left Mrs. Langford to come speak with me?"

"Of course I did. Monroe is entertaining her."

Jane pressed her nose to the cushion. "The turncoat."

Upton made his way around to the front of the settee and Jane slowly turned to face him.

She spied a book sitting on the table in front of the settee. Desperate, she yanked it into her lap and quickly held it open in front of her face. "I'm sorry you came all the way in here. I cannot talk at the moment, Upton. I'm highly engrossed in this book."

"*The Care and Feeding of Swine*?" came his sarcasm-tinged reply.

She slowly tipped the book to the side to read the cover. *Drat.* Poor choice, that. "Yes." She nodded. "I've found I'm quite interested in the daily care of pigs of late."

"It's upside down." More sarcasm.

She exhaled, flaring her nostrils. There was no help for it. "Be that as it may—"

He snatched the book from her hands and flung it across the room. It landed with a thwack against the far wall. Upton stood in front of her with his feet braced apart and his hands on his hips. A muscle ticked in his jaw. "No you don't. You may hide from the world behind your precious books but you're not going to hide from me. Not tonight."

Jane's hand flew to her throat. She forced herself to push up her chin and meet his gaze. His eyes shot green sparks. The reckoning was upon her. "Very well, Upton. Say what you must." She clasped her hands in her lap.

He remained facing her, hands still on his hips. His breathing was labored. He searched her face. "I know it was you in the drawing room the other night."

"Yes. You've already said as much." She tried to keep her dastardly knees from shaking.

"Are you going to deny it?"

Jane fought her blush. "As much as I'd like to, what would be the point?"

"Thank you for that." His shoulders relaxed a bit. He expelled his breath and let his hands drop to his sides.

In an attempt to distract him from her shaking legs, she plucked at the folds in her green gown. "I'm not doing you a favor, Upton. I'm merely attempting to spare myself more shame."

He stood towering above her. "Did you know it was me? That night?"

She craned her neck to look up at him. "Please sit. You're making me nervous." How on earth was she supposed to answer his question?

*And ye shall know the truth, and the truth shall make you free.*

The Bible verse rang in her head. Mocking her. Oh, she knew her Bible verses. Perhaps she didn't agree with all of them. Or most of them. But she knew them.

She took a deep breath. It was time for the truth. "Yes, I knew it was you."

Upton slid onto the settee next to her, leaned forward, and braced his elbows on his knees, staring ahead into the darkened room. "The entire time?"

"No. I discovered it about halfway through. That's why I didn't want to remove my mask." She took another deep breath. She might as well ask him the same. "Did you know it was me?"

"Not until the next morning." He hung his head. "I don't know what to say," he murmured.

"Exactly why I didn't feel we needed to have this conversation," she replied with a slight, humorless laugh.

"Jane, I—"

She held up a hand to stop him. He was either going to tell her he loved her, which she somehow couldn't picture happening, and also knew she couldn't hear, or he was going to tell her it had been a mistake, which she already knew. Neither needed to be said aloud.

"There's nothing to say, Upton. It's over. We needn't mention it ever again."

His eyes were wide as he turned to look at her. "Needn't mention it again? Did it mean so little to you? Do you do that sort of thing often?"

Indignation flooded through her. She stopped plucking at her gown. Her hands turned into fists along the tops of her thighs. "*You're* questioning *me*? I am not the one who should have to answer for my behavior. I'm not the one who brought his *mistress* to a wedding!"

Upton's face contorted with amazement. "My *what*?"

Based on his reaction, Jane immediately had her doubts, but she'd already said the vile word and she wasn't about to back down. "You heard me. Your *mistress*."

He sat up straight and leaned closer to her, his face still registering disbelief. "Who, pray tell, do you believe is my mistress?"

She turned her face away and sniffed. "Don't insult my intelligence, Upton."

"I would never dream of it," he said through clenched teeth.

"Then you know I mean Mrs. Langford," she replied through equally clenched teeth.

"I can assure you, Mrs. Langford is unequivocally *not* my mistress. I do not *have* a mistress. It's not my style, but if it was, I certainly wouldn't dishonor the widow of my deceased friend by making her my mistress. And I would never dishonor Cassandra and Swifdon by inviting a light o' love to their wedding. Have you gone mad?"

Jane snapped her mouth shut. He sounded so convincing. Could she have made a mistake? Oh, God. Of course she could have. "But Mrs. Langford said . . ."

"She said she was my mistress?" Surprise tinged his voice.

"Not precisely, but she implied . . . She said you were 'quite close.'"

Upton pinched the bridge of his nose, closed his eyes, and shook his head. "Look, Jane, I admit Isabella seems to be interested in me, and she's been quite rude to you, but she is not now nor has she ever been my mistress."

"So, I'm the only woman you've kissed at this house party?" The words sounded ridiculous as soon as they left her mouth but she truly wanted to know the answer.

His laugh was a short, wry chuckle. "The one and only. Despite what you think of me and my reputation, I don't make a habit of passionate interludes with ladies at my friends' house parties. You were stunningly beautiful that night. To be entirely candid, I've dreamed about it since."

The air left Jane's body in a whoosh. *Stunningly beautiful? Dreamed about it?* Her hands trembled in her lap where she'd resumed the plucking of her skirts. Perfect. Now in addition to her legs, her hands were trembling. This had to be the precursor to apoplexy. His words reverberated throughout her body. *Dreamed about it since.* Oh, God. She'd dreamed about it too.

*Stunningly beautiful.* Those two words played in Jane's head like a song. She opened her mouth to speak and closed it again. She opened it and closed it once more.

"I hope you're proud of yourself, Upton," she finally managed. "You've done the impossible. You've rendered me speechless. What do you think of that?"

He turned his head and flashed her a grin. "That is a good start, but the more serious question is, what are we going to do about the fact that we kissed each other? I must confess, I enjoyed it immensely. I know you did too. You wouldn't let me stop, after all. So the more important question is . . . when are we going to do it again?"

# CHAPTER TWENTY-FIVE

Garrett arrived at the stables the next morning exactly as planned. It was bloody early for an outing, but he'd agreed to this at dinner last night when Cassandra had suggested they all go for a ride. A dozen or so of the party guests were already wandering around the stables by the time he strolled into the large building.

There had been no nightmares last night. He hadn't slept. Instead, he'd spent the night thinking about his confrontation with Jane. What had he expected to come of it? He couldn't answer that. He'd only known he had to confront her to see if he could detect any sign of her supposed love for him. He'd seen nothing other than shock, which made him wonder if it were true.

Garrett admired Jane for matter-of-factly admitting to being Lady Blue. She hadn't said anything when he'd asked her when they would do it again. He'd been half jesting, half trying to determine if she did, indeed, have strong feelings for him. Jane had announced she had to get to bed and then she'd nearly flown from the room.

Frankly, the entire evening had left Garrett more confused than before.

Jane was in the stables already. She stood with Cassandra and Lucy, wearing a blue riding habit that did little for her figure. It didn't matter. Her figure was burned in his brain.

A loud laugh drew his attention to the right. Mrs. Langford came strolling toward him. "Mr. Upton, there you are."

He squared his shoulders and turned to face her. Isabella had been rude to Jane yesterday. Jane could more than take care of herself, but he refused to allow Isabella to imply to his friends there may be something indecent between them. Whatever she'd said, it had been enough for Jane to draw the conclusion that Isabella was his mistress. Guilt or no, he refused to allow that misconception to continue.

"Good morning, Mrs. Langford." He gave her a tight smile.

She wore a smart emerald-green riding habit that hugged her every curve. Why was Jane's frumpy one making his breeches tight? He looked back at Jane. She turned away. He let out his breath and forced himself to turn back to Isabella. Extracting himself from her company this morning would be difficult.

"Where are we riding to?" Isabella slid a gloved hand over his arm.

"I believe we're riding to the church in the village and back." Garrett could not resist glancing back at Jane again, who was absorbed in conversation with her friends.

"Sounds delightful," Isabella replied. "I do hope you'll help me mount." She looked into his eyes. He didn't like the way she had said the word "mount." Garrett turned his attention to where the stable boys and grooms were preparing the horses. "Isn't that your footman?"

A scowl flitted across Isabella's face. "Oh, Boris, that dolt. I'd much rather have you assist me, Mr. Upton." She batted her eyelashes at him. There was no mistaking the invitation in the depths of her pale green eyes.

He cleared his throat. "Very well."

The team of grooms and stable boys began helping the ladies to mount. When Garrett looked again, Boris was gone. Garrett pasted on a smile and helped Isabella onto the frisky gray filly Cassandra had provided for her. He swung himself up onto his own mount. By the time he finished, Jane was already seated atop her own high-stepping filly. She had a smile on her face and the sunlight glinted off her spectacles. Was her hair looser in the knot today? She was lovely—frumpy riding habit notwithstanding.

Surprisingly, Isabella waited for Jane to come alongside them before she nudged her own mount into a trot. "Do you ride often, Miss Lowndes?"

"Not as often as I should, Mrs. Langford."

"Good morning, Miss Lowndes," Garrett interjected, feeling like an utter arse. Why was Isabella always near when he was trying to speak with Jane?

"Good morning, Mr. Upton." Jane lifted her reins as if to make to move past the two of them, but Isabella stopped Jane with her words.

"Do you ride often enough to race, Miss Lowndes?"

Jane blinked. She let the reins settle back against the saddle. She turned her head to the side. "Race *you,* Mrs. Langford?"

"Yes," came Isabella's overconfident reply.

Garrett tightened his grip on his own reins. The hairs on the back of his neck stood up. Jane couldn't say no to a challenge, especially not from someone she disliked.

"I'm not sure—" Garrett began.

"Do you ride often, Mrs. Langford?" Jane pursed her lips and regarded Mrs. Langford over the top of her spectacles.

Isabella's smug laughter followed. "On the contrary, I rarely ride. But something tells me I could best *you*, Miss Lowndes. You seem more interested in books than horses."

Garrett winced. There was no chance Jane wouldn't scoop up Isabella's gauntlet and slap her with it.

"By all means, then." The gleam of competition shone in Jane's eyes. "I'm eager to show you how wrong you are. Where shall we race to?"

Garrett rubbed the back of his neck. Jane wasn't about to listen to reason coming from him. Excusing himself, he rode to where Lucy was trotting ahead of Cassandra, Claringdon, and Swifdon. "Jane's accepted a challenge to race Mrs. Langford."

Lucy's brows shot up. "Has she?" A sly smile settled on her face.

"Yes," Garrett replied grimly.

"Excellent, we'll have something to divert us," Lucy said.

Garrett pushed his hat back on his forehead. "You think it's a good idea?"

"I don't see why not. I'll be interested to see it. Jane never loses at anything she sets her mind to."

Garrett groaned. "You don't plan to stop her, then?"

"Stop her?" Lucy laughed. "I intend to wager upon her."

Garrett shook his head. By the time he returned to where Jane and Isabella cantered next to each other, they were busily discussing the details.

"See that field in the distance?" Jane pointed to a meadow a half-mile away.

A quick single nod from Isabella. "Yes."

"Shall we race to the other side of it? There's a tree at the far end. Do you see it?"

Garrett followed Jane's gaze. A lone tree stood at the far corner of the field.

Another nod from Isabella.

"That shall be the finish," Jane declared.

"Perfect." Isabella's face was wreathed in a smile. She turned in the sidesaddle and called to the group. "You must all stop and watch us, everyone! Miss Lowndes and I intend to race to that tree." She pointed with her riding crop.

A great deal of murmuring ensued while Lucy led the betting. The entire company lined up along the side of the meadow.

"Make the call to start, Mr. Upton," Isabella prompted with a too bright smile.

Removing his hat, Garrett scrubbed his hand through his hair. He turned his attention to Jane. "You insist upon doing this?"

"Of course," Jane replied.

Garrett let out his pent-up breath. "Very well."

Claringdon drew up his mount beside Garrett. "One has the distinct feeling they're racing over you, Upton."

Garrett grimaced. "Two ladies racing sidesaddle across a field? It's bloody dangerous."

Claringdon grinned at him. "Quite. Who do you think will win? The horseflesh appears to be evenly matched, but I've got five pounds on Jane."

Garrett didn't answer. He turned back to the two ladies, who had brought their mounts to the head of the field.

"When I drop my arm, you may go," Garrett called, raising his right arm high in the air.

Jane was bent low over her horse's neck, whispering to the beast, a determined gleam in her eye. Isabella, however, seemed completely relaxed, nearly disinterested. She, too, had a gleam in her eye, but it looked more wicked than determined.

Garrett lifted his chin. So be it. If they were set on doing this, they might as well get it over with and get on with the day. "On your mark . . . set . . . go." His arm slashed downward. Jane kicked her mount with her booted heel and slapped the crop against the horse's flank. Isabella made a show of kicking and slapping, too, but she didn't go nearly as quickly. Jane was already three full lengths ahead of her across the field.

Garrett exchanged an exasperated look with Lucy and Cassandra. He shaded his eyes to watch Jane's progress. She was galloping as if the devil chased her. Her horse's hooves pounded the grass and kicked up tufts of dirt and leaves. She improved her lead by another length.

She'd made it three quarters of the length across the field when her saddle tilted crazily to the side and she flew off into the high grass.

"No!" Garrett kicked his mount into a gallop and made straight for Jane. His heart raced in a frantic rhythm along with his horse's thundering hooves. He slowed to a stop just before the spot where he'd last seen Jane and vaulted to the ground, frantically searching for her in the tall grass. Her horse had trotted off but remained grazing nearby.

"Jane. Jane!"

A low groan caught his attention and he whirled around. She was lying in the grass, her leg bent at an unnatural angle. Her eyes were closed. *God, please don't let her die.*

He lunged toward her and fell to his knees beside her.

Her face was turned to the side, a large dirt smudge was smeared across her cheek, and her spectacles were nowhere to be seen.

Mrs. Langford's mount galloped to a halt next to them. "Is she all right?" came Isabella's breathless voice.

Garrett put his fingers to the pulse in Jane's neck. It was there, thank Christ. "I don't know," he replied through clenched teeth.

Lucy, Cassandra, Swifdon, and a few others arrived moments later. They dismounted and hovered in a circle around Jane while Garrett cradled her head in his lap. "Derek's gone to the village to fetch the doctor," Cassandra said.

Garrett nodded. Nothing else seemed out of place, but Jane's leg was surely hurt. Her ankle was already bruised and swelling. He leaned down and pressed his ear to her lips.

"She's breathing," he announced. A collective sigh went up among them.

He stroked her cheek. "Miss Lowndes." He leaned closer. "Jane." She looked so helpless and vulnerable. And so pretty without her glasses. Just like the night he'd kissed her. Her hair had come askew out of her topknot. He traced her cheekbone with his fingertips, heedless of what the others might think. Seeing her silent and helpless and hurt brought out a fierce protective streak in him. One he hadn't known he possessed.

"Jane," he whispered again. Her eyes fluttered open and regarded him with their usual dark, sparkling intelligence.

"Garrett?"

Something stirred deep in Garrett's belly when she called him by his Christian name.

"Yes, it's me," he replied softly, pulling a bit of grass from her hair and tossing it aside.

She made as if to sit up but winced and lay back down.

"Stay still. Claringdon's gone to fetch the doctor."

Jane smiled and let her head rest in his lap again. "Upton?" she asked softly.

He bent to hear her. "Yes, Jane?"

Her voice was a croak. "Did I win?"

# CHAPTER TWENTY-SIX

Later that afternoon, Jane sat propped up in bed with her foot on a pillow. She could boast a small lump on the back of her head, but it only hurt when she touched it. She also had a painful twist of her ankle, but the maids brought cold compresses to wrap it, and Lucy brought her hot buttered rum.

Jane stared at the bright white blur that was her stockinged foot. Without her spectacles, she couldn't read. Regardless, resting comfortably in bed was much preferable to house party outings. The doctor had informed her she'd most likely be able to walk after a day or two, assuring her she could attend the wedding.

A knock sounded on her bedchamber door, and Jane stretched and yawned. It was high time for her afternoon nap. "Who is it?"

The door opened and shut and the dark blur of a man strode toward her. She gasped and pulled the covers to her neck. "Sir, who are you?"

Garrett's laughter followed. "You don't recognize me?"

It was Upton? What was he doing here? "I don't

have my spectacles," she admitted sheepishly, "but you shouldn't be in here. It's shamelessly inappropriate."

It was better this way, without her spectacles. If she couldn't see how handsome he was, she was much less likely to fantasize about kissing him again, and that was good for everyone. Ever since he'd adamantly and convincingly denied that Mrs. Langford was his mistress and then called Jane stunningly beautiful, well, that in itself had been a bit irresistible. But it had really been too much when he'd asked her when—not if—they would repeat their interlude in the drawing room. The fact was she'd been distracted by that thought far too much since he'd said it.

Upton's laughter was warm and genuine. "I like that, the perpetrator of the Mrs. Bunbury plot telling me what is shamelessly inappropriate. I had to come see how you're doing, didn't I?"

Jane continued to clutch at the covers. "But I'm in my night rail."

"Yes. I saw a bit of it unfortunately. It's a night rail that looks like something my grandmama would wear and you have blankets up to your neck on top of that. I have absolutely no hope of catching so much as a glimpse of your skin."

She had to laugh. He was right. The frothy lace of her long night rail was anything but revealing. She pushed the covers back down to her waist and nestled back against the pillows. "You are shameless, Upton. Don't allow anyone to ever tell you differently."

"Duly noted," he replied. "Where are your spectacles?" He sounded nearly . . . caring.

Jane sighed. "I'm afraid they were hopelessly bent. Cass has sent to London to fetch me another pair."

"You look . . . pretty without your glasses." He cleared his throat. "Quite pretty."

Heavens. Had Upton just called her pretty? *Quite* pretty?

"How is your ankle?" he asked. She could see enough of his blurry form to know he'd pulled a chair close to the edge of her bed and taken a seat.

"Twisted. And sore. Lady Moreland offered me a bowl of cream as if I were a cat. I told her I'd be ever so much more interested in a teacake. I suppose I should consider it a victory as long as she doesn't send a servant with a bit of salmon. Mrs. Cat would love a bit of salmon."

"Who is Mrs. Cat?"

"A cat. Not my cat. I don't own a cat. She's just a cat I feed sometimes."

The flash of his white teeth was unmistakable. "I hate to tell you this but if you're feeding her, she's your cat."

"No. She's not. I'm certain of it."

"I know better than to argue with you," he said with a laugh. "But tell me, why are you feeding her if you care so little about her?"

"I didn't say I didn't care about her. She's a perfectly good cat. But you see, there are kittens, and well, I couldn't allow *them* to go hungry."

"Why, Jane Lowndes, you are tenderhearted."

Her eyes widened. "No. I'm not."

"Yes, you are. You're quite tenderhearted if you're feeding a mother cat in order to care for her kittens."

Jane glanced away but she couldn't keep the smile from her face. "It's just a cat, Upton."

"If you say so." Upton leaned back in his chair, the grin still on his blurry face. "I'm sorry your ankle is hurt, but you don't fool me. The spill you took from that horse is merely your attempt at causing a scandal, isn't it?"

She laughed at that too. Since when did Upton make her laugh? In a good way?

"If I had planned it, Upton, rest assured I would have

won before I fell. Not to mention I would have planned a more graceful descent. That saddle was faulty, I tell you."

"I don't disagree. Lord Moreland has asked the stable master to look into the matter."

Jane sighed. "As for a scandal, I'd say having a gentleman in my bedchamber is much more scandalous than falling from a horse."

"Oh, no. Don't involve me in your schemes. I'm merely here to check on you." He leaned forward and his voice took on a more serious edge. "We were quite worried about you."

Jane traced her finger along the top of the coverlet. "I know. Cass nearly cried. I hope my foibles don't ruin her wedding. She's pledged to have a team of footmen carry me to the ceremony upon a litter if necessary."

Upton chuckled. "Don't test her. She's a determined bride."

Jane smiled. "I wouldn't dream of it."

Upton appeared to be fumbling with his coat. "I brought you something." Did his voice sound sheepish? Imagine that.

"Brought me something?" she echoed, blinking.

"Yes. I—I forgot you lost your spectacles and cannot read, but—" He placed something rectangular and hefty atop her lap. She touched it. Ran her fingers over its smooth surface. She'd know the feel of it anywhere. "A book?"

"Yes, a book." There was humor in his voice.

"Which book is it?" She lifted it in front of her face and squinted at the golden title. She still couldn't make it out.

*"A Vindication of the Rights of Woman."*

Jane gasped. She hugged the book to her chest. "Mary Wollstonecraft? You brought me Mary Wollstonecraft?"

She blinked and blinked again. She had no idea what to make of it. Of course she'd already read this book. Read it and owned it and loved each and every page of it, possibly memorized entire passages, but the fact that Upton had brought it to her. Well, it just showed he'd been . . . paying attention.

Upton cleared his throat again. "I know she is your favorite author and—"

"How did you know?"

"Everyone knows that."

"No, they don't." Just who was he referring to as "everyone"?

"At any rate, I assumed you already have this one, but this is a first edition and—"

Jane squeezed the book. She could hardly breathe. "You've brought me a first edition Mary Wollstonecraft? Printed in 1792? How did you get it?"

He shook his head. "It's not important how I got it, and why am I not surprised you know the exact year of its publication?"

"It's important to me, Upton. I've wanted a first edition Wollstonecraft for an age. They are not easy to find. How did you find one?"

She could see the outline of his form rubbing a hand through his hair. "Are you always this inquisitive when someone gives you a gift?"

She placed the book carefully in her lap again. "I'm truly curious, Upton, and I'm not about to allow you to leave this room without telling me how you were able to procure this book."

"Fine. My mother purchased it when it was first published; when I was old enough, she gave it to me to read."

"I knew I loved Aunt Mary, but honestly, you've read it?" Her hand fell to the mattress with a thump. "I may need smelling salts for the first time in my life."

"I doubt that." She could hear the smirk in his voice.

"You've read Mary Wollstonecraft?"

"Twice."

"That's it! Fetch me the salts! I can hardly fathom it."

He groaned. "Yes, I've read it. After your accident, I rode over to my estate and got it . . . for you."

Her hand was back at her throat. "You rode over to your estate and got it, for me?"

He pretended a long-suffering sigh. "I thought there was something wrong with your ankle, not your hearing."

She pressed her palm to her cheek. "I am astonished, Upton. I had no idea you had any interest in the rights of females."

"You are wrong. I do indeed. 'Virtue can only flourish among equals,' after all."

Jane nearly squealed. She was quite certain she was experiencing a heart palpitation. "Now you're *quoting* Mary Wollstonecraft!" She put her hand to her chest. "Stop it, Upton. I may never recover from learning that you own Wollstonecraft, but learning that you've memorized her is beyond the pale."

This time he laughed. "I've hardly got every word memorized, I simply—"

"No. No. Don't deny it. There is no retreating from this. You know and now I know you know. We can never go back to our previous thoughts about each other."

"Dare I hope by that you mean you no longer think me a simpleton whose only pleasure is in drinking and gambling?"

Jane sobered. She pressed her lips together, contemplating his words for a moment. It was true. Her opinion of him *had* changed.

She took a deep breath. "I suppose I must grudgingly admit it, Upton, yes."

His voice was even. "I never thought I'd see the day you admitted that."

"There's a first time for everything, I suppose." To her chagrin, her tone was a bit breathy and confused. Why couldn't she stop plucking at the bedsheet? Upton was turning her into a plucker.

"Might I further hope that you don't dislike me as much as you pretend to?" he asked.

She allowed the hint of a smile to play across her lips. "That entirely depends."

"Upon what?"

"Upon whether you're willing to admit you don't dislike *me* as much as you pretend to."

He grinned at her, she knew even without her spectacles. She felt it in her knees.

"With pleasure," he replied.

"Very well, then I admit it. And I must thank you, also," she said.

"For what?"

"For your help today. You quite came to my rescue."

"Any time, my lady. I ask for only one small favor in return."

Her fingers stilled against the sheets. Her heart fluttered in her chest. A favor? "What's that?"

"Call me Garrett."

# CHAPTER TWENTY-SEVEN

Yesterday, he'd brought her a book. Today he brought her . . . flowers. Bloody flowers. Textbook, poetry-inducing flowers. Would she mock him? Would she laugh? Damn it. Garrett didn't know how she would react. The lilacs had bloomed early this year and he'd gone out into the gardens and gathered them himself. Daphne Swift had helped him find a matching lavender ribbon to tie around the stems and here he was on his way back to Jane's bedchamber to deliver them. He shook his head. Flowers? He was turning into a walking verse of bad poetry.

Garrett stood outside Jane's door and thought for a moment. The odds were quite high that she would mock the flowers. She was a mocker, after all, and they were flowers. Daphne had assured him, however, that all ladies enjoyed flowers, even Miss Lowndes.

He took a deep breath. There was more to discover behind that door than whether Jane would enjoy the flowers.

Did she love him?

Why couldn't he stop thinking about that? Despite Cassandra's insistence, nothing in Jane's demeanor up till now indicated it. Yesterday, they'd got on well enough. Admitting she didn't dislike him and asking him to admit he didn't dislike her was still a far cry from *love*. So here he stood, bloody gullible fool that he was, outside her bedchamber door, clutching a bouquet tied with a bow. That's right, a bow.

He couldn't linger in the corridor all morning and risk someone seeing him pay a call to her bedchamber. It was a precarious thing to do as it was.

He knocked.

"Come in," Jane called.

He pushed open the door and strode inside. She was sitting up in bed wearing a new white night rail, still of the grandmama variety, but her hair was down around her shoulders. It was splendid and lush and dark brown with a slight curl to it. His mouth went dry. He licked his lips.

Her spectacles were back, perched upon her nose. The book he'd given her was propped upon her lap, but as soon as she saw him she pushed it aside.

"Upton," she said, and blushed—actually blushed. Jane!—and then more softly, "Garrett."

He strode to stand before the chair that still sat next to her bed. "These are for you." He held out the flowers at a ninety-degree angle.

A small smile wiggled its way onto her lips. She took the bouquet and hugged them to her. "Lilacs are my favorite."

"Mine too," he murmured.

"I find it difficult to believe you have a favorite flower." She pressed the blooms to her nose, closed her eyes, and inhaled deeply.

"Likewise."

She opened her eyes again and blinked at him. "I suppose that's fair."

They both laughed.

"I'm beginning to wonder about you," she continued. "You know my favorite food is teacake and my favorite author is Mary Wollstonecraft, and now you know my favorite flower is a lilac. If I didn't know better, Upton"— she paused for a moment and he could have sworn that she blushed again—"I mean, Garrett, I'd say we were becoming . . . friends."

Friends? Being a friend was a far cry from being in love. He took a seat and leaned back in the chair next to the bed. "You didn't even mention the fact that I've been sneaking into your bedchamber to get a glimpse of you in your unmentionables."

"That *is* quite friendly," she agreed, studying her night rail that covered her more decently than any gown she'd worn at the house party so far.

"What would you say if I told you I also know your favorite color is blue?" he asked.

Jane's eyes widened. "Now, that is *much* too personal. Seeing me in my grandmotherly night rail is one thing, but knowing my favorite color is altogether indecent."

He grinned at her. "But it is, isn't it? Blue?"

"Yes," she replied, setting the flowers on the coverlet next to her. "Appropriate for a bluestocking, is it not? Now that you know so much about me, it's only sporting if you tell me something about you."

"Really?" He arched a brow. "Like what?"

"The obvious things, of course, like what is your favorite food?"

"Beefsteak."

She nodded. "A bit predictable, but very well."

"Predictable?"

"I was hoping you'd name something outlandish like turtle soup."

He grimaced. "I abhor turtle soup."

"So do I, but it's an interesting favorite food, you cannot deny it." She didn't pause for his response. "What is your favorite book?"

*"Candide."*

She sucked in her breath. "You've read Voltaire?"

"I have."

"You're teasing me." She plucked at the ribbon on the flowers. She'd been doing a great deal of plucking in his company of late. He'd never noticed that about her before.

"No, I'm not teasing," he replied. "I've read *Candide* at least three times. If you care to quiz me on its contents, my lady, I'm at your disposal."

She paused for a moment before saying, "Oh, no. That's silly."

"Yes, but you considered it just now, didn't you?"

"How could you tell?"

"You had a certain look on your face. A competitive look. I've seen it before."

She pushed her nose into the air. Very fetching, that. "I only considered it because I enjoy discussing books."

His grin returned. "As do I."

"You do?"

"Don't look so surprised. Contrary to what you might think, I actually enjoy books."

She bit her lip. "Books have always been my closest friends. At least they were when I was a child. They were my only friends. Though now, happily, I have Lucy and Cass."

"And me." His voice was soft.

She averted her gaze, still plucking at the ribbon.

Garrett spoke again to fill the silence. "Why were books your only friends when you were a child?"

Her fingers stilled. "You don't want to hear about that."

Settling back in his chair, he crossed his booted feet at the ankles. "Yes I do. I've got all the time in the world. They're planning a hunt today and I'd rather be boiled in oil than go hunting."

Jane shook her head at him. "That may be, but would you rather sit here and listen to me? You could be doing a host of other things."

"I'm delighted to sit here and listen to you." If he didn't know better, he could have sworn she blushed again. He could get used to making her blush. She was adorable when she did so. "Tell me, Jane. Why were books your only friends?"

She sighed and her shoulders lifted and fell. "Suffice it to say, I wasn't a popular child."

"I wasn't either." He snorted. "I only had a small set of friends I ran with at Eton and—"

"No. I mean to say I had *no* friends. None whatsoever."

He wrinkled his brow and looked at her. "None?"

"Not one. I was an only child and the house was quite lonely. Mama and Papa sent me to school at first, but the other children made such awful fun of me . . . Then Papa was knighted and I was tutored at home and I was so much happier."

Garrett narrowed his eyes on her face. "Why did the other children make fun of you? Because you were so much more intelligent than they were?"

She resumed her ribbon plucking. "No." The way she said the word made his heart tug. "When I was a child, I didn't allow anyone to know I was intelligent. I desperately wanted to be accepted, and being intelligent was not the way to become admired, especially for a girl."

"Then why did they make fun of you?"

This time there was no mistaking the pink blush that crept across Jane's pretty freckled cheeks. "I didn't look like the rest of them. They didn't like that."

He furrowed his brow even deeper. "Didn't look like the rest of them? I don't understand. Were they all blond?" How could she not look like the rest of them?

The edge of her mouth quirked up. "I was quite a portly child. Mama called me plump, but portly was a much more apt description."

Garrett uncrossed his ankles and sat up straight. He couldn't imagine it. Jane? Pretty, intelligent, simple, sarcastic Jane? Portly?

"I don't believe it."

"I can assure you it's true." She sighed.

"Your mother called you plump?"

"Quite often, actually. She thought it was a kind word."

"It's not kind at all." There was a slight growl in his voice. Where had that come from?

"Yes, well, I ate even more teacake as a girl than I do now, I'm afraid, and it didn't melt away the way it does now when I take a good healthy walk every day. Cass will most likely have to roll me from this bed when my ankle has healed."

He was still trying to conjure the image of Jane being portly. He knew she'd been a wallflower. She'd been inordinately pleased about that fact ever since he'd met her. He'd believed she preferred to be a wallflower, was one by choice. "You said the other children . . . They . . . made sport of you?"

Jane tugged at a dark curl that had fallen over her shoulder, and Garrett had to resist the urge to reach out and stroke it too. "They did indeed," she replied. "That's why it was so much better after I remained at home. I only had to endure their teasing when I went out with Mama or at church on Sundays."

Garrett lurched in his chair and planted both boots on the floor. "They made sport of you at *church*?"

"Oh, my, yes. At every opportunity. Being a portly child is a grievous sin."

"No it's not, Jane." His voice was low. He met her gaze.

She glanced away and laughed a shaky laugh. "Tell that to those children. I suppose they're all hideous adults now. I see some of them from time to time and I want to hide from them."

"Still?" The rough edge to his voice remained.

"Yes. You know what the worst part is?" she asked with a wry smile.

"What?"

She scrunched up her nose. "The truth is it makes me want to eat even more teacake."

Without thinking, he reached out and squeezed her hand. "Those children were wrong, Jane. You are even more lovely than the lilacs."

Her breath hitched a bit and she slowly pulled her shaking hand away and placed it on her lap. "Yes, well, that's why books have always been my closest friends. They never tease you, they're always there for you, and they couldn't care less how many teacakes you have gobbled."

He looked at the flowers where they rested on the white coverlet. "I should have brought you teacake instead of lilacs."

She laughed. "It's probably best that you did not." She waved a hand in the air. "Enough about me and my sad past. Speaking of hideous adults, has Mrs. Langford asked about me?"

He shook his head. "Only to inquire as to whether

you'd be able to attend the wedding. I assured her you would."

"I'm certain she's delighted." Ah, Jane's sarcasm had returned full force.

"I truly wish she hadn't come here," Garrett murmured.

Jane met his gaze with her own steady one. "I think she sees me as competition for you. You say she's not your mistress, but what exactly is she to you, Garrett?"

He expelled his breath. Hearing his name on her lips did something unexpected to his insides, but how had this conversation taken this turn? "It's complicated."

Jane nodded softly. "But it's not . . . intimate?"

"No, nothing like that. She's Harold's widow."

"It seems she would like to be more," Jane replied. "Do you want more too?"

Was that regret in her voice? Or was he merely reading that into it? "No. I've been sending her— I feel a responsibility toward Harold. That's all."

Jane nodded. "I see. So you've been kind to her, and she's interpreted that as opening the door to a courtship."

"I don't believe I've done anything to lead her on, to allow her to hope . . . The widows of deceased soldiers have been treated poorly by the government. That's why I'm in support of Swifdon's new bill."

"A noble cause to be sure," Jane murmured. Once again, she looked him directly in the eye. "What happened over there, Garrett? Were you with Harold Langford when he died?"

# CHAPTER TWENTY-EIGHT

Garrett hadn't answered. He'd said something vague about war being hell and promptly left the room. But Jane was certain Garrett knew more about Harold Langford's death than he wanted to say, something that tied him to Harold's widow.

Frankly, Jane had her suspicions about the widow when it came to the accident. She'd seen Mrs. Langford's footman in the stables and wondered if he'd done anything to tamper with her saddle. Tampering with a saddle and then challenging your opponent to a race? A bit predictable, was it not? Of course there was no way to prove it without accusing Mrs. Langford outright. Perhaps that was what Jane deserved for being so quick to race that woman. She shouldn't have trusted her for a moment. She wouldn't make that mistake again.

Jane rang for Eloise to help her put the lilacs in water. Then she settled back against the pillows to continue reading her book. She didn't have much more time to enjoy the peace and quiet. Mama would be here this afternoon. Jane could only hope the Mrs. Bunbury plan would work. As for the idea of starting a scandal, she was beginning to realize how dangerous that particular plan had been. She'd do well to stay far away from scandal until the house party ended.

Thankfully, by the late afternoon, Jane was able to walk on her ankle again. It was still a bit tender and she had to rest it more than she would have liked, but she was no longer confined to bed.

After the hunt, the wedding guests began to arrive. Along with Jane's parents, Lucy's parents, Lord and Lady Upbridge, came. Garrett's mother, Lucy's Aunt Mary, bustled in, hugging everyone and declaring that Cass had never looked more lovely. Derek's brothers, Adam and Collin Hunt, arrived as well, and so did Lord Berkeley, one of Garrett's good friends from school whom they had all met in Bath the previous summer.

The wedding was to be held the next morning and the festivities would last well into the night. Jane was torn. Part of her was relieved that the house party would soon be over and she could go back to reading her books and ensuring that Mrs. Cat and her kittens had enough to eat. But another part of her . . . a part she didn't want to fully admit to, was a bit melancholy over the thought of leaving the party, and Garrett.

Though, admittedly, Jane had little time to think about Garrett. Well, less time than usual. She was busy bustling around—as best she could on her tender ankle— in an attempt to keep her mother from meeting Mrs. Bunbury.

Jane hobbled a few doors down to her mother's room to greet her.

"Your father's in the study with the other gentlemen," her mother announced. "What is it about gentlemen and studies?" She shook her head.

"It's lovely to see you, Mama." Jane kissed her on the cheek.

"How is your leg, dear?" her mother asked, watching her slow progression across the room. "I nearly had an apoplexy when Lady Cassandra's footman came to fetch your spectacles."

"It was just a small tumble from a horse. My pride was hurt much more than my ankle."

A worry line creased her mother's brow. "Oh, Jane, please don't tell me you were racing gentlemen on horseback. That's hardly the behavior one looks for in a wife and—"

It was typical of her mother to be more worried about her daughter's reputation than her health. "No, Mama. I was racing another *lady* on horseback. I would have won, too, if the saddle hadn't given way."

Her mother put her hands on her hips and clucked her tongue. "Where was Mrs. Bunbury when this was going on?"

Jane nearly winced. "Mrs. Bunbury was there. She approved. It was all in good fun."

"I'd like to meet Mrs. Bunbury at the first opportunity."

"And so you shall," Jane replied. "She's, uh, gone off to the village just now, to fetch some supplies for the poultice she's been using on my ankle. Lucy swears by it." *Must remember to ask Lucy to make me a poultice.*

Her mother wrinkled up her nose. "The Morelands don't have the necessary ingredients for a poultice?"

"Er, not this poultice. I believe it requires eye of newt or something like that."

Jane's mother shook her head again. "There you go again with that wild imagination. Gentlemen are rarely interested in ladies who are humorous."

"That's a shame," Jane mumbled under her breath.

"What was that, dear?"

"Come downstairs with me, Mama. I'll lean on you so I may greet Papa. Perhaps I can coax him out of the study."

"We should get you a cane," her mother replied.

"No, thank you. I'm not old enough for a cane, and I refuse to succumb to such accoutrements before it's time."

Jane's mother rolled her eyes. Hmm. Perhaps that's where *she* got it. The thought made Jane smile. But thankfully, Hortense agreed without any more questions about the poultice, the cane, or Mrs. Bunbury, and the two made their way downstairs.

As they slowly progressed along the corridor, Jane relaxed a bit. Goodness. This concentrating on her mother and the Mrs. Bunbury plot bit was good for her. She hadn't thought about Upton in entire minutes.

Garrett had spent most of the afternoon greeting various acquaintances as they arrived. In addition to Garrett's mother, Rafferty Cavendish, one of the top spies for the War Office, was greeted by Cassandra and Julian as if he were their brother. Rafe had been with Donald Swift when he'd died. The younger man had taken it hard. He blamed himself, but everyone knew he couldn't have saved Donald. The fact that Rafe was still alive was a miracle in itself.

Jane's mother and father had arrived too. Sir Charles was a known academic. Apparently he'd passed his keen abilities to his only child. Jane's mother seemed less cerebral, but she was certainly a good-looking lady and was pleasant enough. Garrett wondered at the type of woman who would make a little girl feel bad for being overweight. Sometimes parents were cruel.

Garrett was greatly looking forward to the dance that

evening. He never looked forward to dances. It was fine to see friends and have a good time, but there was something else about tonight. Something different, special. If he were honest, he would admit he was looking forward to seeing Jane again. He'd left her bedchamber abruptly earlier, which was probably for the best. He shouldn't have been in there in the first place, but he hadn't been able to help himself. When she mentioned Harold, the memories had been too much for him. The walls had seemed to be closing in around him. What could he say? The man had died in front of him. Died *for* him. That wasn't something Garrett wanted to revisit during waking hours. He did it often enough in his dreams.

Jane had sent him a note this afternoon. She wanted to be there for the pleasantries, she'd written.

Learning about her and her childhood had been enlightening. Now he had a glimpse into why Jane had such a tough exterior. Her childhood might have been privileged, but it had also been sad. No wonder she and Lucy had become fast friends. They were quite alike, both rejected by the Society they'd been told they must be a part of.

But tonight was for celebrating Cass and Julian's wedding. Even if Jane couldn't dance with him, he'd bring her a teacake or three. He'd coax another smile out of her and perhaps a blush. Garrett whistled as he strolled down the corridor.

"Mr. Upton."

He stopped short at the sound of Isabella's voice. He turned to see her standing behind him.

"Yes." He moved toward her slowly, dread tugging at his gut.

"May I speak with you, privately, for a moment?"

Garrett sucked air through his nostrils. "Very well."

He moved to the side of the corridor near the wall, stepping behind a table to ensure he kept a distance between the two of them.

He watched her carefully. After seeing Isabella's footman in the stables, Garrett had his suspicions as to what had happened to Jane's saddle. But until he had proof, he intended to give the widow a wide berth. "What is it?" he asked.

Isabella let a hand trail along the edge of her décolletage. "Mr. Upton . . . Garrett." She looked up at him shyly. "May I call you Garrett?"

"I don't think that's—"

"You know I came here, to Surrey, I mean, to see you. I'm not particularly well acquainted with Lady Cassandra or Lord Swifdon."

"Yes, I know," Garrett replied, struggling to remain polite. "I wondered why you felt it necessary to follow me here." He lowered his voice even though they were alone. "If you need more money or—"

Isabella squeezed her eyes shut, a pained expression on her face. She held up a hand. "No. It's not about money. You've been quite generous to us. It's just that . . ." She opened her eyes, braced a hand on the table, and stared at him. Garrett had the uneasy feeling many a lesser man had fallen prey to that beautiful face. Like Harold Langford, perhaps. "You must know I've developed feelings for you, Garrett."

Garrett took a step back. "Feelings?"

"Yes. We've been in each other's company a great deal in London of late and I—I've come to care for you."

Garrett cleared his throat. "I hope you won't be offended when I tell you this is a surprise to me, Isabella."

She arched a brow and stepped back, folding her arms over her chest. "Don't play coy, Garrett. You must have noticed my interest in you."

He nodded. "Since we've been here in Surrey, yes, but earlier, in London—"

"I'm telling you now." She stamped her foot, but then smiled at him sweetly and allowed her arms to fall to her sides. "Don't you think I'm beautiful, Garrett?"

Sweat beaded on his forehead. "That is hardly the point, Mrs. Langford."

"You called me Isabella before." She quickly moved around the table in a swish of skirts and pulled his hand to her bosom. "Don't stop."

Garrett pulled his hand from her grasp. "I don't think that's wise."

Her chest rose and fell. Her eyes searched his face. "Why? Because you feel guilty for falling in love with me? Because of Harold?"

Garrett stared off, out the window. "I do feel guilt, terrible guilt, but it's not for the reason you think."

"What reason then?" Isabella demanded, staring up at him, her lips quivering.

Garrett cursed under his breath and turned his head sharply to face her. "Isabella," he whispered, "it's high time I told you. Your husband died saving my life."

# CHAPTER TWENTY-NINE

Isabella's face drained of color. Her pale pink lips continued to tremble and her eyes searched Garrett's face as if she'd learn the rest of the story there.

"What do you mean?" she whispered sharply.

Garrett shoved his hand through his hair and paced toward the window. "It's true. He died saving my life. Your husband is dead because of *me*."

"I don't understand."

Garrett closed his eyes. The guilt pummeled him. "As you know, we were at Zornova. I went down, a bullet in my shoulder and another in my thigh. It was bad, but I was able to crawl."

Garrett expelled his breath in a deep rush. It all came back to him, the haunting memories, the awful screams of men dying around him, the acrid smell of the thick, nearly impenetrable smoke. And the sickening sweet smell of . . . blood.

"I was wheezing, grabbing at my chest. I looked up through the smoke to see another French soldier with his rifle aimed at me. I was wounded too badly to move quickly. I said my prayers."

Isabella gasped.

Garrett took another deep breath. "Harold saw it too. He ran toward me. He launched himself in front of the fire. He saved my life, the brave, mad fool. He gave his life for mine." Garrett turned to look at Isabella. Would she hate him? Could she forgive?

"It sounds like something Harold would do." Her voice sounded more full of pique than hatred.

Garrett hung his head. "He was the best man I ever knew. I owe him my life."

"And that's why you refuse to have anything to do with me?"

Garrett furrowed his brow. How could she be worried about that after what he'd just said? "You haven't known the truth about me, Isabella. Now you do. I expected your hatred or at least your anger. I deserve both."

"What if I told you I forgive you? If I said I still want to be with you?"

Garrett shook his head. "I'd say I don't understand. But regardless, when I see you, I'm reminded of Harold. There are few moments when I'm not reminded of Harold but you're his widow and I just can't—"

"I understand," Isabella said. She picked up her skirts and swept away down the corridor, leaving Garrett with the distinct impression that she didn't understand at all.

# CHAPTER THIRTY

Jane stared at the sparkly silver gown that encased her body. Tonight's grand dance wouldn't rival the one to be held the following evening, but it would be unforgettable just the same.

"That gown looks stunning on you," Lucy declared.

Jane nearly blushed. "It's far, too, ahem, tight. Even after Eloise helped me with the seams."

Not only was the décolletage far more risqué than she would normally wear, the sparkle was far more sparkly than anything she'd ever owned. Of course she couldn't help smiling at herself in the reflection in the looking glass. Would Upton think she was *stunningly beautiful* tonight?

"It looks much better on you than it ever did on me," Lucy added. "Now, here, take this." She handed Jane the vial of lilac perfume.

Jane took the tiny glass bottle, her stomach clenching into excited knots. She promptly dabbed a bit behind both ears. Would Garrett Upton lick it off later?

A blush heated both her ears. She couldn't look at

Lucy when she had those thoughts. She should have told Lucy and Cass about her feelings for Garrett, but she just couldn't. Not yet. Not when it was all too new.

The perfume-licking bit wasn't Jane's only scandalous thought. She intended to kiss Garrett again. She would have to elude her mother's watchful eyes to accomplish it, but she had years of experience in that quarter.

Something had happened between her and Garrett since he'd come to her room and brought her lilacs and Mary Wollstonecraft. Jane's belly fluttered. Whatever it was, it was there, and undeniable. She wanted to kiss him again, desperately. Tonight.

She caught her reflection one final time. "Too bad I don't have a more elegant pair of spectacles, but at least they match the silver of my gown." She chuckled at that thought.

Lucy looked up at her and blinked. "Why, Jane Lowndes, did I just hear you say something to indicate that you give a toss about how you look?"

Jane promptly snapped her mouth shut. She needed to be more careful about what she said in front of Lucy. "Let's go. I need your help making it to the ballroom."

Lucy gave Jane a sly look that indicated she was not entirely through with her previous question but she held out her arm, nonetheless, for Jane to lean on.

Jane took a deep breath. It was time. Time to go to the ballroom and find Garrett, and time to put her Mrs. Bunbury plot into action with Lucy. Jane felt confident on both counts.

She leaned on Lucy's arm, and the two women slowly made their way down to the ballroom. Once inside, Jane barely had a chance to scan the room for Garrett, before her mother found her. Thankfully, Mama was speaking to Cass.

"Jane, come join us," Cass called, motioning her over with her fan. Jane and Lucy slowly made their way over to the two of them.

Mama eyed her up and down. "What are you wearing, miss?"

Jane winced. "I—"

"Isn't it lovely, Lady Lowndes?" Lucy interjected. "It's one of mine. I think Jane looks absolutely stunning in it."

Jane's mother's eyes were wide, but there was definitely a smile lurking in their depths. "I just have never seen Jane in anything so . . . so . . ."

"Silver?" Jane supplied, hoping her mother would let the subject drop. Jane gave Cass a pleading look.

"I was just telling your mother how much we've enjoyed getting to know Mrs. Bunbury," Cass announced with a quick smile in Jane's direction.

Lucy nodded. "Oh, yes. She's a delight but *such* a quick one. I swear I've seen her half a dozen times this evening, but at present I cannot seem to locate her." Lucy stood on tiptoes and made a grand show of scanning the ballroom for the elusive Mrs. Bunbury.

Jane's mother merely nodded. "If you see her again, Your Grace, do point her out immediately."

"Mama, I saw her in the corridor just before I came in," Jane added. "She said she might go and lie down. She wasn't feeling particularly well. She wanted to ensure that I found you and was properly chaperoned this evening."

"Of course you are," Jane's mother huffed.

"She said to give you her regrets that she has been unable to make your acquaintance." Jane shared a knowing look with Lucy.

Hortense fluttered her silk fan in front of her face. "I am sorry to hear she's feeling unwell. I suppose there's always tomorrow at the wedding to meet."

"Yes, of course," Lucy said brightly.

Jane winked at Lucy. She'd never been much of a winker before, but this little victory called for a wink if anything did.

"Janie, come with me. Let's take a turn around the room. We'll go slowly for the sake of your ankle," Lucy said. "You'll excuse us, won't you, Lady Lowndes? There is a certain gentleman I've been wanting Jane to meet."

Jane's mother looked as if she'd just been told that Jane's engagement was imminent. A smile spread across her face. "Oh, yes. Yes, of course. Please go. Have fun."

"I shall see you later, Mama," Jane said, waving as they left, arm in arm.

"That was a nice touch with the bit about the gentleman, Lucy," Jane said with a laugh, after they were well away from her mother.

"She's predictable, the poor dear," Lucy replied with a sigh.

They made their way slowly around the room while Jane continued to test the strength of her ankle. They were nearly to the other side of the large space when she spotted a small group of people that unfortunately included Mrs. Langford.

The widow was wearing purple this evening. Jane snorted. Typical. She thought she was a queen.

Mrs. Langford's head snapped up and she spotted Jane and Lucy.

"Miss Lowndes," she called, leaving the group of gentlemen who were paying her homage and coming to stand near the two ladies. "May I have a word?"

"I suppose so," Jane replied, wanting to be anywhere but in Mrs. Langford's odious company. Reluctantly, Jane relinquished Lucy's arm and painstakingly followed Mrs. Langford over to the wall where there was a bit of privacy.

The widow turned to face her. "I wanted to say one thing."

Jane sighed. "Very well. Say it so that I may limp back over to my friend."

Mrs. Langford's eyes narrowed. "Fine. I'll be blunt. I want Garrett Upton. And I intend to have him."

Jane placed a steadying hand against the wall. She took a breath, concentrating to keep a blank look on her face. So there it was, the ultimate challenge, and stated in such a way that it sounded absurd. "What are you planning to do? Toss a sack over his head and abduct him?"

Mrs. Langford smirked. "Such a wit, Miss Lowndes, and such a child. I am a full-grown woman and, believe me, I know the way to bring a man to heel."

Jane's eyebrows shot up. "To heel? Like a dog, you mean?"

"If need be." She tossed her head and barely shrugged one shoulder. "I'm willing to do whatever it takes."

"Like tampering with a saddle and challenging someone to a race?"

The widow gasped and took a step back. "What are you implying?"

Jane eyed the woman. She had no intention of getting into an argument with Isabella in the middle of the ball at Cass's wedding party, but she also refused to allow the widow to think she was fooling anyone. "Don't count your victory quite yet, Mrs. Langford. I, too, have read *Secrets of a Wedding Night.*" Jane brushed past the widow and made her way back to Lucy. Admittedly, her departure would have had a superior impact if she hadn't had to half limp, but an exit was an exit, was it not? The words were more important than the walking.

Lucy had managed to find Garrett, and they were standing together when Jane returned. She smiled at him brightly and he rushed to offer his arm. "How is your ankle?" he whispered in her ear, causing gooseflesh to pop up. Hopefully he'd got a good whiff of that magical perfume.

"Not perfect but much better," she replied.

To Jane's chagrin, Mrs. Langford sauntered up and joined their group. The woman's strident voice rang out behind them. "Your Grace, it's lovely to see you again."

Lucy rolled her eyes but turned to greet the widow. "Mrs. Langford." She inclined her head.

They turned to face one another in a small circle. Jane kept her arm firmly wrapped around Garrett's.

Mrs. Langford touched her elegant fingers to the strand of pearls at her neck. "It's really too bad you cannot dance this evening, Miss Lowndes. I do hope your ankle heals eventually."

"I'm sure you do, Mrs. Langford," Jane replied, a false smile on her face.

"I myself would love to dance." Mrs. Langford eyed Garrett expectantly.

Jane's grip on his arm tightened. For one awful moment she thought he would be obliged to offer.

"I'd be honored if you'd dance with *me*, Mrs. Langford." Owen Monroe was there. Jane couldn't stop her sigh of relief. The man had a knack for materializing at the precise moment he was needed. A helpful chap indeed.

Mrs. Langford gave Owen a tight smile, but she had no choice but to accept. She took his arm and allowed Owen to lead her to the floor.

"I'm off to find my handsome husband." Lucy gave Jane and Garrett a small wave as she trotted off.

"I'm sorry you cannot dance," Garrett said as soon as they were alone.

"I'm not."

He raised a brow. "You're not?"

"No."

"Why not?"

She leaned up to get closer to his ear so only he could hear. "Because I'd much rather . . . go look at the paintings in the upstairs drawing room."

His Adam's apple bobbed as he swallowed, but otherwise, his face remained a mask. "I see. And would you allow me to accompany you on such a mission?"

"I was counting upon it."

He made to offer his arm, but Jane shook her head. "We shouldn't be seen leaving together," she whispered. "I'll meet you there in ten"—she studied her ankle—"no, fifteen minutes."

The journey to the upstairs drawing room took Jane longer than fifteen minutes. First, she had to wait for her chance to leave the ballroom without anyone noticing, a particularly difficult task given that everyone kept coming to inquire after the health of her foot. By the time she actually made her way from the room, she was still favoring her ankle more than she'd realized. She hobbled out of the ballroom, down the corridor, and up the stairs.

When she finally pushed open the door to the upstairs drawing room, she breathed a sigh of relief. Garrett was waiting for her on the settee in the middle of the room. He faced the portrait they'd pretended to look at the other night. A brace of candles on the mantelpiece illuminated one side of his handsome face. Jane was suddenly shy to be back here, remembering what they'd done on that settee.

*Be bold.* Wasn't that Lucy's favorite saying? Jane had become quite bold indeed. And she was about to become even bolder.

She opened her reticule, pulled out a key, and locked the door.

"What do you have there?" Garrett called, his voice warm.

"The key." She glanced over her shoulder, giving him a positively flirtatious look—one she was not certain she'd heretofore had in her.

He whistled, his eyebrows lifted. "The key?"

"Yes. I came prepared this time. We don't want anyone walking in on us, do we? I asked a footman for it earlier. I gave him a guinea for his trouble."

"Not Mrs. Langford's footman, I hope."

"Certainly not."

She sauntered over to Garrett—as well as one could saunter when one's ankle was doing poorly. She felt more feminine than she ever had in her life. Feminine and romantic. The gown was lovely, the room was cast in shadows, the man was handsome and dashing and . . . she wanted to kiss him. The thought made her shiver.

"How did you get away from your mother?" He took her hand and helped her to sit next to him.

"I told her my ankle was hurting and I needed to prop it upon pillows. Mama said she'd send a servant to check on me, but Lucy volunteered."

"What about Mrs. Bunbury?" he asked, his mouth quirking into a sensual grin.

Jane laughed. "Don't worry. My chaperone is rubbish. Believe me, we'll be completely safe from her."

Garrett's lips twisted into a beautiful smile. "I suppose we cannot expect too much out of her in that she doesn't exist."

He slid across the velvet seat until his thigh touched Jane's. "You look absolutely stunning in that gown," he breathed. His warm breath caressed her neck. She shuddered.

"Thank you."

"I may like it better than the blue one and I hardly thought that possible."

"Thank you." Her good leg shook furiously beneath the silvery folds, but she refused to pluck. *Be bold. Be brave*.

She took a shaky breath. "What should we talk about? Portraits?"

His hand moved to her shoulder. He lightly stroked the column of her neck with one finger. Jane closed her eyes. She couldn't think. His touch did funny things to her insides.

"Seeing as how you've locked the door," he whispered. "I was thinking of something else."

"Something . . . el—else?"

"A lesson."

A shiver chased its way down her spine. She opened her eyes again and focused them on him. "A lesson?"

"Yes." His lips hovered near her ear. "You like to learn new things, do you not?"

She turned her head. Their mouths were only inches apart. She watched his lips. "I do. But what can *you* teach *me*?"

His other hand came up to rub her opposite shoulder. "Ah, you may think you know everything, but believe me when I tell you there is a thing or two that a supposed rake could show you."

Her breath came in short pants. "Is that right?"

"Yes."

Her head tipped back. "By all means, then, show me."

He carefully reached behind her ear and unhooked the wire bar of her spectacles. Facing her, he put his other hand behind her opposite ear and pushed that one up too. He carefully pulled the spectacles away from her face. For a moment, Jane felt naked, vulnerable.

He set the spectacles on the table in front of the settee and turned back to face her. His thumb rubbed across the underside of her eye.

"I like your freckles," he said.

Her throat went dry. "Oh, they're just—"

"Charming," he finished.

"I thought you said something about teaching me a lesson?"

"So I did." He pulled her to him, his mouth capturing hers. His lips slanted over hers, and his tongue plunged inside. Jane fiercely wrapped her arms around his neck. He quickly maneuvered them so she lay on the settee and he was on top of her, kissing her, pressing his hardness against her softness.

He braced himself on one elbow and, using one hand, untied his cravat, uncoiled it quickly, and ripped it from around his neck.

"What are you going to do with that?" she whispered against his rough cheek.

"Tie you to the settee."

Jane's eyes flared. Her heart fluttered in her chest. She'd never heard of anything like that, but she was intrigued. More than intrigued. Ooh, perhaps a rake did have a few lessons to share after all. She met his eyes in a challenge. They'd turned a dark, mossy green. "You wouldn't dare."

He'd arched a brow. "Wouldn't I? Try me." Clutching the rumpled cravat in his fist, he stared her in the eye. "Say the word."

"What word?" Her breath was a heavy pant against his firm chin. Her chest rose and fell rapidly with her excitement.

"Yes," he whispered.

"Yes," she breathed.

\* \* \*

That was all Garrett needed to hear. He pulled Jane's arms above her head and wrapped the cravat around them, securing them at the wrist. Then he wove the top of the material around the settee's open wooden arm. He made a tight knot. He'd never been so thankful for his army training before. He might not be a sailor, but damned if this knot wasn't good enough for his purposes.

Jane's eyes sparkled, but a hint of apprehension lurked in them. He didn't want her to have any doubts.

He kissed her temple. "If you want me to stop, just say so."

"It depends," she breathed, her gorgeous chest rising and falling. Garrett couldn't look away. He wanted her naked and writhing beneath him. But tonight he'd settle for caressing those gorgeous breasts.

"On what?" he answered, his voice muffled as he kissed the tops of both.

"On what you intend to do with me."

His mouth met hers again in a fierce tangle. Then he pulled away and his gruff voice sounded in her ear. "I intend to make you come."

Jane closed her eyes. "You . . . you do?"

"Yes. Do you know what that means?"

All she could do was nod. "I've . . ." She bit her lip. "I'm very well read." She turned to the side.

"Let me assure you," he said, as his fingers made quick work of the buttons on the back of her gown. "This is one thing that's *much* better to experience than to read about."

Jane twisted to help him unbutton the gown. He pulled it down to her waist. Her stays and chemise were all that remained between the two of them. "I'm quite sorry for this," he said, just before he pulled something from his boot.

"For wh—"

The quick flash of a blade before her eyes told Jane he had a knife. He sliced her stays down the middle in one quick maneuver. She sucked in her breath, hard. How had he done that so quickly and effortlessly? Were rakes trained in this manner? Impressive, to be sure.

Still bracing himself on one elbow, he peeled away the remnants of the stays and then slowly, so excruciatingly slowly, he cut the straps of her chemise, first off one shoulder, then the other. His finger traced the line of the fabric where it hovered just over the tips of her nipples. She shuddered.

"Garrett, please."

The knife dropped to the carpet with a soft thud. His hot mouth fell to the exposed skin above the shift. "That's right. Say my name. Beg me."

Jane closed her eyes and arched into his hot mouth. This was the most erotic thing that had ever happened to her. Not that bluestocking spinsters had much occasion for erotic things to happen to them, but suffice it to say she was glad she'd asked this man to meet her in the upstairs drawing room tonight.

"Garrett, please," she whimpered, closing her eyes, feeling every touch, every kiss, every lick with every bit of her soul.

His lips moved lower, nudging the fabric away from her breast. Jane gasped. His wet mouth covered her nipple and . . . sucked. Oh, God. Yes! She clenched her jaw and twisted her head to the side. The pleasure was exquisite. So good. So, so good.

His mouth and teeth tugged at her while his hand came up to play with the other peak of her breast through the fabric of her shift. Somehow the soft scratch of the fabric with his thumb flicking back and forth made her mad with wanting. "Please," she begged.

"Please what?" he murmured against her scorching skin.

"My other breast."

His smile burned against her. "What do you want, Jane?" He moved his mouth an inch, two. "Do you want my mouth here?" He flicked his thumb against her sensitive nipple again.

"Yes. Please. Now." She tugged at the bonds that held her hands above her head. He gave her what she wanted. His mouth scorched across her nipple and Jane closed her eyes and moaned.

Why was this so incredible? Who knew that being trussed up like a hare while the most handsome man in the world did amazingly sensual things to your body was this much fun? None of her books had taught her *that*.

But she wanted to touch him, wanted to run her fingers through his dark hair, pull his mouth up to hers, wrap her arms around his broad shoulders, kiss him again.

His mouth tugged again and again on her breast. His thumb flicked achingly back and forth against her other nipple. She moaned again and strained against the bonds.

"Easy," he said hotly against the soft flesh of her breast. "We've barely got started yet."

Her breath left her body in a whoosh. Her eyes rolled back in her head. "Barely even—" Her breath was a rush of heat and lust.

"That's right." His grin was positively wicked.

One hand left her breast while his hot, wet mouth still tugged at the other.

She shuddered as his free hand moved down, down, down, outlining her legs beneath her silvery skirts. He found the bottom of the fabric and flipped it up, his hand moving slowly back up her leg, along her stockings, only this time it skimmed along the hot skin of her inner thigh.

A tremor racked Jane's body. *Oh, God. Oh, God. Oh, God.* He was going to touch her. *There.*

His hand slowed as it made its way unerringly toward the juncture between her thighs.

She tugged against her bonds again, but it didn't matter. She wouldn't have stopped him even if she could have. It was delicious torture to be unable to touch him. Instead, she mentally begged him to find just the right spot.

And he did. Oh, God, he did. His finger stroked against her once, twice, before settling between the slick folds and finding the—sweet Jesus—*exact* right spot. Jane bit her lip. Her hips arched off the settee.

His mouth never ceased its gentle assault on her nipple and a pressure built between her legs. Ecstasy shot down from her breast, making the exquisite torture worse, much worse.

His finger slowed, then stopped.

"No," Jane cried out.

Then the tip of his finger touched that perfect spot again, the one that made her eyes roll back in her head. "Yes, Garrett, yes," she breathed.

"Yes, what?" he murmured against her breast, nipping at her skin.

"Yes, *please.*"

His finger circled that spot, again and again, while her hips rocked in a rhythm she was completely helpless to stop. She strained against the bonds that held her wrists, her teeth clenched, her eyes closed.

"God, Jane, you're so hot. So hot and wet and—" He groaned. His erection pressed tightly against her outer thigh. She wanted to rip her bonds away and reach for him, feel him, stroke him. But the circling of his finger couldn't be denied. She arched her back again, pressing her breast more fully into his demanding mouth.

Her breath came in short, shallow pants as the pressure between her legs built. "Oh, God. God," she cried, twisting her hips away, but Garrett followed their movements with his finger. He didn't allow her to break their contact.

"Garrett, I can't—" She bit her lip, her head turning fitfully from side to side.

"Yes you can," he whispered huskily against her neck. The stubble along his tight jawline was abrasive against the softness of the top of her breasts and that was driving her slowly mad too.

His finger continued its relentless assault, again, again. "Garrett!" she called, just before she spiraled into oblivion, a feeling unlike any she'd ever known consuming her body.

When Jane finally surfaced from her haze, she realized that Garrett had pulled down her skirts and was tenderly unwrapping the cravat from around her wrists. They were a bit sore, but deliciously so. He rubbed them individually and carefully pulled her hands back down to her sides. He gathered one of her hands in his, brought it to his lips and kissed her knuckles. He was still breathing heavily. He pressed his slick forehead to hers.

She reached for his hips, wanting to feel his erection, but he pulled her hand away, pinning it over her head again. "No," he said huskily. He kissed her again fiercely. "Not unless you want me to take you tonight, right here on this settee."

Truthfully, she'd considered it for a moment. If him taking her on this settee was anything like what he'd just done to her, she was definitely interested. But that would complicate things. Complicate them a great deal. Instead, she kissed him back. The man had just given her the most amazing moments of her life. A kiss in return seemed inadequate.

"That was . . . incredible." The word seemed insufficient, even to her own ears.

"I'm obsessed with your perfume," he murmured. His breathing was still hot and heavy in her ear. He kissed her there, running his tongue along her earlobe, and she bucked beneath him again. Gooseflesh covered her neck and arms. Oh, what this man did to her.

"So?" he asked, nuzzling beneath her ear.

"So?" she echoed, barely able to discern his words with his mouth still on her skin.

"What do you think?"

Her eyes were still closed, but she had to smile at that. She took a long, shuddering breath. "You're right, *so* much better than reading a book."

"And?" he prompted.

"And it seems rakes *can* teach bluestockings a thing or two."

She felt his answering smile against the skin of her neck.

"Furthermore," she added, clearing her throat self-consciously. "I think we're going to need to do *that* again."

"Really?"

"Yes. I'm not entirely certain I caught all the nuances in that first lesson. I may need remedial work."

He captured her mouth with his again. "Happy to be your tutor."

# CHAPTER THIRTY-ONE

Jane sat next to Lucy in the second row of the quaint, stone village church for the wedding of Lady Cassandra Monroe to Julian Swift, Earl of Swifdon. The weather was glorious—cool and bright—for the ceremony that was held at ten o'clock in the morning. The vicar stood in front of the crowded pews, his white vestments gleaming and a broad smile on his face. No doubt his little church hadn't seen this much excitement since Cass's own parents had wed.

"She looks breathtaking," Lucy whispered to Jane, tears in her eyes. "Look at me, I'm crying already."

"She does look beautiful," Jane replied in a whisper. Indeed, Cass was magnificent in a glorious white and silver-beaded gown with a long train and a matching veil. "Thank heavens, the red spot on her nose disappeared."

"Yes, quite courteous of it, was it not?" Lucy said with a laugh.

Julian looked every bit the handsome soldier turned earl in his dashing military dress uniform.

Cass's mother, Lady Moreland, sat in the front row.

The woman nearly convulsed in a fit of joyous tears while her husband tried to comfort her.

"At least she'll stop hating me," Lucy whispered to Jane from where they sat in the row behind the Morelands. "I may have married a duke, but the Swifdon title is far older and more prestigious than Claringdon's. That must be why she's crying."

"I resent that," Derek said from beside his wife. Lucy elbowed him.

Jane gave Lucy a warning look but couldn't entirely stop her smile.

"What did your mother say when you told her Mrs. Bunbury had to leave this morning?" Lucy whispered.

"Shhh," Jane countered. Her mother was sitting just two spots away, on the other side of her father. Jane lowered her voice even further. "I told her Mrs. Bunbury had been overcome with a fit of heat yesterday and had compounded that error by eating something that did not agree with her." Jane smiled slyly. "She's well on her way to London by now."

Lucy pressed her lips together and nodded. She, too, kept her voice especially low. "I'm ever so glad to hear it."

Derek eyed the two ladies skeptically and shook his head.

It was true. Now that Mrs. Bunbury had been dispatched, Jane was happily free of her first and biggest problem. Her second problem, Mrs. Langford, remained of course, but that woman didn't frighten her. Now that Jane knew what the widow was capable of, she intended to stay well away from her. After tomorrow, when all of the houseguests returned to London, doing so would be quite simple. Mrs. Langford might have declared her intentions toward Garrett, but if there was any doubt as to where Garrett's affections lay, he'd proven them to Jane last night.

Jane took a deep breath and concentrated on watching Cass and Julian standing up at the altar together declaring their love for each other. It was beautiful, truly. The smile on the faces of both the bride and the groom declared to the entire assembly how deeply in love they were. Lucy was crying. Even big, strong war hero Derek looked a bit choked up. Jane had never been one to cry. Her stiff upper lip was something of which she was particularly proud, but listening to Cass and Julian take their wedding vows did tug at her heart.

The vicar's voice boomed through the church. "Julian Nicholas James Swift, wilt thou have this woman to thy wedded wife, to live together after God's ordinance in the holy estate of matrimony? Wilt thou love her, comfort her, honor, and keep her in sickness and in health; forsaking all others, keep thee only unto her, so long as ye both shall live?"

Jane caught her breath. The back of her throat burned. She'd never experienced anything like it during a wedding. Lucy made a sobbing noise and Derek patted his wife's knee.

Julian's eyes shone with love and pride. "I will," he intoned.

The vicar turned to Cass. "Cassandra Elizabeth Louisa Monroe, wilt thou have this man to thy wedded husband, to live together after God's ordinance in the holy estate of matrimony? Wilt thou obey him, and serve him, love, honor, and keep him in sickness and in health; and, forsaking all others, keep thee only unto him, so long as ye both shall live?"

Cass's voice was strong and sure. "I will."

Lucy pushed her handkerchief up to her mouth to absorb another sob.

Jane pressed her lips together, hard. Other than the obey part, that had been lovely. Truly lovely. And she'd never seen Cass so happy. Pure radiant joy shone from her face. All the years Cass had written Julian, hoped he'd come back from war safely, had culminated in this beautiful moment. Jane had to shake her head against the burn behind her eyes this time. A movement to the left caught her attention. She glanced over to see Garrett leaning slightly forward, smiling at her softly. He and his mother were sitting farther down the long row.

Jane returned his smile with a tentative one of her own before returning her attention to the ceremony. Garrett looked especially fine today in his formal morning coat. His dark hair brushed the collar and the black brought out the color in his eyes. They looked dark green.

*Perhaps marriage wouldn't be so awful after all.* The thought came out of nowhere and struck Jane in the chest. She gasped. Lucy gave her a quick, questioning look but Jane barely shook her head to indicate nothing was amiss.

She surreptitiously looked over at Garrett again. So far she hadn't thought beyond the house party and their little, ahem, flirtation, but they would have to have a talk at some point, the two of them. That much was clear. Would he be contemplating proposing marriage? Jane plucked at the neck of her gown. She couldn't think about that now. It was too much.

The fact was, in addition to Mrs. Bunbury, and Isabella Langford, Jane had a third problem, and it might well be the most pressing. She had the nagging feeling that she was falling in love with Garrett Upton. It seared her brain every time she had the thought, coming back to haunt her again and again. Each time she tried to push it away, it returned, more insistent than before.

She was surprised to think it. Upton had proven to be funny, intelligent, and well read. The well read part alone was enough to send her halfway to being in love with him. If the first edition Mary Wollstonecraft hadn't got her, quoting it certainly would. Add to that the fact that the man was gorgeous and knew how to do amazing things with his mouth and fingers, and she was nearly without hope.

She couldn't tell Upton she loved him. Could she? Lucy had convinced her he loved her, but Jane wanted to hear it from him. It was far too frightening a pronouncement for her to be the first to make it. But butterflies, of all poetry-dwelling, nauseatingly happy things, fluttered in her belly every time she thought about Garrett. When she caught his gaze again and he gave her that sensuous half-smile of his, the butterflies doubled.

She mustn't think about such things right now. All she needed to do was enjoy the ceremony and look forward to tonight. Her ankle was still sore, but perhaps she could muddle through a waltz with Garrett. Just one. She'd remember it forever. A sly smile spread across her lips. Aside from the waltz, she hoped tonight would be similar to last night actually.

She was going straight to hell for thinking about it in a church of all places, but ooh, last night. Heat rushed between her legs at the memory. The things they'd done. The things they'd *almost* done. She'd nearly begged him to take her right there on the settee in her friend's drawing room. Not very ladylike and certainly not very bluestocking spinsterish of her, but that was perhaps the best part. She plucked at the neck of her gown. It was getting warm in the church with such a large crush. Her thoughts were not helping.

Jane turned her attention back to the ceremony and watched with delight as her two beloved friends promised their lives to each other.

# CHAPTER THIRTY-TWO

After the wedding, the entire party had a breakfast feast on the lawn at the Moreland estate. Tables were set up and covered with huge white linens. Lilacs and white roses festooned each of them. Colorful ribbons of green and lavender had been strung above the tables with poles and children ran and shouted and laughed. There was nary a cloud in the sky and the smell of the fresh flowers along with the slight breeze made the entire affair magical.

Jane was stuck sitting next to a family member of Cass's, some sort of knight. She couldn't help glancing over at Garrett's table time and again. They sat only a few yards from each other. He was usually watching her.

The rest of the day was a blur with Jane and Cass and Lucy all hugging one another, wishing Cass the best, and congratulating her groom. Jane and Lucy helped Cass prepare for the wedding ball, and then they all settled in to take naps so they might be refreshed for the dancing.

Jane snuggled beneath her coverlet, just about to nod off, when her mother came into her room. "Jane, dear, you haven't said. Have you met anyone special since you've been here? A gentleman perhaps."

Normally Jane would have rolled her eyes or pretended to be asleep already. Her mother asked her this same question of every party she'd been to since her come-out. For the first time in forever Jane could actually say yes.

She breathed in the lavender scent from her pillow and squeezed her eyes closed. She wasn't ready to admit it to her mother yet. She didn't want to engage her mother's hopes for a . . . what? A marriage? Jane hadn't considered that possibility, herself. She'd barely begun to enjoy kissing Upton. Marriage was far too much to consider at present.

"I've met some wonderful people here, Mama, and come to know some of them better than before," she replied cryptically. "I'll see you tonight." She rolled over and pulled the covers to her chin.

The wedding ball was spectacular. The dancing was marvelous. There were several sets of La Boulangère, cotillions, quadrilles, and even a Scottish reel or two. The waltzes came and went while Jane waited for her ankle to comply. At least that awful Mrs. Langford had the good sense to stay far across the room. Owen Monroe, it appeared, was taken with the widow. He was spending a great deal of time in her company, poor man. When Owen wasn't there, Daphne Swift seemed to take up the task of speaking with the woman. Poor, sweet Daphne.

Garrett had helped his mother get a plate of food and danced with her to one of the reels while Jane and Lucy watched and laughed and clapped along. Aunt Mary, for her advanced years, was a wonderful sport. She'd hugged Cass soundly and declared how happy she was about her wedding to Lord Swifdon. "I must admit, dear, when you were in Bath last summer, I was convinced you should take the duke up on his courtship, but all's well that ends well, isn't it?" The older woman patted Cass's arm.

"Yes, Aunt Mary. That's absolutely right," Cass replied with a laugh.

Julian pulled his bride's hand to his mouth and kissed the back of it. His eyes sparkled with love and admiration. "I couldn't agree more."

Aunt Mary sighed. "You two are so perfect for each other. I just wish my darling Garrett would find someone special. I'd like to meet my grandchildren before I'm too old to know who they are."

Garrett's eyes nearly bulged from his skull. "Don't get any ideas, Lucy," he growled as Lucy opened her mouth to speak. "Mother, please do not encourage her."

"Lucy needs no encouragement," Aunt Mary replied with a wink.

Soon afterward, their little party broke up to speak and dance and share time with others, but Garrett remained by Jane's side. He ensured she had a proper chair to sit in along the sidelines and that her foot was propped up, and he brought her a glass of champagne and a plate of teacakes.

"You *do* know the way to a lady's heart," Jane said, laughing when he returned with the teacakes.

The look Garrett gave her was so serious, so sincere. She wished she hadn't mentioned her heart. Had it been too much?

"Dance with me," he whispered as another waltz began to play. "We'll mind your ankle."

She stood and placed the plate of teacakes on the chair. "I should like nothing better."

The dance was lovely. They didn't speak. No ribbing or word play or teasing or taunts. Garrett whirled Jane around and around and they stared into each other's eyes as if they were the only two people in the room.

After the music ended, Garrett escorted her back to her seat. "How's your ankle? The dancing didn't make it worse, I hope."

"It held up just fine."

"Excellent." He tugged at his cuff and arched a brow at her. "In that case, would you care to . . . see the portraits?"

Jane returned his knowing smile. "I do still have the key."

"I'm *quite* glad to hear that."

He left the room first, and Jane followed ten minutes later. She had to remind herself not to run up the stairs and risk hurting her ankle again. Once she got there, she took a deep breath and entered the room. Garrett was there, just inside the door. He immediately pulled her into his arms and kissed her. She kissed him back with all the pent-up longing and emotion she felt.

"Wait. I should lock the door," she whispered against his mouth.

"No, Jane. Not tonight. I've thought about it. We can't do this here again. It's too dangerous. Meet me later? In my bedchamber?"

Jane stood on her tiptoes and kissed him again. Her thoughts were a blur. He wasn't just asking her for a few kisses. He was asking her to spend the night with him. Nerves had replaced the butterflies in her stomach, but her entire being was screaming *yes*.

Garrett cleared his throat. "I know we need to have a talk first, a serious one, and I—"

"No." Jane couldn't think about that part. It was too much. She only wanted to live in this magical place for one more night. "Not tonight. Let's not talk tonight."

"Fine, tomorrow morning then. But you'll come to my room, tonight?"

Jane took a deep breath. She wanted it. She wanted him. She was a spinster, after all. What did she care about her useless virginity? The only thing that concerned her was the danger of becoming heavy with child.

"Garrett, if we— I don't want to have a baby."

"Don't worry." He whispered into her mouth. "I have something for that."

She nodded.

He kissed her again. "Jane, have you ever?"

She shook her head. "No."

He traced her cheekbones with his fingers. "Of course not." He seemed tender, so tender. "Don't worry. It's going to hurt . . . a bit, at first, but I can make it good for you. I promise."

"I know it's going to hurt, Upton, I've read about it."

He couldn't help his smile. "It's just like you to think you know all about something you've never done before."

She laughed. "I'll have to get away from Mama. Perhaps I'll tell her I'm going to bed sick." She smiled. "I must have eaten whatever Mrs. Bunbury ate."

Garrett pressed his forehead to hers. "Perfect. Come after the ball. Two o'clock?" he whispered, kissing her once more.

Jane rubbed her nose against his. "I want to . . . I do, but . . ."

"Think about it. If you're not there, I'll know you changed your mind."

# CHAPTER THIRTY-THREE

Jane hurried back down to the ballroom. Her belly was performing somersaults, but a thrill shot through her. She and Garrett were going to make love. She wanted it. She wanted it very much. It would complicate things to be sure, but it would also be the perfect opportunity for him to tell her he loved her. Surely he would. Wouldn't he? He'd mentioned having a serious talk in the morning, that had to be about love and marriage. A man like Garrett would never take his cousin's friend to bed without knowing the consequences of such an act.

As Jane made her way slowly down the stairs still favoring her ankle, the clocks chimed one. An entire hour to wait, an eternity.

Garrett returned to the ballroom as well. He smiled and laughed and danced with Cass and wished her well and joked with his cousin. Aunt Mary had already retired, but the rest of the friends enjoyed themselves, while Lucy noticeably dodged her parents.

The entire time, Jane couldn't keep her gaze from Garrett. He was so handsome. So handsome and he would be . . . Ooh, he would be touching her in a little while. Touching her everywhere and anywhere and making her feel all of those amazing things he'd made her feel before . . . and more.

Jane bit her lip. How would she ever tell Lucy and Cass about this? She *couldn't not* tell Lucy and Cass, but not tonight. Tonight she wanted to keep it to herself. A special secret only she and Garrett would share.

When Garrett turned and winked at her minutes later before he left the ballroom, Jane nearly came undone. Oh, she desperately wanted to tell Lucy and Cass.

Thankfully, Jane's mother had retired as well. She'd insisted that Jane stay and have a good time dancing, with Lucy as her chaperone. Apparently, Jane's earlier admittance that she'd met some wonderful people had given her mother hope. Jane had never before wanted to stay at a party longer than her mother; no doubt the woman had been saying a prayer of thanksgiving as she hurried from the room.

Jane took a deep breath. She counted ten. She would go upstairs and change into her night rail. No, upon second thought, her night rail wasn't exactly enticing. Oh, she was clearly not prepared for midnight assignations with gentlemen at house parties. What self-respecting bluestocking spinster was? Very well. She'd leave on her chemise and cover herself with her dressing gown. Yes. Perfect.

"Cass, dear. I'm going up to bed," she said to her friend, hugging her closely.

"Frankly, I'm surprised you made it this long. And we're not far behind you," Cass said, grinning back and returning her hug. "I love you, Janie. I hope your ankle feels better soon."

"I love you too, Cass. I'm so happy for you and for

Julian. As for my ankle, I'm only glad a litter wasn't involved."

"Don't think I wouldn't have arranged it," Cass replied.

"I have no doubt." Jane took her leave of Julian, Lucy, and Derek and made her way out of the ballroom and up the stairs to her room. By the time she arrived at her door, she was trembling with nerves. She rang for Eloise, who quickly helped divest her of her gown. Jane made it a point to dismiss the maid before she removed her chemise. She took a step over to the wardrobe and grabbed her dressing gown. She clutched it in both hands, staring at herself in the full-length mirror. She looked altogether different in her chemise. In fact, she'd never exactly studied herself this way before, with her hair down and her feet bare. Would Garrett think she was pretty enough? Would her naked body be acceptable to him? Would he think her thighs were too plump? Her backside too round? She'd never cared what anyone thought about her appearance before, but tonight she cared. She cared deeply.

"If you're not there, I'll know you changed your mind," Garrett had said.

For a brief awful moment she thought of him there, waiting for her if she didn't come. She took a shaky breath. She had this moment, this *one* moment to decide. The clock on the mantelpiece struck two and she stared at her reflection in the glass. Her heart pounded so loudly she could hear it in her ears.

She was frozen, paralyzed. What if he thought she wasn't good enough? Wasn't pretty enough? She couldn't take rejection. Not from him.

She squeezed her eyes shut. She couldn't do it.

When Garrett left the ballroom, he went directly to the wine cellar. He needed a bottle of red for tonight. He'd be sure to send over a replacement to reimburse the Morelands, though he doubted they'd mind. The earl and countess had a vast and extensive collection of wine.

The kitchens had been humming with servants bringing courses to and fro, but the evening had died down and a much smaller group remained hard at work. After getting the approval of the butler and assuring the good man that he did not need his help, he asked the hall boy for direction to the wine cellar.

"Just down the way, sir," the boy replied, pointing toward a darkened room at the far end of the basement. Garrett grinned at him and tossed the boy a pound coin for his trouble.

Whistling softly to himself, Garrett used the key the butler had given him and entered the cold, dry wine cellar. He lit a small candle so that he might better see. He stared up at the long rows of bottles. The reds were on one side, the whites on the other. He turned toward the rows of reds. Port, elder wine, madeira. He had to find the perfect thing. He'd stop and get two glasses on his way back through the kitchens. The servants might wonder who he was entertaining, but they wouldn't find out. He grinned.

He pulled out a bottle of madeira. A fine year. Still whistling to himself, he began to turn back toward the door . . . and the entire world went black.

Fifteen minutes later, Jane was still standing in front of the looking glass, hating herself. Tears pooled in the back of her eyes and she glared at her reflection.

"Fatty, fatty." The voices of the children from her days in the schoolyard taunted her.

Finally, she tugged her eyes from her body and met her own gaze in the mirror. That was in the past. This was now. She was no longer that plump little girl she'd been years ago. She might not be willowy or thin, but she wasn't plump any longer either.

She threw her dressing gown over her shoulders. She might be nearly twenty minutes late, but she was going to do this, take the risk, change her life. She would experience making love for the first time with Garrett. Because he wanted her. Because she wanted him. Because he was Garrett.

She hurried to the door of her bedchamber, pushing her arms through the sleeves of her dressing gown. She wrapped it around her waist and cinched the belt around her middle.

Garrett had given her directions to his room on the opposite end of the manor, but Jane was familiar enough with the house to know there was a much more private corridor that led to that end of the property. Perfect for a midnight assignation, she thought with a wry smile. She opened the door to her bedchamber, and peeked both ways to ensure the corridor was empty. Then she slowly tiptoed out.

Even favoring her ankle and keeping to the shadows, it didn't take her long to make it through the corridor and to Garrett's room. Her hand trembled as she placed it on the door handle. What if he'd changed his mind? What if he was angry with her for taking so long? Or hurt? Perhaps he'd assumed she wasn't coming and had fallen asleep.

She slowly turned the handle and pushed open the door. Holding her breath, she moved quietly into the darkened room. The light from a single candle on the mantelpiece cast the bedchamber in a warm glow. She'd barely taken two steps inside when she saw them. There, standing next to the bed facing her was Isabella Langford, and she was passionately kissing Garrett!

Jane clamped a hand over her mouth to stifle her scream.

She took one more awful look and saw his broad shoulders, his dark, curly hair, and his mouth on Isabella's breast as he bent his head to her chest. That was enough. Isabella's chin was thrown back and her eyes were tightly closed.

Covering her mouth this time because she thought she might retch, Jane whirled and ran. She ran out of the room, heedless of the pain that throbbed in her ankle, heedless of anyone who might see her rushing from Garrett's bedchamber in her dressing gown. She didn't even bother to go back the way she'd come. She ran down the long corridor, around the corner, and down a second long corridor, back to her bedchamber. She had to get inside her room. She had to hide. Had to—

She'd nearly made it to her door when her ankle gave way. She collapsed to the floor. The pain in her leg and the pain in her heart collided, causing the floodgates to open. Tears poured down her cheeks. She swiped them away with the backs of her hands and forced herself to stand. She dragged open her door and staggered to the bed where she fell on the mattress, her head jerked to the side.

She sobbed and sobbed as her heart broke into a thousand tiny pieces.

# CHAPTER THIRTY-FOUR

Somewhere around the time dawn cracked above the horizon and spread its insistent tendrils past the curtains, Jane rolled over and groaned. She'd cried so much her face was puffy and her eyes felt as if they bulged from her skull.

She'd been haunted by the horrifying moments in Garrett's bedchamber again and again. She wanted to believe it wasn't true. But when she replayed the awful scene in her mind's eye, she knew it wasn't a dream. Jane had *seen* it. Nothing about the scenario Jane had stumbled onto appeared to be forced. Quite the opposite actually, it was entirely apparent that both the participants had been greatly enjoying themselves.

Betrayal twisted like a knife in her belly. What was wrong with Garrett? She'd been late, yes. She'd been torn, hadn't decided to come right away. But once she'd decided, she couldn't get there fast enough. Obviously, she'd been too late. Obviously, he'd decided she wasn't coming. It hadn't taken him long to replace her in his bed. *Disgusting*. How could she have been so wrong about him? For heaven's sake, she'd actually fancied herself in *love* with him. Thank heavens she hadn't told him, or anyone else. If she'd mentioned it to Cass or Lucy, she'd feel twice the fool right now.

Garrett Upton was revolting, the worst kind of reprobate. But in a way, he'd done her a favor. A sick sort of favor, but a favor nonetheless. If she'd been on time last night, she would have made love to him. She might have given him her innocence, never knowing what kind of man he really was. No doubt she would have found out sooner or later, but not until after she'd made the biggest mistake of her life.

She pressed her palms against her aching eyes. There was no help for it. Life must go on. She intended to get up, wash her face, assist Eloise in packing her bags, and return to London today where she would set about forgetting any of this had ever happened.

She pushed herself up from the bed and hobbled over to the looking glass. Her hair was a tangled mess and her eyes were indeed swollen. As much as she was a disaster on the outside, her insides were a larger mess. In addition to her heart, her pride had taken a severe blow. She'd let down her defenses. She couldn't forgive herself for that. She'd actually convinced herself that someone like Garrett could really fancy someone like her. Preposterous. She hated herself for letting him in even a little, for being weak. She'd spent the last sennight pretending, pretending to enjoy suitors and fripperies, and gowns and balls for once. This is what had come of it. But most of all, more than everything else, she was incensed. Incensed at Garrett Upton . . . for being a liar.

Garrett had spent the better part of the wee hours of the morning pounding on the door of what was obviously a soundproof wine cellar. The brick lining the high walls was thick, thick enough to prevent him from summoning any help, thick enough to keep him from breaking down the bloody walls. Lord knows he'd tried. He'd damn near dislocated his shoulder in the attempt. That is, after he woke with the devil of a head from the bottle of wine that had been broken over it. He'd found himself lying in the shards of glass with a wet head, stained cravat, and ruined coat.

Whoever the hell had ambushed him would deal with his reckoning later. His first thought was getting to Jane.

When a servant finally happened by to unlock the door, Garrett rushed past the footman who'd freed him. "Thanks, chap." Without slowing down, he called, "What time is it?"

"Nearly eight o'clock, sir," the servant returned.

Eight o'clock? Bloody hell. Where would Jane be at this hour?

His first stop was the breakfast room where Lucy, Claringdon, and some of the other guests were eating breakfast.

Lucy's eyes went wide when she saw him. "Garrett, what are you doing here? What happened to your cravat? Why are you wearing your evening attire at this hour? Forgive me for saying so, but you look dreadful."

Garrett tried to catch his breath. "I'll explain later. Have you seen Jane this morning?"

This time Lucy narrowed her eyes. "Yes. She was up with the sun, quite unusual for Jane. She said she and her parents wanted to get an early start back to London."

Garrett cursed under his breath. "Have they gone already?"

"I believe their coach is just now being pulled around," Claringdon added.

Garrett sprinted for the door. He flew down the hallway, his footsteps echoing against the marble, and came to a sliding stop near the front door where Lord and Lady Moreland were taking leave of their guests.

"Are Sir and Lady Lowndes and Jane still here?" he asked, not pausing for the answer.

"Their coach is pulling away right now," came Lord Moreland's reply.

Garrett ripped open the front door and raced out onto the gravel drive. "Miss Lowndes!" he called at the top of his lungs. The coach, which was already moving past the drive onto the lane that led up to the house, came to a stop. Garrett didn't wait. He sprinted toward the vehicle, completely winded by the time he got to it.

The window opened and Jane's mother stuck out her head. "Mr. Upton, is that you?"

"Y—yes," he managed, desperately trying to catch his breath.

"May I ask what you're doing?"

Garrett bent over and braced his hands on his knees, breathing quickly and struggling to remain calm.

"I—I must speak with Jane."

There was a bit of discussion inside the coach, which allowed him time to right his breathing. It still wasn't perfect but was markedly improved by the time Jane stuck out her head. "Go away, Upton."

"No. I won't. I must speak with you."

More discussion in the coach ensued. By the time the door opened, Garrett was able to straighten himself. Jane emerged from the entrance, and Garrett held out his hand and helped her down onto the gravel. She was still favoring her ankle and behind her spectacles her face looked a bit red. Had she been crying? Damn it.

"Very well. What would you like to say to me?" she asked, her voice flat and calm. Too flat and calm.

"Can we go over there?" He gestured to a shady spot

several lengths away from the coach next to a hedgerow. He could already imagine her mother listening to this conversation and he wanted to spare Jane that.

Jane nodded jerkily.

There was a distinct harrumph from inside the coach as the two walked away. Jane had to lean on his arm a bit heavily. "Is your ankle worse?" he asked.

"It will be fine," she replied in the same flat voice.

As soon as they came to a standstill near the hedgerow, Jane released him, crossed her arms over her chest, and glared at him. He couldn't blame her for being angry. He'd left her waiting for him last night. She deserved an explanation.

"I'm sorry," he breathed. "About last night, I was—"

"Please, Upton. I don't want to discuss it. I find the entire thing distasteful in the extreme and I'd prefer to pretend that none of it ever happened."

He searched her pretty face. The spectacles he knew so well covered eyes that were full of anger and a bit swollen. "You can't mean that, Jane."

"I do indeed mean it, Upton."

She was back to calling him Upton and her face was a mask of ice.

"Jane, I'm sorry. I truly—"

"What are you sorry for? I'm the one who should apologize to you."

He furrowed his brow. "What do you mean?"

"I never came to your room last night. I changed my mind."

His face fell. "Wh—what?"

"I changed my mind."

"That's all right, Jane. I didn't mean to do this here, but—" He fell to one knee. "Marry me."

Jane's mouth fell open. "Upton." She gasped. "This

is really beyond the pale. You think you can fix all of this by proposing to me?"

"I'm not trying to fix it. I'm telling you that I love you and I want to marry you. Please say yes, Jane. Please."

He could have sworn there were tears in her eyes, but her face quickly reverted to stone.

"No, Upton. Never."

He searched her face, lowering his voice. "What about what we did the night before the wedding?"

She blushed but anger remained etched in her features. "Yes, as to that, thank you, that was informative, but I don't want to repeat it and I certainly don't intend to marry over it. No one *needs* to marry. I consider it a learning experience only, Upton. Good day." She turned away from him.

"What the devil are you talking about, Jane? I thought we had something together," he said as she left him kneeling by the hedgerow.

She whirled around to face him and shrugged even though he could tell she was fighting back tears. She carefully limped back closer to him, no doubt so her mother wouldn't overhear. "Something? What something? You're experienced, Upton. Far more experienced than I. Do you propose marriage to every lady whom you kiss in a drawing room?"

His head snapped to the side as if she'd slapped him.

"No." His voice was harsh, hard.

"We suffered a bout of temporary insanity, you and I." Jane's voice crackled with ice. "I promise you it will never happen again."

# CHAPTER THIRTY-FIVE

*London, two days later*

Garrett rubbed the top of the dog's head. He sat in the wide leather chair behind his desk in his study. It was nice to be home, back into the routine of things. He had a stack of correspondence half a foot high. He'd thrown himself into his work like a madman, anything to keep from thinking about Jane.

Jane. What the hell had happened with Jane? Would he ever understand women? That woman in particular? Why had her defenses reappeared so quickly? She hadn't even allowed him the chance to explain. Not that it mattered. He had asked her to spend the night with him without a promise. That had been poorly done. But he'd done the right thing as soon as he'd been able. He'd fallen to his knee on the bloody front lawn of the Morelands' estate, and she had thrown it in his face as if it meant nothing.

He scrubbed his hand through his hair. Somehow he'd lulled himself into believing something special had developed between them.

She was frightened. He knew that. She was feeling

things she'd most likely never felt before. Perhaps her refusal of him had been her way of keeping him at a safe distance. Wasn't that Jane's specialty? The entire world was at a distance from her, viewed from behind those silver-rimmed spectacles or from behind the pages of a book. She hid from people, hid from the world, hid behind her cloak of intellectual superiority. Only he'd been able to coax her out, just a bit, but then she'd slammed the door right back in his face.

She'd been cold to him that morning she'd left. So cold. He'd never seen her that way before. But that cold woman wasn't Jane. Not truly. He knew how warm she could be.

He cursed under his breath. Why had he proposed? Because it was the right thing to do? Because he had developed feelings for her? But was it . . . love? He didn't know what love felt like. Damn it. Jane had supposedly been in love with him, or so Cass had claimed. Was that even true? Perhaps Jane was right. Perhaps they had both suffered a bout of temporary insanity. At any rate, it was over now. She'd been quite emphatic in her response. He would do well to forget about it and move forward.

The second dog came up and wagged his tail. Garrett patted him on the head as well. "Let's see to all of these letters," he murmured, firmly pushing thoughts of Jane Lowndes from his mind.

On the top of the stack was a recent letter from Isabella Langford. He broke the seal and unfolded it.

*Please pay me a call, Garrett. I must speak with you at your earliest convenience.*

*Yours,*

*Isabella*

Garrett tossed the letter on the desk and stared blindly out the window. It was time to make it clear to Isabella once and for all that he would not be courting her. He owed it to her to say it to her face, confront the awkwardness of the house party. Tell her that her rudeness to Jane was untenable, and if he ever found out she or her dastardly footman had anything to do with the saddle on Jane's horse being tampered with, he'd make them both pay.

He'd briefly wondered if she had had anything to do with his being conked over the head in the wine cellar. But that made little sense. What possible use could she have for knocking him out and locking him in a wine cellar all night? Given her motives, if she'd been involved he would have no doubt awoken in her bed with her insisting upon a proposal. His gold pocket watch had been missing when he'd awoken. The culprit was likely some desperate servant. Lady Moreland had assured him she'd look into the matter. Apparently, she hadn't yet been able to find the thief.

Garrett ordered the coach put to and paid an afternoon call to Isabella. Her expensive butler ushered him into the drawing room. Isabella soon joined him and asked the butler for tea.

"Thank you for coming." She gave Garrett a bright smile.

"Isabella, I—"

"No. Let me speak first, please."

He nodded. "Very well."

"I know you don't have tender feelings for me, not in the same way I do for you. But I think it makes sense for us to marry, nonetheless."

He opened his mouth to interrupt her.

"Hear me out, please."

He nodded.

"We may not be a love match, but the children need a father. I need a husband. And you will need a wife, an heir."

Jane's words echoed in his head. *No one needs to marry.*

"I understand that, Isabella. Believe me, you are beautiful and I'm certain you would make someone a fine wife, but—"

Isabella took a deep breath. "I know you're hesitant because of Harold. Because of what you told me at the house party."

"That's one reason, yes, but—"

Isabella's voice was strained. "There's something I must show you."

# CHAPTER THIRTY-SIX

"I sent your mother a note telling her that Mrs. Bunbury was feeling ever so much better. I even signed Mrs. B's name to it." Lucy's announcement was accompanied by a wide smile as she served Jane tea in her London drawing room.

"Did you disguise your handwriting?" Jane dropped an extra lump of sugar into her cup. Since she'd returned from the countryside, her ankle had healed, but she was still sore on the inside. She was struggling to seem normal for Lucy's sake.

"Of course I disguised my handwriting," Lucy answered. "Though I doubt your mother's taken much notice of mine over the years."

"Show me," Jane replied. "I'd wager I can tell it's yours."

"You and your study of handwriting," Lucy said with a laugh, as she stood and made her way over to the writing desk in the corner. She took out a piece of parchment, grabbed a quill, and scribbled away.

While Lucy wrote, Jane considered for the one-hundredth time telling her friend what had happened between herself and Garrett. Part of it at least. But she decided against it. Again. Telling one bit would necessitate telling the whole sordid thing and that was a complicated story Jane had no intention of repeating. It had been difficult enough convincing Mama that Mr. Upton had not, in fact, proposed. It was deuced difficult to come up with a plausible explanation as to why a gentleman would stop a coach in such a dramatic fashion, ask to speak to a young lady privately, and then fall to one knee, but somehow Jane had managed to convince her mother that Mr. Upton had simply wanted her recommendation on a book she'd been reading and had lost something in the grass while they'd been discussing it in earnest.

Of course, her father didn't believe it for a moment. He raised both brows over his spectacles, shook his head, and went back to his columns and figures. Thankfully, Papa had never believed that marriage was the goal to which every young lady should aspire. He wasn't about to interfere. Her mother, however, had taken a bit of convincing.

Lucy dropped the quill back into the inkwell and trotted over with the note. "I give you Mrs. Bunbury's handwriting."

Jane set her teacup on the table and took the letter, eyeing it carefully. She quietly contemplated it for a few moments. "Aha. You've given yourself away."

"Where!" Lucy demanded, craning her neck to look over Jane's shoulder.

"Right here." Jane pointed to the top of a letter *p*. "The large circle here with the tail on the end of it is purely Lucy Hunt."

Lucy scowled. "I do that?"

"Yes, but not to worry. While I noticed it, I doubt Mama would. I'd advise you never to attempt to disguise your handwriting in a message to me." Jane laughed.

"You are quite clever. I'll give you that. Though I cannot say such a skill sounds the least bit worth suffering through something that sounds as dreadful as *Montague's Treatise on Handwriting and Whathaveyou*."

"Graphology," Jane said.

"Dull," was Lucy's answer.

Jane set the letter on the table in front of her. She lifted her teacup and took a sip. She sighed. "At any rate, it seems the Mrs. Bunbury plot at the wedding worked well enough, and I see no reason why it should not continue to work for a good, long while. Mama expects me to begin attending the events of the Season and I intend to tell her Mrs. Bunbury is accompanying me. Then I shall come here and read books in your library all evening."

"Yes, well, as to that . . ." Lucy's voice drifted off on a bit of a guilty note.

"What is it?" Jane asked, her teacup frozen in midair.

Lucy set down her cup and folded her hands in her lap. She looked so serious Jane's palms began to sweat.

"It seems there's been a bit of a complication."

"Complication?" Jane echoed.

"Yes, I—"

"Out with it, Lucy. What is it?"

"I hate to be the one to tell you this and heaven knows I would have dragged Cass here with me to deliver this news if she weren't already off on her honeymoon, but it seems that . . ."

"Yes," Jane prompted.

"It seems that you might have created the scandal you wished for after all."

Jane blinked. "Scandal? Me?" The teacup remained frozen.

"Yes."

"What scandal?"

Lucy patted her coiffure. "There's no easy way to say it so I'll just come out and ask you." She pursed her lips. "Were you running about the bachelors' quarters in your dressing gown in the wee hours on the night of the wedding?"

Jane's teacup clattered to the tabletop, tipped over, and spilled its contents across the rug.

Lucy bit her lip. "I'll take that as a yes."

Jane could barely breathe. She stooped to sop up the mess with a napkin, desperately trying to think of what to say. Finally, she righted herself again and faced Lucy. "How do you—"

"Apparently one of the guests thought she saw you and, well, I must admit, I wondered for a moment if it might actually be a good thing, the scandal bit, I mean."

Jane counted three. *Breathe. Breathe. Breathe.* Lucy was being a good friend, not pressing her for the details, which was quite unlike Lucy, actually.

"I suppose my reputation has suffered," Jane ventured.

"It's not good." Lucy shook her head. "But at this point it's mostly just gossip. Apparently a servant did say he was under the impression that Garrett might have proposed to you. How preposterous is that?"

That was it. If Jane had still had the teacup in her hand at the moment, she no doubt would have tossed the thing in the air. "Garrett? Proposed?"

"Yes. One of the servants reported that Garrett appeared to be down on one knee in front of you in the drive the morning you left. I admit I was curious as to why he was so determined to see you." Lucy fluttered a hand in the air.

Jane managed a shaky laugh. "At the house party, you did tell me he's in love with me, after all."

"Yes, I know." Lucy's voice was oddly high.

"Did you ever tell Cass about that ridiculousness?"

"No." Something in the way Lucy refused to look at Jane made her suspicious.

"Lucy?" Jane dragged out the word. "What do you know?"

Lucy folded her hands in her lap. A bad sign to be sure. "First, I must tell you I was quite convinced of it."

"Convinced of what?" Jane's voice took on a tremulous note.

"That it was true. That Garrett loved you."

Jane planted both fists against her hips. "Lucy Hunt! You must tell me what you've done and tell me right away!"

Lucy pressed her lips together and finally met Jane's gaze. "We only told you because we thought— Again, we were quite convinced—"

"Who is *we*?"

"Cass and I."

"What did you do?" Jane gave Lucy her most formidable glare.

Lucy twisted her hands together. Another bad sign. "We saw you together, the night of the masquerade, looking at the portraits in the upstairs gallery."

Jane caught her breath. What else had they seen? "Upton and me?"

"Yes," Lucy replied, still acting sheepish. "I was looking for Garrett and I followed him and . . . then you went into the drawing room together and shut the door. Well, we had to wonder—"

"Wonder what?" A sinking feeling spread through Jane's middle.

Lucy shrugged. "Wonder if you were, you know, *doing* anything?"

Jane forced herself to keep her face blank. "What did you discern?"

"We didn't discern anything. We left soon after. It was all conjecture on our part, but we decided to find out if you and Garrett might have developed a *tendre* for each other. You quite shocked us, you know."

"Just because we went into the drawing room together? Why didn't you come out and ask me what was going on?" Jane slapped a hand against her forehead. "Wait, I know the answer to that already. Because it would be too simple. When Lucy Hunt is involved, complicated escapades are always preferred to directness."

"I take offense to that," Lucy replied, pointing her nose in the air. "And we *did* ask you, or tried to. The next morning, don't you remember? Cass and I came to your room and asked where you'd been the night before. You didn't mention Garrett once. It seemed suspicious to us."

Jane crossed her arms over her chest. "And so you . . . ?"

Lucy winced. "We decided to tell each of you that the other had developed a *tendre*."

"You did what!" Jane slammed her palms against the tabletop. The silverware bounced.

Lucy kept one eye closed and eyed Jane carefully out of the other. "Cass told Garrett that you had developed a *tendre* for him, and I told you that Garrett had developed a *tendre* for you."

Jane's breath came in short spurts. She tried to count three but she couldn't manage it. She waved a hand in the air. "Why in heaven's name did you do that, Lucy?"

Lucy worried the end of her napkin. "We hoped it might serve to flush out the truth. We thought if you both believed the other had feelings, it might help you to confess to your own."

Jane was convinced her eyes were wild. She *felt* wild. "Confess to my own? What in heaven's name made you think I had my own?"

"You must admit that you and Garrett make a fine-looking couple."

"We can barely stand to be in the same room with each other!"

"You were doing an admirable job of it that night in the upstairs drawing room. And everyone saw how enchanting you were dancing together the night of the wedding."

The memory of that dance felt like a punch to her middle. Jane clenched her jaw. "Lucy, I swear, if I didn't know you were the biggest meddler in the entire kingdom, I'd warn you right now to run far and fast. It would only be sporting to give you a head start."

Lucy bit her lip again. "But because you *do* know I'm the biggest meddler in the entire kingdom? Oh, don't hate me, Janie, please."

"I'm absolutely incensed. Truly. But I have to admit, it explains a great deal." She took a deep breath, then another one. "You are known for your schemes and if I were to remain angry with you, I might as well be angry with the sky for being blue."

Lucy nodded so rapidly her black curls bounced. "That is true."

"You're not going to get out of it that easily, Lucy. Tell me, what else did you do? Who else was involved in this little scheme of yours?"

"What makes you think anyone else was involved?" Lucy tossed her napkin back on the tea tray.

"You *always* involve others in your schemes. I know because I'm usually one of them."

Lucy's eyes twitched back and forth.

"Lucy?" Again, Jane dragged out the word.

"Very well, in addition to Cass and myself, Owen Monroe and Daphne Swift were involved."

"Owen and Daphne?" Jane breathed. "What was their involvement?"

Lucy drummed her fingers against the wooden arm of her chair. "Owen was to make Garrett jealous by paying special attention to you and Daphne was to keep Mrs. Langford occupied when necessary."

Jane sat stunned. Her mouth fell open. She felt as if Lucy had hit her over the head with an iron poker. She'd been duped. Duped by the best of them, Lucy Hunt. "So that's why Owen was constantly appearing out of nowhere and Daphne was always speaking with Mrs. Langford."

Lucy's lips twisted. "Of course, they were forced to improvise upon occasion, like the time they jumped in the rowboat together at the lake so that you would be forced to ride with Garrett. Too bad they couldn't have dragged Mrs. Langford off with them."

"I shouldn't be surprised, but I am." Jane rubbed her forehead. The devil's own headache was forming behind her right eye. "Tell me one more thing. Have you admitted this subterfuge to Upton?"

Lucy tugged at the neck of her gown. "Actually, Derek is on his way to do that as we speak."

# CHAPTER THIRTY-SEVEN

Garrett tossed back his third brandy. Brooks's was quiet this afternoon. He'd holed up in a club chair in a corner and ordered drink after drink. He'd been attempting to read the paper but he'd been looking at the same paragraph since he'd arrived. He was preoccupied, preoccupied by Isabella Langford and what she'd shown him.

She'd left the drawing room earlier and returned a few minutes later holding a letter.

A letter from Harold.

As soon as he'd seen his friend's familiar bold scroll on the parchment, an ache formed in Garrett's chest. It was as if the bullet that had torn through his shoulder ten years ago was an open wound again.

Isabella cleared her throat and handed him the letter. "This is addressed to you."

"Me?" Garrett's heart jackknifed in his chest. "How could that be?" He squinted at the date on the top. Years ago, when they'd been together in Spain.

Garrett searched Isabella's face. "Why am I just now seeing this?"

"Harold wrote it to you, but he sent it to me," she replied softly. "He asked me to give it to you in the event that he . . ." Her gaze dropped.

"Have you read it?" he asked.

"Yes."

Garrett made his way to the large window at the front of the drawing room. He took a deep breath and bent his head toward the letter. His eyes scanned the page.

*Upton,*

*If you are reading this, the worst has happened. We've shared many awful days together, my friend, and there's no one else I'd rather die next to. You're a good patriot, a good soldier, and a good man. If you find your way home, please take care of Isabella and the children. That is my dying wish. I could think of no better man to be in my stead. I must know that my family is taken care of. Always. They mean everything to me. I know you will do right by them. You have my eternal thanks.*

*Yours,*

*C. H. Langford*

Garrett rubbed his thumb across Harold's familiar signature. He still missed him. He folded the letter and slid it into his inside coat pocket, pressing it against his shoulder. A crushing weight settled over him as the import of the words he'd read hit him square in the chest. Harold had wanted Garrett to take care of his family.

Why in the hell hadn't Isabella given him this letter long before now?

"There's something else," Isabella whispered.

"What is it?" Garrett had asked quietly.

Isabella took a deep breath. "I am with child."

Garrett's brows snapped together and his head jerked up to face her. "What?"

She pressed a handkerchief against her nose. Her eyes filled with tears. "I'll be ruined if I don't marry quickly."

Garrett stepped closer to her and searched her face for the truth. "You weren't planning on telling me that before now? What about the baby's father?"

"I'm sorry, Garrett. I'm desperate. I don't know where to turn. The baby's father is not in a position to marry me, and I wouldn't have him if he was." She turned away abruptly on a sob, pressing the handkerchief to her mouth.

"Isabella, I—"

Her voice shook with her tears. "The children and I will be outcasts. We'll have to leave London." She turned and dropped to her knees in front of him. "Garrett, you must save us. We need you. Please."

The import of her words pressed on Garrett's stomach. He felt as if he were going to retch. Isabella was asking him to make the ultimate commitment to ensure she and the children were taken care of for good, safe from scandal.

His thoughts turned to Jane. Did he love Jane? Yes. But Jane obviously wanted nothing to do with him. Despite what Cass had told him, Jane didn't love him back. What sort of man of honor would he be if he ignored this letter from the grave? Turned Isabella away? Let her family fall to ruin? Even if he continued to provide them with an income, they would be treated like outcasts. Harold's children would have no hope of good futures.

Sometimes, what you wanted to do and what you should do were two entirely different things.

He helped Isabella up to sit next to him on the settee. "Why are you just giving me this letter now?"

Isabella cast her gaze toward the floor. She seemed so sad and small and vulnerable. "At first, I needed time to grieve. I spent years in disbelief. I know it sounds senseless, but I actually believed Harold might walk through the door one day."

Garrett nodded grimly. "That must have been hell for you. I'm sorry."

She looked up at him. "I know you don't love me. I know it's an enormous thing to ask you to raise another man's children, but we could be happy together. Our feelings might develop, over time."

Garrett watched her carefully. Isabella wasn't stupid. There would be no false pretenses between them. Successful marriages had been based on far less than a promise to a friend to whom one owed one's very life.

Garrett grimaced. The parson's noose tightened around his neck.

Garrett's meeting with Isabella had been several hours ago, and after three brandies at the club, marriage to her still didn't sound like a good idea. He'd have to drink fifty bloody brandies to wrap his mind around it. He hadn't given her an answer, yet, but it was hardly something he could think about for weeks. She was with child and the sooner a marriage took place the better for her reputation. But there was something else to consider. If the child was a boy, he would be named Garrett's heir, the future Earl of Upbridge. However, if Harold Langford hadn't saved his life, the title would have gone out of the family, to a distant cousin, and there was always the chance the child would be a girl.

"Upton, there you are. I thought I might find you here this afternoon."

Garrett looked up to see Derek Hunt and Rafe Cavendish making their way toward him. He stood to greet them. "Claringdon, Cavendish, good to see you."

"A bit early in the day for a drink, don't you think?" Claringdon asked as soon as he was close enough to spot Garrett's brandy.

"I'm not certain that's possible," Rafe added.

Garrett grinned. He'd always liked that Cavendish.

"You should listen to the lad, Claringdon. Care to join me for a drink?" He turned to Rafe. "I didn't know you were a member here, Cavendish."

Rafe flashed his own grin. "I'm not. Just taking advantage of my influential friend here." He clapped Claringdon on the back.

"Welcome," Garrett replied, gesturing to the seats near him.

The other two men sat while Garrett returned his attention to his brandy.

Claringdon relaxed against his seat and crossed one booted foot over the opposite knee. "There's something I need to tell you, Upton. It involves Lucy and—"

Garrett groaned. Setting his drink on the table next to him, he dropped his forehead into his hands. "If it involves Lucy, it's going to be messy, isn't it?"

"A bit," Claringdon replied, tugging at his cuff.

Rafe had busied himself ordering a drink of his own from a passing footman.

Garrett straightened up and took another swig. "Out with it then, Claringdon."

"Lucy informed me last night that she and Cass were up to something at the house party," Claringdon said.

Garrett waved away his words. "If this involves Mrs. Bunbury, I—"

Claringdon shook his head. "It's not that. Apparently, Lucy and Cass thought it would be a good idea if they both"—Claringdon winced—"if they told you Jane was in love with you and told Jane you were in love with her."

Rafe Cavendish whistled. "Now *that* is up to something."

Garrett's stomach dropped. He squeezed his glass. "What do you mean?"

Claringdon wiped a hand across his brow. "Did Cassandra tell you Jane was in love with you?"

Garrett's throat went dry. "Yes."

"Lucy told Jane you were in love with her," Claringdon continued.

The room spun. Garrett clutched at the arm of his chair. "What in the devil are you talking about?"

"I'm deuced sorry to say it," Claringdon continued, "but apparently, they became convinced you and Jane were perfect for each other and set about their plan in a misguided attempt at matchmaking."

Garrett clenched his jaw. "My God. It was never true? Any of it?" he whispered.

"Afraid not."

The footman returned with the brandies just then, and Rafe, good chap that he was, had the decency to remain silent and sip his drink.

Garrett's mind raced. What did this mean? Not only did Jane not love him, but she had been under the mistaken impression he had been in love with her? If she'd been told around the same time he'd been told, that would have been before the picnic at the house party. What the hell had Lucy and Cass been thinking?

"Does Jane know?" Garrett swallowed the lump that had unexpectedly formed in his throat.

"Yes," Claringdon said. "Lucy intends to tell her today. I doubt Jane will be pleased."

"The feeling is mutual." Garrett pressed the back of his hand against the throbbing pain in his head.

"At the risk of offending you, Your Grace," Rafe interjected, "it sounds as if you've got your hands full with your new duchess."

Claringdon's mouth quirked up in a half-smile. "You don't know the half of it, Cavendish." He settled back in his chair and steepled his fingers over his middle. "That's it, Upton. I thought you should know."

Garrett closed his eyes briefly. "Thank you for telling me, Claringdon. I assume Lucy sent you so she wouldn't have to face my wrath."

Claringdon inclined his head. "Something like that. She also had the nerve to ask me to tell you she still believes you and Jane make a fine couple and you should seriously consider marrying her."

Garrett's throat tightened. "It's too late." He shook his head and stared, unseeing, into the fireplace across the room. "You must congratulate me, fellows. I have just decided to marry Isabella Langford."

# CHAPTER THIRTY-EIGHT

"But Lucy told me specifically that you adore *Much Ado About Nothing* and you would certainly agree to accompany me," Daphne Swift said the next afternoon as she and Jane took a turn around Jane's parents' garden. Jane would have preferred a stroll through the park, but considering how gossip about her behavior at the wedding house party was spreading through town, she thought better of such an outing today. It was only a matter of time before her mother found out. And possibly dismissed Mrs. Bunbury. Which was ridiculous, of course, but entirely probable.

"Please, Jane," Daphne continued. "It's been so dreadfully dull since Cass and Julian left on their honeymoon. I've nothing to entertain me."

Jane gave her a sideways stare and pressed her lips together to keep from smiling. "What about Captain Cavendish? He looked as if he were entertaining you at the wedding ball."

Daphne pushed her small nose in the air. "Captain

Cavendish makes me more angry than entertained. The man drives me quite mad."

"I know the feeling," Jane said on a sigh. When Lucy had informed Jane this morning that Upton would be announcing his engagement to Mrs. Langford, she'd done an admirable job of taking the news in stride. It was true she'd briefly lost her mind and fancied herself in love with the man, but after his quick defection to Mrs. Langford, he was no longer someone she even bothered thinking about . . . mostly.

It was her own fault, really, not Upton's. Upton had never made her any promises. He'd never pretended to be anything other than who he was. If Lucy couldn't change her ways, neither could her cousin. Jane never should have believed for one moment the man wasn't a rake. While Lucy seemed convinced Garrett had some-how been forced into proposing to Mrs. Langford, Jane knew better. She'd seen Garrett's attraction to the widow with her own eyes. God help her.

"I do adore *Much Ado About Nothing,* Daphne, but I cannot go with you to the theater. My reputation is in shreds. I'm sure to be treated like *persona non grata* were I to attend."

"Oh, fiddle. You'll be with me and no one will dare cut you. Not to mention you have the backing of the Count-ess of Swifdon and the Duchess of Claringdon as well."

"But Lucy and Cass won't be with me."

Daphne threaded her arm over Jane's. "No, but I will, and I'll make Mother come, too, if it'll help."

Jane laughed. "There's no need to drag your poor mother into it."

"Please, Jane. Please come with me."

Unwinding her arm from Daphne's, Jane bent to pluck a violet from the path next to their feet. "I don't know." She smiled up at Daphne. "I'm still miffed at you for your part in all this, you know. Lucy told me she recruited you."

Daphne returned her smile. "I can only plead that Lucy Hunt can be quite convincing when she wants to be. She told me I'd be doing you a favor to keep Mrs. Langford occupied."

Jane stood and twirled the violet between her fingers. "Hmm. That part was true, actually. Perhaps I shouldn't be miffed at you at all."

"That's right." Daphne nodded happily and the two resumed their stroll. "If you don't come to the theater tonight for yourself, do it for me."

Jane blinked. "For you?"

A soft pink blush crept over Daphne's cheeks. "I heard Captain Cavendish will be at the performance tonight and I . . ." Daphne bit her lip and glanced away.

Jane arched her brow. "Aren't quite as indifferent to him as you'd like everyone to believe?"

Daphne shook her head and gave a miserable shrug. "Including myself."

That night, Jane sat in the Earl of Swifdon's box at the theater with Daphne Swift at her side. She could *feel* the disapproving eyes of the *ton* staring at her from the other boxes.

"At least a dozen sets of quizzing glasses are trained in our direction," Jane said, wanting to slink back into the shadows.

"Ignore them," Daphne replied. "Those awful people. If anyone has anything to say about you, they'll have to say it to me first." She nodded firmly.

Daphne fluttered her hand in the air. "Let's talk about something ever so much more pleasant, like how lovely you look this evening." She turned to give Jane a once-over. "Your hair is different, isn't it?"

"Thank you." Jane self-consciously pushed a curl away from her cheek. She'd asked Eloise to arrange her hair in a chignon tonight, not unlike the one she'd worn at the masquerade ball. She'd grown a bit tired of the severe topknot.

"And your gown," Daphne continued. "It's . . . not blue."

Jane smoothed a hand down her pink dress. It was the softest shade of blush. She'd allowed Mama to purchase it, which that lady had done with great glee. Now Jane was feeling awkward. Blue felt like armor. Pink? Pink felt like . . . naked skin. "Thank you," she murmured. "I thought I'd try another color for a change."

"It suits you. You look beautiful. *That's* probably why the quizzing glasses are trained our way. They're all positively green with envy."

Jane had to smile, though she also had to severely doubt it.

Daphne craned her neck to see out the side of the box. "Look, it's Captain Cavendish. He's only a few boxes down."

Jane nudged Daphne with her elbow. "Go over and say good evening."

"I wouldn't dream of it." Daphne sat back down and pressed her hand to her throat. "If he doesn't have the good grace to come and greet *me*, then I intend to completely ignore him."

"You came here specifically to speak to him," Jane pointed out.

"No." Daphne shook her head and her blond curls bobbed. "I came to be *seen* by him. That's quite different from speaking to him."

"That makes no sense at all."

The curtain behind them ruffled and Lord Berkeley

poked in his head. "Lady Daphne, Miss Lowndes, may we come in?" the viscount asked.

Jane smiled widely at him. Lord Christian Berkeley was a friend of Lucy's, well, Garrett's really. In Bath last summer, Lord Berkeley had briefly and unsuccessfully attempted to court Lucy, but they remained friends. Berkeley had even made an appearance at last autumn's house party where Cass had pretended to be Patience Bunbury. Berkeley was a good man and a tremendous sport.

"Lord Berkeley! Of course, do come in," Jane replied.

Lord Berkeley strode in with Garrett Upton behind him.

Jane sucked in her breath and concentrated on calming her pitter-pattering heart. She should have known Garrett would be with Berkeley. Garrett hadn't looked at her. She stared down at her slippers.

"Lord Berkeley, Mr. Upton," came Daphne's bright voice. "It's ever so good to see you. I didn't realize you were at the theater tonight."

"Upton, here, cannot resist a performance of *Much Ado About Nothing*," Berkeley replied with a laugh. "As soon as I saw you two lovely ladies, I told him we had to come and greet you."

"Funny." Jane kept her eyes trained on Lord Berkeley. "I had the impression *Much Ado About Nothing* is Upton's least favorite of Shakespeare's plays."

"No. That would be *Romeo and Juliet*," Upton bit back.

"A close second then, is it not?" Jane replied with a tight smile.

Lord Berkeley waded into the deafening silence. "I rarely come to town, you know, and when I do, I always enjoy the theater."

"Then you must come more often, my lord," Daphne replied.

"As it is I don't plan to stay the entire Season. I'm returning to Northumberland in a few weeks' time and plan to spend the autumn and winter at my hunting lodge in Scotland."

"That sounds dreadfully remote," Jane said.

"And cold," Daphne added.

"It is both," Lord Berkeley agreed. "And that's exactly why I enjoy it."

"Lord Berkeley," Daphne said. "I am just now about to go in search of Captain Cavendish. Have you seen him this evening?"

"I believe he's in Lord Mountbank's box."

"Would you escort me there, please?"

Jane squeezed her reticule so tightly her fingers ached. *Now* Daphne wanted to leave? "Daphne, I don't think—"

"You don't mind keeping Mr. Upton company, do you, Jane? Whilst we visit Captain Cavendish? *Please?*" For a moment Jane wondered if she was helping Daphne or if Daphne was tricking her into spending time with Upton. At any rate, it would be beyond rude to say that she minded. Instead, she nodded tersely, sat back down, and faced the theater.

"Thank you for staying with Jane, Mr. Upton," Daphne said with her usual friendly smile. "And for escorting me, Lord Berkeley." The viscount held out his arm and Daphne wrapped her small one around it.

A moment later, the two had gone, and Jane was forced to concentrate on keeping her disobedient leg from shaking. She stared into the crowded theater completely unseeing.

"Do you mind if I sit?" came Upton's even voice.

She turned her head slightly to the side but her gaze did not follow. "Not at all."

"Thank you."

Out of the corner of her eye, she watched as Garrett pushed up his black coattails and took the seat next to hers. She couldn't turn to face him. What could they possibly say to each other? Discussing the weather seemed asinine, and discussing the play was covered territory. What else was there? Perhaps silence was the best policy. Apparently Upton didn't agree.

"How is your ankle?"

"Recovered, thank you."

"And your cat?"

"*The* cat is quite well. Her kittens too."

"Glad to hear it." She heard him take a deep breath. "I assume you were also told that we were duped?"

Jane didn't take her gaze off the far wall. "Duped?"

"Yes, Claringdon informed me that while we were at the house party Cass told me that you fancied me while Lucy told you the same."

Jane nodded once. "Yes, Lucy told me."

Upton's voice was unironic. "Seems I've finally fallen victim to my cousin's penchant for trouble."

"That's a pretty way to say 'lies.'"

"They were indeed lies." He paused. "Are you angry with Lucy?"

"Lucy cannot help herself. Any more than you can."

His head snapped to the side to face her. "What is *that* supposed to mean?"

Jane pushed a lock of hair behind her ear. Perhaps she shouldn't have said that. She desperately needed to change the subject. She blurted out the first thing that came to mind. "Lucy tells me you intend to marry Isabella Langford."

"Jane, I—"

"I think it's for the best. I wish you both well."

She took a shaky breath. She didn't love him. He

didn't love her. So why did the thought of Garrett with Isabella make Jane sick to her stomach?

Thankfully, Daphne and Berkeley returned then. "Captain Cavendish sends his greetings, Jane," Daphne said.

"I should have come with you," Jane replied. *Then I wouldn't have had to sit here and have this excruciating conversation with Garrett.*

"Ladies, what do you have planned for the remainder of the week?" Lord Berkeley asked.

"I intend to go shopping on Bond Street tomorrow," Daphne announced. "But I cannot seem to convince Miss Lowndes to come with me."

Jane laughed. "You cannot convince me because I'd rather have my eyes gouged out with hot pokers than go shopping. Unless a bookstore is involved, of course."

"Is that so?" Lord Berkeley whistled. "A lady who doesn't enjoy shopping. You are a rare find indeed, Miss Lowndes."

Jane tilted her head and grinned at him. "My lord? You've never met a bluestocking spinster before?"

Berkeley laughed aloud at that. Then he asked, "What do you intend to do with yourself tomorrow then, Miss Lowndes?"

"I've been looking for an old book. I'm going to the library to search for it. I don't have much hope of finding it, of course, but I do intend to try."

"What book is it, Miss Lowndes?" Lord Berkeley asked.

"It's called *The Art of Penmanship,*" Jane replied. Surely Lord Berkeley was only being polite by asking.

"I have it." Upton's reply sounded curt.

A silence ensued.

"Pardon?" Jane finally offered.

"I have that book at my town house," Upton said.

Jane turned to face him. "You have *The Art of Penmanship*?"

"Yes."

"Mr. Upton, I could not be more astonished," Jane said.

He met her eyes. "If you come to my house tomorrow, you're welcome to borrow it."

# CHAPTER THIRTY-NINE

Jane stood outside the imposing door to Upton's town house for five entire minutes. Eloise was waiting in the coach. Jane was unable to either step forward and rap upon the door or flee back to the vehicle. Instead, she stood, hands folded, reticule dangling from her wrist, as she contemplated the possibilities. She could knock on the door and be ushered into the town house where she would simply tell Upton she'd come to borrow his book. Or, she could turn away, go back home, and pretend she'd never made this journey. Then Upton wouldn't think she gave a fig about him or his book collection. That would show him.

However, she wanted that book.

Her arrival had absolutely nothing to do with seeing Garrett. Nothing at all. She was here in search of a book.

Yes, this was strictly professional.

She squared her shoulders and took one small step closer to the door. She rapped upon it three times and stood back, staring at it expectantly.

The door swung open moments later and a

distinguished-looking butler and two well-behaved dogs stood at attention in the entryway. Upton had dogs?

"Yes?" the butler said, giving Jane a not unfriendly once-over.

She cleared her throat. "I'm Miss Jane Lowndes, here to see Mr. Upton. I am borrowing a book." The last part was completely unnecessary, but seeing as how she was an unmarried female, she felt it wise to explain she wasn't here for some sort of mid-afternoon assignation. God only knew what sort of women arrived on Upton's doorstep at all hours of the day and night.

"Come in." The butler stood aside, allowing Jane to move past him into the house. The dogs politely moved to the side as well. She studied them. They were some type of spaniel. One was red and white and the other, black and white. They looked quite handsome. Upton had never given her any indication that he owned dogs.

She'd never been here before, actually. She used to visit Lucy at her Aunt Mary's town house, which wasn't far. Upton had had this particular house before his father died, and while he was often at his mother's house, this was his main residence in London.

The butler shut the door behind her.

"What are their names?" she asked, gesturing toward the canines.

"Miss?"

"The dogs? What are their names?"

The butler straightened to his full height, which was impressive indeed. "Dogberry and Verges, miss."

Jane's eyes went wide. "Dogberry and Verges?" she echoed. "From *Much Ado About Nothing*?"

"Indeed, miss."

Jane stared at the dogs. She couldn't help but smile to herself.

"Mr. Upton is not in at the moment," the butler

continued. "But he left instructions to show you to the library."

"He left instructions?" Jane pointed to herself. "For me?" And then, "Did you say 'library'?"

"Yes, miss. He specifically told me that if Miss Lowndes paid him a call, to show you to the library and inform you that he intends to return shortly."

Jane shook her head. She and the dogs trotted behind the butler. Upton's house was well appointed. She would give him that. It was tastefully decorated in hues of blue and brown. Not overly stuffed or stuffy. A lovely home, actually. The butler had said "library." *That* had piqued her interest. How had she never known Upton had a library?

Where was Upton? Was he with Isabella Langford? The thought flashed across Jane's mind without her permission. Oh, what did she care? Hopefully, she'd find the book and be gone before the scoundrel made it back from whatever degenerate pursuit he was about.

The butler led her down a corridor and paused before great mahogany double doors. The dogs stopped and sat at attention. The servant grabbed the handles and pushed open the doors. The room beyond stole Jane's breath.

She walked into the large space and spun in a wide circle. Library indeed. The room was perhaps the largest she'd ever seen in a town house aside from a grand ballroom. It was deliciously, perfectly, pleasantly, rightly lined with scores and scores and scores of books. Books! Books! Books!

Jane may have squealed. She only guessed as much because the dogs and the butler stared at her with heads cocked to the side. "Oh, I— My, I . . . didn't know Mr. Upton had such a big . . ." She couldn't stop staring at the rows of books.

The butler cleared his throat and shuffled his feet. What had she been saying? Oh, yes. Books! "I had no idea Mr. Upton had such a vast collection of books."

"Reading is one of Mr. Upton's favorite pastimes," the butler added.

Jane nearly tripped over the thick carpet she'd been traversing in order to get a better look at the contents of the room. Reading was one of Upton's favorite pastimes? Were they speaking of the same Mr. Upton? She hadn't stumbled upon the home of one of Garrett's cousins or . . . no, Garrett had no living male cousins. Not to mention the portrait on the far wall looked a great deal like Garrett. It must be his father. The man had passed away not very many years ago.

"Mr. Upton enjoys *reading*?" she asked, strictly for clarification's sake. Perhaps he was just someone who hoarded books or had become obsessed with collecting things. For all she knew he had a collection of dolls or tin soldiers or something equally odd elsewhere in this town house.

"Yes, miss," the butler replied. He shook himself as if he realized he'd already said too much about his master's personal habits. "I'll leave you to it. Mr. Upton says to inform you everything is alphabetized in the order of the author's last name. Please ring if you'd like me to bring tea."

Jane opened her mouth to say, "That won't be necessary," but she took another look at the huge collection and changed her mind. She could happily die here. She'd need sustenance. She thought her father had a large collection, but nothing in her house could compare to even one small part of the literary feast in front of her.

"Tea would be lovely, thank you." She pulled off her gloves and unhooked her pelisse. This was going to involve some serious inspection. She might as well get started.

"Yes, miss." The butler bowed slightly, gathered her pelisse, and left the room. The dogs stayed with Jane.

"This is Mr. Upton's library?" she asked the dogs.

The handsome animals blinked back at her.

"Mr. *Garrett* Upton?"

They merely cocked their heads to the side.

"And you are Mr. Upton's dogs?" she asked them. "Mr. Garrett Upton's dogs?"

One of the dogs was kind enough to stick out his tongue and pant a bit, which at least led Jane to believe he was listening. She turned back to the room and clasped her hands. When one was presented with one's idea of heaven, where exactly did one begin?

The butler returned with a tea tray. He set the elaborate service on the table in the center of the room.

Jane pursed her lips. Only one thing would make this beyond heaven. "You don't happen to have any teacake, do you?"

"We do, miss. I shall be pleased to fetch some for you." He left again and Jane had to force herself not to clap her hands. Teacakes and a giant library? She might just stay in here indefinitely and devil take Upton if he tried to forcibly remove her.

Jane set her reticule and gloves on the side of a settee and took a deep breath. Like an athlete preparing for a sport, she needed to ready herself. She marched up to the closest wall and ran her fingers along the titles of the leather bound volumes. Alphabetical by author, he'd said. The book she wanted was written by a fellow named Brandon.

She turned toward the far wall. She'd just pop over there and see how close she was to the *B*s.

Fifteen minutes later, Jane had eaten two teacakes and

realized that finding a book in the vast expanse of Upton's library was not nearly as simple a task as one might expect. She'd managed to narrow her search to the *BR*s and had climbed up a spiral staircase to the third level—third level!—in search of the book. Upton, she thought with some irony, was sorely in need of a librarian. Surely any of his friends or acquaintances who came into this room would require similar assistance. Of course, his affianced bride wouldn't pose much trouble. The woman didn't read. Jane doubted Upton had many copies of *La Belle Assemblée* tucked away in here.

Regardless, a librarian was in order. Perhaps he'd hire Jane. She could spend all day in here sorting and browsing and reading and—

The dogs barked as the door opened. Jane swiveled on the balcony. *Had the butler returned with more teacake?* What a helpful chap.

"Jane?"

She sucked in her breath.

*Upton.*

She briefly considered her original plan. Could she hide in this house for the rest of her natural life or was she, indeed, required to declare herself? "We don't know what became of Jane," she could hear her mother's voice saying years from now at a party. "She went out to the library one afternoon and never returned." Because she had told her mother the library was her destination. She just hadn't mentioned *which* library. Mrs. Bunbury, that poor darling, remained in bed with a head cold.

In the end, she decided she must make her presence known. If for no other reason, the idea of the future Mrs. Upton being told that Jane had gone missing in the library would no doubt spur that particular lady into launching an all-out search that would not end until Jane was discovered.

"I'm here," she called back softly.

He tilted his head and looked up at her. His smile was warm and welcoming. "I'm glad you came," he said. Her heart, that traitorous organ, beat quickly, and for a moment she could almost believe he meant it. Almost. But the memory of him kissing Isabella Langford rendered in Jane's mind. She wished she could scrub it away, but it remained like a hideous scar.

The dogs wagged their tails, obviously waiting to be greeted by their master. Garrett bent over and slapped his hands on his thighs. The dogs wiggled up to him and he petted each of them in turn.

Jane slowly made her way down the staircase. She came to stand a few paces from Garrett. She arched a brow. "Dogberry and Verges?"

His grin hit her in her middle. "The stars of the play if you ask me."

"Not Hero and Claudio?"

"Certainly not."

She tapped her slippered foot against the rug. "What about Beatrice and Benedick? They would be the names I'd choose. You surprise me, Upton. I didn't know you were partial to dogs."

"I'm not. My friend, the Countess of Merrill's sister, Miss Andrews, gave me these two. She works with the Royal Society for the Humane Treatment of Animals and she's forever rescuing animals in need. When I saw these two little scoundrels, I couldn't say no."

"They are darling," Jane allowed, scratching Dogberry behind the ear.

"Would you care to sit?" Garrett asked her.

Jane followed him to the settee near the center of the room. She sat on one end. He sat on a chair at right angles to her. He looked handsome today, blast him. Unbearably so. His long legs were encased in buckskin breeches, his feet in black top boots. He wore an emerald green coat and white shirttails and cravat. His dark hair was a bit mussed and it looked as if he hadn't shaved in a day or two, which Jane quite liked, actually.

"You've been keeping a large secret from me, Upton."

His forehead burrowed in a frown, but his hazel eyes sparkled. "Secret?"

She spread her arms to indicate the room. "I had no idea you had . . . this."

Half of his mouth quirked up in a smile. "You never asked."

"I would never have guessed. I can't understand why Lucy never mentioned it to me."

One of the dogs rested his large paw on Upton's lap. "Would you believe me if I said I asked Lucy not to tell you?"

Jane blinked at him. "Why would you do that?"

"Because you've always enjoyed giving me endless grief over the fact that I'm not a reader."

She wrinkled her nose. "But you *are* a reader, or so your butler says."

Garrett leaned back and crossed his booted feet at the ankles. "You find that so difficult to believe?"

Jane made a show of reaching for a third teacake. "I've never seen you with a book in your hands."

"Some of us read despite being able to conduct ourselves in polite Society without hiding behind books."

Jane stiffened. She dropped the teacake back to the plate. "I don't hide behind books."

"Don't you?"

"No." She stood to leave with jerky movements. Why had she even come here? She should have known nothing good could come of it.

"Don't go," he said, standing also and reaching out to her.

She crossed her arms over her chest. "Why should I stay?"

He shoved his hands in his pockets and bent his head. His words were quiet. "Jane, why didn't you come that night? Why did you change your mind?"

She turned around, facing away from him. She couldn't look at him. "What does it matter?"

"It matters very much. I thought we had something special. I thought we were becoming close."

She nudged her spectacles and turned her face to the side but still didn't look at him. She laughed a humorless laugh. "Closer? Special? That's rich considering what you did that night."

"What do you mean?" His voice was full of confusion.

She whirled to face him, anger replacing the sadness in her chest. "Don't pretend you don't know, Upton. It's not becoming."

"I thought I missed our assignation and I apologized for that. I was unavoidably detained, but you said you didn't come so what did it matter?"

"Unavoidably detained?" She snorted. "Is that what you call it?"

He scrubbed a hand through his hair, obviously frustrated. "What else should I call it? I spent the night locked in the blasted wine cellar, attempting to break down the bloody door and hoping you wouldn't hate me forever."

His use of such profanity shocked her. She snapped up her head to look him in the eye and searched his face. "Wine cellar? What are you talking about?"

He rubbed the back of his neck and paced to the windows. "I went to the cellar to get a bottle of wine for us.

While I was there, someone clubbed me over the back of the head and the next thing I knew, I woke up with a hell of a lump on my skull and no way to get out. I nearly tore off my arm trying to break down that door."

Jane sat down hard, her skirts whooshing around her. She rubbed a fingertip between her eyes. "Wine cellar? You weren't in the wine cellar."

"Yes, I was. God knows I wish I wasn't."

She crossed her arms tightly over her middle. "No. You were in your room. I saw you."

"What?"

"You were there. I saw you."

"You said you didn't come."

Tears stung the backs of her eyes. "I lied. I came. Only I was nearly half an hour late. But by the time I arrived you were . . ." She studied her slippers where they rested on the carpet, Verges snuggled up next to her foot.

"I was what?"

Jane closed her eyes briefly. "You were making love to Mrs. Langford."

"What!" Garrett's face went ashen pale. "Mrs. Langford was there? In my room that night?"

"Yes. I *saw* you, the two of you."

Garrett knelt in front of her. He grabbed her hand. "Think hard, Jane, think. What exactly did you see? I wasn't there that night. I swear it. Someone locked me in the wine cellar."

Jane searched her memory. What exactly *had* she seen? "I saw . . . I saw Mrs. Langford standing near your bed and you . . . or someone . . . kissing her. I only saw the back of his head. He looked like you, tall, dark-haired, and he was in your room."

Garrett's face was grim. He cursed under his breath. "Isabella's footman is tall and has dark hair. He's not un-like me physically."

"But how did she know? How would she have known we planned to—"

"I don't know. But I bloody well intend to find out."

Jane cupped her hand over her mouth. She was going to be sick. "You're betrothed to her."

"We haven't announced our betrothal yet, but this changes everything. Besides, you must know, I never would have offered for her if it wasn't for—"

"What? What does she have over you, Garrett? Lucy seems to think she's forcing you somehow."

"No. Not that. I wouldn't allow that. She . . . showed me a letter. But it doesn't matter. I must speak to Isabella. If she did what we think she did, it is beyond the pale."

"What letter?"

Garrett took a deep breath. "In Spain. Harold Langford. You asked me once if I was there when he died. I was. In fact . . ." Garrett hung his head. "He died for me."

Jane grabbed his hand and squeezed it. "Tell me. What happened?"

Garrett moved into the seat next to her, his hands clasped in his lap. He took a deep breath and recounted the same story he'd once told Isabella.

When he'd finished, Jane set a trembling hand on his. "I'm sorry, Garrett. So sorry."

He stared at her, unseeing. "I relive that moment every night in my dreams."

"It must be hell for you." She rubbed her hand against his. "But you have to know that Captain Langford made that choice. He wanted you to live."

"That doesn't make the guilt go away. In the dreams, I try to make it right. I attempt to save him, push him away, tell him no. Harold had two children. He had a wife. Isabella deserved better than to have the father of her children die for me."

"You've been taking care of her, haven't you, Garrett?"

He nodded, once. "It's the least I could do . . . for Harold and the children."

Jane's heart ached for him. If only Isabella Langford deserved him. "Why do you think Mrs. Langford did what she did at the party?"

Garrett searched her face. "I think she was jealous of you, Jane. She'd obviously decided before she came that she wanted a proposal from me. I told her no. I wasn't willing to do it." He hung his head again. "Until she showed me the letter."

"What does the letter say?"

Garrett rubbed a knuckle across his forehead. "It's from Harold. He wanted me to take care of Isabella and their children. He asked me to. How could I refuse? I owe the man my *life*."

Jane took a shaky breath. "I cannot imagine how difficult this must be for you."

He shook his head. "It's not just the letter. Isabella told me . . . she's with child. Now I suspect her footman may be the father."

Jane gasped.

"I must go see her. I must ask her what she's done, get her to admit her guilt." Garrett turned and looked Jane in the eye. "I have to know something, Jane. Could there ever be a future between you and me?"

# CHAPTER FORTY

The sharp raps on Jane's bedchamber door tore her from her sleep. She blinked open one eye. Estimating by the amount of sunlight streaking through the window, it was, regrettably, morning, far too early to rise. She'd been up all night piecing together everything that had happened.

Isabella Langford was absolutely dreadful. What sort of a woman did things like tampering with saddles and conking people over the head with wine bottles? Then to stage a scene like the one she had in Garrett's room. With her own *servant*? It was positively revolting. Now Garrett was betrothed to that hideous woman, and she was increasing with another man's child.

Garrett's sense of honor ran deep, Jane knew, but deep enough to marry a woman like Isabella? She doubted it. She also doubted Isabella would admit to the things she'd done, and there was no way to prove any of them.

Garrett intended to confront Isabella, but that was between them. What Jane couldn't stop thinking about was his question to her. Could they have a future together?

Could they? She'd spent the night contemplating that question and still didn't have an answer.

Another sharp rap sounded at her door, pulling Jane from her thoughts.

"Who is it?" she called.

"Your mother!"

Jane groaned and pulled the pillow over her head. Mama knew better than to bother her at such an ungodly hour. If she was rapping on Jane's door this early, it wasn't going to be good.

"Come in," Jane managed to reply, though her words were horribly garbled by the pillow.

Her mother marched into the room. Jane dragged the pillow from her face and blinked one bleary eye.

"Miss?" Her mother crossed her arms over her chest. Another bad sign.

"Yes?" Jane stuffed the pillow behind her head and managed to sit up.

"Did you do something you ought not at the wedding house party?"

Jane blinked. Panic rose within her. Stalling was the best tactic. "Pardon?"

"Lady Elrod just left. She said she was distressed to report she'd heard some unsavory gossip about your behavior at the house party."

"What in the world is Lady Elrod doing paying calls at this time of day? It isn't even noon, is it?" More stalling. Well done.

"It *is* nearly noon, young lady, and that is not the point. Were you or were you not gallivanting about the corridors of the Morelands' estate in the middle of the night in your dressing gown?"

"Gallivanting? I'm not even certain how one goes about gallivanting, Mama."

Her mother stamped her foot. "Answer me, Jane!"

Jane rubbed her sweaty palms against the bedsheets. "I'm trying to answer you. I don't know what you are implying."

"Lady Elrod informed me there is a rumor that you were seen in the bachelor wing of the house far past a decent hour wearing only your dressing gown and night rail."

It was her chemise, actually. "I'd like to know how Lady Elrod knows anything about it," Jane replied. "She wasn't even invited to the house party."

"Jane, I'm not going to ask you again. Is there any truth to this rumor?"

Jane took a deep breath. She had two choices. She could admit that she had, indeed, been gallivanting about in her dressing gown, which might give her mother an apoplectic fit. Or she could deny she had been gallivanting about in her dressing gown, which she doubted her mother would believe at the moment. The latter might convince her mother to leave her alone, temporarily at least, until more gossip reached her ears. But the former might cause her mother to realize that the scandal was well on its way to ruining Jane's reputation, and that alone would be reason enough to keep Jane from attending any of the Season's events. Oh, yes. That was the obvious choice, then.

"Yes, Mama," Jane said with a nod. "I *was* gallivanting about in the middle of the night wearing nothing other than my night rail and dressing gown." It probably wasn't prudent to mention the chemise.

Her mother gasped. Her hands fell to her sides. "You were not!"

Jane winced. "You asked and I told you the truth. What did you want me to say?"

"I wanted you to say it was a complete fabrication."

Jane concentrated on picking lint off the coverlet. "I'm sorry, Mama, but it's true."

Her mother paced in front of the large window that looked down over the gardens in the back of the town house. She wrung her hands. "What are we to do?"

"What is there to do?" Jane offered.

"I cannot face my friends and tell them this isn't true, knowing that it is. You'll be ruined!"

Jane settled back into the pillows. "I doubt there's much to be done other than my forgoing social events for the foreseeable future. I'll just remain here and read. A pity."

Her mother stopped pacing, put her hands on her hips, and glared at her. "No you don't. You're not going to get away with this. Your chaperone will be held accountable for this. Where was Mrs. Bunbury when you were gallivanting about in the middle of the night?"

"I'm certain she was asleep, poor woman." Jane's fingers itched to pick up the book she'd left off reading last night.

Hortense Lowndes's voice simmered with outrage. "If your reputation is ruined, she'll never find work in this town again. I demand to see Mrs. Bunbury immediately!"

# CHAPTER FORTY-ONE

How Jane managed to sneak out of her town house and make it to Lucy's, she would never know. It was a miracle as far as Jane was concerned. After she'd convinced her mother she would have to write Mrs. Bunbury a note and ask the woman to pay them a visit as soon as she was feeling up to it, Jane had slipped out of the back door. She scurried past the mews, nodding to Mrs. Cat, and managed to hire a hack near the corner to take her the several streets to Lucy's town house.

Once she arrived on Lucy's doorstep, Jane rapped on the huge black-lacquered door. The duke's butler, Hughes, soon answered it.

"I've come to call on Her Grace," Jane announced.

The butler gave her a condemning glare, but ushered her into the blue salon at the front of the house before going to alert his mistress that she had a visitor. Jane paced while she waited for Lucy.

"Jane, dear, what is it?" Lucy asked as she hurried into the room moments later.

"Lucy, it's terrible. Mama found out about the scandal and now she's demanding to confront Mrs. Bunbury. What shall we do?"

Lucy merely nodded. "How did she find out?"

"Apparently, Lady Elrod told her," Jane replied.

Lucy's pretty face crumpled into a scowl. "What does Lady Elrod know about it?"

Jane tossed her hands in the air. "It doesn't matter. The fact is, Mama knows and she's incensed. She says she plans to ensure Mrs. Bunbury doesn't work in this town again. She refuses to give her a good reference."

Lucy clucked her tongue. "Not much of a threat, dear."

Jane shook her head. "Also, not the point. Mama demands to see her."

Lucy pursed her lips. "Well, that's not possible."

Jane struggled to keep from raising her voice. "Of course it's not possible. The question is, what are we going to *do*?"

Lucy shrugged one shoulder. "Stall her."

"The time for stalling is over, Lucy. Mama is beside herself. I've never seen her so angry. I managed to tell her that I had to write to Mrs. Bunbury and ask her to pay us a call. Then I came here, but Mama won't believe me for much longer. If I don't produce Mrs. Bunbury soon, she'll know it's all a ruse."

Lucy tapped a finger against her cheek. "It seems we have only two choices."

"And they are?"

"To produce Mrs. Bunbury or admit she doesn't exist."

Jane pinched the bridge of her nose. "Heaven help me. Which of those two do you suggest?"

"Let me think on it a bit. Don't worry, dear. We'll sort it out. Perhaps Mrs. Bunbury can die in a freak accident. Or leave suddenly for France."

Jane ignored her friend's prattling. She had something

even more pressing on her mind. "There's something else I need to tell you, Lucy. Something I should have told you long before now." Jane bit her lip. "It's about Garrett."

Lucy raised both brows. "You're calling him Garrett now?"

"Yes."

"Oh, this is serious."

"I went to his town house alone yesterday." She paused. "Why didn't you tell me he had a giant library?"

"If you think that's giant, you should see the one at his country estate. What were you doing at Garrett's town house?"

"He invited me."

"Invited you?"

"Yes, to borrow a book and I—I wanted to see him, too, if I'm being honest. Oh, Lucy, you won't believe it." She pressed her hands to her cheeks.

"Believe what, dear?"

"I think you need to sit."

Eyeing Jane carefully, Lucy sat.

Jane spent the next twenty minutes telling Lucy every single sordid thing that had happened between her and Garrett. Well, not *every* sordid thing. She left out the more private details, but shared enough for Lucy to get the essence. Afterward, Jane dropped her head into her hands. "Lucy, what am I to do?"

"This is not surprising to me in the least," Lucy said.

"It's not?"

"I'm not surprised you and Garrett have shared a *tendre* for each other. I thought as much during the house party. That's why Cass and I did what we did."

Jane groaned. "But you didn't know for certain."

"True. I only had my suspicions. I admit, those often get me into more trouble than they should. At any rate,

I agree with you that Mrs. Langford is behind whoever locked Garrett in the wine cellar."

"He says he's going to confront her about it, but he's already committed to marrying her. Apparently, he did so because of a letter."

"A letter?"

"Yes, from Harold Langford. Captain Langford asked Garrett to take care of Isabella if anything happened to him."

"Why would Garrett do that?"

Jane tugged at her sleeve. "Because Harold Langford took a bullet that would have ended Garrett's life. The letter means a great deal to him."

"I've always known Garrett feels terribly guilty over something that happened in Spain, though he's never told me what that was," Lucy said. "I think his guilt is severely clouding his judgment. Captain Langford couldn't possibly have known he would die in that fashion. We must find out more about this. I have a feeling Mrs. Langford is behind that letter too."

Jane nodded. "I don't doubt it, but how could we ever prove such a thing?"

Lucy tapped her cheek again. "We must see the letter for ourselves. Did you borrow your book?"

"No. I didn't find it and then Garrett told me the story about Isabella and the wine cellar and I completely forgot about the book. He did say I could come back whenever I wished, however."

Lucy smiled slyly. "That's perfect. Return to Garrett's house to borrow that book, and while you're there, look for the letter."

Jane gasped. "I can't do that."

"Whyever not?"

"You want me to root around in his private things?"

Lucy nodded. "Yes, exactly."

"I can't do that, Lucy."

"I'd do it. Be bold."

Jane groaned.

Lucy patted her shoulder. "Think of it this way, dear, what would Lucy Hunt do?"

Jane pressed her palm to her forehead. "She'd go to Garrett's town house and search for that letter."

# CHAPTER FORTY-TWO

Garrett had gone straight to Isabella's town house as soon as the hour had been decent. She wasn't in, or so the butler had said. Garrett had left more frustrated than before. He wanted to confront her, to ask her why she'd done what she'd done. How had she known he and Jane were planning to meet in his room that night?

After his talk with Jane yesterday, he had more to think about than ever. Jane had not answered him when he'd asked if they could have a future together. He didn't blame her. He'd made a complete mess of things. He'd proposed to her too late at the house party, and now he was asking her about their future while he was supposed to become formally betrothed to another lady. The wrong lady. A lady who would apparently stop at nothing to get what she wanted. How the devil had things got so complicated in such a sort amount of time?

"Sir, would you like to go home?" the coachman said as Garrett reentered the vehicle.

"No, John. Take me to my mother's."

Ten minutes later, Garrett was sitting in his mother's drawing room. Mary Upton came pattering in, a wide smile on her face. "To what do I owe the pleasure?"

"I thought I'd stop and see how you are."

His mother arched a dark brow. "I think the more important question is, how are *you*, my son?"

Garrett wrinkled his brow. "What do you mean?"

"I may be getting on in years but I still keep abreast of the latest news. There is quite a lot of talk about you lately."

"Talk? About *me*?"

"You, the house party, Miss Lowndes?" His mother dragged out the last two words in a dramatic fashion.

"What about Miss Lowndes?"

"Seems the gossips are saying she was spotted in her night rail near the bachelors' quarters the night of the earl's wedding."

Garrett struggled to keep his face blank. His mother eyed him carefully. "You wouldn't know anything about that, would you?"

He didn't meet his mother's gaze. "Why would you think I'd know about that?"

His mother had picked up her stitching, one of her favorite pastimes. She shrugged one shoulder. "Oh, I don't know. Perhaps because I heard that you and Jane looked quite enamored with each other when you danced on the night of the wedding."

Garrett widened his eyes. "Enamored?"

His mother shrugged the other shoulder. "Yes, and what's this about you going and getting yourself engaged to Isabella Langford?"

"It's not yet official."

"I'm glad to hear that."

His head snapped up. "Mother?"

His mother kept her eyes trained on the embroidery

in front of her. "I don't care for that woman, Garrett. Jane Lowndes, however, would make a fine wife. I've always liked her quite a lot."

"Mother! I never knew—"

"I know. I know. I tend to keep my mouth shut and allow you to go about your business without any unnecessary interference from me. You are a grown man, after all. But you're still my son, and if I see you making a mistake, it seems I can't keep quiet. Marrying Isabella Langford would be a mistake. Not to mention I've never noticed you to be a bit infatuated with the woman."

"I'm not," he admitted. "But it's not quite that simple."

"Oh?"

Garrett laughed. "You're completely transparent, Mother. I can tell how desperately you want to ask me why."

Her eyes sparkled with mirth. "Well, now that the question is on the table."

Garrett took a deep breath. "Harold Langford . . . he . . ." Garrett closed his eyes.

"He what, dear?"

"He died saving my life." There it was. It had been a secret he'd carried so long and now he'd told two different women in as many days. He had to admit to himself, it felt good to say it, to finally have it off his chest.

His voice quavering slightly, Garrett recounted the tale of the day Harold died. She listened intently with tears in her eyes before setting her embroidery aside, leaning over, and squeezing his hand. "I'm sorry, Garrett. Sorry for you and sorry for Harold Langford and his family. But you didn't make the decision that day, he did."

"You can't know the guilt I feel, have always felt."

"Guilt is a terrible master. I know because your father carried it with him."

Garrett shook his head. "Father?"

"Yes.

"Your father cried like a babe the day your cousin Ralph died. He was devastated for his brother and for Lucy and her mother."

"But Father couldn't have done anything to save Ralph."

"That's true, but it didn't stop him from feeling guilt. And don't think I don't know you've carried a bit of that same guilt, too, over your cousin's death."

Garrett hung his head. "I have."

"If you weren't alive, Garrett, there would be no one to take over the earldom. Think of that. The estate would be passed to a distant relative. I have no doubt Ralph would have grown into a fine earl. But I know there could be no better man to take over the responsibility of the Upbridge estates and titles than you, my son. Your father felt the same way. He told me."

"He told you?"

"Yes. He was proud of you, Garrett. So very, very proud."

A lump formed in Garrett's throat. He squeezed his mother's hand. "Thank you for that, Mother."

"I love you, Garrett. I know you'll do the right thing. You always do."

No drinking today. Garrett waved away the footman who hovered near him. He was back at Brooks's, but he needed his wits about him. He intended to confront Isabella this afternoon.

Adam and Collin Hunt were playing cards nearby. Since their brother had been named a duke, the Hunt brothers had come up in Society. Garrett was about to go greet them when Claringdon and Cavendish came strolling through the door.

"Upton," Claringdon said. "Fancy seeing you here again. We were just meeting my brothers."

"And I'm happy for any excuse to drink in the middle of the day," Cavendish added.

"Good to see you both," Garrett replied.

"Come join us," Claringdon insisted.

Garrett made his way over to the card table where the other men were settling. He greeted the Hunt brothers, who resumed their play, while Claringdon, Cavendish, and Garrett sat together in a small group of large leather chairs.

"You look as if you have something on your mind, Upton," Rafe said. "Not a happy bridegroom?"

Garrett scrubbed his hand across his face. "That is an understatement."

Claringdon's eyebrows shot up. "Trouble already?"

"It was always trouble," Garrett replied.

Claringdon waved down a footman and ordered three brandies.

"The last thing I need is a drink. I have important decisions to make," Garrett said.

"On the contrary, sounds as if the *first* thing you need is a drink," Rafe replied, with a wicked grin.

"Care to tell us the trouble?" Claringdon asked.

"Suffice it to say I owe someone an enormous favor and the price may be entirely too great to pay," Garrett replied.

Claringdon steepled his fingers. "You're talking about Harold Langford."

Garrett eyed the duke carefully. "You know?"

Claringdon nodded. "I know what happened in Spain. Langford took a bullet for you. But it was no more than what any of us would have done for each other, you must know that."

Garrett briefly closed his eyes. "You cannot know the guilt I feel."

"You're right. I cannot. I do know that you're directing your guilt into something useful by helping Swifdon champion the soldiers' bill. You cannot pay with the rest of your life for something that was neither your fault, nor your choice."

Garrett took a glass from the footman. "Easy for you to say, Claringdon. You don't have another man's blood on your hands."

"I do." Rafe Cavendish's two words fell like lead to the rug.

Both men's heads turned to face him.

"I have another man's blood on my hands," Cavendish continued, staring unseeing into the depths of his newly acquired brandy glass. "I know exactly what the guilt feels like."

Upton shook his head. "No, Cavendish. Everyone knew Donald Swift never should have gone to France. He volunteered and there was no stopping him. He said as much in his letter to Julian. You did your best to protect him."

"I failed, and an earl died because of me. The man had no children, no heirs." Cavendish's voice was heavy.

"He had Julian. Julian is the earl now."

"You think I shouldn't feel guilt? Is that what you're telling me, Upton?" Cavendish asked, a wry smile on his face.

Garrett shook his head again. "No one blames you. No doubt Donald remained alive as long as he did because you were with him."

Rafe tossed back his drink. "Perhaps, but the guilt gnaws at my soul." He set his empty glass on the table and looked Garrett in the eye. "The same as it does yours."

Garrett sucked air through his nostrils. "I understand, Cavendish. I do. But you shouldn't blame yourself."

Cavendish cocked a brow. "Perhaps you should take your own advice, Upton."

Garrett strode down the club's stone steps minutes later. He'd had that drink, after all, and another. What Rafe Cavendish said resonated. Finally. Through all the years and all the nightmares. All the people telling him it wasn't his fault when he'd believed damn well it was . . . he finally felt . . . free. Damn Harold Langford for taking that bullet. Damn Isabella Langford for being conniving. And damn him for allowing his guilt to push him in a direction he had no business going.

It was true. No one blamed Cavendish for Donald Swift's death. The earl had recklessly volunteered to go on a mission to France for the War Office under the guise of diplomacy. Rafe was one of the best spies the War Office had. Donald gave them away. It had ended in their capture and torture. Rafe barely escaped with his life and had spent the past six months slowly recuperating. Rafe was alive in *spite* of Donald, not the other way around. But Rafe felt guilt. He was the only other man who understood, the only other person who could absolve Garrett.

"Perhaps you should take your own advice." Garrett repeated Cavendish's words. The captain was damn right. Garrett could no longer live in the past, blaming himself for the actions of another man.

After ten years of allowing guilt to ride him, control him, today he was done. Harold Langford had chosen Isabella. Harold Langford had chosen to throw himself in front of that bullet.

Garrett Upton had his own choices to make.

# CHAPTER FORTY-THREE

Garrett's invitation to come back to the library whenever she liked was an enticement Jane couldn't resist. If looking about Upton's town house led to the opportunity to search for a certain letter, so be it. Of course, she'd pointed out to Lucy that she might just *ask* Garrett for the letter, but nothing was simple when Lucy Hunt was involved.

Jane had come straight from Lucy's house, in fact. Less chance to encounter her mother and be forced to explain why Mrs. Bunbury hadn't yet materialized. One problem at a time.

Cartwright and the dogs greeted Jane at the door again and ushered her into the library. "Mr. Upton is not here at present," the butler intoned. "We expect him back at any moment."

"Thank you. I'll be happily entertained by the books," she replied.

Cartwright served the tea tray and Jane partook of a teacake. She waited twenty entire minutes before tiptoeing to the door—tiptoeing seemed appropriate when one was engaged in clandestine activities—and peeking into the corridor. The dogs, who remained at her heels, peeked out too.

"The study is just down the way, is it not?" she asked the dogs, who merely wagged their tails in reply.

She took a deep breath. *Be bold*. Jane straightened her shoulders, closed her eyes briefly, darted out of the room, down the corridor, and slipped into the far door on the right.

The dogs ran with her, and moments later, all three were happily behind the closed study door.

"Thank you for not barking," she said to them. "That was well done of you."

The dogs each took a turn getting a pat on the head. Then Jane glanced around the study. Decorated in masculine hues of dark blue, it smelled vaguely like Upton. She took a deep breath to savor the scent. A large mahogany desk sat in front of a bay window, two large leather chairs in front of it. A few dark wooden bookshelves lined the walls—more books!—and a large comfortable-looking chair rested on a round rug in front of the fireplace. A cozy and useful space.

She hurried to the desk and scanned the tabletop. It was neatly arranged. A pile of what appeared to be out-going mail, an inkwell, several quills, a large square glass paperweight. Nothing appeared to be correspondence, however. She tiptoed again, this time around to take a seat in the large chair. She closed her eyes. The lemony scent of furniture polish and a hint of ink filled her nostrils. It felt like Upton in here. Peaceful, calm, sensible. She suddenly missed him.

She took another deep breath. "I am not proud of myself for doing this," she announced to the dogs. "I assure you, I'm not usually the type of person who sneaks about and pries into other people's belongings."

The dogs looked at her with wide, trusting eyes.

"I'm doing this for you too. You don't want that horrible woman as your stepmother."

This elicited more wagging of tails.

Jane turned her attention back to the desk. There were three drawers on each side and one in the middle. She'd just take a quick peek inside each. "Please let it be here," she whispered.

She slowly slid the middle drawer out first. More quills. A tray of sand. A seal and some wax. No letters. No paper at all.

She closed the drawer and pulled open another on the bottom right. A quick perusal of the large stack of important-looking papers inside told Jane it was mostly contracts and estate-related paperwork.

She pulled out the next drawer and the next. They were neatly arranged, but did not contain a letter from Harold Langford.

She chewed on her bottom lip. What if she didn't find it? But then, what was she planning to do with it if she did find it? She took another deep breath. *Be bold.*

She pulled open the bottom drawer on the left. A box sat in the center of the drawer, full of what appeared to be . . . letters. Trembling, she pulled the box from the drawer and placed it on the desktop. The letters stood on their sides, stacked together.

Jane pulled out the first few. Missives from Aunt Mary, one or two from Lucy, one from Lord Berkeley. She slid them back into place and took out the next set. More from Aunt Mary, half a dozen from other friends, none from Harold Langford.

Jane scanned the room. Upton might return at any moment, or a servant might venture in to clean or something. She didn't have time to rummage through all of the letters.

Something told her the one she was looking for wouldn't be like the others, wouldn't be with less important correspondence. Upton would do something special with it, because of what it meant to him. Using both hands, she lifted the entire group of letters, and set them carefully in a large stack on the desktop. Then, she peered into the bottom of the box.

A single letter was there. Underneath them all. Not stacked like the others. Hidden away. With a hand that continued to shake, she pulled out the lone letter. She unfolded it, holding her breath.

Harold Langford's name was scrolled across the top with a date from nearly ten years ago. She slid it onto the desktop and expelled her pent-up breath.

She'd done it. She'd found it. Now she needed to get out of here.

Closing her eyes and briefly saying a prayer, just in case there was a heaven, Jane gathered up the large stack of letters, placed them back in the box, and replaced it in the drawer. She shut the drawer, grabbed the letter, and jumped to her feet.

The door to the room cracked open and Isabella Langford sauntered in.

The beautiful widow narrowed her eyes and put her hands on her hips. "Miss Lowndes, explain yourself. What are you doing in my future husband's study?"

# CHAPTER FORTY-FOUR

Garrett bounded up the stairs to his town house and flung open the door. He'd sent Isabella a note earlier, asking her to meet him here. Unfortunately, he'd been detained at his solicitor's office.

He didn't slow as he made his way toward his study, the dogs jumping at his heels. "Cartwright, is Mrs. Langford in the study?"

"She is, sir."

"Has she been waiting long?"

"Not very, sir. And, sir?" The butler cleared his throat.

Garrett stopped and turned to face him. "Yes?"

"Miss Lowndes just left."

Garrett blinked. "Miss Lowndes was here?"

"Yes, sir. She came to have a look at the library again."

"Ah, I trust you made her comfortable."

"I did, sir. Tea and cakes were served immediately upon her arrival."

Garrett had to smile. He was sorry he'd missed Jane, but it was probably for the best. What he had to say to Isabella needed to be said in private.

"Thank you, Cartwright. That will be all for now."

Garrett continued his brisk pace down the corridor to the study, opened the door, and marched inside. Isabella sat on the settee, a cup of tea suspended in her hand. The moment she saw Garrett, she turned to face him. "There you are. I've been waiting."

"No teacakes?"

"I never eat those things. They're bad for my figure."

They were quite good for Miss Lowndes's figure. A devilish grin spread across his face. "I see."

"Why was Jane Lowndes in this house when I arrived?" Isabella demanded.

Garrett managed to keep his voice steady. "Miss Lowndes is welcome to use my library at any time."

"That will change once we're married."

"No it won't."

Isabella's jaw tightened but her voice softened and she pretended to smile. "We can discuss it later, after the wedding."

"There's not going to be any wedding, Isabella."

Her teacup clattered to the saucer. "Not going to be—" A questioning look spread across her face, part fear, part confusion. "Are you saying you'd prefer to marry by special license? That can easily be arranged. I know someone who—"

"No, that's not what I mean." Garrett took a deep breath. "I have made mistakes in my life. More than one. Some more grievous than others. I'll never forget the day Harold died, and I will always honor him and thank him. I can never repay him. It's not possible."

Isabella's brows had snapped together over her pale,

green eyes. She watched him carefully. "Yes, you can repay him. You can repay him by marrying me."

"Our marriage will not bring back Harold. I refuse to compound one mistake with another. We'd make each other miserable, Isabella. We cannot marry."

Her mouth dropped open. "You cannot be serious. You're tossing me over?"

"We haven't formally announced our engagement. There will be little talk."

"But . . . I've begun planning. I—"

"I'm sorry, Isabella. Don't worry. I'll ensure you and the children are looked after financially until the bill passes in Parliament."

"The bill?"

"The one Swifdon and Claringdon are sponsoring to ensure the families of the dead and wounded are provided for."

Her mouth turned into a white line. "A pension from the government cannot keep me in the manner to which I've grown accustomed. How can you do this? What about Harold's letter? What about the baby?"

"The baby belongs to your footman, Boris, doesn't it? He should do the honorable thing and marry you."

Her face paled to match her lips. "You expect me to marry a footman?" She sneered. Her eyes narrowed to tiny slits. "Harold would turn over in his grave if he knew you were abandoning us."

Her words hurt, as Garrett had expected them to, but he no longer felt the wrenching guilt. "If you ever need anything monetarily for the children, all you need do is send me a note."

"That's it? You plan to foist us off with a promise based on a note? You have no honor, Garrett Upton!"

Garrett winced and clenched his jaw. It was the most hurtful thing she could say to him. He'd also been prepared for that. "I shall always do right by you and by the children, for Harold's sake. You have my word."

"Your word is as good as dirt," she spat.

"I'm sorry you feel that way. But it does not change my mind."

She set down her teacup and stood. Moving toward him, she held out her palms in supplication. "Please, Garrett." Her voice had turned wheedling. "Please marry me."

"I can't, Isabella. I do not trust you. I also happen to be in love with someone else."

Her eyes rounded in shock. "Don't *trust* me? Why in heaven's name not?"

"Don't feign innocence. I know you had Boris tamper with Miss Lowndes's saddle the day you raced each other. I also know he hit me over the head with a bottle of wine and locked me in the wine cellar the night of the wedding."

She looked away. "I have no idea what you're talking about."

"Don't you? What if I told you Jane *saw* you in my bedchamber that night?"

Her head snapped up and her eyes flared. "It's her, isn't it? She's the one you think you're in love with. What are you saying? That your precious, virginal Miss Lowndes was in your bedchamber that night? What would the *ton* have to say about that?"

He clenched his fists at his sides. "Isabella, if you tell anyone about this—"

"You'll what?"

"I'll tell them about everything you've done, including the fact that you're breeding."

"You have no proof about anything I've done. If you refuse to marry me, I'm already ruined, but the damage to your precious Miss Lowndes's reputation will be done by then. There are already rumors swirling about her behavior at the party. One word from me, someone who was actually there, and she will be ruined completely."

"You wouldn't dare."

"Try me."

A muscle ticked in his jaw. "What do you want?"

"I want you to marry me."

"I refuse to be manipulated, Isabella."

"Even for your precious little bluestocking? She won't be received in any decent drawing room in London by the time I'm through telling my tale."

"Not if I marry her first."

# CHAPTER FORTY-FIVE

If Hughes, the butler, thought it was odd that Miss Jane Lowndes kept appearing at the Duke of Claringdon's doorstep at all hours of the day without an escort, he did not acknowledge his concern, as a good duke's butler should. With Lucy as the duchess, the man was assured a lifetime of odd happenings in his household.

This time, he ushered Jane into the blue salon with barely a lift of his haughty brow. Lucy came in moments later.

"Well." Lucy rushed over and sat next to Jane on the settee. "What happened?"

Jane couldn't hide her smile. "I just came from Garrett's town house."

"And?" Lucy searched her face.

"And I found it!"

Lucy clapped her hands with glee. "Let me see it."

Jane tugged open the drawstring to her reticule and pulled out the crumpled letter. "I barely made it out of there," she said in a rush, excitement making her words tumble over themselves. "Isabella came in and found me in the study."

Lucy scrunched her nose as if she smelled something awful. "What was Isabella doing there?"

"She said she came to speak with her future husband. I wanted to retch. I made a quick excuse as to why I was standing behind his desk when she saw me and then I left immediately."

Lucy covered her laughing mouth with her hand. "You did not. What did you say?"

Jane leaned in. "I told her I was playing a game of hide-and-seek with the dogs."

"No!"

"Yes."

"Did she believe you?" Lucy's eyes danced with mischief.

"What do I care? I slipped the letter into my reticule and left, but not before informing her that Garrett had told me I might have the use of his library whenever I like. I couldn't resist." She slapped her knee to punctuate her words. "That harlot."

"That's perfect. Did she have an apoplectic fit?"

"She gave me a stare that could turn water into ice. I believe she reminds me of Medusa."

"She reminds me a great deal of Medusa. Though admittedly her hair is more fetching than snakes." Lucy waved a hand in the air. "Enough about her. Show me the letter. Have you read it?"

"Not yet. I haven't had a chance. I was so nervous. I'm still shaking." Jane held out her trembling hand for her friend's inspection.

"You did an excellent job. Mission accomplished. Now, let's see the letter."

Sitting side by side, the two unfolded the letter and

both scanned the page. Lucy sucked in her breath. Jane gasped. They turned to look at each other.

"So sad," Lucy said, shaking her head.

"It is sad, but I don't believe for one moment that Harold Langford actually wrote this." Jane jabbed a finger at the paper.

"I don't either," Lucy agreed. "But how would we prove such a thing?" She tapped her finger against her cheek.

"If I knew what Mrs. Langford's handwriting looked like, I could compare the two. I'm certain she disguised it."

A slow smile spread across Lucy's face. "Aren't you the expert in that particular field?"

Jane frowned. "Yes, but how can we get a writing sample from Isabella?"

Lucy snapped her fingers. "I have one!"

"What?"

"I have one. She wrote to thank me for my kindness at the house party." Lucy rolled her eyes.

"Ugh. She did?"

"Yes. Obsequious, wasn't it? I get that quite a lot now that I'm a duchess."

"Where is her letter?" Jane asked frantically.

"I'll be right back." Lucy hurried out of the room while Jane struggled to remain calm. She would love to prove something Mrs. Langford had done wrong. Make her stand accountable for just *one* of her devious schemes.

Lucy returned waving the other letter in her hand. "Here it is."

Jane took the two letters and hurried to the writing desk, where she flattened them side by side. She studied the writing of first one, then the other.

"Well?" Lucy prodded, impatiently tapping her slipper.

"Give me a moment." Jane narrowed her eyes. "It's definitely not Isabella's handwriting on this letter from Harold."

"But . . . ?"

"Look, here, the line of the *l* is quite similar. The *a* also looks suspiciously like hers. She may have copied the words from letters from Harold, but she cannot entirely disguise her own penmanship." Jane continued to study the letters intently. "The *h*. There's an extra tail on the top. Just like hers."

Lucy peered over Jane's shoulder. "So you *do* think it's a forgery?"

Jane lifted her gaze and pushed up her spectacles. "Yes. She forged this letter."

Lucy pressed her lips together and crossed her arms over her chest. "That evil minx. How dare she try to play on my poor cousin's sense of guilt?"

"Your cousin can take care of himself," Jane replied. "But I refuse to allow her to get away with this." Jane stood and straightened her shoulders. "I intend to do something about it."

"What are you going to do, Jane?" Lucy asked.

"I'm going to confront Medusa. And make her eat this letter." She waved the fake letter in the air.

"And then?" Lucy prodded.

"Then I'm going to ask your cousin to marry me."

Lucy's mouth fell open. "Do you mean it?"

Jane nodded slowly and took a deep breath. "Yes. Marriage has always frightened me. I never wanted to answer to a man. But Garrett is my equal. He'll be my partner. He's always treated me with kindness and respect. I don't fear marriage any longer, Lucy. I *covet* it. How do you like that?"

Lucy's eyes shimmered with tears. "Oh, Janie. I'm so happy for you."

Jane shot Lucy an impudent look over her shoulder. "First, I need you to help me with the scheme to end all schemes, Your Boldness. It will solve the problem with my mother, my scandal, and Isabella Langford all at once." She waved the fake letter again. "I'm going to need this, and we're going to need Derek's help with something. Something big!"

# CHAPTER FORTY-SIX

"I must say I'm surprised you would come here, Miss Lowndes." Isabella Langford strutted across her purple silk drawing room toward Jane. The room was nearly as garish as the woman herself, with opulent oil paintings and huge palm trees in pots in all four corners. *No accounting for taste.*

Jane had waited in the salon on Charles Street for the better part of an hour before the woman finally deigned to grace her with her company.

Jane straightened her back to compete with Isabella's haughty stature. "Why are you surprised, Mrs. Langford? You haven't known me to back down from a fight before today, have you?"

Isabella shrugged one shoulder. "If you're here to threaten me about—"

"I'm not here to threaten you. I'm here to tell you something."

"What's that?"

Jane crossed her arms over her chest and firmed her jaw. "Leave Garrett Upton alone."

Isabella laughed loud and long. Jane had to fight the urge to cover her ears, the sound was so strident. "You haven't spoken to him recently, have you?"

"What does that have to do with anything?"

"No matter. Suffice it to say the last time I spoke with him, he was suffering from a temporary bout of insanity. But I still intend to have him, Miss Lowndes. Mark my words."

Jane raised her chin. "Don't pretend you love him."

Isabella laughed again, a short bark this time. "Of course I don't love him. Who said anything about love? Love has little place inside a marriage. I never loved Harold either, though the poor sop loved me. He loved me desperately." She sighed.

"You're hideous."

"You're naïve."

"Why do you want to marry Garrett if you don't love him?"

"Good God. You're more naïve than I thought. I'm not certain if he told you, but Garrett's been paying my bills, Miss Lowndes." She gestured to the gaudily decorated room. "Look around you. I've grown quite accustomed to this way of living. Better than any I could have afforded as the wife of a soldier. Harold and I never lived this way."

"So you're using Garrett for money?"

"I quite enjoy living like a countess." Isabella smiled tightly. "Inheriting the title one day also won't be half bad."

"Why don't you just find some other rich man to marry?"

"So easy is it? Is that why *you've* been unsuccessful in the marriage mart?"

Jane clutched her reticule so tightly her knuckles turned white. "I haven't been attempting to marry."

"So you say. It's not as easy as it seems, I assure you. With Garrett, I have the upper hand."

Jane narrowed her eyes on the widow. "The upper hand?"

"Guilt, Miss Lowndes. It's extremely useful."

Jane counted three. She desperately wanted to slap Medusa but that would hardly be helpful. "You mean Garrett's guilt over Harold's death?"

"Of course."

Jane loosened the strings on her reticule. "I know you forged the letter from Harold to Garrett and I can prove it."

If the widow was surprised, her face didn't register it. She looked bored instead. "Really? How can you prove it?"

Jane pulled the letter from the purse. "I compared the letter with your handwriting."

Isabella sneered. "Is that what you were doing in Garrett's study yesterday? Sneaking around stealing letters?"

"Garrett deserves to know the truth."

"Even if you were right, Miss Lowndes, what do you want me to do about it?"

"I want you to admit it."

"Fine, I admit it. Who cares?"

"I care. Garrett cares. I intend to show Garrett the letters and tell him you confessed. He'll never marry you."

A slow smirk spread across the widow's face. "What if I told you he already knows?"

Jane sucked in her breath. "No he doesn't."

"Yes he does. But he'll still marry me. I'm certain of it. I have one final card to play. He's beautiful, my future husband. I'll give him that. Beautiful, but stupid."

"How dare you! You don't even know him. Garrett's far from stupid."

The widow tapped a tapered fingernail against her

chin. "I used to think so too, but now . . . I'm not so cer-tain."

"He already knows you tampered with my saddle the day of the race. He knows you had your footman lock him in the wine cellar."

"Yes, and he knows the letter is a fake. At least he suspects it. But he'll marry me nevertheless. That's how naïve you are, Miss Lowndes. You actually think the truth matters. Besides, what do you care? I thought you believed him to be a reprobate."

"He's not a reprobate. He's intelligent and funny and opinionated. He loves to attend the theater and he's won-derful with his dogs. He's kind to servants and he's good to his mother. He gave me a first edition Mary Woll-stonecraft, and he's allowed your husband's death to make him sick with guilt all these years. He's a strong, good, noble man. You don't deserve him, Isabella."

Another sharp bark of laughter from Isabella. "You *do*?"

"No. I don't deserve him either, but at least I'll spend every day of my life trying."

Isabella's lip curled. "People who fancy themselves in love make me ill."

"Stay away from him." Jane's voice simmered.

Isabella rolled her eyes. "I'm going to have to ask you to leave." She rang for her butler. "Garrett Upton is going to be my husband and I insist that *you* stay away from him."

Jane raised her chin and glowered at Isabella. "What-ever your so-called one final card is, I wish you well, Mrs. Langford, because you're going to have to fight me for him, and I never lose."

# CHAPTER FORTY-SEVEN

Garrett strode into the church. With each step, anger and bile rose in his throat. He was through playing Isabella's games. He'd received a letter from her this morning with a vague threat, demanding he meet her at St. George's at ten o'clock. He was here, but only to tell her once and for all that if she didn't leave him alone, he would have her arrested for every vile thing she'd done.

Isabella Langford was beyond evil. How had Harold, the good man that he was, stood being married to her?

Garrett squinted. The church was dim . . . and empty. Isabella hadn't yet arrived. He'd tried to see Jane last night but her mother had informed him that she was with Lucy. A visit to Lucy's house had revealed that the two women were not at home. No matter. Garrett intended to go straight to Lucy's house this morning after he finished this odious task. He would beg Jane to marry him. No, he would demand it. No, he would ask. She had to say yes, didn't she? She loved him as much as he loved her. He was certain of it.

The door at the side of the altar opened and a bride dressed in white, a veil covering her face, came walking out. The vicar came out, too, dressed in grand vestments. He made his way to the center of the altar.

Garrett sucked in his breath. Isabella had gone too far this time. If she thought he would marry her merely because she'd lured him to a church and arrived wearing a wedding gown, she was sorely mistaken.

Garrett made his way up to the altar. He took a deep breath and glanced at Isabella. He couldn't see her evil face through her veil. "Reverend, you don't understand. I can't—"

"Would you please uncover your bride's face?" the vicar asked.

"I'd rather not," Garrett replied. If the man thought it was odd, so be it.

"I insist upon it, my son," the vicar replied in a firm, steady voice.

Garrett took another deep breath. Very well. He would uncover her face, but that hardly changed the fact that he refused to marry her.

He turned toward her and placed both hands at the bottom of the thick veil. He lifted it slowly, trying to decide how best to handle the next few awkward moments. Finally, he flipped the veil over her head in one swift motion and took a step back.

It wasn't Isabella. It was . . . Jane.

She smiled at him brightly. "Thank you. It was quite hot under there, Upton. I was concerned my spectacles would fog."

Garrett's jaw dropped. "Jane, wha—"

"I forged the letter asking you to meet here today," Jane whispered.

Garrett only had a moment to process that before the door on the side of the altar opened again and his mother,

Daphne Swift, Owen Monroe, Rafe Cavendish, the Hunt brothers, Lucy, and Claringdon all came strolling out.

Jane nodded to the vicar. "Will you please give us a moment, Reverend?"

"Of course." The vicar nodded and moved into the small group of people.

Jane fell to one knee. She clasped Garrett's hand. "Would you do me the honor of marrying me, Upton?"

His face broke into a huge smile. He pulled her back up to her feet, still clasping her hands. "Are you jesting?"

"Of course not. I know Mrs. Langford has threatened to ruin my reputation but, as Lucy says, I can hardly be a scandal if I *marry* the man with whom I was scandalous."

"But—"

"Mother and Father have already approved. They're thrilled actually. They never thought I would marry." She turned toward the door in the altar. "Come out and tell Mr. Upton how thoroughly you approve of him, Mama. I think he needs to hear it."

The door opened and Sir Charles and Lady Lowndes came out. Jane's mother had a wide smile on her face.

"We do. We truly do," Lady Lowndes said.

"It's quite true, young man," Sir Charles agreed.

"I need to give Mrs. Bunbury a raise," Lady Lowndes added.

Jane and Lucy exchanged sly glances just before Jane turned back to Garrett to hide her laughter. "You see? They're thrilled," she whispered. "I hate to please my mother quite this much, but I suppose there can be no help for it."

He squeezed her hand. "Why's that?"

"Because I'm desperately in love with you, Upton. I'm told that when one is desperately in love, one marries, regardless of the title one may acquire in so doing."

"That is true!" Lucy called.

"You're not supposed to be listening, Lucy," Jane called back.

"Oh, quite right. I'm sorry. Carry on."

Garrett swallowed the lump in his throat. He searched Jane's face. This was a great deal to absorb, but he had no doubts. There was only one problem. "As much as I'd like to say yes, we don't have a license."

Jane nodded. "Yes, we do. Derek procured one for us last night. It's extremely convenient to know a duke."

Garrett turned toward Claringdon. "You got us a license?"

"Indeed," came Claringdon's reply. "Deuced awkward to wake the archbishop in the middle of the night, but he appreciated the coin I gave him. You owe me a drink the next time I see you at the club. Several drinks."

Jane smiled a satisfied smile. "See, there? You have no more excuses."

The door to the church opened then and Isabella Langford, wearing all black, came strolling down the center aisle.

She crossed her arms over her chest and tapped her fingers along the opposite arm. "Well, well, well. Isn't this a pretty sight?"

Garrett and Jane turned to face her.

"Isabella?" Garrett's voice was grim.

"Boris has been following you, Garrett. He told me I might find you here this morning," Isabella replied.

"Please leave," Garrett demanded, pointing toward the doors.

"I don't think so, my dear. I have something quite important to say."

"Go ahead and say it," Jane interjected, lifting her chin. "Then get out."

Isabella's eyebrows rose. "Aren't you a brave one, Miss Lowndes?"

Jane straightened her spine. "I told you once, I'm not one to back down from a fight."

Isabella shrugged one shoulder. "Regardless, I doubt very much you'll like what I have to say."

Garrett made a move toward the woman but Jane held his arm. "Let her speak."

Isabella raised her nose in the air. "I'm here before God and man to declare that the groom has impregnated me."

A shocked gasp went through the church. The vicar turned a white that matched his robes.

"That's not true!" Garrett snapped.

"Yes it is. I know it's inconvenient given your marriage plans, darling, but the church cannot possibly marry you, knowing this," Isabella purred.

Jane's hands were clenched into fists at her sides. "Isabella, get out of here. You're a liar and we all know it. You don't love Garrett and he doesn't love you. Stop this madness."

Isabella laughed again, a short bark this time. "I refuse to allow the father of my baby not to own up to his responsibilities."

"I will own up to them!"

Everyone's head swiveled to the left. Boris came marching in. Isabella's face was a study in shock. "Boris, no!"

"Yes," Boris replied. "I've asked you to marry me half a dozen times and you've refused. But I won't allow you to ruin another man's life over a mistake we made together."

"Shut up, you fool. You don't know what you are saying." Isabella's voice was high and strained. Her face was quickly turning a mottled shade of red.

"I know exactly what I'm saying and it's high time I

spoke up." Boris faced Garrett and Jane. "I'm sorry for what I've done, Mr. Upton. Isabella told me she saw the two of you in the upstairs drawing room the night of the masquerade. She asked me to cut the strap on Miss Lowndes's saddle."

Jane shook her head. "I knew it."

Boris nodded guiltily but kept talking. "She also overheard you planning to meet the night of the wedding. She told me to follow you to the wine cellar, Mr. Upton, and to ensure you didn't make it back to your room."

Garrett glared at Isabella.

"Shut up, you imbecile!" Isabella hissed.

Boris turned back toward Isabella. "I'm sorry to have done those things. I did them because I loved you, and I thought you loved me. But now I must make things right." He walked up to Garrett and handed him something.

Garrett clutched the gold pocket watch in his fist.

"I only took it so you'd think one of the Morelands' servants had done it," Boris said. "I'm sorry."

The vicar stepped forward. "Are you certain, young man? You swear you are the father of this woman's unborn baby?"

"Yes, Reverend. I must confess and I have no doubts."

Isabella tore at her hair and ran shrieking from the church. Boris quickly followed her.

"Best of luck with that one," Lucy called after him.

The vicar cleared his throat and nodded toward Garrett. "Well, then, now that that unpleasant business is settled. Do you wish to proceed?"

"Just one more moment, Reverend." Garrett turned back to Jane.

"Jane," Garrett whispered, this time swallowing the

even larger lump in his throat. She'd done all this for him, and she loved him. "Are you sure? Are you certain this is what *you* want?"

She leaned up on her tiptoes and kissed his cheek. "You were right about me, Garrett. I've been hiding behind books all my life. It's high time I became brave enough to take a chance in the real world, in a real story, my own story. I want my happy ending to be with you."

Garrett cupped her cheeks and kissed her. The small crowd behind them cheered. "By all means, my love, let's get married."

# CHAPTER FORTY-EIGHT

Garrett carried her over the threshold of his town house. It was a silly, sentimental thing to do, and Jane adored it. She'd worn her mother's wedding gown, which had made her mother's eyes moist with tears, but Jane was in a hurry to get the uncomfortable thing off . . . for more than one reason.

They'd spent the remainder of the morning and all the afternoon celebrating with their friends at Derek's town house, but now they were home. Alone.

She'd been looking forward to this all day. The butterflies had winged in her middle since she'd first seen Garrett at the church. When he set her down in the marble foyer of his home and tenderly kissed her, her traitorous legs began shaking again.

"I sent a note. The servants have all been dismissed for the evening," he whispered in her ear.

"That's . . . nice." Her voice trembled. Apparently the servants had taken the dogs with them.

Garrett rubbed his thumb along her cheekbone and tipped up her chin. "Don't be nervous, Jane."

"I don't want to be. Truly, I don't."

He nuzzled her ear, and Jane closed her eyes.

"Come upstairs with me," he murmured.

"Yes," she breathed. Oh, yes. How she wanted to make love to this man.

He led her by the hand to his bedchamber. The room was sparse and masculine and very Upton. Two candles in a silver brace flickered atop the mantelpiece, casting the room in a shadowy glow. A large bed against the back wall was covered in silken, emerald sheets. A dark cherrywood wardrobe, a matching writing desk, a portrait of a black-and-white spaniel on the wall.

"That's not Dogberry or Verges, is it?" Jane asked.

"No, that's Henry. I had him when I was a boy. I miss him still."

An unexpected rush of tears stung the backs of Jane's eyes. This was why she loved him. On the outside he was witty and carefree, but on the inside he cared . . . deeply, about everyone and everything in his world.

Jane kicked off her white satin slippers and rolled off both stockings before whirling around. "Unbutton me."

He chuckled. "Not the most romantic way to begin."

"No, it's not that," she answered with a laugh. "This gown is terribly uncomfortable."

"I'm happy to comply," he said softly, his lips moving to the back of her neck. Jane felt the tug of his fingers against the long row of buttons along her back, but all she could concentrate on was his mouth on the soft spot beneath her ear. She tilted her head to the side.

He turned her slowly. The bodice gaped away. She held it to her with both hands.

"You're unbuttoned, my lady."

Nerves took over then. "Th—thank you."

Gently cupping her shoulders, he pressed a kiss to her forehead. "Would you like to keep your spectacles?"

Jane looked up into his face and realized he was teasing her. "It would make things easier to see. What if I miss something important fumbling around blind as a mole?"

"I won't let that happen," he breathed, slowly pulling her spectacles over each ear. He pulled them away from her face and led her to the bed, where he placed them on the table next to the huge mattress.

Jane clutched at the front of her gown.

"Wouldn't you like to remove it entirely?" he asked, turning back to face her.

"Yes." She nodded. She let go and the gown pooled around her waist in waves of white satin. She pushed it over her hips and it fell to the carpet in a whoosh of fabric.

Her stays remained and her chemise beneath that. She took a shaky breath. The voices in her head returned to haunt her. Would Garrett think she was too plump? Not beautiful enough?

"You are gorgeous," he whispered, pulling her into his arms and kissing the column of her throat. Jane's head fell back, the hint of a smile on her lips. Well, it certainly bolstered her confidence to be told she was gorgeous.

"Would you like me to help you with your stays?" he asked.

"They're not easy," she warned.

"I remember."

A flash of heat spiked through Jane's body. "Do you have a knife in your bedside drawer?"

"No, but we should remedy that as soon as possible."

That caused another rush of heat, this time between her legs. "Are you going to tie me up?" she asked, another shadow of a smile on her lips.

"Do you want me to?"

"I did enjoy it. Perhaps I'll tie *you* up next time."

"That can be arranged." His voice was positively devilish.

He'd been busily pulling the ties of her stays loose, one by one, but stopped and turned her to face him. "Jane, do you know what happens between a man and a woman in bed?"

Jane fought her blush. "Yes. I told you. I am extremely well read. And, er, Lucy mentioned a thing or two."

His face relaxed. "Please do not tell me a word Lucy said."

"Don't worry. I won't."

He rubbed Jane's shoulder. "All I ask is that you trust me."

A shiver chased through her. "In case you use a knife or tie me up?"

"Nothing like that." He kissed her tenderly again. "Tonight I want to make you touch the clouds."

Jane's shivering increased. "It sounds positively delightful."

He finished unlacing her stays, and Jane faced him wearing only her chemise. "I refuse to remove another piece of clothing until you do, sir."

He grinned wickedly. "With pleasure."

Jane climbed onto the massive bed and propped herself against the pillows. "I'm going to need my spectacles for this." She rummaged on the side table to locate them.

Garrett began by slowly untying his snowy white cravat. His eyes didn't move from hers, and he didn't say a word. He tugged the bow at his neck and unwrapped the material from his throat. He pulled it away and tossed it on the foot of the bed. Then he undid his shirtsleeves, removing the links of his cuffs one by one and setting them on the bedside table.

Jane watched in fascination, her tongue darting to wet her lips.

Next, Garrett tugged his shirttails from his breeches and used both hands to pull the white linen shirt over his head in a crisscross motion. He crumpled the fabric into a ball and tossed it onto the foot of the bed as well.

He stood before Jane, naked from the waist up. The broad expanse of his chest mesmerized her. She let her gaze play over it, memorizing every detail. She winced at the scar from the bullet that had nearly taken his life, but the imperfection did nothing to detract from his pure, male beauty. Her fingers ached to touch him.

He took a seat on the edge of the bed and removed first one dark boot and then the other. By the time he was done, his tight breeches were all that remained.

"I believe we're even," he said, sliding toward her on his hands and knees.

Jane panicked. "Usually when I'm up this late, it's be—because I'm reading. Then I find I'm unusually tired in the morning." It was a ridiculous thing to say, but nerves had quite got the best of her.

"You know what I think?" he asked, hovering over her.

"Wh—what?" she managed.

"You should be tired from being made love to all night. Not from reading."

Jane's throat went dry. All she could do was stare at the wide expanse of chest above her. Then he pulled her into his arms. His hands pushed into her hair and savagely tore out the pins. She didn't even feel the slight pain.

His mouth was on hers, mastering her. His groin pushed against her most intimate spot. He was hot and hard and heavy, reaching for her. She pressed her lips together and looked up at him. "I want to see all of you."

His smile was downright sinful. He rolled onto his back, undid the buttons under the fall of his breeches, and used both hands to pull them over his hips. The garment was gone in one quick movement, tossed to the end of the bed.

Jane's gaze scoured him. He lay with his hands crossed under his head, entirely nude. "Look all you like," he said in a teasing voice Jane found irresistible.

So look, she did.

The man was stunning. His broad shoulders and wide muscled chest tapered down into the flat plane of his abdomen and then . . .

His member looked enormous. Far too big to . . . fit, but she'd worry about that later. For now, she was preoccupied staring at her husband's unbearably handsome body. *Her husband.* His legs were long and muscled. The was another scar at the top of his right leg. Amazing that he walked without a limp. She wanted to touch it. To kiss it. Her brave, strong Garrett. Her gaze trailed off at his ankles and his feet. He even had beautiful feet.

Levering up on one elbow, he pulled her spectacles from her face and placed them back on the table.

She sighed. "I suppose you're going to want to see *me* now."

He snorted. "God, Jane. You make me laugh. I love that about you."

Jane shrugged. "Mama says gentlemen are rarely interested in ladies who are humorous."

"With all due respect, your mother is wrong."

"That's what I said." Jane pushed herself to her knees. "So is that a yes? You do want to see me naked?"

He grinned and quirked a brow. "If it's not too much trouble."

With shaking hands, she gathered her chemise in both fists near her knees and slowly pulled it up.

Garrett's eyes turned a mossy green.

She pulled the garment over her head and tossed it aside, shivering as the cool air found her naked flesh.

He moved up to sit beside her, his eyes focused on her breasts. "Jane, you are . . . magnificent."

Magnificent? She closed her eyes and smiled to herself. That was a promising start.

He leaned over her and followed her down. His mouth finding hers, his sleek, warm tongue sliding against hers.

"Can I touch you, Garrett?"

"All you like," he whispered into her hair.

She wrapped her arms around his neck first, sliding her fingers through the dark curls. Then she skimmed along the broad column of his neck and across his muscled shoulders. His skin was bundled silk beneath her fingertips. She trailed her hands down his chest and pride swelled in her heart as his muscles jumped in response to her touch. He closed his eyes and Jane stroked his rough cheek. She ran her thumb along the firm line of his jaw.

"Stopping there?" His voice sounded strained.

Jane kissed his chest. She reveled in the feel of his hot skin beneath her lips. He smelled like soap and masculinity. "You want me to go lower?" she asked, the hint of a smile in her voice.

"If you insist," he replied in a mock-resigned voice.

With pleasure, Jane resumed her exploration. She pushed her hand along the hard outline of the six muscles that stood out along his abdomen. Then she let her hand trail lower, and lower still, until she wrapped her fist around him.

Garrett groaned.

Instinctively, she slid her hand up and down. He groaned again. His forehead bunched into a look resembling pain. He pulled her hand away. "You are too good at that," he said in a shaky voice that made Jane's insides melt. "Let me touch you first."

She trembled but lay back against the pillow and allowed him to scan her from top to toe.

"I was wrong," he murmured, his tongue flicking against her nipple. Jane gasped. "You are beyond magnificent. You're perfect."

His other hand didn't remain still. It cupped her opposite breast and played with the pink crest. Jane pushed her fingers through his hair, holding his mouth to her aching breast. She arched her back to allow him to draw the swollen bud deeper into his torturous mouth. She moaned.

His hand moved lower, skimming the outside of her waist, playing along the rise of her hips, and finally, sweeping between her thighs to find the place she desperately wanted him to.

He stroked between her cleft and parted the springy hairs there. He stroked again, once, twice, before settling in the exact perfect spot. The spot that made her entire body tremble.

He lowered himself between her legs. His head moving down until his mouth was at her navel. "Jane," he whispered against the soft skin of her belly.

"Yes," she managed, but she could hardly think with his finger doing magical things to her, let alone speak.

"You're really going to enjoy this next bit."

She sucked in her breath. "I am?"

"Yes. A lot."

"Show me," she breathed.

He continued his slow movement down her body until his hot, wet mouth hovered above her most sensitive place. He drew his finger away. She cried out at the loss but the location of his mouth promised better things. Surely he didn't mean to—

"Are you about to . . . ?" Jane couldn't bring herself to say the words.

"Yes." The feel of his warm breath against her sensitive skin made her shudder. She was about to come off the bed. She hadn't ever read about *this*.

"Do you mind?" he asked.

"Not at all," she answered. Then she couldn't think because his mouth was on her, his tongue owning her. She grabbed the bedsheets with both fists and arched her back off the mattress. "Oh, God," she murmured, her head tossing against the pillow. "Upton, I swear, if you stop now."

His warm laugh touched her thigh. "I wouldn't do that to you, Jane."

The use of her first name was her undoing. There was something so sweet, so lovely, so sincere about it. His tongue nudged once more in her center and she came apart, grabbing his head and crying a keening wail.

He pulled himself up and his mouth was on hers again, insatiable. "How did I know you'd be a screamer?" he said against her mouth between ravenous kisses.

"I can't believe what you just did . . . what you made me feel."

"You haven't felt half of it yet."

A shudder racked her body.

His mouth moved to her breast and he teased her, played with her, sucked her until her back arched off the bed again and she wrapped her fingers through his hair. "Upton."

"Will you please call me Garrett when I'm making love to you?" His voice was piqued, but heavy with lust.

"Garrett," she breathed.

He groaned and slid one finger into her hot wet warmth.

"Oh. God. Yes." Another keening wail from her that he covered with his mouth.

His finger touched the most sensitive spot between her legs, rubbing her in tiny circles, and her hips matched his movements. "Garrett, I—"

"Don't talk. Just feel."

"I'm feeling too much." Her hips kept up their circular motion. She was a puppet on his string.

"That's not possible."

She pressed her forehead to his, hard. "What are you doing?

"Stop talking."

"Tell me."

"I'm going to make you come again."

Her eyes rolled back in her head. His finger was magical, perfect. He knew exactly where to touch, how long, and how much pressure to exert. Her hips bucked. She sobbed against his shoulder. She wanted to bite him. "Please," she whimpered. "Please."

"Please who?" he whispered fiercely into her ear. "Say my name." He slid another finger into her and Jane came apart in a thousand pieces.

"Garrett," she cried as she came. "Oh, Garrett."

Garrett lay with her head against his shoulder for a few moments, allowing the self-satisfied smirk to remain on his face. He'd never been half the rake he'd been accused of, but tonight he was bloody proud of the experience he did have. Jane had come twice, and they hadn't even made love yet. Happy wedding night to her.

There was still much left to teach her. His cock ached. He wanted to bury himself in her, but he didn't want to frighten her.

Jane was beyond gorgeous. He'd nearly spilled his seed just watching her take off her chemise. Her skin

was like porcelain, her breasts full and round and perfect. Her waist was small and her hips flared enticingly.
And her backside. Oh, her backside. Poems should be
written about Jane's backside.

"How about another lesson?" He drew his finger
across her pebbled nipple.

She stretched her arms over her head and arched her
back. "Yes, please."

"Let's start by you kissing me, here." He pointed to
his shoulder.

Jane smiled a lazy, satisfied smile. "Yes."

She moved to her knees and pushed him back against
the pillows. Then she leaned over him, those full, gorgeous breasts making his mouth water. They pressed
against his chest, making his skin tingle as she bent her
head to kiss his shoulder.

His breathing hitched. "Now, here." He pointed to his
nipple.

Jane's dark eyes flared. She moved lower and her pink
tongue darted to lick his nipple. She was learning fast.
*Thank God for intelligent women.*

His voice wavered a bit this time. "Now, here." He
pointed to his abdomen.

Jane gave him the most sensual smile he'd ever seen,
before lowering herself even farther, letting her tongue
find its way to the spot he'd pointed out. She nipped at
the tight skin there.

He clutched the bedsheets and swallowed hard. She
might be learning a bit *too* fast.

"Now." Damn. His voice shook like an untried lad.
"Here." He took his cock in his hand and stroked it once,
twice.

The sound Jane made was a throaty moan. His hand
moved away and her tongue dipped again. She closed
her entire mouth around his tip.

"God," he breathed. "That's so good."

Her lips began a slow descent and he clutched both hands in the bedsheets. "So damn good," he groaned, his forehead beading with sweat. Yes, she was a fast learner, his wife. *His wife.*

Her mouth rose and fell, and rose and fell again, her hot, wet tongue rubbing against his scorching skin over and over until Garrett was mindless. His hips arched off the bed and he clenched his eyes shut.

"Grab my balls," he demanded, and Jane complied, squeezing them in her torturous hand.

The ache between his legs was unholy. "Jesus, Jane, I—"

Her lips came off his cock with a sucking noise that was strangely erotic. "You what?"

Her scent was driving him mad. "I can't wait," he breathed, pulling her roughly into his arms and rolling on top of her. He grabbed the back of her head by her hair and tugged, exposing her neck and nipping at it. "I have to have you *now*."

He pushed his rough thigh between her soft legs and Jane spread open for him. "I'll do my best to make this as painless as—"

"Take me!"

He pushed into her warm wetness and took a deep breath. He wanted to control himself, but the overwhelming feeling of being inside her made him mad. He thrust again, rocking a bit farther this time. Then he kissed her mouth and slid in to the hilt.

Jane winced.

Not moving inside of her, he kissed the side of her eye, her ear, her cheek. "Are you all right?" he whispered.

"I will be. Show me the rest."

That was all Garrett needed. He pulled out slowly and plunged in again. He repeated the action, watching her face for any sign of discomfort. Instead, a slow smile soon spread across her face.

He pressed his forehead hard against hers and stroked into her again and again. He clenched his jaw. He needed to make this good for her too.

His hand worked its way between her legs and found the little nub of pleasure there. Jane's eyes widened. He rubbed her up and down, over and over until she slid into another climax.

Her inner muscles clamped him and Garrett was lost. He pumped into her again one final time and wrapped his arms around her fiercely. He groaned her name while shudders racked his entire frame.

"That was . . . incredible," Jane said moments later, tugging the sheets over her still-trembling body.

He pulled her into his arms, cradling her against his belly. "That's what you said the last time we were intimate."

"I'm much more eloquent when you're not touching me."

He traced his finger along her collarbone. "That's too bad, because I find that I cannot stop touching you."

"You're v—very good, you know." Jane did her best to concentrate, despite the fact that he was already making her hot and wet again.

"Are you saying you prefer a rake after all?"

"I suppose I do."

"Then I hate to disappoint you, but I am not and never have been a rake."

She leaned up on one elbow to look at him. Her dark hair fell over one shoulder. "What are you talking about? Lucy always said how popular you were with ladies and—"

"Popular as a friend, yes, and I do admit to a certain

amount of experience, but hardly of the sort you convicted me of in your head."

Jane fell back to the mattress and bounced slightly. "I suppose that's what I get for being such a know-it-all."

He buried his nose in her hair and nipped her ear. "I never called you that."

"No, but you were thinking it."

He rested his chin atop her head. "You do tend to pontificate upon every subject. However, if you weren't such a know-it-all, Isabella may have thought she'd got away with her handwriting subterfuge."

Jane smiled. "That's true." She smoothed a hand over the pillow and sighed. "Being a know-it-all was how I dealt with being different when I was a child. I tried to impress people with my knowledge rather than my appearance."

He lifted the sheet and stole a quick peek. "You're doing a fine job of impressing me with your appearance."

She laughed and swatted at his hand. "Be serious, you rogue. No one ever . . . wanted me the way a man wants a woman."

Garrett's face sobered and he pulled her back into his arms and kissed her forehead. "You are as lovely as you are intelligent. I love you for both."

Her eyes filled with tears. "You love me?"

"Of course I do, my darling. I think I've loved you since you argued with me about *Much Ado About Nothing*. I'd never met a woman I couldn't charm before I met you."

"And I never met a man who argued with me so vehemently. I cannot tell you the number of times I dreamed of tripping you."

His crack of laughter bounced against the far wall. "Do I need to watch my step?"

"Never." She wrapped her arms around his neck and kissed him soundly. "I love you, Garrett. I love you very much."

"And I love you, my Jane."

She pulled away and gave him a sidewise smile. "So, no knives or tying me up tonight?"

He cocked a brow. "Interested?"

She shrugged. "Perhaps."

Garrett pulled her into his arms again. "Whatever you say, Lady Blue. Why don't we—" He whispered something positively indecent in her ear.

Jane shivered with delight. "Ooh, as you wish, Lord Green."

# CHAPTER FORTY-NINE

*One month later*

"You cannot possibly have an objection to the plot of *Much Ado About Nothing* any longer, Garrett," Jane said as they sat in the gardens behind Julian's town house playing cards. Julian and Cass had recently returned from their honeymoon trip and Jane and Garrett had come to visit, along with Lucy and Derek.

"That's ridiculous." Garrett tossed a card on the small table the footmen had set up for their game. "Why would you think I no longer object to it? I've objected to it for years."

Jane played her next card. "Yes, but correct me if I am wrong, you objected to it based upon the argument that the plot was so outlandish, it could never possibly happen to two sane, intelligent people like Benedick and Beatrice."

"That's right," Garrett replied with a nod, waiting for Julian to place his card. "Especially Benedick. Just because you're my wife now, doesn't mean I'm going to agree with you about everything. I do hope you'll resolve to show me the same courtesy."

"Not to worry. I am resolved to agree with you on as little as possible." Jane flashed her new husband a smile. "But if two sane, intelligent people could not possibly fall for the antics in *Much Ado About Nothing,* how do you explain what has happened between us?"

Garrett's forehead wrinkled in a frown.

"She's got you there, Garrett," Lucy replied from her seat on an iron bench across the pebbled walk. The duke and duchess were sitting out this particular game of whist.

"We all went to a house party," Jane continued, waiting for Cass to set her next card on the table. "You and I were told the opposite one loved us, and in the end, you were even momentarily convinced you'd arrived at a church in order to marry a different bride."

Garrett's mouth fell open, astonishment etched across his features. "I— But I—"

"Don't argue with her, Upton. Believe me when I tell you married life is much more agreeable when one admits the lady is always right," Derek declared with a laugh.

"And don't even get me started on the bit about Mrs. Langford and her footman," Jane said. "Or the fact that your dogs are named Dogberry and Verges."

Garrett leaned over and kissed his wife on the cheek. "You're perfectly right, my love, we'll just have to find something else to argue about. I've no doubt we can think of something."

"Excellent." Jane gave him a saucy smile. "I already have an idea. Now that we've resolved that eternal argument, just think of the fun we'll have trying to come to an agreement on what we'll name our children."

Garrett rubbed her shoulder. "What did you have in mind?"

"It's quite simple. If we have a daughter, she will be named Mary for Mary Wollstonecraft."

Garrett raised both brows. "What if he's a son?"

"Then just Wollstonecraft, of course."

Garrett shook his head and studied his cards. "I don't mind what we name the children. I'm merely content that you're my wife, and one day will be my countess."

"I'm the unlikeliest lady, to be sure, but Mama is pleased. Though it is a bit of a shame I must relinquish my former title as the head of the wallflowers. Being a bluestocking spinster was not my destiny, it seems." Jane laughed. "Do you know I told Mama that Mrs. Bunbury's excellent matchmaking skills are to thank for our wedding?"

"You didn't," Cass said with a gasp.

"I most certainly did. She's promised to give her a glowing reference. Too bad the poor dear won't be able to use it. She's retiring to the countryside, don't you know?"

"That's convenient," Julian replied.

"Isn't it though?" Lucy asked with a sigh. "That particular bit was my doing. Mrs. Bunbury's sister took horribly ill and she was needed to take care of the children immediately. I doubt we'll hear from her for quite some time."

"Or until someone else needs a nonexistent chaperone," Julian added.

"Why, Julian, I believe you're finally learning how our minds work," Lucy said with a laugh.

"That is a terrifying thought," Derek interjected.

"You never know when we'll need to be up to our schemes," Lucy said.

"No more schemes for me," Jane replied. "I intend to settle down into married life and use my influence to promote the cause of the rights of ladies."

"You do, do you? Who do you intend to influence?" Garrett asked.

"Why, you, of course. You're going to have to battle that horrid Lord Bartholomew one day."

Garrett leaned over and whispered in her ear. "Lord Bartholomew doesn't frighten me, my love. And now that I'm sleeping through the night, no longer waking up with nightmares, I daresay I'll be even more prepared to take him on."

"I only hope things settle down for a bit," Cass said. "All those plots made me so nervous."

"Don't worry, dear," Lucy replied. "Now that you, and I, and Jane, and Garrett are all happily settled, there should be no more cause for intrigue. In fact, I only hope things won't become dull around here."

"I doubt that's possible, my love," Derek said. "Which reminds me. Swifdon, congratulations are in order on the bill being passed. I know how hard you worked on it."

Julian inclined his head. "Thank you, Your Grace. Of course Upton here had a great deal to do with it as well."

Garrett nodded. "The families of the soldiers deserve it."

Lucy's eyes lit up. "Speaking of families of the soldiers, did you hear Mrs. Langford ran off to Gretna Green and married last week?"

"No!" Jane gasped.

"Yes." Lucy's nod was so vigorous one of her curls bounced out of her coiffure.

Garrett groaned. "Whom did she marry? I pity the chap."

"No one I've ever heard of," Lucy replied.

Jane leaned her head on her husband's shoulder. "At least she'll no longer be reliant on you for money, Garrett."

"There is that to consider," Garrett replied. "Though

if the children ever need anything, I'll certainly provide it."

Jane lifted her head and kissed his lips. "That's why I love you so. You're generous and kind."

"*That's* why you love me. I'm pleased to hear it. I wasn't certain whether you married me for me, or for my libraries."

Jane shrugged. "Both, Garrett, I married you for both. I'm awfully fond of the dogs as well."

Garrett sighed. "Now that Mrs. Cat and her kittens are ensconced in our house, we've got a practical menagerie."

"Who knew the two of you would be such unabashed lovebirds?" Cass asked with a happy smile. "I can hardly believe my eyes. I go off on my honeymoon trip and miss every bit of the excitement."

The back door of the house opened and Daphne Swift came hurrying out.

Cass turned to her sister-in-law. "Good morning, Daphne. Is something the matter?"

Daphne clasped her hands together. "Good morning, everyone." She bobbed a quick curtsy to the group at large, then she turned her attention to her brother, her teeth tugging her bottom lip. "Julian, there's something I must tell you." Her voice shook a little.

Concern flitted across Julian's features. "What is it, Daphne?"

Daphne slowly smoothed her pink skirts. "Remember that time I asked you for a favor? You promised me there'd be no questions asked?"

Julian's face took on a thunderous expression. "That was a long time ago, last autumn if I remember correctly."

Daphne absently tugged at the neck of her gown. "It seems that I . . ."

"Yes?" Cass prompted, concern written across her face.

Daphne took a deep breath. "It just so happens . . ."

"Go on," Lucy prompted this time. Like the others, she was perched on the edge of her seat.

Daphne glanced away. "It seems I may be legally married to Captain Cavendish and I need your help to get an annulment."

Lucy made a strangled sort of squeaking noise.

Jane turned to Cass with wide eyes. "What were you saying about missing all the excitement?"

Thank you for reading *The Unlikely Lady*!
I hope you enjoyed Jane and Garrett's story. These two
were so much fun to write!


I'd love to keep in touch.

- Visit my website for information about upcoming books,
  excerpts, and to sign up for my e-mail newsletter: www
  .ValerieBowmanBooks.com.
- Join me on Facebook: http://Facebook.com/
  ValerieBowmanAuthor.
- Follow me on Twitter at @ValerieGBowman, https://
  twitter.com/ValerieGBowman
- Reviews help other readers find books. I appreciate all
  reviews whether positive or negative. Thank you so
  much for considering it!

*Coming soon...*

Look for the next novel of delightful romance by
**VALERIE BOWMAN**

*The Irresistible Rogue*

Available in November 2015 from
St. Martin's Paperbacks